SPAN
PORT
Short Stories

SPANISH & PORTUGUESE
Short Stories

SENATE

Spanish & Portuguese Short Stories

Stories selected from
*The Masterpiece Library of Short Stories, Volume XVIII,
Spanish and Portuguese,* issued by
Allied Newspapers Ltd., in association with
The Educational Book Company Ltd, London.

This edition published in 1995 by Senate, an imprint of
Studio Editions Ltd, Princess House, 50 Eastcastle Street,
London W1N 7AP, England

ISBN 1 85958 146 3

Printed and bound in Guernsey by
The Guernsey Press Co. Ltd.

SPANISH
Short Stories

Contents

CONTENTS

JUAN MANUEL

1282–1347

A YOUNG MAN AND HIS MANY FRIENDS

FROM " EL CONDE LUCANOR "

A CERTAIN good man had a son; and among other matters which he advised, he enjoined him always to endeavour to obtain a great number of friends; and the son did as he was told. He began to keep much company, and to share his substance among different individuals whom he esteemed as his friends, and ready to do anything in their power to pleasure him;—nay, insomuch as to venture their lives and substance, if need be, in his behalf.

And one day this young man, conversing with his father, was asked whether he had done as he had been commanded, and had yet obtained many friends.

And the son replied that he had; and in particular, that among others, there were ten of whom he was most assured, that never in any difficulty or necessity whatever would they be led to desert him.

When the father heard this, he said he was greatly surprised that his son had been able in so short a time to obtain so many friends; and such as he, who was an old man, had never been fortunate enough to possess during his whole life, at all events never counting more than one friend and a half. And the son began to argue with him, maintaining that what he had said of his friends was only the truth.

When the father saw that his son was so eager on their behalf, he said that he ought to proceed to prove it in the following manner. First, that he should kill a pig, and having put it into a sack, should go with it to the house of one of his friends, and when admitted there, tell him secretly,—not that it was a pig, but a man whom he had unhappily killed. Further, that if this fact should be made known, it would be quite impossible for him to escape with his life; and that all those who knew of it would be likely to share with him in the same fate. That his son should

1

enjoin them, since they were his friends, not to reveal the fact; and that if need be, they should unite with him and defend him.

And the youth did this: going to the house of his friends, he informed them of the fatal accident that had befallen him. They all, one after another, declared, that in all other matters they would serve him to the utmost, but that on such an occasion, which would endanger both their lives and property, they dare not assist him; beseeching him, at the same time, for the love of God, not to breathe to a single being that he had been at their houses. Some of them, indeed, said that they would go to solicit on his behalf; and others observed that they would do as much, and, moreover, would not desert him even till after his execution, and that they would then give him honourable interment.

And after the youth had thus tried the sincerity of all his friends, without finding any to receive him, he returned to his father, and related what had happened. And when the father saw that it so fell out, he said to his son, that he might now very well see how those who had lived long, and seen and experienced much in such a matter, knew more than their sons. He then added, that he himself had only one friend and a half, and that he might go and try them.

The young man went accordingly to prove what his father had meant by half a friend, and he took the dead pig along with him. He called at the door of his father's half friend, and recounted to him first the unlucky adventure which had befallen him; that he had spoken with all his friends in vain, and beseeched him, by the regard he bore his father, to assist him now in this his utter need.

And when his father's half friend saw this, he said that he had a regard for the father, but had no sort of love for or acquaintance with the son; but that for his father's sake, he was willing to assist him, and to conceal the affair. He then took the sack with the pig, and carried it into his orchard, where he deposited it in a deep furrow, and covered the spot with weeds and vegetables to conceal it from every eye.

The youth then returned and acquainted his father with what had occurred in regard to this his half friend. He next ordered his son, on a certain day, when they should all be engaged in council, to start some question, and discuss it with this same friend very warmly, till at length he should deal him a hard blow in the face, which, when the opportunity served, was accordingly done.

But the good man, on being smitten, only said, " By my faith, young man, thou hast done ill; yet thou mayest be assured, that neither for this or other injury thou canst do, will I reveal what happened in the garden."

The son afterwards reported this to his father, who then told him to go to the house of his other friend, and he did so.

And again he recounted all that had happened; and the good friend of his father directly said, that he would do all to save his life and his reputation. And it by chance happened that a man had been killed in that town, and none knew by whom; but several people having noticed the youth going along at night with the sack upon his shoulders, they concluded that he was no other than the murderer.

In short, they informed of him, and the youth was taken and pronounced guilty of the offence; but his father's friend all the while exerted himself to compass his escape. And when he saw that there was no way left to save him from death, he said to the Alcalde, that he did not wish to have the sin of killing that young man upon his conscience, for, in fact, it was not he who had killed the man, but a son of his own, and the only one he had; and in this way did he succeed in saving the life of his friend's son, by the hard sacrifice of his own.

JUAN MANUEL

THE NAKED KING

THREE impostors came to a King and told him they were cloth-weavers, and could fabricate a cloth of so peculiar a nature that a legitimate son of his father could see the cloth; but if he were illegitimate, though believed to be legitimate, he could not see it.

Now the King was much pleased at this, thinking that by this means he would be able to distinguish the men in his kingdom who were legitimate sons of their supposed fathers from those who were not, and so be enabled to increase his treasures, for among the Moors only legitimate children inherit their father's property; and for this end he ordered a palace to be appropriated to the manufacture of this cloth. And these men, in order to convince him that they had no intention of deceiving him, agreed to be shut up in this palace until the cloth was manufactured, which satisfied the King.

When they were supplied with a large quantity of gold, silver, silk, and many other things, they entered the palace, and, putting their looms in order, gave it to be understood that they were working all day at the cloth.

After some days, one of them came to the King and told him the cloth was commenced, that it was the most curious thing in the world, describing the design and construction; he then prayed the King to favour them with a visit, but begged he would come alone. The King was much pleased, but wishing to have the opinion of some one first, sent the Lord Chamberlain to see it, in order to know if they were deceiving him. When the Lord Chamberlain saw the workmen, and heard all they had to say, he dared not admit he could not see the cloth, and when he returned to the King he stated that he had seen it; the King sent yet another, who gave the same report. When they whom he had sent declared that they had seen the cloth, he determined to go himself.

On entering the palace and seeing the men at work, who began to describe the texture and relate the origin of the invention, as also the design and colour, in which they all appeared to agree, although in reality they were not working, when the King saw how they appeared to work, and heard the character of the cloth so minutely described, and yet could not see it, although those he had sent had seen it, he began to feel very uneasy, fearing he might not be the son of the King who was supposed to be his father, and that if he acknowledged he could not see the cloth he might lose his kingdom; under this impression he commenced praising the fabric, describing its peculiarities after the manner of the workmen.

On the return to his palace he related to his people how good and marvellous was the cloth, yet at the same time suspected something wrong.

At the end of two or three days the King requested his " Alguacil " (or officer of justice) to go and see the cloth. When the Alguacil entered and saw the workmen, who, as before, described the figures and pattern of the cloth, knowing that the King had been to see it, and yet could not see it himself, he thought he certainly could not be the legitimate son of his father, and therefore could not see it. He, however, feared if he was to declare that he could not see it he would lose his honourable position; to avoid this mischance he commenced praising the cloth even more vehemently than the others.

When the Alguacil returned to the King and told him that he had seen the cloth, and that it was the most extraordinary production in the world, the King was much disconcerted; for he thought that if the Alguacil had seen the cloth, which he was unable to see, there could no longer be a doubt that he was not the legitimate son of the King, as was generally supposed; he therefore did not hesitate to praise the excellency of the cloth and the skill of the workmen who were able to make it.

On another day he sent one of his Councillors, and it happened to him as to the King and the others of whom I have spoken; and in this manner, and for this reason, they deceived the King and many others, for no one dared to say he could not see the cloth.

Things went on thus until there came a great feast, when all requested the King to be dressed in some of the cloth; so the workmen, being ordered, brought some rolled up in a very fine linen, and inquired of the King how much of it he wished them to cut off; so the King gave orders how much and how to make it up.

Now when the clothes were made, and the feast day had arrived, the weavers brought them to the King, informed His Majesty that his dress was made of the cloth as he had directed, the King all this time not daring to say he could not see it.

When the King had professed to dress himself in this suit, he mounted on horseback and rode into the city; but fortunately for him it was summer time. The people seeing His Majesty come in this manner were much surprised; but knowing that those who could not see this cloth would be considered illegitimate sons of their fathers, kept their surprise to themselves, fearing the dishonour consequent upon such a declaration.

Not so, however, with a negro, who happened to notice the King thus equipped; for he, having nothing to lose, came to him and said, "Sire, to me it matters not whose son I am, therefore I tell you that you are riding without any clothes."

On this the King commenced beating him, saying that he was not the legitimate son of his supposed father, and therefore it was that he could not see the cloth. But no sooner had the negro said this, than others were convinced of its truth, and said the same; until, at last, the King and all with him lost their fear of declaring the truth, and saw through the trick of which these impostors had made them the victims.

When the weavers were sought for they were found to have fled, taking with them all they had received from the King by their imposition.

ANONYMOUS
15TH CENTURY

THE BITER BIT

Who thinks to take another in
Is oft in his turn taken in.

Two townsmen and a countryman, on a pilgrimage to Mecca, agreed to share provisions till they should reach Mecca. But the victuals ran short, so that they had nothing left but a little flour—enough to make a loaf.

And the townsmen, seeing that, said one to the other:

"We have but little food, and our companion eats much, how shall we bring about that he shall eat none of the bread, and that we alone eat it?"

And they took this counsel—they would make the loaf, and whilst it was baking should all go to sleep, and whoever dreamed the most marvellous thing in that time, he should alone eat the bread.

This they did, thinking to betray the simple rustic, and they made the loaf and put it to bake, and then lay down to sleep. But the rustic saw through their treachery, and when the companions were sleeping took the half-baked bread, ate it, and turned to sleep.

Then one of the townsmen awoke as one dreaming and afraid, and called to his companion; and the other said, "What hast thou?"

"I saw a marvellous vision: methought two angels opened the gates of heaven, and bore me before the face of God."

And his companion said, "Marvellous is that vision. But I dreamed that two angels seized me, and, cleaving the earth, bore me to hell."

The rustic heard all this and pretended to sleep, but the others called out to him to awake, and he discreetly, as one amazed, replied, "Who are ye that are calling me?"

They replied, "We are thy companions."

And he said, "Have ye returned?"

And they said, "Whence wouldst thou have us return?"

And the rustic said, "But now methought I saw two angels take the one of you to heaven, and then two other angels take the other to hell; and seeing this, and thinking you would neither return, I got up and ate the loaf."

7

DIEGO HURTADO DE MENDOZA
1503-1575

HOW LAZARO BECAME THE SERVANT OF AN ESQUIRE

ONE day in Toledo I accidentally encountered a certain esquire in the street; he was of a good appearance, well dressed, and walked with an air of ease and consequence. As I cast my eyes upon him, he fortunately took notice of me, and said:

" Are you seeking a master, my boy? "

I replied that I was.

" Then follow me," said he; " you have reason to thank your stars for this meeting: doubtless you have said your prayers with a better grace than usual this morning."

I followed him, returning thanks to Providence for this singular good turn of fortune, for, if one might judge from appearances, here was exactly the situation which I had so long desired. It was early in the morning when I was engaged by this kind master, and I continued to follow him, as he desired, till we made the tour of a great part of the city. As we passed the market, I hoped that he would give me a load to carry home, as it was then about the hour that people usually made their purchases of that nature; but he passed by without taking the slightest notice.

" Peradventure," quoth I to myself, " these commodities are not exactly to his taste; we shall be more fortunate in some other quarter."

It was now eleven o'clock, and my master went into the cathedral to hear prayers, where I likewise followed him. Here we stayed until the whole service was finished and the congregation were departed; and then my master left, and proceeded towards one of the back streets of the city. Never was anybody more delighted than I, to find my master had not condescended to trouble himself about supplying his table, concluding, of course, that he was a gentleman whose means enabled him to consign to others such inferior domestic cares, and that on our arrival at home we should find everything in order,—an anticipation of great delight to me, and, in fact, by this time almost a matter of necessity. The

8

clock had struck one, when we arrived at a house before which my master stopped, and throwing his cloak open, he drew from his sleeve a key with which he opened the door.

I followed my master into the house, the entrance of which was extremely dark and dismal, so much so, as to create a sensation of fear in the mind of a stranger; and when within found it contained a small courtyard and tolerably sized chambers. The moment he entered, he took off his cloak, and inquiring whether I had clean hands, assisted me to fold it, and then, carefully wiping the dust from a seat, laid it thereon. He next very composedly seated himself, and began to ask me a variety of questions, as to who I was, where I came from, and how I came to that city; to all which I gave a more particular account than exactly suited me at that time, for I thought it would have been much more to the purpose had he desired me to place the table and serve up the soup, than ask me the questions he then did.

With all this, however, I contrived to give him a very satisfactory account of myself, dwelling on my good qualities, and concealing those which were not suitable to my present auditory. But I began now to grow very uneasy, for two o'clock arrived, and still no signs of dinner appeared, and I began to recollect that ever since we had been in the house I had not heard the foot of a human being, either above or below. All I had seen were bare walls, without even a chair or a table,—not so much as an old chest like that I had such good occasion to remember. In fact, it seemed to me like a house labouring under the influence of enchantment.

" Boy, hast thou eaten anything to-day? " asked my master at last.

" No, sir," I replied, " seeing that it was scarcely eight o'clock when I had the good fortune to meet your honour."

" Early as it was," returned my master, " I had already breakfasted, and it is never my custom to eat again till the evening; manage as you can till then; you will have the better appetite for supper."

It may be easily supposed that, on hearing this, my newly-raised hopes vanished as rapidly as they had risen; it was not hunger alone that caused me to despond, but the certainty that Fortune had not yet exhausted her full store of malice against me. I could not but weep over the incidents of my past unfortunate career, and anticipate its rapidly approaching close; yet withal, concealing my emotion as well as possible, I said:

" Thank God, sir, I am not a boy that troubles himself much about eating and drinking; and for this quality I have been praised even to this very day by all the masters whom I have ever served."

" Abstinence is a great virtue," returned my master, " and for this I shall esteem thee still more; gormandising is only for swine, men of understanding require little to allay their appetite."

" I can understand that sentiment right well," quoth I to myself; " my masters have all advised the same course; though the devil a bit do *they* find the virtues of starvation so very pleasant, by all that I have seen."

Seating myself near the door, I now began to eat some crusts of bread which I had about me; they were part of some scraps I had collected in my career of charity.

" Come here, boy," said my master, " what are you eating? "

I went to him, and showed him the bread. He selected from the three pieces which I had, the best and largest, and said, " Upon my life, but this seems exceedingly nice bread."

" Yes, sir," I replied, " it is very good."

" It really is," he continued, " where did you get it? was it made with clean hands, I wonder? "

" That I can't answer for," I replied, " but the flavour of it does not come amiss to me."

" Nor to me either, please God! " said my poor devil of a master; and, having finished his scrutiny, he raised the bread to his mouth, and commenced as fierce an attack on it, as I quickly did on the other.

" By heavens! but this bread is beautiful! " exclaimed he; and I, beginning to see how matters stood with him, redoubled my haste with the remainder, being well assured that if he finished first, he would have little hesitation in assisting me; but luckily we finished together. He then carefully picked up the crumbs which had fallen, and entering a small chamber adjoining, brought out an old jar with a broken mouth. Having drunk therefrom he handed it to me, but to support my character of abstemiousness, I excused myself, saying, " No, sir, I thank you; I never drink wine."

" The contents of the jar will not hurt you," he said; " it is only water! "

I took the jar, but a very small draught satisfied me, for thirst was one of the few things from which I suffered no inconvenience.

Thus we remained till night, I anticipating my supper, and my master asking me many questions, to all of which I answered in the best manner I was able. Then he took me into the chamber whence he had brought the jar of water, and said:

" Stay here, my boy, and see how to make this bed, as from henceforth you will have this duty."

We then placed ourselves on each side of this bed, if such it can be called, to make it; though little enough there was to make. On some benches was extended a sort of platform of reeds, on which were placed the clothes, which, from want of washing, were not the whitest in the world. The reeds showed like the ribs of a lean hog, through an old covering which served to lie upon, and the colour of which one could not exactly praise.

It was night when the bed was made, and my master said, " Lazaro! it is rather late now, and the market is distant; likewise the city abounds with rogues; we had better therefore pass the night as we can, and to-morrow morning we will fare better. Being a single man, you see, I don't care much for these things, but we will arrange better in future."

" Sir, as to myself," I replied, " I beg you will on no account distress yourself. I can pass a night without food with no inconvenience, or even more, indeed, if it were necessary."

" Your health will be all the better for it," he said, " for take my word for it, as I said to-day, nothing in the world will ensure length of life so much as eating little."

" If life is to be purchased on such terms," said I to myself, " I shall never die, for hitherto I have been obliged to keep this rule, whether I will or no; and, God help me, I fear I shall keep it all my long life."

My master then went to bed, putting his clothes under his head, instead of a pillow, and ordered me to seek my rest at his feet; which I accordingly did, though the situation precluded all hope of sleep. The canes, of which the bedstead was composed, and my bones, which were equally prominent, were throughout the night engaged in a continual and most unpleasant intimacy; for considering my illness, and the privations which I had endured, to say nothing of my present starving condition, I do not believe I had a single pound of flesh on my whole body.

Throughout that day I had eaten nothing but a crust of bread, and was actually mad with hunger, which is in itself a bitter enemy to repose. A thousand times did I curse myself and my unhappy fortunes—the Lord forgive my impiety; and what was a sore addition to my misery, I dared not to move, nor vent my grief in audible expressions, for fear of waking my master; many times during this night did I pray to God to finish my existence!

As the morning appeared, we arose, and I set about cleaning my master's clothes and putting them in order; and helped him to dress, very much to his satisfaction. As he placed his sword in his belt he said, " Do you know the value of this weapon, my boy? The gold was never coined that should buy this treasure of me. Of all the blades Antonio ever forged, he never yet made its fellow."

And then drawing it from the scabbard and trying the edge with his fingers, he added, " With this blade I would engage to sever a bale of wool! "—" and I would do more than that with my teeth," said I to myself; " for though they are not made of steel, I would engage to sever a four pound loaf and devour it afterwards."

He then sheathed his sword and girded it round him, and with

an easy, gentlemanlike carriage, bearing himself erect, and
throwing the corner of his cloak over his shoulder, or over his arm,
placing his right hand on his side, he sallied forth, saying:

" Lazaro, see to the house while I go to hear mass, and make the
bed during my absence; the vessel for water wants filling, which
you can do at the river which runs close by; though take care to
lock the door when you go, lest we should be robbed, and put the
key on this hinge, in case I return before you, that I may let myself
in."

He then walked up the street with such an air of gentility that a
stranger would have taken him for a near relation of the Count of
Arcos, or, at least, for his *valet de chambre*.

" Blessed be the Lord! " said I, " who, if he inflicts misfortunes,
gives us the means of bearing them. Now who, on meeting my
master, would dream but that he had supped well and slept well;
and, although early in the morning, but that he had also breakfasted well?   There are many secrets, my good master, that you
know, and that all the world is ignorant of.   Who would not be
deceived by that smiling face and that fine cloak? and who would
believe that such a fine gentleman had passed the whole of yesterday
without any other food than a morsel of bread, that his boy had
carried in his breast for a day and a night?   To-day washing his
hands and face, and, for want of a towel, obliged to dry them with
the lining of his garments—no one would ever suspect such things
from the appearance before them.   Alas! how many are there in
this world who voluntarily suffer more for their false idea of honour
than they would undergo for their hopes of an hereafter! "

Thus I moralised at the door of our house, while my master paced
slowly up the street; and then, returning within, I lost no time in
making the tour of the house, which I did, though without making
any fresh discovery whatever; or finding anything of a more con-
solatory nature than my own gloomy thoughts.

I quickly made our bed, such as it was, and taking the water-
jar, went with it to the river.   There I saw my gay master in one
of the gardens by the river-side, in close conversation with two
ladies, closely veiled, for there were many who were in the habit
of resorting thus early in the morning to enjoy the fresh air, and
to take breakfast with some of the gentlemen of the city, who likewise frequented the spot.   There he stood between them, saying
softer things than Ovid ever did; while they, seeing him apparently
so enamoured, made no scruple of hinting their wish to breakfast.
Unfortunately his purse was as empty as his heart was full, therefore this attack on his weaker position threw him somewhat suddenly into disorder, which became evident from his confusion of
language, and the lame excuses of which he was obliged to avail
himself.   The ladies were too well experienced not to perceive, and

that quickly, how matters stood; it was not long, therefore, before they exchanged him for a more entertaining gallant.

I was all this time slily munching some cabbage stalks, for want of a better breakfast, which I despatched with considerable alacrity, and then returned home, without being seen by my master, to await his orders respecting breakfast on his return.

I began to think seriously what I should do, still hoping, however, that as the day advanced my master might return with the means to provide at least for our dinner, but in vain. Two o'clock came, but no master; and, as my hunger now became insupportable, without further consideration I locked the door, and, placing the key where I was told, sallied out in search of food. With a humble subdued voice, my hands crossed upon my breast, and the name of the Lord upon my tongue, I went from house to house begging bread. The practice of this art, I may say, I imbibed with my mother's milk; or rather, that having studied it under the greatest master in all Spain, it is no wonder that I was so great an adept in all its various branches.

Suffice it to say, that although in this city there is no more charity than would save a saint from starvation, yet such was my superiority in talent, that before four o'clock I had stowed away nearly four pounds of bread in my empty stomach, and two pounds more in my sleeves and in the inside of my jacket. Passing then by the tripe market, I begged of the women that keep the stalls, who gave me a good-sized piece of cow-heel, with some other pieces of boiled tripe. When I got home, I found my good gentleman already arrived, and having folded and brushed his cloak, he was walking about the courtyard. As I entered, he came up to me, as I thought, to chide me for my absence, but, thank God, it was far otherwise. He inquired where I had been, to which I replied :

" Sir, I remained at home till two o'clock; but when I found that your honour did not return, I went out, and recommended myself so well to the notice of the good people of this city, that they have given me what you see."

I then showed him the bread and the tripe which I had collected. At the sight of these delicacies his countenance brightened up.

" Ah! " said he, " I waited dinner for you some time; but as it grew late I finished. You have nevertheless acted very properly in this matter; for it is much better to ask, for the love of God, than to steal. I only charge you on no account to say you live with me, as such proceedings would not exactly redound to my honour—although I hardly think there is any danger, seeing that I am known so little in this city."

" Do not alarm yourself, sir, on that head," said I, " for people thought as little of asking who was my master as I of telling them."

" Eat away, then, you young rogue," said he, " and with the blessing of God, we shall not have long need of such assistance, though I must say, since I have been in this house, good fortune has never visited me.   There are houses, from some reason or other, so unlucky that every one who occupies them becomes infected with their ill-fortune, and this is without doubt one of them; but I promise you that directly the month is up, I will leave, even if they should offer it to me for nothing."

I seated myself on the end of the bench, and commenced my supper with the tripe and bread.   My poor unhappy master all the time eyed me askance, and never once took his eyes from my skirts, which at that time served me instead of a dinner-service.   Providence had that day so favoured me, that I resolved my master should partake of my abundance, for I could well understand his feelings, having experienced them of old, and to that very day, indeed, I was no stranger to them.   I began to think whether it would exactly become me to invite him to my repast, but as he had unfortunately said he had dined, I feared lest he might take it amiss. However, I very much wished that the poor sinner might have the benefit of my labour, and break his fast as he had done the day before, particularly as the food was better, and my hunger less. My good wishes towards him were speedily gratified, as they happened to jump with his own humour, for directly I commenced my meal he began walking up and down the room, and approaching me rather closely.

" Lazaro," said he, " I really cannot help remarking the extreme grace with which you make your meal.   I don't think I ever saw any one eat with more natural elegance; certain it is, that observers might benefit by your example."

" Doubtless, my good sir," thought I, " it can only be to your extreme amiability that I am indebted for this compliment."   Then, in order to give him the opportunity which I knew he longed for, I said, " Good materials, sir, require good workmen.   This bread is most delicious, and this cow-heel is so well cooked and seasoned that the smell alone is sufficient to tempt any one."

" Cow-heel, is it? " said he.

" It is, sir," I replied.

" Ah," said he, " cow's heel is one of the most delicate morsels in the world; there is nothing I am so fond of."

" Then taste it, sir," said I, " and try whether this is as good as you have eaten."

He seated himself on the bench beside me, and laying hands on the cow-heel, with three or four pieces of the whitest bread, commenced in such good earnest that one might easily see his rations were not disagreeable to him—grinding every bone as ravenously as a greyhound.

" With a nice sauce of garlic," said he, " this would be capital eating."

" You eat it with a better sauce than that, my good sir," thought I.

" By heavens," said he, " anybody would think, to see me eat, that I had not touched a morsel to-day."

" I wish I was as sure of good luck as I'm sure of that," said I to myself. He asked me for the water-jug, and I gave it to him, which, by the way, was a sure proof he had eaten nothing, for it was as full as when I brought it from the river. After drinking, we went to bed in the same manner as on the night before, though it must be confessed in a much more contented mood.

Not to dwell too much on this part of my story, I shall only say, that in this manner we passed eight or ten days, my worthy master taking the air every day, in the most frequented parts, with the most perfect ease of a man of fashion, and returning home to feast on the contributions of the charitable, levied by poor Lazaro.

With all this, however, I liked him very much, seeing he had not the ability to do more—in fact, I was much more sorry for his unfortunate condition than angry at the situation in which his deficiencies placed me; and many times I have been reduced to short commons myself that I might bring home a certain share for my unlucky master. But he was poor, and nobody can give what he has not got—an excuse which I cannot make for the old scoundrels I served before,—though as God is my witness, to this very day I never see a gentleman like my master strutting along as though the street was hardly wide enough for him, without marking the singular way in which Fortune apportions her favours.

I pitied him from my heart, to think that with all his apparent greatness he might at that moment suffer privations equally hard to endure. But with all his poverty, I found greater satisfaction in serving him than either of the others, for the reasons I have stated. All that I blamed him for was the extravagance of his pride, which, I thought, might have been somewhat abated towards one who, like myself, knew his circumstances so intimately. It seems to me, however, that the poorest gentlefolk are always the most proud; but there is consolation in the thought that death knows no distinction, but at length most generally places the commoner in higher ground than it does the peer. I lived for some time in the manner I have related, when it pleased my miserable fortune, which seemed never tired with persecuting me, to envy me even my present precarious and unhappy condition.

It appeared that the season in that country had been unfavourable to corn; therefore it was ordained by the magistracy that all strangers who subsisted by alms should quit the city, or risk the punishment of the whip. This law was enforced so rigidly, that only four days after its promulgation, I beheld a procession of miserable wretches who were suffering the penalty through the streets of the city; a sight which so alarmed me that I did not dare for the future to avail myself of my accustomed means of subsistence.

It can hardly be possible to imagine the extreme necessity to which our house was reduced, or the mournful silence of those who were expiring within; for two or three days we neither spoke a word, nor had we a mouthful to eat. With regard to myself, there were some young women who earned their living by cotton-spinning, and making caps, and with whom, being near neighbours of ours, I had made some slight acquaintanceship; out of their pittance these poor girls gave me a morsel, which just served to keep life within me.

I did not, however, feel my own situation so keenly as I did that of my poor master, who, during the space of eight days, to the best of my knowledge, never touched a mouthful; at least, I can say, the deuce a morsel ever entered our door. Whether he ever got anything to eat when he went out I cannot determine; but I know well, that he sallied out every day with a waist as fine as a greyhound of the best breed; and the better, as he thought to evade suspicion, he would take a straw from the mattress, which could even ill spare the loss, and go swaggering out of the house, sticking it in his mouth for a toothpick! He continued to attribute all his ill-fortune to the unlucky house in which we were lodged.

" The evils we have to bear," he would say, " are all owing to this unfortunate dwelling—as you see, it is indeed sad, dark, and dismal: nevertheless, here we are, and, I fear, must continue awhile to suffer; I only wish the month was past, that we might well be quit of it."

It happened one day, suffering, as I have described, this afflicting persecution of hunger, that by some extraordinary chance, I know not what, nor did I think it dutiful to inquire, there fell into my poor master's poverty-stricken possession the large sum of one real, with which he came home as consequentially as though he had brought the treasure of Venice, saying to me with an air of extreme satisfaction and contentment:

" Here, Lazaro, my boy, take this—Providence is at last beginning to smile on us—go to the market, and purchase bread, meat, and wine; we will no longer take things as we have done. I have other good news, likewise. I have taken another lodging; so that there will be no occasion to remain in this wretched place longer than the end of the month. Curse the place, and he who laid the first brick; by the Lord, since I've been here, not a drop of wine have I drunk, nor have I tasted a morsel of meat, neither have I enjoyed the smallest comfort whatsoever; but everything has been, as you see, miserable and dismal to the last degree. However, go, and quickly, for to-day we will feast like lords."

I took my real and jar, and without another word set out on my errand with the utmost speed, making towards the market-place in the most joyous and light-hearted mood imaginable. But, alas! what enjoyment could I expect, when my adverse fortune so preponderated that the slightest gleam of sunshine in my career was sure to be overtaken by a storm? I was making my way, as I said, in extremely good spirits, revolving in my mind in what manner I should lay out my money to the best advantage, and returning heartfelt thanks to Providence for favouring my master with this unexpected stroke of fortune, when I saw a great crowd at the other end of the street, among whom were many priests; and I soon found to my horror that they were accompanying a corpse.

I stood up against the wall to give them room; and as the body passed I beheld one, who, as I supposed, from the mourning she wore, was the widow of the deceased, surrounded by friends. She was weeping bitterly, and uttering in a loud voice the most piteous exclamations.

" Alas! " she cried, " my dear husband and lord! whither are they taking you? To that miserable and unhappy dwelling! To that dark and dismal habitation! To the house where there is neither eating nor drinking! "

Good heavens! never shall I forget the moment when I heard those words; it seemed in my fright as though heaven and earth were coming together.

" Miserable and unhappy wretch that I am," I exclaimed in an agony of mind, " it is to our house then that they are bearing this body! "

I rushed from the place where I stood, through the crowd, forgetting in my fright the object of my errand, and made with all speed towards home. The instant I arrived I closed the door, barred and bolted it, and cried out to my master with the utmost earnestness of manner to help me to defend the entrance.

He, greatly alarmed, and with the impression that it was something else, called to me, " What is the matter, boy? Why do you slam the door with such fury? "

" Oh, master," said I, " come here and assist me, for they are bringing a dead body here! I met them in the street above, and I heard the widow of the dead man crying out, ' Alas! husband and master, whither do they take you? To the dark and dismal house; to the house of misery and misfortune; to the house where they neither eat nor drink.' To what other house then can they be bringing him than this? "

Directly my master heard these words, albeit in no merry humour, he burst out into such a fit of laughing that it was some time before he could utter a word.

During this time I was holding fast the door, placing my shoulder

against it for better security. The crowd passed with the body;
though still I could not persuade myself but that they intended to
bring it in. When my master was more satiated with mirth than
with food, he said to me in a good-tempered manner:

" It is very just, Lazaro; according to what the widow said, you
were right in thinking as you did; but as they have thought better
of it, and passed on, open the door and go on your errand."

" Stop a little longer, sir," said I; " let them pass the end of the
street, that we may be sure "; but he would not wait, and coming
to the street door, he opened it, and forced me away, for I hardly
knew what I did, with fright, and so he despatched me again to the
market.

We dined well that day, though my appetite was but indifferent;
and it was some time before I recovered from the effect of that mis-
adventure, though it was an excellent source of mirth to my master
whenever it was brought to his recollection.

In this manner I lived some little time with my third and
poorest master, the Esquire; having great curiosity to know what
could possibly have induced him to come to that part of the world,
for I knew he was a stranger on the first day I lived with him, from
the fact of his not knowing a single soul in the city. At last my
wish was gratified; for one day, when we had feasted pretty well,
and were consequently in good humour, he told me a little of his
history. He was a native of Old Castile, and had quitted his country because he had refused to salute a neighbouring gentleman of
consequence, by taking off his hat first, which, according to punc-
tilio, was construed into an insulting mark of disrespect.

My honourable master wished to convince me that, being a gentleman, the other, though superior, had an equal right to doff his
bonnet to him; " for," said he, " though I am, as you see, but an
Esquire, I vow to God if the Count himself were to meet me in the
street and did not take off his hat to me, aye, and entirely off, the
next time we met I would turn into some shop, pretending business,
rather than pay him the least mark of respect. And though you
see me here poorly off, yet in my own country I have an estate in
houses in good condition, and well rented, only sixteen leagues from
the place where I was born, worth at least two hundred thousand
maravedis; so you see that they must be of good size and in good
repair. I have likewise a dovecot which, if it were taken care of,
which it is not, would furnish upwards of two hundred young birds
annually; and many other things I possess, which I have relin-
quished solely because I would not have the slightest imputation
cast upon my honour, by yielding precedence to one who was in
fact no better than myself; and I came to this city hoping to obtain
some honourable employment, though I have not succeeded so well
as I could have wished."

In this manner my master was going on with his narrative, giving me an account of the honourable proceedings by which he had suffered, when he was interrupted by the appearance of an old man and woman; the former came to demand the rent of the house, and the latter that of the bed. They brought the account, and claimed for two months more than he could raise in a year; I think it was about twelve or thirteen reales. He answered them very courteously that he was then going out to change a piece of gold, and should return in the evening. But he made his exit this time for good; and when the good people came for their money I was obliged to tell them that he had not yet returned. The night came, but without my master, and being fearful of remaining in the house by myself, I went to our neighbours, to whom I related the circumstances, and they allowed me to remain with them.

Early in the morning the creditors returned, and inquired of the neighbours. The women replied that his boy was there, and the key of the door ready for them. They then asked me about my master, and I told them that I knew not where he was, and that I had not seen him since he went out to change the piece of gold; but that I thought it was most likely he was gone off with the change.

On hearing this news, they sent for a lawyer and a constable, and called on me and others to witness their taking possession of my master's effects in payment of their demands. They went all over the house, and found just as much furniture as I have recounted before, when they demanded of me, " What has become of your master's property? where are his trunks? and where is his household furniture? "

" I'm sure I don't know," I replied.

" Doubtless," said they, " the property has been removed during the night. Señor Alguacil, take that boy into custody; he knows whither it has been taken."

On this up came the alguacil, and seizing me by the collar, said, " Boy, thou art my prisoner, if thou reveal not where thy master hath hid his effects."

I, as if quite new to this sort of thing, expressed the utmost surprise and terror, and promised to state everything I knew, which seemed a little to disarm his anger.

" That is right," exclaimed all, " tell all you know, and fear nothing."

The man of law seated himself at a desk, and desired me to begin.

" Gentlemen," I continued, " my master is in possession of a good stock of houses and an old dovecot."

" So far well," was the reply; " however little worth, it will meet the debt he owes me; in what part of the city do they lie? "

" On his own estate, to be sure," was my answer.

" That is all the better," they exclaimed; " and where is his estate? "

" In Old Castile," I replied, " as he told me."

Both alguacil and notary laughed out at hearing this, exclaiming, " Quite enough—quite enough to cover your claim, though it were even greater."

The neighbours who had gathered round us, now said, " Gentlemen, this here is a very honest boy; he has not been long in the 'squire's service, and knows no more of him than does your worship; the poor little sinner came knocking at our doors, and for charity's sake we gave him something to eat; after which he has gone to sleep at his master's."

Seeing that I was innocent, they let me go free; but the notary and the alguacil now came on the owners for the taxes, which gave rise to no very friendly discussion, and a most hideous din; the man and woman maintained very stoutly that they had neither the will nor the means to pay them. The others declared they had other business in view of more importance; but I left them without stopping to see the issue of the affair, though I believe the unfortunate owner had to pay all, and he well deserved to do it, for when he ought to have taken his ease and pleasure, after a life of labour, he still went on hiring out houses to increase his gains.

It was in this way that my third and poorest master took leave of me, by which it seems I put the seal to my bad fortune, which, while exercising its utmost rigour against me, had this singularity in it, that though most domestics are known to run away from their masters, it was not thus in my case, inasmuch as my master had fairly run away from me.

MATEO ALEMÁN
1547–1610

HOW GUZMAN EXCITED THE COMPASSION OF THE CARDINAL

HAVING roused myself early one fine morning, according to custom, I went and seated myself at the door of a cardinal, concerning whom I had heard an excellent character, being one of the most charitably disposed in Rome. I had taken the trouble of getting one of my legs swelled, on which, notwithstanding what had passed, was to be seen a new ulcer, one that might set at defiance the most penetrating eye or probe of a surgeon.

I had not omitted to have my face as pale as death; and thus, filling the air with horrible lamentations while I was asking alms, I moved the souls of the different domestics who came in and out to take pity upon me; they gave me something; but I was yet only beating up for game—it was their master I wanted. He at length made his appearance—I redoubled my cries and groans—I writhed in anguish; and I then accosted him in these terms:

" Oh! most noble Christian; thou friend of Christ and His afflicted ones! have pity upon me, a poor wretched sinner. Behold me cut down in the flower of my days; may your excellency be touched with my extreme misery, for the sake of the sufferings of our dear Redeemer."

The cardinal, who was really a pious man, stopped; and, after looking at me earnestly, turned to his attendants.

" In the name of Christ, take this unhappy being, and bear him into my own apartments! let the rags that cover him be exchanged for fine linen; put him into a good bed—nay into my own—and I will go into another room. I will tend on him; for in him do I verily see what must have been the sufferings of our Saviour."

He was obeyed; and, oh charity! how didst thou shame those lordly prelates who think Heaven in debt to them, if they do but look down upon some poor wretch: while my good cardinal, not content with what he had done, ordered two surgeons to attend,

21

recommending them to do all in their power to ease my agony, and to examine and cure my leg; after which they should be well recompensed. He then, bidding me be of good cheer, left me, to pursue his affairs; and the surgeons, to make the best of my case.

They declared at once that it was useless, and that gangrene had already commenced. So seriously did they pronounce this, that, though I knew the effect was solely produced by staining my leg with a certain herb, I almost felt alarmed for the consequences. They then took out their case of instruments, called for a cauldron of hot water, for some fine linen, and a poultice. While these were in preparation, they questioned me as to the origin of my disease, how long I had had it, etc., etc.—moreover, whether I drank wine, and what was my usual diet.

To these, and to a hundred such interrogatories, I replied not a word; so great was my alarm at the terrific processes that appeared to be going on in order to restore me to my pristine health and soundness. I was infinitely perplexed, not knowing to what saint to have recourse; for I was apprehensive there might not be a single one in heaven inclined to interfere in behalf of so thorough-paced a rascal. I recalled to mind the lesson I had so lately been taught at Gaeta, and had my misgivings that I might not escape even on such good terms as I had done there. The surgeons ranked high in their profession; and, after having curiously turned round my leg about twenty times, retired into another room to discuss the result of their observations. I remained in a state of horror not to be described; for it had got into my head that they would decide upon amputation; to learn which I crept softly towards the door to listen, fully resolved to reveal the imposture in so dreadful an alternative.

" Sir," said one, " we may consult here for ever, to little purport; he has got St. Anthony's fire."

" No such thing," replied the other, " he has no more fire in his leg than I have in my hand; we might easily remove it in a couple of days."

" You cannot be serious," said the first speaker. " By St. Comus, I know something of ulcers; and here, I maintain it, we have a gangrene."

" No, no, friend," replied the second, " we have no ulcer—we have a rogue to deal with—nothing is the matter with him I know the whole history of his ulcer, and how it was made. It is by no means very rare; for I know the herbs with which the impostor has prepared it, and the ingenious method in which they have been applied."

The other seemed quite confounded at this assertion; but, ashamed of owning himself a dupe, he persisted in his former opinion: on which a pretty warm colloquy would have ensued, had not the more ingenious of the two had the sense to recommend first to examine the leg, and to end the dispute afterwards.

" Look a little deeper into the matter," said he, " and you will see the fellow's knavery."

" With all my heart. I will confess you are right, when I see there is no ulcer, or rather gangrene."

" That is not enough," replied his colleague. " In acknowledging your error, you must also admit I am entitled to at least a third more fees than yourself."

" By no means," retorted the other. " I have eyes to detect imposture as well as you; and I am of opinion we ought to divide the good cardinal's fees fairly between us."

The dispute now waxed warm, and rather than give up his point, each declared that he would make the cardinal acquainted with the whole business.

In this dilemma I did not hesitate a moment—there was no time to lose—escape was impossible. I rushed into the presence of the faculty, and threw myself at their feet. With well-dissembled grief I thus addressed them :

" Alas! my dear sirs, take pity upon an unfortunate fellow-creature. Think, gentlemen, ' homo sum; nihil humani,' etc. I am mortal like yourselves—you know the hard-heartedness of the great, and how the poor and forlorn are compelled to assume the most horrible shapes in order to soften their hardness; and in doing this what risks and sufferings do we not encounter, and all for so small a remuneration. Besides, what advantage will you get by exposing such a poor miserable sinner? You will certainly lose your fees, which you need not do if you will let us understand each other. You may rely on my discretion; the fear of consequences will keep me silent, and we may each benefit in our respective professions."

Upon this the men of physic again consulted, and at length came to the resolution of pocketing their fees, " secundum artem." Being all of one mind, we now begged to be ushered into the presence of the cardinal, and the surgeons then ordered me to be placed upon a couch, at the side of which they made an immense display of chirurgical instruments, dressings, etc.—again consulted, and after wrapping my leg in a great number of bandages, they desired that I might be put into a warm bed.

His excellency, meanwhile, was full of anxiety to learn the state of my health, and whether there were any hopes of recovery.

" My lord," replied one of the surgeons, " the patient is in a deplorable situation, gangrene has already begun; still, with time and care, there is a chance that he might recover, please God, but it will be a long affair."

" And he is fortunate," said his coadjutor, " in having fallen into our hands; another day, and he was lost for ever; but no doubt Providence must have directed him to the door of your excellency."

This account seemed to please the cardinal; it gave him occasion to display the truest Christian charity, and he desired that neither time nor skill might be spared in the endeavour to restore me to health. He also directed that I should be supplied with everything; and the surgeons on their part pledged themselves to do all that art could effect, and each of them to pay me a visit at least twice in the day; it being necessary to detect the slightest change that might occur in my present condition.

They then withdrew, not a little to my consolation; for I could not but regard them, while present, in the light of two executioners, who might fall upon me at any moment, or publish my imposition to the world. So far from this, however, they made me keep my apartment for three months, which to me seemed like so many ages, so difficult is it to give up the habit of gambling—or begging, with the tone of freedom they seem to include. In vain was I daintily lodged and fed, like his excellency himself; the *ennui* I felt was intolerable. I was incessantly beseeching the doctors to take pity on me, and bring the farce to a close, until they were at length compelled to yield to my importunity.

They left off dressing my leg, and, on its being reduced to its natural size, they acquainted the good cardinal with the fact, who was in raptures at the performance, under his auspices, of so great a cure. He rewarded them handsomely, and came to congratulate me on the miraculous event; and having acquitted myself well in his frequent visits to me, in regard both to my opinions and my principles, he imbibed a real kindness for me; and to give me a further proof of it, he gave me the situation of one of his confidential attendants—a species of honour I was too deeply sensible of to be able to refuse.

MIGUEL DE CERVANTES
1547–1616

THE PRETENDED AUNT

As two young law-students, natives of La Mancha, were one day passing along the streets of Salamanca, they happened to see over the window of a certain shopkeeper, a rich Persian blind, drawn closely down—a novelty which attracted their attention. Fond of adventure, and more deeply read in the noble science of attack and defence than the laws of Bartolus or Baldus, they felt a strong curiosity to know why the articles the shop contained were kept, being marked on sale, so studiously out of view. Why not exhibited in the window as well as at the door?

To remove their perplexity they proceeded to make inquiries—not at the shop, but at one some little distance off, where they observed a babbling old shopkeeper busily serving his neighbours, and, at the same time, retailing the latest news and scandal of the place. In answer to their questions, he ran on with the same volubility.

"My young gentlemen, you are very inquisitive; but if you must know, there is a foreign lady now resides in that house, at least half a saint, a very pattern of self-denial and austerity, and I wish you were under her direction. She has with her, also, a young lady of extraordinary fine appearance and great spirit, who is said to be her niece. She never goes out without an old squire and two old duennas, young gentlemen; and, as I think, they are a family from Granada, rich, proud, and fond of retirement. At least, I have not seen a single soul in our city (and I have watched them well) once pay them a visit. Nor can I, for the life of me, learn from what place they last came hither. But what I do know is, that the young lady is very handsome and very respectable to all appearance; and from the style of living and high bearing of the aunt, they belong to none of the common sort, of that I am sure."

From this account, pronounced with no little emphasis and authority by the garrulous old gentleman, the students became more eager than ever to follow up their adventure. Familiar as they were with the topographical position of the good citizens, the names of the different families and dwellings, and all the flying reports of

25

the day, they were still in the dark as to the real quality of the fair
strangers and their connections in the University.

By dint of industry and perseverance, however, they hoped soon
to clear up their doubts, and the first thing they ascertained was
that, though past the hour of noon, the door of the mansion was
still closed, and there seemed no admittance even upon business.
From this they naturally inferred that, if no tradesmen were admitted, the family could not well take their meals at home; and
that if, like other mortals, they ate at all, they must soon make
their appearance on their way to dinner.

In this conjecture they were not deceived, for shortly they saw a
staid and reverend-looking lady issue from the dwelling, arrayed
all in white, with an immense surplice, wider than a Portuguese
canon's, extending over her head, close bound round her temples,
and leaving only just space enough for her to breathe. Her fan was
in her hand, and a huge rosary with innumerable beads and bells
about her neck—so large indeed, that, like those of Santinuflo, they
reached down to her waist. Her mantle was of fine silk trimmed
with furs; her gloves of the whitest and newest, without a fold; and
she had a walking-stick, or rather an Indian cane, delicately
wrought and tipped with silver.

A venerable old squire, who seemed to have belonged to the times
of Count Fernan Gonzales, escorted his honoured mistress on the
left hand. He was dressed in a large wide coat of velvet stuff without any trimming—ancient scarlet breeches—Moorish hose—a cloak
trimmed with bands—and a cap of strong netted wool, which produced rather a quizzical effect, but which he wore because he was
subject to cold and a dizziness in the head; add to which a large
shoulder-belt and an old Navarrese sword.

These respectable-looking personages were preceded by another
of very different exterior, namely, the lady's niece, apparently
about eighteen, graceful in her deportment, and of a grave but
gracious aspect. Her countenance was rather of the oval—beautiful and intelligent; her eyes were large and black as jet, not without a certain expression of tenderness and languor; arched and
finely marked eyebrows, long dark eyelashes, and on her cheeks a
delicate glow of carnation. Her tresses, of a bright auburn, flowed
in graceful curls round brows of snowy whiteness, combined with
a fine delicate complexion, etc., etc.; and she had on a sarcenet
mantle; a bodice of Flemish stuff; her sandals were of black velvet,
enriched with gilt fastenings and silver fringe; fine scented gloves,
not only fragrant with common essence, but with the richest amber.

Though her demeanour was grave, her step was light and easy:
in each particular she appeared to advantage, and in her *tout
ensemble* still more attractive. In the eyes of the young scholars
she appeared little less than a goddess, and, with half the dazzling

charms she boasted, would have riveted her fetters on the hearts of older and more experienced admirers. As it was, they were completely taken by surprise—astonished, stupefied, overwhelmed, and enchanted. They stood gazing at so much elegance and beauty as if their wits had left them; it being one of the prerogatives of beauty, like the fascination of the serpent, first to deprive its victims of their senses, and then to devour them.

Behind this paragon of perfection walked two ugly old duennas (like maids-of-honour), arrayed, if we only allow for their sex, much in the obsolete manner of their knight companion, the ancient squire.

With this formal and imposing escort, the venerable chaperon at length arrived at the house—the good squire took his station at the door, and the whole party made their entry. As they passed in, the young students doffed their caps with extraordinary alacrity and politeness, displaying in their air and manner as much modesty and respect as they could muster for the occasion.

The ladies, however, took no notice of them, shutting themselves in, and the young gentlemen out: who were left quite pensive and half in love, standing in the middle of the street. From this want of courtesy they ingeniously came to the conclusion that these fair disturbers of their peace had not come to Salamanca for the purpose of studying the laws of politeness, but studying how to break them. In spite, however, of their ingratitude, they agreed to return good for evil, and to treat them on the following night to a little concert of music, in the form of a serenade—for this is the first and only service which poor students have it in their power to offer at the windows of her who may have smitten them.

Seeking some solace, however, for their disappointment just at present, they repaired to a restaurateur's; and having partaken of what little they could get, they next betook themselves to the chambers of some of their friends. There they made a collection of all the instruments of musical torture they could find, such as old wire-worn guitars, broken violins, lutes, flutes, and castanets; for each of which they provided suitable performers, who had at least one eye, an arm, and a leg among them.

Not content, however, with this, being determined to get everything up in the most original style, they sent a deputation to a poet, with a request that he would forthwith compose a sonnet. This sonnet was to be written for, and precisely upon, the name of *Esperanza*, such being the Christian appellation of the hope of their lives and loves; and it was to be sung aloud on that very same night. The poet undertook the serious charge; and in no little while, by dint of biting his lips and nails, and rubbing his forehead, he manufactured a sonnet, weaving with his wits just as an operative would weave a piece of cloth.

This he handed to the young lovers; they approved it, and took the author along with them to repeat it to the musicians as they sung it, there being no time to commit it to memory.

Meantime the eventful night approached—and at the due hour there assembled for the solemn festival nine knights of the cleaver, four vocal performers with their guitars, one psaltery, one harper, one fiddler, twelve bell-ringers, thirty shield-sounders, and numerous other practitioners, divided into several companies; all, however, better skilled in the music of the knife and fork than in any other instrument. In full concert they struck up on entering the street, and a fresh peal on arriving at the lady's house, the last of which made so hideous a din as to rouse all within hearing from their quiet slumbers, and bring them to their windows half dead with wonder and alarm.

This was continued some time just under the lady's window, till the general concert ceased, to give room for the harp and the recital of the poet's sonnet. This was sung by one of those musicians who never wait to be invoked; nor was the poet less on the alert as prompter on the occasion. It was given with extreme sweetness and harmony of voice, and quite accorded with the rest of the performance.

Hardly had the recitation of this wonderful production ceased, when a cunning rogue among the audience, turning to one of his companions, exclaimed in a loud, clear voice:

"I vow to Heaven I never heard a viler song worse sung in all my born days! Did you note well the harmony of the lines, and that exquisite adaptation of the lady's name; that fine invocation to Cupid, and the pretty mention of the age of the adored object —the contrast then between the giant and the dwarf—the malediction—the imprecation—the sonorous march of the whole poem. I vow to God that if I had the pleasure of knowing the author I would willingly, to-morrow morning, send him a dozen pork sausages, for I have this very day received some from the country."

At the word sausages, the spectators were convinced that the person who had just pronounced the encomium meant it in ridicule; and they were not mistaken; for they afterwards learnt that he came from a place famous for its practical jokers, which stamped him in the opinion of the bystanders for a great critic, well qualified to pass judgment upon poets, as his witty analysis of this precious morsel had shown.

Notwithstanding all their endeavours, the windows of the house they were serenading seemed the only ones that remained closed, a circumstance at which our young adventurers were not a little disappointed. Still, however, they persevered; the guitars were again heard, accompanied by three voices, in a romantic ballad chosen for the occasion. The musicians had not proceeded far before they heard a window opened, and one of the duennas whom they had before seen made her appearance. In a whining hypocritical tone she addressed the serenaders:

"Gentlemen, my mistress, the Lady Claudia di Astudillo y Quinones, requests that you will instantly repair to some other quarter, and not bring down scandal upon this respectable neighbourhood by such violent uproar; more particularly as there is now at her house a young lady, her niece, my young mistress, Lady Esperanza di Torralva Meneses y Pachico. It is very improper, therefore, to create such a disturbance among people of their quality. You must have recourse to other means, of a more gentlemanly kind, if you expect to meet with a favourable reception."

On hearing these words, one of the young gallants quickly retorted, "Do me the favour, most venerable mistress, to request your honoured Lady Donna Esperanza to gladden our eyes by presenting herself at the window. I wish to say a few words, which may prove of the greatest consequence."

"Oh, shocking!" exclaimed the duenna. "Is it the Lady Esperanza you mean? You must know, my good sir, she is not thus lightly to be spoken of—she is a most honourable, exemplary, discreet, modest young person, and would not comply with such an extravagant request, though you were to offer her all the pearls of the Indies."

During this colloquy with the ancient duenna, there came a number of people from the next street; and the musicians, thinking the alguacils were at hand, sounded a retreat, placing the baggage of the company in the centre; they then struck up some martial sounds with the help of their shields, in the hope that the captain would hardly like to accompany them with the sword dance, as is the custom at the holy feast of San Fernando at Seville, but would prefer passing on quietly to risking a defeat in the presence of his emissaries.

They therefore stood their ground for the purpose of completing their night's adventure; but one of the two masters of the revels refused to give them any more music unless the young lady would consent to appear at the window. But not even the old duenna again honoured them with her presence there, notwithstanding their repeated solicitations, a species of slight which threw the whole company into a rage, and almost incited them to make an attack upon the Persian blind, and bring their fair foes to terms. Mortified as they were, they still continued their serenade, and at length took their leave with such a volley of discordant sounds as to make the very houses shake with their hideous din.

It was near dawn before the honourable company broke up, to the extreme annoyance and disappointment of the students at the little effect their musical treat seemed to have produced. Almost at their wits' end, they at last hit upon the expedient of referring their difficulties to the judgment of a certain cavalier, in whom they thought they could confide. He was one of that high-spirited class termed in Salamanca *los generosos*.

He was young, rich, and extravagant, fond of music, gallant, and a great admirer of bold adventures; in short, the right sort of advocate in a cause like theirs. To him they recounted very minutely their prodigious exertions and their ill-success; the extreme beauty, grace, and attractions of the young, and the imposing and splendid deportment of the old lady; ending with the small hope they had of ever becoming better acquainted with them. Music, it was found, boasted no charm for them, " charmed they ever so wisely "; nay, they had been accused of bringing scandal upon the whole neighbourhood.

Now their friend the cavalier, being one who never blinked danger, began to reassure them, and promised that he would soon bring their uncourteous foes to conditions, *coûte que coûte*; and that, as he was himself armed against the keenest shafts of the little archer-god, he would gladly undertake the conquest of this proud beauty on their account.

Accordingly, that very day he despatched a handsome and substantial present to the lady-aunt, with his best services; at the same time offering all he was worth—life, his person, his goods and chattels, and—his compliments. Such an offer not occurring every day, the elder duenna took on her the part of the Lady Claudia, and, in her mistress's name, was curious to hear from the page something of the rank, fortune, and qualifications of his master. She inquired especially as to his connections, his engagements, and the nature of his pursuits, just as if she were going to take him for a son-in-law. The page told her everything he knew, and the pretended aunt seemed tolerably well satisfied with his story.

It was not long ere she went, in person, in her mistress's name, as the old duenna, with an answer to the young cavalier, so full and precise, that it resembled an embassy rather than a letter of thanks. The duenna arrived, and proceeded to open the negotiation; she was received by the cavalier with great courtesy. He bade her be seated in a chair near his own; he took off her cloak with his own hands, and handed her a fine embroidered handkerchief to wipe the perspiration from her brow, for she seemed a little fatigued with her walk. He did more; and before permitting her to say a single word on the nature of her errand, he ordered sweetmeats and other delicacies to be set before her, and helped her to them himself. He then poured out two glasses of exquisitely flavoured wine, one for her and one for himself. In short, so delicate and flattering were his attentions, that the venerable guardian of youthful virtue could not have received more genuine pleasure if she had been made a saint upon the spot.

She now opened the object of her embassy with the most choice, demure, and hypocritical set of phrases she could command, though ending with a most flat falsehood to the following purport:

"She was commissioned," she said, "by her excellent young mistress, Donna Esperanza di Torralva Meneses y Pachico, to present to his excellency her best compliments and thanks. That his excellency might depend that, though a lady of the strictest virtue, Donna Esperanza would never refuse to receive so excellent and accomplished a gentleman upon an honourable footing, whenever he were inclined to honour her aunt's house with his presence."

The cavalier replied " that he had the most perfect faith in all he had heard respecting the surpassing beauty, virtue, and accomplishments of her young mistress, qualities which made him only the more eager to enjoy the honour of an interview."

After an infinite variety of reservations and circumlocutions this proposal was acceded to by the good duenna, who assured him there could be no possible objections on the part of either of the ladies, an assertion than which, however, nothing could be farther from the truth. In short, desirous of discharging her duennal duty in the strictest manner, and not content with intercepting the cavalier's presents, and personating Donna Claudia, the wily old lady resolved to turn the affair to still further account. She ended the interview, therefore, with assuring him that she would, that very evening, introduce him to the ladies; and first, to the beautiful Esperanza, before her aunt should be informed of his arrival.

Delighted with his success, the young cavalier dismissed his obliging guest with every expression of esteem, and with the highest compliments to her fair mistress; at the same time putting a purse into the old duenna's hand, enough to purchase a whole wardrobe of fine clothes.

"Simple young man," muttered the cunning old lady, as she left the house; " he thinks it is all finely managed now; but I must touch a little more of his money; he has certainly more than he knows what to do with. It is all right; he shall be welcome to my lady's house, truly; but how will he go out again, I wonder. The officers will see him home, I dare say, but not till after he has paid me well again for being admitted; and my young lady has made me a present of some handsome gowns for introducing so pretty a young gentleman; and her foolish old aunt rewarded me well for discovering the secret."

Meantime, the young cavalier was impatiently expecting the appointed hour; and as there is none but sooner or later must arrive, he then took his hat and cloak, and proceeded where the ancient duenna was expecting him.

On his arrival she nodded to him out of a window, and having caught his eye, she threw him the empty purse he had presented her with, well filled, in the morning. Don Felix was at no loss to take the hint, and on approaching the door, he found it only a little open, and the claws of the old beldame ready to clutch the offered bait before she granted him admittance. It was then opened wide, and she conducted him in silence upstairs, and through a suite of rooms into an elegant little boudoir, where she concealed him behind a Persian screen, in a very skilful and cautious manner. She bade him remain quite still; her young lady, Esperanza, was informed of his arrival, and from *her* favourable representation of his high rank, fortune, and accomplishments, she was prepared to give him an interview, even without consulting her aunt. Then giving her hand as a token of her fidelity, she left Don Felix couched behind the screen, in anxious expectation of the result.

Meanwhile, the artful old wretch, under the strictest promise of secrecy, and a handsome present of new gowns, had communicated to the aunt the important intelligence of the discovery of so unpleasant an affair, relating to the unsullied reputation and high character of her niece. She then whispered her mistress in the ear that she had actually discovered a man concealed in the house, and what was worse, by appointment with her young lady, as she had learnt from a note she had intercepted; but that she dared not disturb the intruder, as he appeared armed at all points. She therefore entreated her mistress to make no noise, lest he should perpetrate some deadly deed before the officers of justice, to whom she had sent notice, should arrive to secure him.

Now the whole of this statement was a new tissue of lies, as the old beldame intended to let the cavalier very quietly out, and had never yet ventured to acquaint her young lady with his presence at all. Having thus carried her point with the old lady, she declared that if she would promise to stay without disturbing herself in that room, she would go in search of Esperanza, and conduct her to her aunt immediately. This being agreed upon, the duenna proceeded to look for her young lady upstairs, and was not a little puzzled to find her seated in her boudoir, and Don Felix near her, with an expression of the utmost pleasure and surprise in his countenance.

What had been his astonishment on Esperanza's entrance, to behold the beloved girl from whom he had been separated by her aunt's cruelty not many months before. What an ecstatic meeting for both; what a dilemma for the treacherous old duenna, should an explanation have already taken place! She had not been many weeks in the Lady Claudia's service, and she would certainly not be many more if the lovers should be thus discovered together.

What was to be done? Ere they could decide, her mistress's step was heard on the stairs; she was calling Esperanza in those sharp, bitter tones to which her niece was too well accustomed, and she had already reached the ante-room ere Don Felix was safely ensconced behind the screen. Esperanza hastened towards her, and found her seated in an easy arm-chair, in a sad flurry of mingled rage and alarm.

She cast ominous and perturbed glances towards the boudoir whence her niece had just issued, and then looked out of the window, impatient for the arrival of the police. She did not venture to allude to the cause of her dismay; bidding her niece sit down, a portentous silence ensued. It was now late, the whole household, even their protector, the ancient squire, had retired to rest. Only the old duenna and her young mistress were wide awake, and the latter was particularly anxious for her aunt to retire. Though only nine, she declared she believed the clock had struck ten; she thought her aunt looked jaded and unwell; would she not like to go to bed? No reply; but dark, malignant glances sufficiently attested what it would have been had she dared to speak out. Though unable, however, to deal in particulars, she could not refrain from making some general observations which bore upon the case.

In a low tone, therefore, she addressed her niece as follows: " I have often enough warned you, Esperanza, not to lose sight of the exhortations I have invariably made it my business to give you. If you valued them as you ought, they would be of infinite use to you, as I fear time and experience will, ere long, sufficiently show "; and here she again looked out of the window.

" You must not flatter yourself we are now at Placentia, where you were born; nor yet at Zamora, where you were educated; no, nor at Toro, where you were first introduced. The people of those places are very different from what they are here; there are no scandals, no jealousies, no intriguing, my dear; and (in a still lower tone) no violence and uproar such as we heard in the street last night. Heaven protect us from all violent and deceitful men; from all house-breaking, robbery, and assassinations. Yes, I say, I wish we were well out of Salamanca! You ought to be aware in what a place you are; they call it the mother of sciences, but I think it is the mother of all mischief; yes, of everything bad, not excepting some people whom I know; but I mention no names just now," she added, with a look of suppressed malice and vexation; " though I could if I pleased. But the time will come! " and she here muttered some low unintelligible threats about grates and convents. " We must leave this place, my dear; you perhaps don't know there are ten or twelve thousand students here, young, impudent, abandoned, lost, predestined, shameless, graceless, diabolical, and mischievous wretches, the scum of all parts of the world, and addicted to all evil courses, as I think we had pretty good proof only last night. Though avaricious as misers, when they set their eyes upon a young woman, my dear, they can be extravagant enough. The Lord protect us from all such, I say! Jesu Maria save us from them all! ''

During this bitter moral lecture, Esperanza kept her eyes fixed upon the floor, without speaking a word, and apparently quite resigned and obedient, though without producing its due effect upon her aunt. '' Hold up your head, child, and leave off stirring the fire; hold up your head and look me in the face, if you are not ashamed, and try to keep your eyes open, and attend to what I say. You require all the senses you have got, depend upon it, to make good use of my advice; I know you do.''

Esperanza here ventured to put in a word : '' Pray, dear aunt, don't so fret yourself and me by troubling yourself to say any more. I know all you would say, and my head aches shockingly—do spare yourself, or I think my head will split with pain.''

'' It would be broken with something else, perhaps, if you had your deserts, young miss, to answer your affectionate aunt in such a way as that! To say nothing of what I know—yes, what I know, and what others shall know, when somebody comes ''; and she glanced very significantly towards the door.

Of this edifying conversation Don Felix had partly the benefit, as it occurred so near his place of concealment. The old duenna, meantime, being desirous, after the discovery that had taken place, of ingratiating herself with the lovers, and finding there was no hope of Donna Claudia retiring to rest till the arrival of the police, thought it high time to bring the young cavalier out of his dilemma. It was her object to get him safe out of the house, and yet preserve the good opinion of her venerable mistress, who might wait, she thought, till doomsday for the police.

As it was impossible to speak to Don Felix, she hit upon the following expedient to make him speak for himself, trusting to her own and her young lady's discretion for bringing him off safely. She took her snuff-box, and approaching his hiding-place very slyly, threw a good handful into his face, which taking almost immediate effect, he began to sneeze with such a tremendous noise that he might be heard in the street.

She then rushed, in apparent alarm, into the next room, crying out : '' He is coming! he is here;—guns and pistols—pistols and guns—save yourselves, my dear ladies! Here, you go into this closet ''; she pushed the old aunt into it, almost dead with fright, and closed the door. '' You come with me,'' she continued to Esperanza, '' and I will see you safe here.'' Saying which, she took the young lady with her, and joined her lover, who had already found his way downstairs.

Unluckily, however, to make the scene more complete, and to

impose the better upon her old mistress, she opened the window, and began to call out, " Thieves! thieves! help! help! " though in as subdued a tone as possible.

But at the very first cry, the corregidor, who happened to be walking close to the house, entered the door, followed by two of his myrmidons, just as Don Felix opened it to go out. They instantly pounced upon and secured him before he had time either to explain or defend himself, and, spite of the entreaties of Esperanza and the duenna, he was borne away.

They followed, however, to represent the affair to the chief alguacil; and they had gone only a little way when they were met by a strong party, headed by the identical two students, who came prepared for a fresh serenade, on the strength of their friend the cavalier's support and assistance. What was their surprise and dismay to behold him in such hands, and followed by the lovely Esperanza herself, the cause of all their anxiety and exertions.

Love and honour at once fired their breasts, and their resolution was taken in a moment. Six friends, and an army of musicians, were behind them. Turning to them, out flew their own swords, as they called on them to draw in aid of honour and beauty, and rescue them from the hands of the vile alguacils. All united in the cry of rescue—the musicians in the rear struck up the din of war; and a hideous peal it was—while the rest rushed on with as much haste and spirit as if they had been going to a rich banquet. The combat was not long doubtful; the emissaries of justice were overpowered by the mere weight of the crowd which bore upon them; and unable to stir either hand or foot, they were mingled in the thick of the engagement, pressed on all sides by halt, and maimed, and blind, and stunned with the din of battle from the rear.

While this continued, Don Felix and his fair companion had been the especial care of the students and their friends, by whom they had been early drawn off into a place of comparative safety. Here a curious scene took place:—After the first congratulations upon their victory, the two students took their friend Don Felix by the hand, expressing the deep gratitude they both felt for the eternal obligation he had conferred upon them, having so nobly redeemed his pledge of bringing the lady to terms, and placing her in their hands.

The speaker then continued that *he*, having had the good fortune to bear her away in safety from the crowd, was justly entitled to the prize, which he hoped would not be disputed, as he was then ready to meet any rival. The other instantly accepted the challenge, declaring he would die sooner than consent to any such arrangement. The fair object of their strife looked at Don Felix, uttering exclamations of mingled terror and surprise, while the

young cavalier, just as the students were proceeding to unsheath
their weapons, burst into a fit of uncontrollable mirth.

"Oh, miracle of love! mighty power of Cupid!" he exclaimed.
"What is it I behold? Two such sworn friends to be thus meta-
morphosed in a moment! Going to fight; after I have so nobly
achieved the undertaking! Never,—I am the man you must both
run through the body, for verily I am about to forfeit my pledge.
I, too, am in love with this lady; and with Heaven's permission
and her own, to-morrow she will be mine—my own wedded wife;
for, by Heaven! she returns no more to Aunt Claudia and her
duennas."

He then explained to the astonished students the story of their
love; how, when, and wherefore they had wooed—their separation
and sufferings—with the happy adventure that had crowned their
hopes. Then, imitating the language of the students, he took their
hands, assuring them of his deep gratitude for the eternal obligation
they had conferred upon him.

On the ensuing day, Esperanza gave her hand to Don Felix, and
the venerable Aunt Claudia was released from her hiding-place and
all further anxiety on her niece's account.

FRANCISCO DE QUEVEDO
1580–1645

THE VISION OF THE CATCH-POLE POSSESSED

On going the other day to hear mass, at a convent in this town, I found the doors closed, and a world of good people pressing and praying to get in. Upon inquiring what was the matter, they told me there was a demoniac about to be exorcised, which made me the more eager to see the ceremony; but all to no purpose, for after having been nearly stifled in the crowd, I was glad to make my escape, and betake myself once more to my lodgings.

As I went, I met a particular friend of mine at the end of the street, belonging to the same convent, who gave me the same information. Observing my curiosity, he told me to follow him, and having a general passport, he took me through a little door at the back of the church into the vestry. Here we found a miserable, dogged-looking fellow, with a fur tippet round his neck, as slovenly as any beggar you meet—all in rags and tatters, his hands bound, and stamping and roaring in a most horrible manner.

" Bless me! " I exclaimed, crossing myself, " what is all this? "

" This," replied the good father, who was to expel the devil—" this is a man possessed with an evil spirit."

" That's an infernal lie," cried the demon that tormented him; " with all respect to the present company, it is not a man possessed with a devil, but a devil possessed with a man! You ought to take care what you say, for it is quite evident, from both the question and answer, that you are little better than a set of fools. Know that we devils never get possession of the body of an alguacil if we can help it; it is in spite of ourselves if we do. To speak correctly, therefore, say that you have here a devil *catch-poled,* and not a *catchpole* possessed. To give you your due, you men can outwit us devils better than you do the catchpoles, for we take fright at the cross, while they make use of it as a cloak for their wicked purposes.

" Still, while we thus differ in our humour, we are much of a mind in regard to the duties we have to fulfil; for if we bring men into judgment and tribulation, so do the bailiffs; we pray for the

37

progress of vice and all its societies, and so do they; in fact, they
are the more zealous of the two, because they make a livelihood by
it, and we only for the sake of company. Here you see the catchpoles are worse than the devils, for they are bent upon devouring
their own species. We are angels, though black ones, compared
with them, and were only changed into imps for setting ourselves
upon an equality with the Most High. The generation of catchpoles live, like worms, upon corruption; so you may as well leave
off, my good father, plying this wretch with beads and reliques—
you will sooner snatch a soul from damnation than anything out
of his clutches. In short, your catchpoles and we devils belong
both to the same order, only we are of the *barefoot*, like the
reverend father (having a hard footing in the world), while they
go warm shod—both shoes and stockings."

I was rather astonished to find so great a sophist in the devil;
but, spite of all, the holy man persisted in his exorcism, and to
stop the demon's mouth, he washed his face in some holy water,
so that the demoniac became ten times madder than before. He
began to howl so horribly as to deafen the whole company, and
make the floor tremble.

" Perhaps," he exclaimed, " you think all this the effect of your
holy water; no such thing; the pure element itself would have done
as much; for a catchpole hates nothing so much as cold water.
They may well be called alguacils, from Pagan descent; and as so
much more suitable to their behaviour."

" Come, come," retorted the good father, " we must not listen to
this villain; give his tongue free scope, and you will hear him revile
the government, and the ministers of justice themselves, because
they keep the world in order, and put down villainy—all which
goes to spoil his own market."

" Chop me none of your logic, old fool," replied the devil, " for
there is more in our philosophy than you are aware of; but if you
like to do a poor devil a good turn, be quick and give me my *exit*
out of this accursed bumbailiff. Were I not a devil of some rank
and reputation, I should be better able to endure the scoffs and
taunts that will welcome my return back for keeping such sorry
company."

" You shall leave it this very day," cried the holy father; " in
pity to this tormented wretch, I will expel thee, spite of thy infernal
obstinacy; wilt thou persist in torturing him, I say? "

" It is nothing," returned the devil, " but a trial between us
which shall prove the greater devil of the two."

The priest did not in the least relish these keen and wicked replies,
which turned the laugh against him; but to me it was very amusing; and addressing myself to the good father, I said:

" We are all friends, I believe, here, and I wish you would let

me put a few questions to this merry demon; I may be able, perhaps, to get something good out of him, even against his will, if
you will just stop his hand a little on this poor wretch."

The exorcist granted my request, and the merry devil resumed
with a laugh:

"We shall never, I see, want a friend at court while a poet
resides there; and it would be very ungrateful in the whole race if
we did, after the treatment they have experienced from us below."

"Have you many?" inquired I.

"Whole lots," he replied; "and there is nothing so pleasant as
the first year of a poet's novitiate; he brings letters of recommendation for our ministers, and inquires for Rhadamanthus, Charon,
Cerebus, Minos, etc., etc., with a grave face."

"What punishment do you inflict?" I asked, rather anxiously.

"A great deal, and of a very proper kind," he replied. "We
praise the works of their rivals; some are employed for a thousand
years in revising a few hackneyed stanzas upon jealousy; others
beat their heads with their empty palms, or bore their noses with
a hot iron to get a new thought. They split a hair, and torture a
word into every absurd complication of sound; they bite their nails,
or stand transfixed in a brown study. But your comic poets fare
the worst, for the villainous tricks they play upon the stage in
coupling high-born ladies with clowns and lackeys, and princes and
nobles with the refuse of the other sex. We do not find room for
these satiric wits along with the others, but with pettifoggers, and
common dealers in the arts of shuffling, cheating, and forging.

"As to the discipline employed, those who come, for instance,
by the way of fools, we place among the astrologers; a man condemned for manslaughter finds his seat among the physicians; merchants who have negotiated a vile business take their chance with
Judas; and corrupt ministers of every class pitch their tents close
to those of the great robbers of the earth. A certain dealer, who
declared he had lived upon the immaculate sale of cold water, took
up his station with his friends the publicans. Indeed, the whole of
our kingdom is divided into separate districts, to accommodate all
classes of colonists. The blind, who would fain rank with the poets,
we include among the lovers; a sexton, and a cook who roasted cats
for hares, we send to the pastry shop."

"And have you many lovers," I inquired, "in your domin-
ions?"

"Marry! that we have; and all are great admirers of themselves;
some busied with their money, some with their own discourses,
others with their own works; but very rarely one that can be said
to like his own wife. No wonder, indeed; for the women generally
bring them to the stool of repentance, and then the devil may take
his own way. But for true sport, give me your fashionable, genteel

lovers—your men of colours and favours—so trimmed and laced as to make a most admirable sign for the tailor or the mercer. Some you would mistake for carriers, bending under the burden of love-letters; some are horned, some flaming like comets; and best of all to behold are the antics of your maiden lover, with open mouth, and hands extended, embracing the air for his visionary mistress.

" There are also a kind of empty-handed, befooled pretenders, ever on the watch, snatching at the shadow, but who can never reach the substance; while some, worse than these, condemn themselves for ever for a Judas kiss. One storey lower is the asylum of contented cuckolds, a rank poisonous place, strewed with the relics of reputation and paved with horns. But, resigned to their sorry destiny, the inhabitants never so much as question the justice of the sentence to which they are doomed; but far more difficult to keep in order are the admirers of old women, who occupy the adjoining apartment, whose luxury and depravity of taste are consigned to perpetual bondage.

" To leave all this, let me give you a word of advice—not to persist in making caricatures of us devils in your shows and pictures, if you wish me to indulge your curiosity. Why should you give us claws and talons like a vulture or a griffin—why tails— why saucer eyes and horns—nay, why even crowned with a coxcomb? You might take us for hermits, philosophers, or corregidores! Think better of it; paint us as we are; and one good turn will bring another. The other day we had Geronimo Bosco with us; and on inquiring what had led him to make such frightful representations of us in his visions, he made answer, it was because he had never really believed that there were demons, though he now found that it was but too true.

" What we consider still worse, is the usual style of your discourse when you wish to reflect upon any one's ill behaviour; as, for instance, ' See how this devil of a tailor has spoiled my coat; how this devil of a fellow has made me wait; and how this devil of a rascal has taken me in! ' all which is very unhandsome, thus to rank us with the scum of mankind. Tailors, indeed! a set of wretches that serve us for fuel, and who are obliged to beg hard for the honour of being burnt! You have another bad custom, too, of giving everything to the devil which you do not like yourselves: as, ' the devil take it; go to the devil; and the devil give you good of it '; as if he had nothing else to do than to take possession of what you choose to give him; if they are so ready, let them come themselves, and depend upon receiving a hearty welcome."

In the same strain the devil rambled on some time, when suddenly was heard a scuffle which had befallen between two conceited coxcombs about a point of precedence. On turning to look, I beheld some objects in the distance that appeared to carry something in the shape of crowns.

" Are there kings in hell? " I inquired; and the demon satisfied my doubts by observing that it abounded with them; some condemned to subjection under those whom they had oppressed—some for extreme cruelty, and desolating their kingdoms in a way more terrific than the great plague. Others are expiating their avarice, for making deserts of populous villages and smiling plains; while many find their way thither by means of corrupt ministers, more base and cruel than themselves. It is delightful to see them suffer; and their torments are redoubled, inasmuch as they most frequently bring half their kingdom with them, bringing down upon the world universal ruin.

" It is thus, then, that kings find themselves a royal road to perdition, while your great merchants reach it by a bridge of silver. Next to these, I may mention your judges! "

" What, are there judges there? "

" Are there! " returned the demon, " why, the judges are like game to our palates—the choice morsels—the most prolific fish that supply our great lake; for what are the bailiffs, the proctors, barristers, attorneys, and clerks, that arrive every day in shoals, but the fry from these mighty judges; and sometimes, in a lucky season for cheating, perjury, and forgery, we are so full that we can nowhere find room for our guests."

" What! would you say that there is no justice on the face of the earth? " I inquired.

" I do," replied the devil; " and if you will listen, I will tell you, if you have never heard the story."

" I have not," was the answer.

" Then open your ears, and here you have it," retorted the devil with a smile. " Once, in days gone by, Truth and Justice happened to meet in their peregrinations over the earth; the one was naked, the other was very frank, and sour of aspect; and neither found the least hospitality or good reception in any quarter. After wandering about miserably in the open air, Truth was compelled to take up a lodging with a mute; and Justice, seeing that her name was generally used as a cloak for villainy, and that she was held in no regard, made up her mind to return to heaven. She took her departure from the great courts and cities and went into the country, where she met with some simple villagers, who afforded her the best entertainment in their power; but malice and persecution still followed her, and she was driven even thence. She then resorted to many other places, and people everywhere asked her who she was. She told them plainly she was Justice; for she would not tell an untruth. ' Justice! ' they all cried, ' she is an entire stranger to us—there's nothing for her here—go, shut the door!   After this wretched reception on earth, she indignantly took wing and returned to her native heaven, without so much as leaving even a trace of the path by which she had passed.

" The fame of her name, however, did not become extinct; and we still behold her depicted with the sceptre of power in her hands, while she is, moreover, called Justice.   But let us call her by what name we will, it is in her name the fires are kindled in the realms below; and the sleights of hand performed under her disguise sur- pass everything to be achieved by the most accomplished jilts, rogues, pick-pockets, or cut-throats in this wide world; in short, the power of avarice has reached such a height as to bid defiance to all other passions, and to absorb the whole faculties of body and soul in schemes of imposture and plunder.   First in the list of iniquity, does not the seducer, under the pretence of her consent, steal the honour of her he vows to love?   Does not the attorney dive into your pockets, and show both a law and a rule for it?   the comedians run away with your time as well as your money, while contriving to live on the recitation of other men's productions? Love outwits you with his eyes; the orator with his tongue; the soldier keeps you at arm's length; the musician beguiles you with his voice and fingers; the astrologer puzzles you with his calcula- tions; the apothecary sickens you with his drugs; the leech draws your blood; and the physician finally bids you take your exit.

" Now in some way or other, these characters all belong to the great class of impostors; but it is the catchpole who combines all; and, in the name of justice, imposes upon and oppresses you with all his might.   Ever waking and on the alert, he watches you with his eyes; he dogs you with his feet; seizes you with his hands; accuses you with his tongue; and, in short, makes you cry out in the words of the Litany, ' from all catchpoles, as well as devils, good Lord deliver us! ' "

" But what is the reason," inquired I, " that you have not included the women among the thieves, for surely you must admit they are both of the same trade? "

" For mercy's sake," interrupted the devil, " not a word of the women, if ye love me; for we are so wearied with their endless importunity and the clatter of their tongues that we take alarm at the bare idea of them.   It is the necessity we devils labour under of finding accommodation for them which makes the infernal abode what it is; for ever since the death of the Witch of Endor it has been their constant endeavour to stir up strife, and in their extreme malice and uncharitableness to set us all by the ears together. Not a few, indeed, have the hardihood to tell us to our face that when we have done our very worst they have still some greater pun- ishment in store for us.   Yet, perhaps, on the whole, we ought to console ourselves that however great an infliction upon *us*, they are still more formidable to *you*, for we have there none of your grand theatres, saloons, parks, and other places of assignation, with which the earth is so abundantly supplied.''

'' You appear then to be in no want of a female population,'' returned I; '' but in which do you most abound, the handsome or the opposite, think you? ''

'' Oh,'' quoth the devil, '' for one beauty we have at least half a dozen frights; and the reason is, that your pretty women, when they have had their way till they are tired, and rung out the changes on all kind of pleasures long enough, generally turn out saints, and repent; whereas your plain people pine themselves to death for spite, and, flying in the face of Providence, so distort their tempers and their very souls that they are enough to terrify the devil himself when they arrive. For the most part, they live to be old, and invariably take leave of the world with a malediction on the younger and fairer part of the creation whom they leave behind. This is the burden of their last sigh.''

'' You have said quite enough; I wish to hear no more of the ladies. But to approach another and a humbler class, what are the kind of mendicants whom you have to find room for in the regions below? have you many? ''

'' Poor people,'' quoth the devil; '' who are they? ''

'' Those,'' I replied, '' who possess nothing in this world.''

'' How is it likely,'' returned the devil, '' that they should be damned for having nothing, when men are only sent to us for sticking too closely to the world? You may look, but will find none of their names in our books; which is no wonder, for if you have nothing, the devil himself will desert you in time of need. To say the truth, where will you find falser friends than are your sycophants, hollow friends, boon companions, envious and malicious acquaintance; than sons, brothers, or other relatives that lie in wait for your life to get at your money, and, while they hang over your couch, sincerely wish you already at the devil?

'' But the poor are never flattered, nor envied, nor attended, nor accompanied by friends. No one longs for their property; and, in fact, they are a class of people who live well, and die better; and there are a few who would not barter their rags for the privilege of royalty itself. They go and come at their pleasure; and be it war or peace, they are as free from cares as they are from taxes, and all burdens and duties that sit so uneasily on the shoulders of the great. For them judgments have no terrors, and executions no steel; they live inviolable, as if they bore a charm to keep intruders at a distance. What thought have they of the morrow? they husband the passing hour, and are content. The past with them is numbered with the dead, and not knowing the future, they fear it not. But stop! it is an old saying, ' that when the devil preaches, the world is near at an end.' "

" This is the work of divine power," exclaimed the holy father, who was busily exorcising the catchpole: " Thou art the father of lies, devil, and withal dost promulgate mighty truth sufficient almost to convert a heart of stone."

" Mind your own business," retorted the devil, " and do not imagine that my conversion is to be brought about by you. If I speak the truth, it is in aggravation of your guilt, in order that when called upon, some future day, you may not plead any ignorance of your duty, my good father. Verily, you most of you shed tears at parting, not from sincere repentance, but a just dread of what you have to expect from your sins. In short, you are little better than hypocrites; and if at any time your reflections trouble you, it is because you know your bodies will not long hold out, and it is then only you begin to pick a quarrel with the sin itself."

" Thou art a base impostor," retorted the exorcist, " for there is many a righteous soul takes its sorrow from another cause. But I see thy drift; thou hast a mind to amuse us to put off thy own evil hour, which is not yet come, peradventure, when thou must quit the body of this poor fellow. It shall not be; I conjure thee in the name of Him thou darest not resist to cease thy tormenting, to quit and give him up, and henceforth to hold thy peace."

The devil, of course, obeyed; and the good priest, turning towards us, " My friends and fellow-countrymen," he cried, " albeit I am thoroughly of opinion that it can be no other than the devil who hath entertained us with this conversation through the troubled medium of this unlucky wretch; yet we may stand excused, one and all, in weighing well what he hath proposed, and reaping some benefit from such discourse. Without referring, therefore, to the authority from which it came, remember that Saul (wicked prince as he was) did prophesy truly of things to come, and that honey before now hath been plucked from the lion's mouth. Please to withdraw, then, and I shall make it my prayer—as it is my lively hope—that this strange and sorrowful exhibition may lead you to a genuine sense of your errors, and ere the close, to a blessed amendment of your lives."

MATÍAS DE LOS REYES

17TH CENTURY

THE DUMB LOVER AND HIS PHYSICIAN

IN the castle of Montcaller, not far distant from Turin, the capital of the Duke of Savoy, lived the widow of one of the principal chevaliers of that country. She was young, beautiful, and accomplished, and her retired and amiable manners shed the lustre of virtue over her personal graces. So unostentatious was her behaviour that she seemed to have been all her life the inhabitant of a village rather than of a court; and determining upon never again marrying, she retained only one domestic, and inhabited a small and lonely country house. Here she employed herself in the humblest duties of life, seldom allowed herself to be seen, except in going to mass on festival days, and lived in a manner altogether below her proper condition.

It is a custom in that country for the ladies in time of peace to entertain any illustrious strangers who may happen to be travelling through it, with all the attentions of domestic hospitality; but Finea, the name of our heroine, abhorred this custom, and on all occasions took advantage of her solitude to prevent the intrusion of company.

But about this time there arrived at Montcaller the cavalier whose misfortune is the subject of our story. He was a knight famous throughout the province for his valour and address, and had come thither on some important public business. Having accomplished his purpose, on the morning previous to his return home he went to hear mass at the church usually attended by Finea. He saw her, was struck with her beauty, and still more with the report of her wisdom and accomplishments. He, in fact, became most passionately enamoured of her, and, according to the usual course of things, his passion was strong in proportion to the difficulties which opposed themselves to its gratification.

Hastening, therefore, to Turin, and completing his official duties, he immediately returned to Montcaller to pursue the conquest of Finea's heart. He spent several days in reconnoitring, but his

45

mistress never made her appearance except, as before, in her walk
to church; and if at any time he attempted to address her she
covered her face with her hands, so as to forbid any conversation.
Piqued beyond bearing at this, the knight felt his love still increasing as her disdain became more manifest. He used every art
of the lover, enlarged his presents as his hopes decreased, multi-
plied his attentions in proportion as she rejected them, and the
more severely she repulsed him the more earnest was he in his
suit.

But neither presents, nor attentions, nor patience availed anything against the firmness and austerity of the widow.   The
miserable lover was able neither to obtain the least sign of success
nor to divert his thoughts a moment from his design. He lost his
appetite, sleep fled his eyes, and he fell into a dreadful sickness.
The physicians, not discovering the seat of the disease, could apply
no remedy, and he went step by step towards the grave. While
in this condition, he was visited by a friend of his, a knight of
Espoleto. To him, Lelio, the name of our hero, related the story
of his love, and the cause of his sickness; particularising and dwelling upon the cruelty and harshness of his mistress, which would,
without doubt, prove the cause of his death.

The knight of Espoleto, finding the origin of his friend's illness,
said to him affectionately:

" Lelio, trust this affair of your love to my hands. Fear not
but that I shall discover some method for bringing this lady to a
more tractable state of mind."

" I ask no more," replied the sick man, " but that you would
speak to her, and tell her the condition into which her cruelty has
thrown me; for I think if she knew it, she would not be so inexor-
able—or so obstinately opposed to my passion. But tell me, how
do you intend proceeding? for I have employed both entreaties and
stratagems to obtain only one hour's interview, yet without
success."

" Attend," said the other, " to your recovery, and leave everything else to me."

Lelio was contented with the promises of his friend, and in a
few days, to the astonishment of his physicians, was in a condition
to leave his chamber. The natives of Espoleto are all great talkers,
and endowed with a ready wit. They are admirable beggars for
Saint Anthony, whose cause they advocate through all Italy, and
are omnipotent in words, gesticulations, and protestations, by
which they make all whom they address converts to their per-
suasion. Lelio's friend was of this notion, and not forgetting the
promise he had made, he set about fulfilling it in the best manner
possible. As, in addition to their occupation already mentioned,
the Espolitans are celebrated for their traffic in all female curiosities,

he thought he might make use of this circumstance to accomplish his designs.

He accordingly brought a basket, furnished it with wares, and having clad himself like a travelling merchant, set out for his destination. On arriving before Finea's house, he loudly recounted his list of articles, and the lady, hearing his noise, stepped to the door herself and beckoned him with her hand. The pedlar was not backward in accepting the invitation; and when he had entered the house, taking advantage of his assumed old age, he began to converse with great ease and garrulousness. The lady put her hand into the basket, and having shown great skill in her judgment of the different articles, at last fixed her attention on a piece of valuable and very beautiful stuff, saying, if she could she would have purchased the whole of it.

" Señora," said the pedlar, " take the whole, ask not the price either of this or anything else here—all is at your service. I am sufficiently paid in finding they are agreeable to your taste."

" Heavens," said the lady, " I require nothing but what I can pay for; women like me must not receive things for nothing; but I thank you for your kindness; tell me the price, I pray you, it is not right you should be so liberal of your property and labour."

" If," rejoined the pedlar, " you have a heart as generous as your countenance is beautiful, you will receive what I offer as coming from one who desires to consecrate them on the altar of your beauty."

Finea, hearing this, blushed like a rose opening its young buds to the first May sun. Looking attentively at the supposed merchant, she said, " You astonish me much by speaking as you do. I should wish to know to what purpose you thus address me, since I am persuaded you are under an error, and mistake the person to whom you are sent."

Then, without changing his appearance, but with eyes bent downwards, he spoke of the sufferings which her disdain had caused to Lelio, how passionately he loved her, and how no one else in the world possessed greater accomplishments, or could be found in the court of Turin with more wealth, valour, courtesy, affability; at length he succeeded so well that Finea agreed to give her lover a secret interview, appointing both the time and place.

Lelio was delighted at his friend's diligence, and hastening at the appointed time to the place assigned by Finea, was conducted by her, in company with a domestic, into a low back apartment, which was sufficiently large to hinder the conversation from being heard by the servant, who was sent to the farther part of it. Lelio began by declaring his intentions, with eyes full of love and tenderness, saying how much he had suffered for her sake, and supplicating her to have pity on him, which, if she granted, would purchase his gratitude for ever.

She replied that she was a widow, that she had ceased to think of love; that she now only regarded the services of religion, and that there were many more beautiful women under no such restraints. At last, after much reasoning, the poor lover, seeing that he was fatiguing himself in vain, and that she was determined not to give him any comfort, with tears in his eyes, and almost ready to die, said:

" Since I see I must resign all hope of pity, and that I am doomed to suffer the extremity of misery, I have still one means left of preferring my request; it is that you would grant me peace for the sake of our common country."

The lady sought a moment to reply. " I question," said she at length, " if your love, Señor Lelio, be as great as you say. But to try it, you shall swear to observe one request which I will make, and which, if you religiously fulfil it, shall obtain my regard in return."

The incautious cavalier solemnly swore to do whatever Finea should require, and besought her to declare her wishes.

" Señor Lelio," said she, " I grant your petition; and you must fulfil mine, according to your solemn oath. That which I require of you then is, that for the space of three years from this time you speak no more with any human being, neither man nor woman, whomsoever it may be—that for this space you live as if you were dumb! "

Wonderful that thus, at the feet of a woman, the spoil of her dexterity, should have fallen all the wisdom and valour of a knight. Well were the sentiments of the wise man and of Saint Hieronimus now exemplified! Lelio was for a moment thunderstruck at his mistress's demand, which appeared mad and foolish, and almost impossible to be observed. However, having taken a most solemn oath, he determined upon fulfilling the promise. Having, therefore, made signs with his hand, placing it on his mouth, and thus assuring the lady of his intention, he departed, after a similar farewell, to his home.

Continuing in the same determination after his return to observe his oath inviolably, he pretended to have become suddenly dumb— a misfortune for which he was greatly pitied by all who knew him. From Montcaller he went to Turin, still pretending to be suffering under the loss of his speech. He then proceeded to Ferrara, whither his fame as one of the bravest and most accomplished chevaliers in Europe had preceded him.

The duke accordingly invited him to his court, where his noble bearing won him the respect of the courtiers and the admiration of the ladies. An opportunity also soon occurred in which he ren-

dered the duke good service by his knightly prowess; and the war
in which the prince was then engaged had no sooner terminated
than he bestowed the highest honours on the good chevalier for his
aid.   But the more he regarded him, the greater was his sorrow for
the affliction under which he suffered, and he determined that no
means should be left untried for his recovery. He therefore made
it known throughout Italy, at all times celebrated for its learned
schools of medicine, that whosoever could discover a remedy for
the dumb knight should receive a reward of fifty thousand florins;
but, to prevent needless trouble, that they who failed should forfeit
as much, or be imprisoned in default of payment.

Numberless were the unfortunate physicians who employed all
the resources of their art in vain, and repented of having ever made
the attempt, in prison.   At length Finea, secretly secure of success,
offered to effect the cure; but all the courtiers ridiculed the idea of
a woman's performing a cure in which so many learned men had
failed.   The duke, however, determined on making the experiment
of her skill, and directed her to be shown the apartment of Lelio,
which was in the most retired part of the palace.

Finea, however, was not met with the ardour which she had, it
may be supposed, expected.   The knight armed himself with reason
and resolution, and resisted every approach of tenderness, with the
suspicion that she had been attracted by the reward rather than by
love and compassion for him.   He called to mind, also, the greatness of the affection he had showed her—the cruel manner in
which she had treated him, and how much he had suffered for her
sake.

Having a little tempered his passion by these means, he determined upon taking vengeance for her cruelty, and making her
suffer in turn.   Finea, therefore, having saluted him courteously,
and mentioned the reasons for desiring to see him alone, without
obtaining the expected reply, said:

" Señor Lelio, do you not know me?   Do you not see that I
am your mistress, Finea, to whom you a little time since made so
many professions of love? "

He answered her by signs that he knew her well, and then,
touching his tongue and shaking his head, gave her to understand
he had not the power of speech.

Finea answered him a little anxiously, that she absolved him
from his oath—that she would keep her promise, and excuse him
the half-year still wanting to complete the period of his silence—
that she had come to Ferrara for the sole purpose of doing this,
and giving him a full assurance of her affection.   To all which
Lelio gave no reply but touching his tongue and sorrowfully
shrugging up his shoulders.

The Señora, seeing the resolution of Lelio, was at a loss what to do; for neither tears, nor promises, nor entreaties were able to effect the miracle she had boasted herself capable of performing. At last, finding nothing of any avail, she was obliged to retire unsuccessful, and in default of paying the fine, was thrown into prison with the rest who had made vain attempts at the cure.

After this occurrence, the cavalier, well satisfied with the revenge he had taken, presented himself before the duke, and unloosening his hitherto tied-up tongue, told him the whole history of the circumstances which led to his long silence. He then besought him immediately to free the persons who had been so unjustly confined on this account, and repaid them for their sufferings and uneasiness with very ample gifts. Finea was then sent for, and in the presence of all the court Lelio said:

"Well do you know, Señora, how long and how faithfully I served you, and how truly I deserved to obtain that return which the highest lady of the land fails not to give her faithful lover; well do you know also how little was the reward I received for my great toil, and how you obliged me, by a solemn oath, to three years' silence. This penance I have observed without the slightest remission; and I would rather have died than have failed in the observance. And now, although your rigour deserved a greater punishment than that you have received, I am determined to use my power with lenity; and I, therefore, publicly say that you ought to receive the reward promised for my cure, and I supplicate His Highness to give it you for a dowry and to permit me to espouse you, hoping that you will in future be more cautious and tractable."

The duke and all his courtiers greatly applauded the address of Lelio, and His Highness immediately ordered the fifty thousand florins to be given to Finea, as being rightly due to her for the cure of Lelio. To the knight he gave fresh assurances of favour and promotion; and the nuptials being celebrated with all due rejoicing, he succeeded in persuading Lelio to settle in Ferrara, where he spent his days with Finea in peace and happiness.

SERAFÍN ESTÉBANEZ CALDERÓN

1799–1867

AN ANDALUSIAN DUEL

THROUGH the little square of St. Anna, towards a certain tavern, where the best wine is to be quaffed in Seville, there walked in measured steps two men, whose demeanour clearly manifested the soil which gave them birth. He who walked in the middle of the street, taller than the other by about a finger's length, sported with affected carelessness the wide, slouched hat of Ecija, with tassels of glass beads and a ribbon as black as his sins. He wore his cloak gathered under his left arm; the right, emerging from a turquoise lining, exposed the merino lambskin with silver clasps.

The herdsman's boots—white, with Turkish buttons,—the breeches gleaming red from below the cloak and covering the knee, and, above all, his strong and robust appearance, dark curly hair, and eye like a red-hot coal, proclaimed at a distance that all this combination belonged to one of those men who put an end to horses between their knees and tire out the bull with their lance. He walked on, arguing with his companion, who was rather spare than prodigal in his person, but marvellously lithe and supple.

The latter was shod with low shoes, garters united the stockings to the light-blue breeches, the waistcoat was cane-coloured, his sash light green, and jaunty shoulder-knots, lappets, and rows of buttons ornamented the camelite jacket. The open cloak, the hat drawn over his ear, his short, clean steps, and the manifestations in all his limbs and movements of agility and elasticity beyond trial plainly showed that in the arena, carmine cloth in hand, he would mock at the most frenzied of Jarama bulls, or the best horned beasts from Utrera.

I—who adore and die for such people, though the compliment be not returned—went slowly in the wake of their worships, and, unable to restrain myself, entered with them the same tavern, or rather eating-house, since there they serve certain provocatives as well as wine, and I, as my readers perceive, love to call things by their right name. I entered and sat down at once, and in such a manner as not to interrupt my Oliver and Roland, and that they might not notice me, when I saw that, as if believing themselves

51

alone, they threw their arms with an amicable gesture round each other's neck, and thus began their discourse:

" Pulpete," said the taller, " now that we are going to meet each other, knife in hand—you here, I there, . . *one, two,* . . *on your guard,* . . *triz, traz,* . . *have that,* . . *take this and call it what you like* . . .—let us first drain a tankard to the music and measure of some songs."

" Señor Balbeja," replied Pulpete, drawing his face aside and spitting with the greatest neatness and pulchritude towards his shoe, " I am not the kind of man either for la Gorja or other similar earthly matters, or because a steel tongue is sheathed in my body, or my weasand slit, or for any other such trifle, to be provoked or vexed with such a friend as Balbeja. Let the wine be brought, and then we will sing; and afterwards blood—blood to the hilt."

The order was given, they clinked glasses, and, looking one at the other, sang a Sevillian song.

This done, they threw off their cloaks with an easy grace, and unsheathed their knives with which to prick one another, the one Flemish with a white haft, the other from Guadix, with a guard to the hilt, both blades dazzling in their brightness, and sharpened and ground enough for operating upon cataracts, much less ripping up bellies and bowels. The two had already cleft the air several times with the said lancets, their cloaks wound round their left arm—first drawing closer, then back, now more boldly and in bounds—when Pulpete hoisted the flag for parley, and said:

" Balbeja, my friend, I only beg you to do me the favour not to fan my face with *Juilon* your knife, since a slash might use it so ill that my mother who bore me would not know me, and I should not like to be considered ugly; neither is it right to mar and destroy what God made in His likeness."

" Agreed," replied Balbeja; " I will aim lower."

" Except—except my stomach also, for I was ever a friend to cleanliness, and I should not like to see myself fouled in a bad way, if your knife and arm played havoc with my liver and intestines."

" I will strike higher; but let us go on."

" Take care of my chest, it was always weak."

" Then just tell me, friend, *where* am I to sound or tap you? "

" My dear Balbeja, there's always plenty of time and space to hack at a man: I have here on my left arm a wen, of which you can make meat as much as you like."

" Here goes for it," said Balbeja, and he hurled himself like an arrow; the other warded off the thrust with his cloak, and both, like skilful penmen, began again tracing S's and signatures in the air with dashes and flourishes, without, however, raising a particle of skin.

I do not know what would have been the end of this onslaught, since my venerable, dry, and shrivelled person was not suitable for forming a point of exclamation between two combatants; and the tavern-keeper troubled so little about what was happening that he drowned the stamping of their feet and clatter of the tumbling stools and utensils by scraping street music on a guitar as loud as he could. Otherwise he was as calm as if he were entertaining two angels instead of two devils incarnate.

I do not know, I repeat, how this scene would have ended, when there crossed the threshold a personage who came to take a part in the development of the drama. There entered, I say, a woman of twenty to twenty-two years of age, diminutive in body, superlative in audacity and grace. Neat and clean hose and shoes, short, black flounced petticoat, a linked girdle, head-dress or mantilla of fringed taffeta caught together at the nape of her neck, and a corner of it over her shoulder, she passed before my eyes with swaying hips, arms akimbo, and moving her head to and fro as she looked about her on all sides.

Upon seeing her the tavern-keeper dropped his instrument, and I was overtaken by perturbation such as I had not experienced for thirty years (I am, after all, only flesh and blood); but, without halting for such lay-figures, she advanced to the field of battle.

There was a lively to-do here: Don Pulpete and Don Balbeja, when they saw Donna Gorja appear, first cause of the disturbance and future prize for the victor, increased their feints, flourishes, curvets, onsets, crouching, and bounds—all, however, without touching a hair. Our Helen witnessed in silence for a long time this scene in history with that feminine pleasure which the daughters of Eve enjoy at such critical moments. But gradually her pretty brow clouded over, until, drawing from her delicate ear, not a flower or earring, but the stump of a cigar, she hurled it amidst the jousters. Not even Charles V.'s cane in the last duel in Spain produced such favourable effects. Both came forward immediately with formal respect, and each, by reason of the discomposure of his person and clothes, presumed to urge a title by which to recommend himself to the fair with the flounces. She, as though pensive, was going over the passage of arms in her mind, and then, with firm and confident resolution, spoke thus:

" And is this affair for me? "

" Who else should it be for? since I . . . since nobody——" they replied in the same breath.

" Listen, gentlemen," said she. " For females such as I and my parts, of my charms and descent—daughter of la Gatusa, neice of la Méndez, and grand-daughter of la Astrosa—know that there are neither pacts nor compacts, nor any such futile things, nor are any of them worth a farthing. And when men challenge each other, let the knife do its work and the red blood flow, so as not to have my mother's daughter present without giving her the pleasure of snapping her fingers in the face of the other. If you pretend you are fighting for me, it's a lie; you are wholly mistaken, and that not by halves. I love neither of you. Mingalarios of Zafra is to my taste, and he and I look upon you with scorn and contempt. Good-bye, my braves; and, if you like, call my man to account."

She spoke, spat, smoothed the saliva with the point of her shoe, looking Pulpete and Balbeja full in the face, and went out with the same expressive movements with which she entered.

The two unvarnished braggarts followed the valorous Donna Gorja with their eyes; and then with a despicable gesture drew their knives across their sleeve as though wiping off the blood there might have been, sheathed them at one and the same time, and said together:

"Through woman the world was lost, through a woman Spain was lost; [1] but it has never been known, nor do ballads relate, nor the blind beggars sing, nor is it heard in the square or markets, that two valiant men killed each other for another lover."

"Give me that fist, Don Pulpete."

"Your hand, Don Balbeja."

They spoke and strode out into the street, the best friends in the world, leaving me all amazed at such whimsicality.

[1] Count Julian, governor of the provinces on both sides of the Strait of Gibraltar, to avenge himself on King Roderick for dishonouring his daughter, the famous La Cava (also called Florinda) of the Spanish ballads, invited (A.D. 711) the Moors into Spain.

ANTONIO DE TRUEBA

1821–1888

THE ARCHITECT'S WIFE

I

TOWARDS the middle of the fourteenth century Toledo was laid under siege by Don Enrique de Trastamara; but the city, faithful to the King surnamed " the Cruel," offered a brave and obstinate resistance.

Often had the loyal and valiant Toledans crossed the magnificent bridge of San Martin—one of the structures of greatest beauty of that city of splendid erections—and had cast themselves on the encampment of Don Enrique, which was pitched on the Cigarrales, causing sad havoc to the besieging army.

In order to prevent the repetition of these attacks, Don Enrique resolved upon destroying the bridge.

The Cigarrales, upon which the army was encamped, were beautiful lands enclosing luxuriant orchards, pleasure gardens, and summer residences. The fame of their beauty had inspired Tirso and many Spanish poets to sing its praises.

One night the luxuriant trees were cut down by the soldiers of Don Enrique, and heaped upon the bridge. At day-dawn an immense fire raged on the bridge of San Martin, which assumed huge proportions, its sinister gleams lighting up the devastating hordes, the flowing current of the Tagus, the palace of Don Rodrigo, and the little Arab Tower. The crackling of the strong and massive pillars, worked with all the exquisite skill of the artificers who created the marvels of the Alhambra, sounded like the piteous cry of Art oppressed by Barbarism.

The Toledans, awakened by this terrible spectacle, ran to save the beautiful erection from the utter ruin which menaced it, but all their efforts were unavailing. A tremendous crash, which sounded throughout the creeks and valleys watered by the Tagus, told them that the bridge no longer existed.

Alas! it was too true!

When the rising sun gilded the cupolas of the Imperial City, the Toledan maidens who came down to the river to fill their pitchers from the pure and crystal stream returned sorrowfully with empty

55

pitchers on their heads; the clear waters had become turbid and muddy, for the roaring waves were carrying down the still-smoking ruins of the bridge.

Popular indignation rose to its highest pitch, and overflowed all limits; for the bridge of San Martin was the only path that led to the lovely Cigarrales.

Joining their forces for one supreme effort, the Toledans made a furious onslaught on the camp, and, after blood had flowed in torrents, compelled the army to take flight.

II

Many years passed since the bridge of San Martin had been destroyed.

Kings and Archbishops had projected schemes to replace it by another structure, of equal strength and beauty; but the genius and perseverance of the most famous architects were unable to carry out their wishes. The rapid, powerful currents of the river destroyed and swept away the scaffolding and framework before the gigantic arches could be completed.

Don Pedro Tenorio, Cardinal Archbishop of Toledo, to whom the city owes her glory almost as much as to her Kings, sent criers throughout the cities and towns of Spain, inviting architects, Christian and Moorish, to undertake the reconstruction of the bridge of San Martin; but with no result. The difficulties to be encountered were judged insurmountable.

At length one day a man and a woman, complete strangers to the place, entered Toledo through the Cambron Gate. They carefully inspected the ruined bridge. Then they engaged a small house near the ruins, and proceeded to take up their quarters there.

On the following day the man proceeded to the Archbishop's palace.

His Eminence was holding a conference of prelates, learned men, and distinguished knights, who were attracted by his piety and wisdom.

Great was his joy when one of his attendants announced that an architect from distant lands solicited the honour of an audience.

The Cardinal Archbishop hastened to receive the stranger. The first salutations over, his Eminence bade him be seated.

" My Lord Archbishop," began the stranger, " my name, which is unknown to your Eminence, is Juan de Arèvalo, and I am an architect by profession."

" Are you come in answer to the invitation I have issued calling upon skilful architects to come and rebuild the bridge of San Martin, which in former times afforded a passage between the city and the Cigarrales? "

" It was indeed that invitation which brought me to Toledo."

" Are you aware of the difficulties of its construction? "

" I am well aware of them. But I can surmount them."

" Where did you study architecture? "

" In Salamanca."

" And what erection have you to show me as a proof of your skill? "

" None whatever, my lord."

The Archbishop made a gesture of impatience and distrust which was noticed by the stranger.

" I was a soldier in my youth," continued he, " but ill-health compelled me to leave the arduous profession of arms and return to Castile, the land of my birth, where I dedicated myself to the study of architecture, theoretical and practical."

" I regret," replied the Archbishop, " that you are unable to mention any work of skill that you have carried out."

" There are some erections on the Tormes and the Duero of which others have the credit, but which ought to honour him who now addresses you."

" I do not understand you."

" I was poor and obscure," rejoined Juan de Arèvalo, " and I sought only to earn bread and shelter. Glory I left to others."

" I deeply regret," replied Don Pedro Tenorio, " that you have no means of assuring us that we should not trust in you in vain."

" My lord, I can offer you one guarantee which I trust will satisfy your Eminence."

" What is that? "

" My life! "

" Explain yourself."

" When the framework of the centre arch shall be removed, I, the architect, will stand upon the keystone. Should the bridge fall, I shall perish with it."

" I accept the guarantee."

" My lord, trust me, and I will carry out the work! "

The Archbishop pressed the hand of the architect, and Juan de Arèvalo departed, his heart full of joyous expectation. His wife was anxiously awaiting his return. She was young and handsome still, despite the ravages of want and suffering.

" Catherine! my Catherine! " cried the architect, clasping his wife to his arms, " amid the monuments that embellish Toledo there will be one to transmit to posterity the name of Juan de Arèvalo! "

III

Time passed. No longer could the Toledans say, on approaching the Tagus across the rugged cliffs and solitary places where in former times stood the Garden of Florinda, " Here once stood the

bridge of San Martin.'' Though the new bridge was still supported by solid scaffolding and massive frames, yet the centre
arch already rose to view, and the whole was firmly planted on
the ruins of the former.

The Archbishop, Don Pedro Tenorio, and the Toledans were
heaping gifts and praises on the fortunate architect whose skill
had joined the central arch, despite the furious power of the
surging currents, and who had completed the gigantic work with
consummate daring.

It was the eve of the feast of San Ildefonso, the patron saint of
the city of Toledo. Juan de Arèvalo respectfully informed the
Cardinal Archbishop that nothing was now wanting to conclude
the work but to remove the woodwork of the arches and the scaffolding. The joy of the Cardinal and of the people was great. The
removal of the scaffolding and frames which supported the masonry
was a work attended with considerable danger; but the calmness
and confidence of the architect who had pledged himself to stand
on the keystone and await the consequences of success or lose his
life, inspired all with perfect trust.

The solemn blessing and inauguration of the bridge of San
Martin was fixed to take place on the day following, and the bells
of all the churches of Toledo were joyously ringing in announce-
ment of the grand event appointed for the morrow. The Toledans
contemplated with rejoicing from the heights above the Tagus
the lovely Cigarrales, which for many years had remained solitary
and silent—indeed, almost abandoned—but which on the day following would be restored to life.

Towards nightfall Juan de Arèvalo mounted the central arch to
see that all was ready for the opening ceremony. He went humming to himself as he inspected all the works and preparations.
But suddenly an expression of misgiving overspread his countenance. A thought had struck him—a thought that froze his blood.
He descended from the bridge and hastened home.

At the door his wife received him with a joyous smile and a
merry word of congratulation. But on beholding his troubled face
she turned deadly pale.

'' Good heavens! '' she cried, affrighted, '' are you ill, dear
Juan? ''

'' No, dear wife,'' he replied, striving to master his emotion.

'' Do not deceive me! your face tells me that something ails
you? ''

'' Oh! the evening is cold and the work has been excessive.''

'' Come in and sit down at the hearth and I will get the supper
ready, and when you have had something to eat and are rested
you will be at ease again! ''

'' At ease! '' murmured Juan to himself, in agony of spirit, whilst his wife busied herself in the preparation of the supper, placing the table close to the hearth, upon which she threw a faggot.

Juan made a supreme effort to overcome his sadness, but it was futile. His wife could not be deceived.

" For the first time in our married life," she said, " you hide a sorrow from me. Am I no longer worthy of your love and confidence? "

" Catherine! " he exclaimed, " do not, for heaven's sake, grieve me further by doubting my affection for you! "

" Where there is no trust," she rejoined in feeling tones, " there can be no true love."

" Then respect, for your own good and mine, the secret I conceal from you."

" Your secret is a sorrow, and I wish to know it and to lighten it."

" To lighten it? That is impossible! "

" To such a love as mine," she urged, " nothing is impossible."

" Very well: then hear me. To-morrow my life and honour will be lost. The bridge must fall into the river, and I on the keystone shall perish with the fabric which, with so much anxiety and so many hopes, I have erected."

" No, no! " cried Catherine, as she clasped her husband in her arms with loving tenderness, smothering in her own heart the anguish of the revelation.

" Yes, dear wife! When I was most confident of my triumph, I discovered that, owing to an error in my calculations, the bridge must fall to-morrow when the framework is removed. And with it perishes the architect who projected and directed it."

" The bridge may sink into the waters, but not you, my loved one. On bended knees I will beseech the noble Cardinal to release you from your terrible engagement."

" What you ask will be in vain. Even should the Cardinal accede to your entreaty, I refuse life destitute of honour."

" You shall have life and honour both, dear husband," replied Catherine.

IV

It was midnight. Juan, worn out with grief and anxious work, at last had fallen asleep; a feverish sleep that partook more of the character of a nightmare than of Nature's sweet restorer.

Meanwhile his wife had for some time made a show of sleeping. But she watched her husband anxiously. When she felt certain that he had at length succumbed to a deep sleep, she softly rose, and scarcely daring to breathe, crept out into the kitchen. She opened the window gently and looked out.

The night was dark; now and again vivid flashes of lightning lit up the sky. No sound was heard save the roar of the rushing currents of the Tagus and the sighing of the wind as it swept in and out among the scaffolding and complicated framework of the bridge.

Catherine noiselessly closed the window. From the hearth she took one of the half-burnt faggots which still smouldered, and throwing a cloak over her shoulders went out into the silent streets, her heart beating wildly.

Where was she proceeding? Was she carrying that burning faggot as a torch to light her path in the dense darkness of a moonless night? It was indeed a dangerous track, covered as it was with broken boulders and uneven ground. Yet she strove rather to conceal the lighted wood beneath her cloak.

At last she reached the bridge. The wind still sighed and whistled, and the river continued to break its current against the pillars, as though irritated at meeting obstacles which it could no longer sweep away.

Catherine approached the buttress of the bridge. An involuntary shudder of terror passed through her frame. Was it because she stood on the edge of that abyss of roaring waters? Or was it because her hand, only accustomed hitherto to deeds of goodness, was now brandishing the torch of destruction? Or rather did she tremble because a tremendous peal of thunder at that moment resounded through the vault of heaven?

Waving the torch to kindle it afresh, she applied it to the dry, resinous wood of the scaffolding. The wood quickly ignited, and the flame, fanned by the wind, ascended with fearful rapidity, spreading and involving arches and framework and the whole structure of the bridge.

Then she quitted the scene swiftly. Aided by the glare of the conflagration and the vivid flashes of lightning which lit up the sky, Catherine soon traversed the space which separated her from her home. She entered as noiselessly as she had left it, and closed the door. Her husband still slept soundly, and had not missed her. Catherine again pretended to be fast asleep, as though she had never left her bed.

A few moments later a noise of many people running arose within the city, while from every belfry the bells rang forth the terrible alarm of fire. A tremendous crash succeeded, followed by a cry of anguish such as had been uttered years before, when the besieging army wrecked the former bridge.

Juan woke in terror; Catherine lay at his side, apparently sleeping calmly. He dressed himself in haste, and ran out to learn the reason of the uproar. To his secret joy he beheld the ruin of the burning bridge.

The Cardinal Archbishop and the Toledans attributed the disaster to a flash of lightning which had struck the central arch, and had, moreover, ignited the whole structure. The general sorrow was intense. Great also was the public sympathy with the despair which the calamity must have caused the architect, who was on the eve of a great triumph. The inhabitants never knew whether it was fire from heaven or an accident that had caused the conflagration; but Juan de Arèvalo, who was good and pious, and firmly believed in the protection of heaven, never wavered for an instant in the belief that the bridge had really been destroyed by lightning.

The destruction of the bridge, however, only retarded Juan's triumph for a twelvemonth. On the following year, on the same festival of San Ildefonso, his new bridge was solemnly thrown open by the Cardinal; and the joyous Toledans once more crossed the Tagus to visit the lovely grounds of the Cigarrales, which they had been deprived of for so many years. On that auspicious day the Cardinal celebrated the event by giving a magnificent banquet. At his right hand sat the architect and his noble wife; and after a highly complimentary speech from the Cardinal, the whole company, amidst a tumult of applause, conducted Juan and Catherine to their home.

Five hundred years have passed since then, but Juan's bridge still stands secure above the rushing waters of the Tagus. His second calculation had no error.

JUAN VALERA
1824–1905

THE FAIRY KISS

I

A VERY remarkable guest had arrived at the Monastery of the
Capuchins in the city about the year 1672. The visitor was celebrated everywhere for the acuteness of his intelligence, the profound
knowledge which he had acquired, and the scientific works which
he had published. It is enough to say, and all that need be said,
that the guest was the Most Reverend Father Antonio de Fuente
la Pena, the former Provincial of the Order.

After having dined with excellent appetite, and enjoyed a good
sleep to recover from the fatigue of the journey, Father Antonio
received in his cell the Superior, Father Domingo, to whom he
spoke of the important matter which had induced him to come
to that holy abode.

"I have happened to hear," he said, "of the strange case of
Donna Eulalia, the only daughter of the distinguished knight, Don
Cesar del Robledal. And after having considered and weighed
everything, I have come to the conclusion that the girl is neither
the victim of demoniacal possession nor is she hag-ridden."

"Your Reverence must pardon me if I contradict you. I do not
see any proof that the girl is neither possessed nor hag-ridden.
Although perhaps I ought not to say it, it is well known that,
thanks be to God, I have a good deal of power over evil spirits, and
I have driven a great many out of the bodies of the people whom
they were tormenting. If those which torment the young Donna
Eulalia do not obey me, it is not because they have not taken
up their abode within her or around her, but because they are
very sly and crafty. If they are within her, they hide and dissimu-
late in such a way that they do not hear my exorcisms, and
if they are around her and are tormenting her, they are always quick
enough to make their escape when I come, and do not return until
I have gone. The symptoms of the evil are very evident, however. The only thing which I cannot quite decide is whether the
girl is possessed of a devil or hag-ridden."

"Well, then," replied Antonio, "my conclusion is quite the

contrary, and the more I think the more I am confirmed in my opinion. Donna Eulalia never speaks Latin or any other language than our own pure and elegant Spanish; her feet always touch the ground when she is not sitting or lying down; instead of being pale, thin, and haggard, I know that she is very pretty and so fresh-looking that she is like a rose in May; and the fact that she refuses to marry any of the suitors whom her father proposes to her, and that she appears sad and thoughtful, as well as the fact that she spends her evenings alone in her room, engaged in mysterious conversations with invisible beings, does not prove that she is possessed by the devil or anything of the sort. Devils are never so gentle and friendly with any human creature. Therefore it is a being of a less wicked and hurtful nature than those fallen angels which has influenced the young lady, Donna Eulalia. Clearly, it is not a devil but a fairy which visits her and talks to her. I am well up in the knowledge of these beings, since I have made it my business to study the subject of fairies, as you know from my celebrated book entitled *The Being Explained,* and so I have come here to see if I can get into communication with the fairy which visits Donna Eulalia, and induce it to leave her, using for this purpose the means placed in my power by my special knowledge."

" It is strange," observed Father Domingo, " that your Reverence should make this statement only on the ground of conjecture."

" It is not mere conjecture," replied Father Antonio. " Although as a punishment for my sins I have never been worthy to have supernatural revelations made to me, still I very often have natural revelations, and that is the case now. We are alone here, and I can speak with freedom, confiding in the indispensable seal of secrecy, as between one priest and another."

Father Domingo made a sign that he would not repeat what was about to be said to him, and Father Antonio continued in a low mysterious tone:

" The fairy which visits Donna Eulalia has talked freely with and has explained everything to me. It is well known that I am esteemed, respected, and even loved by the fairies, whom I have defended from the insults and calumnies heaped on them by ignorant people. I have proved that they are not devils or lost souls, but very subtle and invisible creatures, almost always bright and lively, having their origin in the thinnest of air. As the fairies are pleased with me, is there anything extraordinary in the fact that they should come and converse with me? Again, my studies and investigations with respect to the tiniest and almost least corporeal of beings have sharpened my senses so much that I can see, touch, and hear what remains quite imperceptible to the coarser powers of ordinary mortals. Forgive me this piece of boasting; but when I look around over the universe I can discover ten times as much life and intelligence as the majority of other men can realise. But to keep to our present case, for the last ten years, ever since Donna Eulalia was fifteen, for she will be twenty-five within three days now, she has been solitary, reserved with other people, intractable and obstinate; but I am aware now that the fairy is going to depart from her within these next three days, and then he will appear in the form of a handsome young man. Donna Eulalia will then be relieved of all other trouble, and although she will always be reserved, modest, and well-behaved, still she will lay aside her obstinacy, will cease to be shy and unduly retiring, and will be gracious and approachable like any other girl of her age."

With a slightly sarcastic intonation, although tempered or veiled by respect, Father Domingo exclaimed:

" No doubt this revelation was not made by halves, and the fairy has told your Reverence the place and time of his disappearance and of the appearance of the young man."

" Yes, that is so," replied Father Antonio. " It will take place at midnight, in Donna Eulalia's own room, where we are to go and conceal ourselves, not mentioning the case to Donna Eulalia or to any one else, except Donna Eulalia's father, who is to accompany us, but must be unarmed, lest he should have a sudden outbreak of anger. Your Reverence can be armed with your exorcisms and I shall be fortified with my knowledge of the world of fairies. I feel perfectly certain that all will end happily."

II

At the time fixed on the appointed night, Don Cesar and the two friars stole on tiptoe in the most mysterious silence to the door of Donna Eulalia's room. Father Domingo was armed with his book of exorcisms and with a hyssop sprinkler; Father Antonio had an incense burner, in order to set fire to magic herbs, and scatter smoke around; and Don Cesar was armed only with patience, which he had solemnly promised not to lose and not to be angry, no matter what might happen.

When all their rites and invocations had been performed, Father Antonio and Father Domingo told Don Cesar to knock loudly at the folding doors of Donna Eulalia's room, which was locked, and to order her to throw both doors wide at once, without any excuse or pretext of any sort.

There was no means of refusing or delaying obedience to this command, and the door was suddenly thrown wide open. Through the opening there appeared, like a magnificent portrait by Claudio Coello in its frame, a handsome young man very richly and becomingly dressed in the uniform and decorations of a captain in the army, a long sword by his side, waving plumes adorning the hat which he carried in his right hand, a rich gold chain round his neck, and orders glittering on his breast, and with gold spurs completing his full riding-boots.

Don Cesar, who was very hot-tempered and very jealous of his family honour, would have rushed forward and thrown himself on the stranger if the two priests had not held him back, one on each side.

The young officer, in a calm and dignified tone, then said:

" Compose yourself, Don Cesar, and do not be angry at finding me here at such a late hour. I am Captain Don Pedro Gonzalez de la Rivera, whose station and qualifications have already been described to your worship by my friend the Genoese banker, Jusepe Salvago, and whose exploits in Portugal, in Flanders, in Italy, and in the Far East, where I have borne arms, have been made known to you by other persons of consequence. I aspire to the hand of Donna Eulalia; she has given me proofs that she would like to have me for her husband, and all that we want now is your paternal consent, to be followed by the blessing of the Reverend Father Antonio, who is present, and who, I hope, will not refuse us his benediction."

" All that would be very well," replied Don Cesar with ill-repressed anger, " if your honour did not ask for it after offending my grey hairs, breaking into my house, and trampling down all respect."

" Don Cesar," replied the Captain, smiling, " I have committed this apparent offence in vengeance for another not so apparent which your worship committed against me ten years ago, when you found me in this very same spot, in tender conversation with the young lady, Donna Eulalia, who was not then quite fifteen years of age. I was then a young monkey of sixteen, and your worship drove me out of here with cuffs of anything but a paternal nature. For love of Donna Eulalia I endured all this, and I would have endured even worse insults if worse had been possible. But since then I have given sufficient proof of my valour, and again, Fortune has favoured me, and my honour is well established. The satisfaction which I ask for and expect for past injuries is that your worship will accept me as your son-in-law."

Just then Donna Eulalia came forward and placed herself beside the young officer. She looked most charming in her rich and graceful robe and magnificent jewels, and her youthful blushing face showed the greatest joy and happiness. What was Don Cesar to do? He consented to all, and embraced his two children affectionately, but first of all, he looked at the Captain closely, and said:

" God bless me, my boy, how you have grown and improved in these ten years! Who would ever recognise in you the impish fair-haired boy who was acolyte to the Capuchins and used to ring such lively peals on the bells? "

III

With all his respect and consideration for Father Antonio, the Father Superior could not avoid speaking his mind and saying that it was clear to him that if there had been no devil in the case, neither had there been any fairy, and that the whole affair had only been a little comedy.

Father Antonio, however, defended himself, and before he returned to Madrid, where he usually resided, he spoke to the Father Superior as follows:

" Not only has there been a fairy, but one of the most romantic fairies which could possibly exist in this sublunar world. The young maiden was so pure, so truthful, and so ignorant of evil that at fifteen years of age she seemed an angel rather than a woman. The lad was as good and as honest as she was. Both loved each other with the most sincere affection, without the least thought of evil, without any admixture of the passion which had never been aroused in either of them. They wished to be united in a holy bond of marriage so as to live together until their death, as they had lived side by side since their infancy. The great obstacle to this was the difference in their social positions. Periquito would have to win for himself social station, a name, renown, and fortune. When they separated in order that he might go forth in his noble quest, without the least idea of wrong, with the innocence of children, and the fervent love of heaven in their souls, their lips met in one long kiss. There is no doubt that at that moment there fluttered between their lips a light particle of ether, an indivisible atom, the soul of intelligence and life. The burning flame of their pure love penetrated the atom, gave it form and brightness, and all that there is of beauty and nobility in the world came to be reflected in it as in an enchanted mirror in which everything is purified and rendered sublime. The sacred fire of love in each young soul formed into one shape, and without entirely leaving either of them it became an invisible being with a separate existence and yet with something shadowy, insubstantial, and most resembling the spirit of conscience. The lovers parted. He went very far away, he fought and wandered. During ten years he heard nothing more of her or she of him in the ordinary everyday way of human communication. But the being which represented the aspirations of their souls, the fairy which had taken shape from their kiss, with its wings glittering like those of a butterfly, and its speed more swift than that of lightning, flew from one end of the earth to the other, now alighting on him, now on her, so that they could embrace as if they were really together and thus renew the innocent kiss from which the fairy form had taken shape, not as a vain memory but as something ever new and ever keeping their love alive. Does your Reverence doubt that such a fairy exists or has existed? How else can we explain the tenacious persistence during ten years of the one early mutual love? It was not only on her side. It was not only on his side. It lived in both, but when they parted it separated both to form from the union of their souls a distinct being. This being now has no longer need to exist; it disappears but does not die. We cannot say that death has come or will come to the spark of intelligence, enriched with the vivid representation of all that is most beautiful in earth and heaven, when, having fulfilled the mission for which it was created, it blends into the great ocean of intelligence and of feeling from which we derive harmonious strength, the light of day, and the life which palpitates in the myriads of invisible beings which fill the vast spaces of the universe.''

Father Domingo listened to all this, and to much more spoken by Father Antonio, with attention, and he finally became convinced that there really were fairies; some prosaic, others romantic like that of Don Pedro and Donna Eulalia, and that Father Antonio's theory did not in any way appear incompatible with Catholic truth, since it redounded to the greater glory of God, as far as such a thing can be understood and grasped by the limited power of comprehension of human nature.

JUAN VALERA

THE ARCHBISHOP'S COOK

In the good old days, when Archbishops were rich and powerful, there lived in Toledo an Archbishop who was so austere and self-denying that his table was scantily furnished, and he accustomed himself so much to fast-day food that his diet was fish, vegetables, and cereal dishes.

This venerable vegetarian servant of God allowed himself one luxury, and even that was in accordance with his principles. His cook was accustomed to serve him for luncheon a most delicious and nourishing vegetable soup, made, according to the cook's own statement, solely of lentils, beans, and peas. The cook was so clever in his treatment of this modest fare that the soup appeared, thanks to the skilful flavouring employed, superior to the best soups which could be obtained from the richest materials.

However, it happened unfortunately that this skilful servitor had one great defect. He could not agree with the butler. And as the quarrel was constantly renewed, even on the most trifling pretexts, the cook was dismissed.

Another cook came to provide for the Lord Archbishop's table, and he was instructed to prepare a good vegetable soup for his Grace's luncheon. He did his best, but the Archbishop found the soup detestable, and ordered his butler to engage another cook and to get rid of the incompetent one.

Eight or nine other cooks followed in rapid succession, for none of them succeeded in flavouring the soup in the proper way, and they had to depart, one after the other, in disgrace for their incompetence in providing the proper archiepiscopal fare.

At last a cook was engaged who in addition to his culinary art possessed a certain amount of common sense and acuteness, and before entering on his responsible work, he had the good idea of going to see the original cook and of begging him, for the love of God and all the saints in heaven, to let him know exactly how he had prepared the vegetable soup which the Archbishop liked so much.

The first cook was so generous that he was quite frank with his latest successor, and he honestly confided to him the recipe for the soup, of which he had always hitherto made a mystery.

The new cook carried out the instructions given to him with the greatest care, flavoured the soup exactly according to the recipe, and had it served to the austere prelate.

As soon as the latter tasted it, he uttered an exclamation of joy, and finished his plate of vegetable soup with the greatest relish. Then he said enthusiastically:

" Thanks be to Almighty God! At last He has sent me a cook who can make soup as well as the first one, or even better. It is delicious and most appetising. Bring the cook here. I want to let him know how pleased I am with him."

The cook arrived highly delighted. The Archbishop received him most affably and graciously, and praised his talent up to the skies.

The artist of the kitchen was so flattered that, being a really honest, sincere, and good Christian, he decided to give his kind master a proof not only of his abilities in his professional domain, but also of high moral qualities, on which he prided himself even more than on his merely material functions.

So the new cook said to the Archbishop:

" Your Grace, in spite of the profound respect which I have for you, I think it my duty to tell you that your former cook deceived you, and that it is not right that I should follow his bad example. This soup does not consist only of peas and beans. All that was an untruth; the flavour of the soup is due to a rich stock made up of pieces of ham, chickens' breasts, livers and kidneys of small birds, and the most delicate morsels of mutton. You see, your Grace, how he deceived you."

The Archbishop looked fixedly at his cook, and shaking his finger at him with a smile in which disappointment and amusement were mingled, he said:

" In that case, you rascal, you had better keep up the deception! "

JUAN VALERA

THE ELOQUENT BASQUE

MORE than a hundred years ago the Bishop of Malaga was a man noted for his knowledge and virtue, and a very eloquent preacher. He was also agreeable in person, and his manner was so affable and gracious that he permitted his subordinates to chat with him, and even to make jokes, not only not being annoyed, but even enjoying their conversation.

The Bishop was a Basque, and his friends, in praising his eloquence to the skies, said that it was extraordinary and unique among the sons of the provinces of Biscay, where, according to them there had never been a man who could speak two words of sense, or a priest who was not a dunce and quite incapable of expressing himself in the pulpit.

The good prelate, urged by his Christian modesty, maintained with patriotic fervour that they were wrong, and he asserted that among the Basque priests, his contemporaries, there were at least three dozen who were superior to him in knowledge, skill, and inspiration for composing sermons.

As time passed and no Basque priest was ever sent to that diocese, the dispute appeared never likely to be settled. The Bishop did not give any proof of his assertions by any practical test, and his friends continued wrongly or rightly denying to all Basque clerics, except to his Lordship himself, any capacity whatever for sacred oratory.

At last, however, there arrived in Malaga in search of help and patronage a priest from the Basque province of Guipuzcoa, who had made his studies in the very same seminary as the Bishop himself and had been his greatest friend there. The Bishop received him cordially and made him stay in his palace. When they were alone together, the good Bishop lost no time in telling his old friend of the interminable discussions which he had with the others of his acquaintance, and then he said to him: " It is very lucky that you have come here, because now I can make use of you to prove the truth of my contention. This day week there will be a great ceremony in the cathedral, and you must preach at it. See that your sermon is so eloquent and edifying that it

70

will eclipse, obscure, and reduce to insignificance everything that
I have ever composed.''

'' But how can I do that? '' asked the poor priest in dismay.
'' You know very well that I am anything but learned, and so little
able to preach that I have never dared to mount the pulpit in
my life.''

'' God is good and He can do anything,'' calmly replied the
Bishop. '' Put your trust in God and do not doubt that on this
occasion He will perform a great miracle in your favour and in
mine.''

Trusting in the Divine Goodness and more inspired than ever,
the Bishop, denying himself to all visitors, shut himself up carefully in his study, and that evening wrote a real masterpiece, an
absolutely perfect discourse, perhaps the best which he had ever
written in all his life.

The following morning he gave the sermon to his friend the
priest, enjoining him to learn it thoroughly by heart.

Thoroughly alarmed and despondent lest he should not be able
to commit the sermon to memory, or should forget it after he had
learned it, our priest (so anxious was he to please his good patron)
spent two whole days in learning each word by heart and then,
without hesitating or pausing, he recited it like a parrot to the
Bishop. Two other days were spent in teaching the budding
preacher the intonation, the expression, and the movement of the
hands, so eloquent in Spanish preaching, that must correspond with
the spoken word.

The Bishop was now quite satisfied. He considered the discourse
pronounced by his friend admirable, and anticipated both for himself and for his disciple an overwhelming triumph.

Next, he announced that the preacher would be a compatriot
of his, and full of patriotic pride he said to his friends:

'' Now you will see something good. You will have to admit
that this humble priest of my race and from my town is a better
preacher than I am. He is a modern St. John Chrysostom, a
torrent of eloquence and a well of wisdom. In future you need
not tease me by saying that with the exception of myself there is
no Basque who can preach.''

They were all full of impatience, longing to hear the Basque
preacher. At last the day and hour of the ceremony came. The
cathedral was crammed to its very corners. The Bishop and the
canons sat in state in the choir, surrounded by all the pomp which
befitted the circumstances. In the centre of the edifice and not far
from the pulpit the ladies of high society and greatest piety in the
city were assembled, most of them very pretty and elegant in their
graceful robes and lace mantillas, with roses, pinks, and other
flowers in their hair. The humbler classes, both men and women,

filled the naves.   In fact, the curiosity to hear the new preacher was
universal and most remarkable, seeing that his fame as an orator
had been industriously spread abroad by the Bishop.

At last our Basque appeared in the pulpit and began his sermon
with so much grace and interest that the admiration, the surprise,
and the holy joy which filled all hearts were manifest throughout
the great building.   But alas and alack!   About half-way through
the sermon, fate, or rather Divine Providence, willed that the
preacher, in spite of his careful study, forgot what was to come
next.   He perspired, stopped short, wrung his hands, all in vain.
No doubt he would have to leave the pulpit with his sermon half
finished.   The discredit and the lack of prestige would be awful.
And the worst thing was that the sermon was interrupted at the
very moment of most thrilling interest, when the preacher was
describing the misfortunes which God had sent to afflict our nation,
either as a chastening means or to punish our many sins.

In his frantic despair the Basque lost his head completely, and
turning to the Bishop who sat watching him on his throne, began
to make a furious attack on him with the intimacy of a former
fellow-student.   Luckily in his excitement he made use of his native
Basque, which not another soul in the cathedral except the Bishop
understood.   He uttered prayers and reproaches in the sonorous
unknown tongue, he denounced him as a false friend who had
placed him in this terrible position, which was certain to be his
ruin and would oblige him to abandon the holy office of the priest-
hood in disgrace.

Who knows if it was a miracle of the Almighty?   What is
certain is that all at once, when he had relieved his soul of the
venom of his bitterness against the Archbishop in the language
which only they two could understand, not only did he remember
all the rest of the sermon from the point where he had left off, but
he was moved by a marvellous inspiration, and he exclaimed:

" The words which I have just uttered, my brethren, are taken
from the Lamentations of Jeremiah, and are the expression of his
affliction."

And then, happy in having recovered his thread, he went on
with real eloquence and complete self-possession to finish his admirable discourse.   The whole congregation was edified and amazed.
The Bishop had proved that there were Basques who could preach
as well as he could.   Everywhere the praise of the priest resounded,
not only as a most eloquent preacher, but also as a most learned
man, for had he not quoted an impassioned passage from the Sacred
Scriptures entirely by heart in the original Hebrew?

PEDRO A. DE ALARCÓN

1833–1891

THE TALL WOMAN

I

"WHAT do we know, my friends? What do we know?" exclaimed Gabriel, the distinguished mining engineer, sitting down under a pine tree and near a fountain, on the slope of Guadarrama, about six miles from the Escurial Palace and just on the boundary line between the provinces of Madrid and Segovia. Well do I know the place, the fountain, and the pine tree. I can see them still, but I cannot remember the name.

"Let us all sit down and rest here," said Gabriel. "We have agreed to enjoy the lovely weather as best we can in this charming place, famous for the tonic qualities of this sparkling fountain and for the picnics which have taken place here, where great scientists have come to observe Nature and to find an appetite from time to time. Yes, sit down and I will tell you a true story to bear out my theory. You call me a materialist, but still I maintain that in this world in which we live strange things happen—things so strange that no reason can account for them, nor can science or philosophy give any explanation of such things. Surely there are more mysteries in heaven and on earth than all our philosophy can account for, slightly to alter the words of Hamlet."

Gabriel addressed this lively speech to five friends of various ages, none of them very young and only one elderly. Three of them like him were mining engineers, the fourth was an artist, and the fifth something of a writer. All of them had come up with Gabriel, who was the youngest, on hired mules from the village of San Lorenzo, to spend the day in hunting for specimens in the lovely woods of Peguerinos, gathering interesting forest plants under the pine trees, catching butterflies in gauze nets, finding rare beetles under the bark of the decayed trees, and in all these occupations giving a fair amount of attention to the well-filled hamper of cold provisions and the skin of wine to the cost of which all had contributed in equal shares.

This was in the middle of the hot summer of 1875. I am not sure if it was the festival of Santiago or that of San Luis, but it was

73

a holiday of some sort—I think San Luis. In any case, the day was very hot, and the shade of the pine wood and murmur of the fountain were delicious after climbing the mountain-side. Up there, mind, heart, body, and especially appetite were refreshed by the pure air and the stillness, so sweet after the busy life of the plains which we had left so far below us.

The six friends sat under the shade of the pine trees, and Gabriel continued as follows:

" You may call me a visionary if you like, but it has been my fortune or misfortune through life that I have ever been regarded as a materialist, a man of modern thought, not believing in things unseen, in fact, a positivist! Yes, I may be so, but my positivism includes an acknowledgment of the mysterious influences of Nature —all the strange and inexplicable facts which *are* facts because they happen; all the emotions of the mind which are inseparable from the life of every reasoning creature. I believe in all these things because they are material and natural. They cannot be explained, but still they happen. Now, as to other things, which are supernatural, or extra-natural, just listen to what I am going to tell you and then judge for yourselves. I was not the hero of the strange occurrence which I am going to relate to you—but listen, and then tell me what explanation you can give me—natural, physical, scientific, whatever you think will best explain the case, if explanation be at all possible.

" Now, all of you, give me your close attention. But first of all, give me some wine. It ought to be cool enough now, for the skin has been resting under the flow of the fountain ever since we came on it. It was surely created by Providence for the use of weary and thirsty souls who come here in pursuit of science.

II

" Perhaps you may have heard of an engineer of Public Works named Telesforo de Ruiz, who died in 1860? "

" No, I never heard of him."

" Oh, yes, I have heard of him. He was an Andalusian, very dark and handsome. He was engaged to be married to the daughter of the Marquis of Moreda, and he died of gastric fever."

" Yes, that was he," replied Gabriel. " Well, about six months before he died, my friend Telesforo was a most brilliant young man, as every one said. Tall, strong, handsome, talented and with a first-class diploma from the School of Mines, and excellent prospects, he was very much sought after in the way of his profession by both public and private enterprises, and he was just as much sought after in private life by the fair sex, marriageable or unhappily married, and even by some charming widows anxious

to tempt Providence again. One of these was a well-known conquest of his, who would gladly have accompanied my friend to the
altar. However, she does not enter into this story, and indeed
Telesforo merely amused himself in her case by a very strong
flirtation with her. If she did make herself a bit cheap to him. . . .
Well, he was all the time deeply and seriously in love with the girl
to whom he was engaged, poor Joaquina de Moreda, and so the
poor widow merely filled a temporary gap. . . ."

" Now, now, Don Gabriel! No scandal allowed."

" I am not going to talk any scandal. Neither what I am going
to tell you nor what I may ask you to say later on the subject is
at all suitable for any but the most serious style of conversation.
Juan, give me another glass of wine. This wine is really excellent.
Well, my friends, listen with all your attention, for now I am going
to begin my tale in earnest. Those of you who knew the young
people will remember that poor Joaquina died suddenly when
taking the waters at Santa Agueda at the end of the summer of
1859. I was in Pau when the sad news came, and I was very
much affected on account of my friendship for Telesforo. I had
only met the girl once, at the house of her aunt, General Lopez's
widow, and her extreme pallor, of a bluish tint, struck me as an
indication of weak health, such as one sees in sufferers from aneurism. But she was very graceful, refined, and gentle-looking, and in
addition to her personal charms she would inherit her father's title,
as she was the only child, and she would also have a good deal of
money. So when I heard of her death I knew that her sweetheart would be inconsolable, and when I got back to Madrid, about
three weeks later, I went to see him early one morning. He had
a charming flat in the Calle del Lobo, near the Plaza San Jerónimo,
and he lived there and had his office under the same roof.

" He looked very sad, but was calm, and evidently master of
his grief, as he sat working with his assistants at some plan of a
railway. He was dressed in deep mourning, and when I entered,
he embraced me in silence, then turned to give some instructions
to one of his staff respecting the work in hand. I waited until,
taking my arm, he led me to his private sitting-room at the other
end of the house, saying as we went:

" ' I am so glad you have come. I cannot tell you how much
I have missed you in my present state of mind. Something very
strange and unaccountable has happened to me, and I want just to
tell you about it, for only a friend who knows me as you do will
be able to judge if I am mad or a fool. I certainly wish to have
some sane and calm opinion such as I know that yours will be.
Sit down here,' he went on when we had reached the sitting-room,
' and do not be afraid that I am going to weary you by describing
the grief which afflicts me, and which can only end with my life.

You have not had much personal experience of sorrow or human suffering, but yet you can imagine what I suffer and must always suffer. I do not seek or wish for consolation now or later on, or ever in all time. That subject is ended now. What I want to tell you is something so strange, so terrible, that I must speak of it to some one of calm judgment, some one who will listen and advise me. The whole adventure is like an awful seal set on my present misery, on the agony of my life, and it tortures me to the point of despair. It is all a most frightful mystery, and I think it will alarm you too.'

" ' Speak,' I replied, feeling vaguely anxious and more than half wishing that I had not come to see my unhappy friend. His expression of terror struck a chill to my heart and made me fear for his reason.

" ' Listen to me, then,' said he, wiping the perspiration from his forehead.

III

" ' I do not know if it is a mental twist which I have always had, or if it is the effect of some of those silly tales which old nurses use to frighten children into quiet and obedience, but ever since I was very young nothing caused me so much fright and horror as the sight, or even the thought, of a woman alone out of doors at a late hour of the night.

" ' I assure you that I have never been a coward. Like every other man of the world, I have always been ready to fight a duel if it became necessary to do so, and not very long after I had left the School of Mines I was obliged to quell a dangerous revolt among my workmen on my first important piece of work, by means of blows and even of shots, so that single-handed I reduced them to obedience. All my life, in Jaen, in Madrid, and elsewhere, I was accustomed to go about the streets at any hour of the night, alone and unarmed, and if by chance I did meet any late wanderers of suspicious appearance, I knew that they were merely thieves or human prowlers in search of prey, and I only avoided them or let them pass without notice. But if the solitary form was that of a woman, walking or standing, then, if I was alone, or there was no one else in sight, I was in the most abject state of terror possible to be imagined. You may laugh if you like, but my agony of mind was dreadful; I shivered from head to foot, thought of ghosts or lost souls, apparitions from the other world, wraiths of persons still alive; in fact, of all the terrible superstitious ideas which have ever been invented to torture the credulous, and which at any other time or in any other circumstances would have only provoked my ridicule. Then I hastened my steps or turned back· I made all kinds of detours to avoid meeting the lonely figure, and overcome by repulsion and horror, I fled to my home, never stopping until I was safe within its doors.

" ' Once in the shelter of my own house, I could laugh at my silly fears, and console myself by reflecting that at any rate no one of my acquaintance knew of such folly on my part. I could feel sure then that, as I did not believe in fairies or witches or apparitions of any sort, there was no need to have been frightened by the sight of the poor solitary creature, whom want, or vice, or some other cruel spur had driven away from shelter on such a night and at such a time. I felt that I would have done better to have offered her assistance if she was in need of it, or alms, if I had waited for her to ask me for them. But all this solid reasoning did not prevent my acting in just the same way when the next solitary female form was sighted. When I was twenty-five years of age, I met many such lonely nocturnal wanderers, and though I had always fled from them in the same way, I never had the slightest reason to think that they intended me any harm or were able to injure me in any way, nor had I ever any notable or disagreeable adventure with any one I met in the street late at night. But my fear was indomitable, only vanishing when I was safe at home, and could laugh at or scold myself for my lack of common sense. If I were not alone, or if there were other people in the street, the case was different, for I did not care then. The incident attracted no one's notice, and was soon forgotten, as children forget their terrors of the dark when they have companions by their side.

" ' Now, this brings me to one night about three years ago. I have only too good reason to remember the exact date. It was the 16th of November, at three o'clock in the morning. At that time I was living in a little flat in the Calle de Jardines, near the Calle de la Montera. The night was terribly cold and wet, and I was alone. You will ask me what I was doing out of doors at that hour on a November morning. Well, you will be surprised to hear that I had just left a sort of gambling saloon, unknown as such to the police, but where many people had already been ruined. I had been induced to go there the night before for the first and last time. Gambling was never a vice of mine, and the inducement held out to me by the friend who took me there, and who was a bit of a scamp, was that I would see something of the smart night life of the capital, and make the acquaintance of some interesting members of Bohemian society and ultra-fashionable actresses and other stars of the demi-monde, who dropped in to win or lose a few crowns at roulette.

" ' Well, about midnight the fun waxed furious. People of all classes dropped in, apparently after the theatre or the late receptions of society; play grew high, and I, like all novices, threw prudence to the winds, and staked my all, winning at first and then losing steadily, until at last, after being severely handled by cruel Fortune, I came away without a single coin in my pockets, and with debts to my friend and others, the amounts of which I had jotted down, without having any very clear idea of what they amounted to, but feeling certain that it was utterly out of my power ever to discharge them.

" ' I was going home, half dead with weariness, annoyance and disgust at my own folly, freezing with cold, and also very hungry. I did not know what to do, except to write to my poor father, who was very ill, asking him to send me money, and that would not only grieve but surprise him, for he believed that I was doing well in my profession and already in comfortable circumstances.   Overcome by these sad thoughts, I was just crossing the corner of the Calle de los Peligros to reach my own street, and was about to pass a newly-erected house at the corner, when on looking up, I became aware that in the doorway, erect and still as a pine tree, stood a very tall, stout woman, about sixty years of age, whose wicked bold lashless eyes were fixed on me like two daggers, whilst her huge toothless mouth grinned at me with indescribable malignity.

" ' The terror, or rather, the mad panic, which seized on me then surpassed all I had ever experienced previously. I stood staring at this horrible figure, and each line of her form, each smallest detail of her dress, were indelibly branded in my recollection. The lamp at the street corner shone steadily on the scene, and the apparition, or whatever it might be, and I alone were the occupants of the entire street. I forgot my ruined position, I forgot my folly of that night, there was only room in my brain for one thought, if thought it could be called—a crazy terror of the woman who seemed to fill the whole doorway beside me.

" ' Oh, do not be alarmed, my friend. I was not really mad; I am not mad now. But what shall I be if some consolation is not found for me; some solution of the distress of my soul? It is for that reason that I have asked you to listen to me and to bear with me.

" ' The first surprising thing about this woman, as I must call her, was her great height and the breadth of her bony shoulders; next the size and roundness of her enormous owl-like eyes, the size of her nose, and the hideous gap which served her as a mouth, made still more hideous by the malignant grin which would have disfigured the fairest mouth in existence, and finally, the strange coquetry of her dress; the bright-coloured handkerchief which was draped over her ugly forehead and fastened beneath the chin, and a very small fan which she held open in her hand, and which she flirted in an affectation of modesty before her face and figure.

" ' Nothing could be more grotesque or ridiculous than the sight of that tiny fan in those enormous hands, like a sceptre of weakness to a giantess so old, so bony, so hideous. The same effect was produced by the gay cotton handkerchief in contrast to the huge deformed nose, and the coarse face which made me ask myself for a moment if this were not a man in woman's dress. But no. The expression was that of a wicked woman, of a witch, of a sorceress, of one of the Fates, of a Fury. I cannot express my exact thought, but in that instant I felt that this was the cause and the justification of all the unreasonable fears which had overcome me when I had seen a woman, however innocent-looking, alone in the street at night. It would seem that, from my very birth, I had foreseen the horror of this encounter, and that I feared it by instinct, as all living creatures are given the instinct to recognise their natural enemies, even by their approach, before ever they have received any injury from them.

" ' When I saw now for the first time this sphinx of my whole life, I did not run away, less through shame or manly pride than because I dreaded unreasoningly that my very fear would reveal to the creature that it was I, her victim, who fled, and would give her wings to pursue me, to seize me, to . . . I could not tell what I feared. Panic is a thing of itself, and has no form of thought even to shape the thing it fears or to put into words its own madness.

" ' The house where I lived was at the extreme end of the street, which, as you know, is very long and narrow. Not another soul was to be seen. I was alone, utterly alone, with that awful statue-like figure, which might annihilate me with a word. How was I to get away, to get home? I looked along to where I saw the broad well-lighted Calle de la Montera, where policemen and watchmen are on beat at all times.

" ' Finally, I do not remember how, I resolved to do something to escape from the horrible obsession which dominated me—not to take to flight, but to creep by degrees down the street, even at the cost of years of life and health, to get away, to get nearer to my home, if I did not fall dead on the ground before reaching it.

" ' I had moved thus slowly about twenty steps along the street towards my house, when all at once a new spasm of terror seized me. I did not dare to stop, I could not look round, but what if my enemy were following me. Dared I look round? I stopped and tried to reason calmly.

" ' " One or other thing must happen," thought I with the speed of lightning. " Either I have good cause for this fear, or else it is sheer madness. In the first case, this terrible witch is following me, she will overtake me, and nothing in the whole world can save me. But if this is only a craze, a mania, an access of folly, a groundless panic, then let me face it out, convince myself of its unreality, and thus be cured once for all, and never have to suffer in this way again. I shall feel certain of my silly conduct if I find that this poor old woman is still standing in the doorway sheltering from cold, or waiting for the door to be opened. Then I shall go home, and never again will I permit such groundless fears to torment me.''

" ' Having almost calmed myself by this forced reasoning, I stood still and turned my head.

" ' Oh, Gabriel, Gabriel, how shall I convey my feelings to you at what I saw? The tall woman had followed me with soundless footsteps, she was towering over me, almost touching me with her fan, her head was bent so as nearly to touch my shoulder.

" ' Why? Ah, why, indeed? Was she a pickpocket? Was it a man in disguise? Or was it only a spiteful old woman, who saw that I was frightened and wanted to terrify me more? Was it the spectral reflection of my own cowardice? Was it the sum total of all the deceptions and shortcomings of our human nature?

" ' To tell you all the ideas which ran through my mind at that moment would be impossible. I managed to utter a shriek, which roused me from my stupor as from a nightmare, and I ran like a terrified child of four years old and did not stop until I was in the Calle de la Montera.

" ' Once there, all my fear fell away from me. And yet the Calle de la Montera was deserted too. I looked all along the Calle de los Jardines, the whole of which I could see, and which was sufficiently well lighted by its three lamp-posts and by the reflection from the Calle de Peligros. It would not be possible for the tall woman to hide if she had gone in that direction, but I give you my word there was not a cat or the shadow of a mouse to be seen in the whole street, not to speak of a giantess like my tormentor.

" ' " She has gone into some other doorway," I thought. " But she will not be able to get away without my seeing her if she moves while the lamps are lit."

" ' Just then I saw a night-watchman coming along the Calle del Caballero de Gracia, and I called him without moving from where I stood. To explain my call and put him on the alert, I told him that there was a man disguised as a woman in the Calle de Jardines, that he had gone into that street by the Calle de los Peligros, and must have gone off towards the Calle de la Aduana; that I would remain where I was if he would go to the other end of the street, and that in that way he would not be able to escape. It would be well for us both to capture him, I said, for he must be a robber or other bad character to go about disguised at that hour.

" ' The night-watchman did as I advised. He went down to the Calle de la Aduana, and when I saw his lantern gleam at the other

end of the Calle de los Jardines I went along the other side and
down the next street to meet him.

" ' Neither of us had seen anything in the shape of a human
being, although both of us had looked into the doorway of every
house.

" ' " He must have gone into some house," said the watchman.

" ' " I expect so," I replied, opening my own door, with the
firm determination to change to another street next day.

" ' I ascended the stairs to my flat on the third floor, and opened
the outer door with my latch-key. I never made my good servant
José sit up for me.

" ' However, this time, he was waiting up for me. My troubles
were not over yet.

" ' " Is there anything wrong? " I asked him in surprise.

" ' He seemed rather agitated.

" ' " Sir," he said, " Captain Falcón was here from eleven
o'clock until half-past two. He said he would come back after
daylight, and that if you came back, you were to wait up for him,
as he must see you."

" ' Those words filled me with new terrors. I felt as if my own
death were at hand. Certainly something very serious was on foot.
My dear old father had been very ill for a long time, and as he had
seemed to be much worse lately, I had written to my brothers in
Jaen, where all my family lived, that if matters became very serious
they were to telegraph to my friend, Captain Falcón, who would
let me know at once what had happened. I had no doubt now that
my father was dead.

" ' I sat in an arm-chair, awaiting the dawn and my friend, who
was to be the bearer of sad news. How can I express what I
suffered in those long hours of waiting. Three things, all of terribly
painful association, kept repeating themselves in my mind, as being
inextricably connected with one another, standing apart from the
rest of the world in a monstrous and terrifying group: my ruin at
play, the meeting with the tall woman, and the death of my
honoured father!

" ' When six o'clock struck, Captain Falcón entered my sitting-
room, and looked at me in silence. I flung myself into his arms in
a hysterical outburst, and he said, essaying to calm my grief:

" ' " Weep, my friend. You have indeed cause to weep, for
such a loss as this can only come once in a lifetime." '

IV

" My friend Telesforo," continued Gabriel, after he had drained
another goblet of wine, " paused when he reached this point of his
story, and after a silence of some minutes went on as follows:

" ' If this were all I had to tell you, you might not find anything strange or supernatural in it, and you might tell me what others have told me; men of much common sense of my acquaintance to whom I have spoken of it; that every person of lively and ardent imagination has his or her pet subject of unreasoning terror; that mine was the idea of solitary female night-walkers, and that the old woman in the Calle de Jardines was only some poor old creature who tried to ask me for alms when she was without home or food, and whom I had alarmed by my own strange demeanour; that at the worst, she could only be some associate of thieves or other bad characters, waiting in a quiet street for her companions, and fearful of their being discovered by the night-watchman.

" ' I, too, wished to believe this, and after hearing it constantly repeated, I did almost come to believe it at the end of some months. Still I would have given years of my life for the certainty of never again seeing the tall woman! And now I would give everything I have just to be able to see her once more! '

" ' But why? '

" ' Just to be able to strangle her! '

" ' I don't understand.'

" ' You will understand when I tell you that I met her again three weeks ago, a few hours before I received the fatal news of the death of my poor Joaquina.'

" ' Well, tell me about it.'

" ' There is not much more to tell. It was about five o'clock in the morning, and I had been to an entertainment where I had not been much entertained. I had the unpleasant task of breaking the news of my approaching marriage to a lady with whom I had had a very pronounced flirtation, and who took the news very ill. I had to stand many reproaches and even tears from the charming young widow when I explained that the position was inevitable; my resolution was taken, and my wedding-day fixed. At that moment, though I did not know it, they were burying my promised wife in Santa Agueda.

" ' It was not yet daylight, but there was that faint light in the sky which shows that night is weakening. The street lamps had been extinguished and the watchmen had retired, when, as I was passing by the Plaza de las Cortes to get to my flat in the Calle del Lobo, at the corner of the Calle de Santa Ana, who should cross my path but the terrible woman whom I had seen in the Calle de Jardines.

" ' She did not look at me, and I thought she had not seen me. The same dress, even the same little fan as when I saw her three years ago. And all my previous terror was as nothing in comparison with what took possession of me now. I walked quickly down the Calle del Prado after she had passed, but I did not take my eyes off her to make sure that she did not turn her head; and when I reached the other part of the Calle del Lobo I breathed hard as if I had just breasted an impetuous stream, and my fear giving way to satisfaction, I pressed on, thinking that I had narrowly but completely escaped the notice of the hateful witch, and that now I was free from her baleful proximity.

" ' But just as I was about to enter my house a new terror arose. Surely she was too cunning to allow me to escape like this, and she was only feigning not to notice me in order to be able to track me with more certainty down the dark and silent street and thus find where I lived.

" ' I stopped and looked round. There she was just behind me, her dress almost touching me, her wicked eyes fixed on me, her hideous mouth distended in a spiteful grin of triumph, as she fanned herself with an air of languor, as though ridiculing my childish terror.

" ' That fear gave place at once to the most senseless fury, to the rage of desperation, and I flung myself on the vile creature, seized her by the arms and dashed her against the wall. I held her back by the throat, and rained blows on her until I was obliged to desist, in the conviction that I was really dealing with a human being and a woman.

" ' She had uttered a hoarse cry of mingled pain and rage, and pretended to weep, but I felt that it was but pretence; and then fixing her hyena eyes on me, she said:

" ' " Why do you treat me like this? "

" ' My anger died away and my fear returned.

" ' " Do you not remember," I said, " that you have seen me elsewhere? "

" ' " Indeed I do," she replied sardonically. " The night of San Eugenio, about three o'clock, in the Calle de Jardines."

" ' I shivered involuntarily, but I still kept hold of her.

" ' " Who are you? " I asked. " Why do you run after me like this? What do you want with me? "

" ' " I am only a poor weak woman," said she with a diabolical grin. " You hate and fear me without cause or reason. If not, will you please tell me why you were so overcome with fear the first time you saw me? "

" ' " Because I have hated you ever since I was born," I cried involuntarily. " Because you are the evil spirit of my life! "

" ' " So that you have known me for a long time past? Well, my son, I have known you too."

" ' " You have known me? Since when? "

" ' " Before you were born. And when I saw you pass close to me three years ago, I said to myself: ' Here he is at last! ' "

" ' " But what am I to you? What are you to me? "

" ' " I am the devil," she said, spitting in my face. And with that she suddenly slipped from my grasp, caught up her skirts, and ran from my sight without making the least noise as she disappeared.

" ' It would have been madness to try to overtake her. And it was now broad daylight and a good many people were passing in the streets, both in San Jerónimo Square and in the Calle del Prado. The tall woman continued to run, or as it seemed to fly, until she reached the Calle de las Huertas, now all gleaming in the morning sun. She stopped there and looked back at me, waving her fan at me in a threatening manner, holding it closed like a dagger, and finally she disappeared round the corner of the last street.

" ' No, just wait a moment, Gabriel. Do not give me your opinion yet, for I have not quite finished my strange tale, in which my heart and my life are equally involved. Listen to me for a few minutes longer!

" ' When I reached home, whom do you think I found awaiting me but Colonel Falcón, as he is now, and he had come to bring me the terrible news that my love, my darling Joaquina, all my hope of happiness and good fortune on this earth, had died the day before in Santa Agueda! Her unhappy father had telegraphed to Falcón, knowing what an old friend of ours he was, asking him to break the news to me . . . to me, who had guessed that a great misfortune was in store for me as soon as ever I set eyes on the curse of my life. Now you know why I want to kill the enemy of my happiness, my born foe, that wicked old sorceress, who is the embodiment of the cruelty of my destiny.

" ' But why do I talk like this? Is she really a woman? Is she a human being at all? Why did the presentiment of her existence weigh on me ever since I was born? Why did she *recognise* me when she saw me first? Why have I only seen her when some great misfortune has happened to me? Is it the apparition of Satan? Is it Death? Is it Life itself, for me, with misery? Is it Antichrist? What or who is it? '

V

" Well, my dear friends, I leave you to imagine what remarks I made and what arguments I used in the effort to calm Telesforo, for all that I said was just the same as you are all thinking now and preparing to tell me, so as to prove to me that there is nothing superhuman or supernatural in my story. You will tell me more than that . . . you will say that my poor friend was not in his right mind; that he must have been always a little mad, for he evidently suffered from the moral infirmity which specialists call groundless panic, or as the case may be, intermittent delirium; that even

admitting that all that he said about the strange woman was quite
true, still it was only a case of a singular series of chance coin-
cidences of dates and events; and that perhaps the poor old woman
was mad too, and was excited by his mania. She might have been
an old rat-catcher abroad at her nightly work, or a beggar, or even
a self-styled witch, as the hero of my tale said to himself in an
interval of lucidity and common sense."

" That is about the truth," said the companions of Gabriel in
different ways. " We have all had that idea, and we were just
about to express it to you."

" Well, just listen to me for a moment, and you will see that I
was wrong in thinking that, as you are wrong now. The only
person who was not wrong was Telesforo. Ah! it is much easier to
talk of madness than to find an explanation of many things which
happen on this earth."

" Go on, tell us the rest! "

" I am going to do so, and this chapter, as it is the last, will be
related to you without even a preliminary glass of wine.

VI

" A few days after this conversation with Telesforo I was obliged
to go to the province of Albacete in my capacity of mining engineer;
and not many weeks later I heard from a contractor of public
works that my poor friend had been attacked by a very severe
gastric fever and jaundice. He was green in hue, unable to move
from his chair, and he could not work, nor would he see any one.
His grief and melancholy were pitiable, and the doctors despaired
of his recovery. Then I knew why he had not answered my letters,
and I applied to my old friend, Colonel Falcón, for news. What
he told me was ever more and more depressing.

" After five months of absence, I returned to Madrid on the very
day when the news of the battle of Tetuan arrived. I remember it
as if it were yesterday. That evening I bought the *Correspondencia
de España* to see the news, and the first thing my eye lighted on
was the obituary notice of my poor friend Telesforo, and the invitation to all his friends to attend his funeral on the following day.

" You will readily understand that I would not willingly fail to
show him this last poor tribute. I had a place in one of the carriages nearest to the hearse, and when we alighted in the cemetery
of San Luis I noticed a woman of the poorer class, old and very tall,
who laughed in a most unseemly manner when the hearse arrived,
and who then advanced with an air of triumph towards the pall-
bearers, pointing out to them with a very small fan the way they
were to take to reach the open grave, which was to be my friend's
last resting-place.

" At the first glance I recognised, with grief and fear, that this woman corresponded to the description given by Telesforo of his implacable enemy. She was just what he had described, with her enormous nose, her infernal eyes, her hideous mouth, the bright printed cotton handkerchief over her head, and the tiny fan, which in her hands seemed to be the sceptre of profanity and inhuman mockery.

" She perceived at once that I was looking at her, and she fixed her eyes on me in a peculiar way, as if recognising me whilst she ascertained that I recognised her. I felt that she knew that my dead friend had told me all about the scenes in the Calle de Jardines and the Calle del Lobo. She seemed to send me a challenge, to declare that I had inherited the hatred she had borne to my unfortunate friend.

" I confess that the fear which overcame me was greater than the surprise which I felt at this new coincidence or disaster. It seemed to me to be certain that some mysterious connection had existed in some supernatural way between the appalling old woman and Telesforo previous to this life; but at that moment I saw that my own life, my own good fortune, my own soul even, were in danger if I was to inherit this strange and terrible animosity from beyond the grave.

" The tall woman began to laugh, pointing at me mockingly with her fan, as if she had read my thoughts and wished every one to notice my cowardice. I was obliged to lean on the arm of a friend to avoid falling to the ground, and then she made a gesture of contempt or pity, turned on her heels, and walked into the churchyard, still looking at me with her head turned over her shoulder. She fanned herself and signed to me with the fan at one and the same time, walking with mincing steps among the tombs with a sort of infernal coquetry, until at last I saw her disappear for ever in the crowded heart of that great world of the dead.

" I say ' for ever,' because fifteen years have passed since then, and I have never seen her since that moment. If she was really a human being, she must be dead by now; and if she were not, if she were a supernatural creature, I feel sure that she must have scorned me too much to persecute me.

" Now, my friends! I have told you all I know. Let me have your opinion as to such strange facts. Do you think that they are quite natural? "

.   .   .   .

It is needless for me, the narrator of the strange story which I then heard and which I have just given you to read, to repeat the remarks made by the group of friends and comrades to Gabriel. For indeed the fact remains that every reader will have to use his own judgment as to the conclusion to which he comes, and to his own ideas and beliefs in the matter.

So I will say no more. I leave it to the judgment of every one of my readers to solve a mystery which has never been solved to my satisfaction or that of any other person who considered the strange case. And if it must ever remain a mystery, then I have only to address the most affectionate and faithful greeting to each of the five others who with me spent that unforgettable day on the shady slope of the pine-wooded hill of Guadarrama.

VALDEMORO, *August* 25, 1881.

PEDRO A. DE ALARCÓN

THE PATRIOT TRAITOR

In the little village of Padrón, in Galician territory,[1] about the year
1808, a certain García of Paredes sold toads and snakes and rain-
water for fortune-telling, in addition to his regular business as an
apothecary. He was a misanthropic bachelor, a descendant, most
likely, of that illustrious man who killed a bull with one blow of his
fist.

It was a cold and mournful night in autumn. The sky was over-
cast by dense clouds, and the entire absence of earthly light left
the darkness to hold its own in all the streets and plazas of the
town.

About ten on that dreadful night, which the unhappy circumstances of the country made much more sinister, there arrived in the
plaza, which to-day is called Plaza of the Constitution, a silent
group of shadows, even darker than the obscurity of heaven and
earth. These shadows advanced toward the drug-store of García
of Paredes, which had been completely closed since the ringing
of the " Bells for the Departed," or since exactly half-past
eight.

" What shall we do? " said one of the shades in exceedingly
correct Galician.

" Nobody has seen us," observed another.

" Let us break down the door! " proposed a woman.

" And kill them! " murmured as many as fifteen voices.

" I will take charge of the apothecary! " exclaimed a boy.

" We'll all look after him! "

" For being a Jew! "

" For taking the part of the French! "

" They say that to-day more than twenty Frenchmen are supping
with him."

" Indeed I believe it! As they know they are safe here they have
come in a crowd."

" Ah, if it was in my house! Three lodgers have I thrown into
the well! "

" My wife decapitated one yesterday! "

[1] *Galicia,* formerly a kingdom and afterwards a province in the north-
west of Spain.

88

" And I," said a friar with a coarse voice, " I have asphyxiated two captains by leaving lighted charcoal in their cell, which had been mine! "

" And that infamous apothecary protects them! "

" How respectful he was yesterday when he was walking with those vile outcasts! "

" Who would have expected it of García of Paredes? Not a month ago he was the most valiant, the most patriotic, the greatest royalist of the village."

" Yes, how he sold in his shop portraits of Prince Ferdinand! "

" And now he sells pictures of Napoleon! "

" He used to excite us to defence against the invaders——"

" And since they came to Padrón he has gone over to them! "

" And to-night he gives a supper to all the chiefs! "

" Hear what a noise they are making! It is well they do not cry, ' Long live the Emperor! ' "

" Have patience," murmured the friar. " It is still very early."

" Let us let them get drunk," said an old woman. " Then we will enter—and not one shall remain alive! "

" I say let us quarter the apothecary! "

" Cut him into eighths, if you wish! A sympathiser with the French is more odious than a Frenchman. The Frenchman treads a foreign country under foot; the French sympathiser sells and dishonours his native land. The Frenchman commits an assassination; the French partisan is a parricide! "

While the foregoing scene was taking place at the door of the apothecary's shop, García of Paredes and his fellow-revellers were indulging in the merriest and most unbridled gluttony imaginable.

There were twenty of the Frenchmen whom the druggist had at his table, and all of them were chiefs and officers.

García of Paredes was forty-five years old; he was tall and withered and yellower than a mummy; one would say his skin was long since dead; his forehead reached to the nape of his neck, thanks to the shining baldness that had something phosphorescent about it; his dull, black eyes, set deep in fleshless hollows, were like those lakes, shut in by mountains, that offer only darkness, dizziness, and death to whoever gazes into them; lakes that reflect nothing; that sometimes roar sullenly, but without suffering any change; that devour everything that falls upon their surface; that return nothing; that nobody has been able to sound; that are fed by no river and for which the imagination seeks a bottom in the ocean of the antipodes.

The supper was abundant, the wine good, the conversation cheerful and animated. The Frenchmen laughed, swore, blasphemed, sang, smoked, ate, and drank, all at the same time.

One of them told about the secret love-affairs of Napoleon;
another, about the night of the Second of May in Madrid; another,
the battles of the Pyramids; and still another, the execution of
Louis XVI.

García of Paredes drank, laughed, and chatted like the others, or
perhaps more than they; and so eloquent was he in favour of
the Imperial cause, that the soldiers of Cæsar would have embraced him, have applauded him, have improvised songs in his
honour.

" Sirs," the apothecary had said, " the war which we Spaniards
make against you is as foolish as it is purposeless. You, sons of the
Revolution, come to draw Spain from her traditional abasement,
to free her from prejudice, to dissipate religious darkness, to better
her antique customs, to teach us those useful and incontrovertible
truths, that there is no God, no after-life, that penitence, fasting,
chastity, and the other catholic virtues are quixotic foolishness, un-
suited to a civilised people, and that Napoleon is the true messiah,
the redeemer of the people, the friend of the human race. Sirs!
May the Emperor live as long as I desire that he may live! "

" Bravo! Hurrah! " exclaimed the men of the Second of May.

The apothecary bent his forehead with unspeakable anguish.

Soon he lifted it, as strong and as serene as before. He drank a
glass of wine, and continued :

" An ancestor of mine, a García of Paredes, a barbarian, a Samson, a Hercules, a Milo of Crotona, killed two hundred Frenchmen
in one day—I believe it was in Italy. You see, he was not so
fond of the French as I! He acquitted himself valiantly in the
wars against the Moors of the kingdom of Granada; the Catholic
King himself made him a knight, and he mounted guard more
than once in the Quirinal, when our uncle, Alexander Borgia, was
Pope. Oh, you didn't think I had such illustrious ancestry! For
this Diego García of Paredes, this forebear of mine—who has as a
descendant an apothecary—took Cosenza and Manfredonia, entered
Cerinola by assault, and did good work at the battle of Pavía.
There we took prisoner a King of France, whose sword was in
Madrid nearly three centuries, until it was taken from us three
months ago by that son of an innkeeper who comes at your head,
and whom they call Murat."

Here the druggist paused again. Some of the French seemed to
want to reply to him; but he, arising and imposing on all silence
by his attitude, seized a glass convulsively and exclaimed with a
voice of thunder :

" I drink your health, gentlemen, and may my ancestor be
cursed, for he was a beast and he is now in the depths of hell.
Long live the Frenchmen of Francis I. and of Napoleon Bona-
parte! "

" Long live they! " responded the invaders, with great satisfaction. And all emptied their glasses.

Just then they heard a noise in the street, or rather, at the door of the shop.

" Did you hear? " asked the French.

García of Paredes smiled.

" They come to kill me," he said.

" Who? "

" My neighbours of Padrón."

" Why? "

" Because I sympathise with the French. For some nights they have surrounded my house. But what difference is it to us? Let us go on with our feast."

" Yes, let us go on! " exclaimed the revellers. " We are here to defend you."

And striking bottles against bottles, rather than glasses against glasses, " Long live Napoleon! Death to Ferdinand! Death to Galicia! " they cried together.

García of Paredes hoped that the health-drinking would quiet them, and murmured in a sad tone:

" Celedonio! "

The clerk stuck his pale, frightened face through a door without daring to enter the cavern.

" Celedonio, bring paper and ink," said the apothecary tranquilly.

The boy returned with writing materials.

" Sit down," continued his master. " Now, write the figures which I am going to give you. Divide them into two columns. At the top of the right column put ' Debit,' and at the top of the other, ' Credit.' "

" Sir," trembled the clerk, " at the door there is a tumult. They cry, ' Death to the apothecary! ' And they demand entrance."

" Be quiet and let them alone! Write what I have told you."

The French smiled with admiration to see the druggist occupied in adjusting accounts while death and ruin hovered near him. Celedonio raised his head and made ready his pen, waiting for the figures to put down.

" Let us see, gentlemen," said García of Paredes, addressing his table-companions. " I want you to help me continue our feast with a single toast. Let us begin in order of seats at table. You, captain, tell me, how many Spaniards have you killed since you crossed the Pyrenees? "

" Bravo! Magnificent idea! " exclaimed the Frenchmen.

" I," said the man addressed, sitting up and pulling his moustache petulantly; " I have killed, personally, with my sword—oh, put it at ten or twelve."

" Eleven on the right! " cried the druggist to his clerk.

The clerk repeated, after writing:

" Debit, eleven."

" Go on," continued the host; " and you, M. Julius? "

" I, six! "

" And you, commandant? "

" I, twenty! "

" I, eight! "

" I, fourteen! "

" I, none! "

" I do not know—I have shot blindly."

So each answered as his turn came. And the clerk went on putting down figures on the right.

" Let us see now, captain," continued García of Paredes; " we begin again with you. How many Spaniards do you expect to kill in the rest of the war, supposing it lasts, say, three years? "

" Oh! " answered the captain, " who can estimate that? "

" Calculate it, I beg of you."

" Put another eleven! "

" Eleven to the left," dictated García of Paredes. And Celedonio repeated:

" Credit, eleven."

" And you? " asked the druggist in the same order he had before followed.

" I, fifteen! "

" I, twenty! "

" I, one hundred! "

" I—a thousand! "

So answered the Frenchmen.

" Put them all down at ten, Celedonio," murmured the druggist ironically. " Now add up the columns separately."

The poor youth, who had written the figures with drops of deadly sweat upon him, was obliged to add on his fingers, like old women, so great was his terror.

At the end of a space of horrible silence he said to his master:

" Debit, 285. Credit, 200."

" That is to say," added García of Paredes, " two hundred and eighty-five dead, and two hundred sentenced. Total, four hundred and eighty-five victims."

And he pronounced these words in so deep and sepulchral a voice that the Frenchmen looked at each other in alarm.

Meanwhile the apothecary was settling a new account.

" We are heroes! " he exclaimed on finishing it. " We have drunk seventy bottles, or perhaps a hundred and five and a half measures of wine, which, divided among twenty-one—for each has done his share—gives five measures to each man. I repeat, we are heroes! ''

With this the panels of the door cracked, and the boy, tottering, stammered :

'' Now they are entering! ''

'' What hour is it? '' asked the apothecary with the greatest tranquillity.

'' Eleven. But don't you hear them breaking in? ''

'' Let them. *It is now the hour!* ''

'' The hour? For what? '' murmured the Frenchmen, trying to rise.

But they were so drunk that they could not rise from their chairs.

'' Let them enter! '' they called in drunken tones, drawing their swords with difficulty and without succeeding in standing. '' Let the rabble enter! We will receive them! ''

With this there sounded below, in the shop, the noise of the vessels and phials which the people were breaking, and upon the stairway sounded the unanimous and terrible cry :

'' Death to the French sympathiser! ''

García of Paredes arose, as if impelled by a spring, on hearing that noise within his house, and supported himself by the table, so as not to fall again into his chair. He threw around him a look of inexpressible joy and showed upon his lips the immortal smile of one who triumphs. Thus, transfigured and beautiful, with the trembling of death and of enthusiasm upon him, he uttered the following words, broken and solemn as strokes of a knell of agony :

'' Frenchmen! If any of you or all of you should find occasion propitious for avenging the death of two hundred and eighty-five compatriots and for saving the life of two hundred others in addition; if by sacrificing your existence you might placate the insulted shades of your ancestors, punish the murderers of two hundred and eighty-five heroes, and free from death two hundred brothers, thus augmenting the hosts of the patriot army with two hundred champions of national independence, would you look for even a moment at your own miserable life? Would you hesitate an instant in embracing, like Samson, the column of the temple and dying, as the price of slaying the enemies of God? ''

'' What does he say? '' the Frenchmen questioned.

'' Sir, the assassins are in the ante-room! '' cried Celedonio.

'' Let them enter! '' called García of Paredes. '' Open the door of the parlour for them! Let them all come—to see how a descendant of a soldier of Pavía shall die! ''

The Frenchmen, astonished, stupid, held to their chairs by an insupportable lethargy, believing that the death of which the Spaniard spoke was going to enter the room in the wake of the rioters, made mighty efforts to lift the swords which were lying on the table; but they could not succeed with their weak fingers in even grasping the hilts. It seemed that the iron adhered to the board by an insurmountable force of attraction.

At this point more than fifty men and women, armed with sticks, daggers, and pistols, yelling, and with flashing eyes rushed into the room.

" Let them all die! " screamed some women who entered first.

" *Stop!* " cried García of Paredes with such a voice, such an attitude, such a look, that the cry added to the immovability and silence of the French and imposed cold terror on the crowd, which was not looking for that unresisting and mournful reception.

" You need not flourish your daggers," continued the apothecary in a failing voice. " I have done more than all of you for the independence of the Fatherland. I have pretended to be a French sympathiser! And you see—the twenty chiefs and officers, the invaders—twenty—do not touch them! *They are poisoned!* "

A cry at once of terror and admiration arose from the hearts of the Spaniards. They took another step toward the revellers, and found that the greater number were already dead, with head fallen forward, arms extended upon the table, and hand stiffened on sword-hilt. The others were in the agony of death.

" Long live García of Paredes! " cried the Spaniards, surrounding the dying hero.

" Celedonio," murmured the apothecary. " The opium—has run out. Send for opium—to Coruña."

And he fell upon his knees.

Then his neighbours of Padrón realised that the apothecary also was poisoned.

Now one could see a picture that was as sublime as it was terrible. Women, seated on the ground, sustained on their laps and in their arms the dying patriot, being the first to overwhelm him with caresses and blessings, as they had been first in seeking his death. The men had collected the lights of the table and, kneeling, they held them above that patriotic, tender group. Finally in the shadow lay twenty dead or dying men, some of them falling now and then with a fearful heaviness.

And at each death sigh that was heard, at each falling of a Frenchman to earth, a glorious smile lighted the face of García of Paredes, whose spirit shortly returned to heaven, blessed by a minister of the Lord, and mourned by his brothers of his own land.

PEDRO A. DE ALARCÓN

THE CORNET PLAYER

Where there's a will there's a way

I

"DON BASILIO, play the cornet and we will dance. It is not so hot under these trees."

"Yes, yes, Don Basilio, play the cornet à piston! "

"Bring Don Basilio the cornet on which Joaquin is learning to play."

"It isn't a very good one. Will you play it, Don Basilio? "

"No! "

"Why not? "

"Because I will not! "

"But why not? "

"Because I do not know how to play."

"Not know how to play! Did you ever know such a hypocrite? "

"I suppose he only wants to be coaxed a bit."

"Don't we all know that you have been the chief cornet player of your regiment, Don Basilio? "

"And that no one could equal you as a musician! "

"And that you were sent for to play at the Palace, in the days of Espartero! "

"And that you have a pension! "

"Please, Don Basilio. Do be kind to us! "

"Well, my children, what you say is true. I have played the cornet. I have been a—a specialist, as you say, but it is also true that two years ago I made a present of my cornet to a poor musician who had passed his examination as a cornet-player, but had no instrument of his own. Since then I have not blown a note."

"What a pity! "

"And you a second Rossini! "

"But anyhow, you will play for us this afternoon! "

"Out here in the fields it makes no difference if the cornet isn't very good."

" Grandfather, don't forget that it is my birthday! "

" Hurrah, hurrah! Here comes the cornet! "

" Now, what will he play? "

" A waltz? "

" No, a polka."

" Polka! What nonsense! Let us have a fandango."

" Oh, yes! A fandango, our own national dance."

" My dear children, I am very sorry, but it is quite impossible for me to play the cornet."

" But you are always so obliging, and now——"

" Do not be unkind to us."

" Your little grandson begs you to play."

" And your niece too."

" For Heaven's sake don't tease me. I have told you I cannot play."

" But why? "

" Because I have forgotten how to play, and what is more, I have sworn never to learn again."

" To whom did you swear? "

" To myself, to a dead man, and to my daughter, your poor mother."

The whole party grew serious on hearing this, and kept silence.

" Ah, if you only knew what it cost me to learn to play the cornet! " added the old man.

" Oh, tell us! It is a story, then? "

All the young people gathered round.

" A story indeed," said Don Basilio, " and a strange one. Listen, and then you can judge whether I can play the cornet or not."

He sat under a tree, and the interested group sat round him, while he related the story of how he learned to play the instrument for which he had been so celebrated.

Just in such a way did Byron's hero, Mazeppa, relate to Charles XII. one evening, under another tree, the terrible story of how he learned to ride.

Let us listen to Don Basilio.

II

" Just seventeen years ago the civil war broke out in Spain.

" Carlos and Isabel both claimed the crown, and the people of Spain, divided into two parties, shed their blood in a fratricidal struggle.

" I had a friend, named Ramón Gomez, a lieutenant of chasseurs in the same battalion in which I was, and he was the most charming man of my acquaintance. We had been brought up together, we left school at the same time, we fought together from the beginning of the war, and both of us were ready to die for freedom. He was more eager for the freedom of our country than even I and all the rest of the army put together.

" One day our Colonel offended Ramón by some arbitrary order; one of those brutes of authority which sometimes interfere with the most promising careers. I do not know exactly how this came about, but the result was that the proud and freedom-loving lieutenant of chasseurs abandoned the ranks of his comrades, deserted even his bosom friend, went over to the enemy, and all that he might have the right to kill his Colonel in fair warfare! Ramón was not the man to stand insult or injustice from any one under the sun.

" Neither my threats nor my entreaties were of any use to make him change his mind. He had fully decided. He would exchange the Queen's uniform for that of the Carlists, the helmet for the rebel cap, in spite of his mortal hatred for the party who were disturbing our country—the faction fighters, as we called them.

" At that time we were in the Prince's district, three leagues distant from the enemy. Ramón had determined to desert that night. It was miserable weather, cold, wet, and dreary, and next day there was to be a battle.

" About midnight Ramón came to my quarters. I was asleep, but he called me softly.

" ' Basilio! '

" ' Who is it? '

" ' It is I. Farewell! '

" He caught hold of my hand.

" ' Listen,' he said. ' If there is a battle to-morrow, as we expect, and if we meet in it——'

" ' Well, of course we shall meet as friends.'

" ' No. We shall embrace first, and then we shall fight. I shall certainly die to-morrow, for I shall stop at nothing until I have killed the Colonel. As for you, Basilio, do not expose yourself to danger. Glory is nothing but smoke.'

" ' And what about life? '

" ' That's true,' exclaimed Ramón. ' You should be the Colonel yourself. Our pay is not smoke, however, at least until we have spent it. Well, everything is over with me now! '

" ' What gloomy ideas,' said I, but I was sad enough too. ' We will both survive to-morrow's battle.'

" ' Well, let us make an appointment to meet after it is over.'

" ' Where? '

" ' In the old hermitage of St. Nicholas, at one o'clock in the morning. If one of us does not come, it will be because he is dead. Do you agree? '

" ' Yes, of course I agree.'

" ' Well, good-bye, then.'

" ' Good-bye.'

" A hearty embrace, and we parted. Ramón disappeared in the surrounding darkness.

III

" As we expected, the Carlists attacked us next day. The battle lasted from three in the afternoon until night fell, and there was great slaughter on both sides. About five o'clock my battalion was engaged in severe fighting with a force of troops from Alava, commanded by Ramón.

My friend wore the rebel uniform and the white cap of the Carlists!

" I ordered my troops to fire on his men, and he gave a similar order to those under his command. We fought hand to hand, but at last my side conquered, and Ramón was obliged to retreat with the remnants of his force. Not, however, before he had killed his former Colonel with his own hand, shooting him down without remorse.

" At six o'clock the tide of battle turned against us. Part of my company was cut off, surrounded, and I and my men were taken prisoners, brought to the little town in the neighbourhood which had been occupied by the Carlists since the beginning of the campaign, and nothing seemed more certain than that we would all be shot at once! for no quarter was given in that war to prisoners by either side.

IV

" I heard one o'clock strike as I sat in my prison cell—the hour of my appointment with Ramón. I was shut up with my companions in the town prison.

" I asked one of my guards about Ramón.

" ' Oh, he is a brave fellow. He killed a colonel with his own hands. But we think he must have been killed, too, at the end of the battle.'

" ' Why do you think so? '

" ' Because he has not come back from the battlefield, and none of his men know what has become of him.'

" Ah, what I went through that night!

" One hope remained to me. Ramón might have gone to the hermitage of St. Nicholas, and thus not returned to the scene of the battle.

" ' How sad he will be,' I thought, ' if I do not go to meet him.
He will think I am dead. And indeed I am not far from my end
now. The Carlists always shoot their prisoners, just as we do.'

" At dawn a chaplain entered the prison.

" All my comrades were asleep.

" ' Are we to die? ' I asked on seeing the priest.

" ' Yes,' he replied in a sad and gentle tone.

" ' Now? '

" ' No, in three hours' time.'

" A minute later he awakened my comrades, and the prison resounded with cries, prayers, sobs, and curses.

V

" When a man is near death, he usually becomes possessed with
one idea, which dominates him above all others, and of which he
cannot get rid. This happened to me, like a nightmare, a feverish
dream or madness. I could not turn my thoughts from Ramón.
Living or dead, in the other world already or in the hermitage
waiting for me, his image never left me, and I did not trouble about
my own fate for fretting and chafing to know what had become of
my friend.

" The Carlists took away my captain's uniform and put the
clothes and cap of one of their own men on me, a worn-out
suit too.

" I was marched to my death with my nineteen comrades in
misfortune. There had been twenty-one of us, but one had been
pardoned, because he was a musician. The Carlists were very
short of musicians for their regimental bands, so they spared the
lives of all musicians whom they captured."

" So that was how you were saved, Don Basilio," all the young
people cried out in joy. " You say you cannot play, and yet you
were saved because you were a musician! "

" No, my children," replied the old man. " I was not a
musician.

" To go on with my story. The firing party arrived, and the
rest of the regiment was drawn up in a hollow square. We were
ranged in a row to await our death. I was the eleventh from the
beginning of the row. That is, I was to be the eleventh to die. I
thought of my wife and my daughter; you and your mother, my
child! Then the shots began. My eyes were bandaged, so that I
could not see who fell.

" I began to count the shots to see when my turn would come. I
wished to be able to know when my last moment on earth was at
hand. But my head was swimming; I grew confused, and I lost
count!

" Those shots will ring for ever in my ears. I can hear them now; I can feel again the torture which the suspense inflicted on my brain. Each time I thought, ' My turn is surely next,' but another shot rang out and I was still alive.

" At last I had no longer any doubt. Something struck or seized me. I felt no pain, but confused murmurs filled my ears. I staggered and fell, and I remembered nothing more. I seemed to fall into a deep sleep, from which I only woke to dream, and my first dream was that I had been shot and killed.

VI

" Still in a dream I found myself on a couch in the prison. I could not see.

" I raised my hand to my eyes, thinking that they were still bandaged, but there was nothing there. Had I died, or was I blind?

" No. The fact was that the prison was perfectly dark.

" I heard a bell tolling. It was a church bell.

" ' It is nine o'clock,' I thought. ' But what is the day? '

" Something bent over me; a shadow still darker than the heavy air of the prison. It took the shape of a man.

" I asked, ' What has become of the other nineteen? '

" They have all been shot.'

" ' And I? Am I still alive, or is this death, too? '

" I groped towards the shadow and murmured the name which came first to my thoughts.

" Ramón? '

" ' What is it? ' asked the voice of the shadow, the voice of my friend.

" ' Ramón! ' I exclaimed, trembling. ' Am I in the other world? '

" ' No,' replied the voice.

" ' Ramón, are you still alive? '

" ' Well, yes, so far.'

" ' And I? '

" ' The same.'

" ' But where am I? Is this the monastery of St. Nicholas, the hermitage where we were to meet? Am I not a prisoner? Or did I dream everything? '

" ' No, Basilio, you have not dreamed anything. Listen.

VII

" ' As you know, yesterday I killed the Colonel in fair fight. I am avenged. I was mad with rage, and I went on killing my own former comrades until night fell and I could see no one else on the battlefield.

" ' When the moon rose, I thought of you. I directed my steps to the hermitage of St. Nicholas, intending to wait for you there. It was just ten o'clock. We had agreed to meet there at one, and the night before I had not closed my eyes. I slept heavily until the sound of a clock awoke me.

" ' It was one o'clock.

" ' I looked round and found I was alone. I thought you must be dead. But still I waited, full of anxiety and distress.

" ' Two, three, four o'clock. What a terrible night of waiting!

" ' You did not come before the dawn. No doubt you would never come; you were dead. I left the hermitage and went down to the town to where the Carlists were. The sun was rising when I got to their barracks. All thought that I had been killed the day before, so that they greeted me with joy, and the General heaped attentions on me. Among other news, I was told that twenty prisoners were about to be shot. A presentiment darkened my mind.

" ' " Is Basilio among them? " I wondered.

" ' I ran at once to the place of execution. The firing party had been drawn up, and I heard some shots. I tried to distinguish the faces of the prisoners, and at last I saw you through a mist of agitation and anxiety which nearly blinded me. There were still two others to be shot before your turn came. What was to be done?

" ' I dashed forward like a madman. Catching you in my arms, I called out frantically:

" ' " Not this one, General. You must not shoot this one! "

" ' The General, who was directing the firing party, and who recognised me from the evening before, asked in surprise:

" ' " And why not? Is he a musician? "

" ' A sudden inspiration came to me, the one hope which existed flashed on me like sunshine on a blind man. The opportunity must not be lost. I was dazzled by the idea, and I cried out at once:

" ' " Musician, General! Why, he is one of the best musicians in the whole royalist army. He is a great musician! "

" ' You had fallen at my feet in a swoon, and you still lay unconscious.

" ' " What instrument does he play? " asked the General.

" ' Another inspiration. I looked at the regimental band, and thought some instruments were not there.

" ' " The . . . the . . ." I ran my eyes over the band. " The cornet à piston, General."

" ' " We do want a cornet à piston, don't we? " asked the General, turning to the bandmaster.

" ' How impatiently I awaited the reply.

" ' " Yes, General, we want one badly," answered the bandmaster.

" ' " Take this man away, and shoot all the others," said the Carlist General, coolly lighting a cigarette.

" ' So then I had you carried back to the prison here.'

VIII

" As Ramón stopped speaking, I rose and embraced him, saying in a choked voice:

" ' You have saved my life.'

" ' I don't know about that,' replied Ramón.

" ' Why, what now? '

" ' Can you play the cornet? '

" ' No.'

" ' Well, then, not only have I not saved your life, but I have lost it and my own as well.'

" I shivered, seeing what he meant.

" ' Do you know anything of music? ' asked he, after a pause.

" ' Very little.   You remember they taught us some at school.'

" ' That was very little indeed; we might say less than nothing. They will certainly shoot you, and they will shoot me, too, as a traitor, for deceiving them.   Just think.   In a fortnight's time they are going to have the regimental band complete, and you are to be a member of it.   It is all settled.'

" ' A fortnight? '

" ' Yes, indeed.   And as you will not be able to play the cornet, for the age of miracles is past, we shall both be shot for certain.'

" Then I sprang up.

" ' Shot! ' I exclaimed.   ' Just wait.   I don't want to be shot, and I will not let you be shot either, as you have saved my life.   In a fortnight I will understand music, and I will know how to play the cornet.'

" Ramón laughed at my promise.

IX

" There is not much more to tell, my children.

" We found out a music master in a small town a little way off, and, under pretext that, as I had lost my instrument in the battle, I wished to practise on his cornet, I was allowed to go to him under the charge of my friend Ramón, who gave his word that I would not try to escape.   Oh, that fortnight.   Day and night I studied, and every hour of day was spent with that musician, learning his infernal cornet à piston.   In a fortnight I had mastered it well enough to become a member of the band and practise with the others.

" I know you will ask me why I did not run away.   I could not. I was a prisoner of war, and Ramón was responsible for me.   He might have escaped without me, but he would not go alone, and it was too risky for both of us.

" I could not speak, eat or even think. I played, played, until I really believe I went mad. I must have done so, for my one thought in this world was my music.

" I had made up my mind to learn and I did learn. Where there's a will there's a way.

" If I had been dumb and had wished to speak, I would have spoken; if I had been paralysed and had wished to walk, I would have walked; if I had been blind and had wished to see, I would have seen! So great was my will to save my friend's life and my own.

" I willed to do it and I did it. To will a thing is to have the strength to do it. Children, do not forget this; there is always a way if there is a will. My whole mind went into what I willed, and I succeeded.

" But indeed I went mad.

" I thought of nothing but music. My new cornet, which they gave me when I became a member of the band, was like a child, like a live creature to me. For three years it scarcely left my hands. My whole world was made up of the notes of the scale and their combinations.

" Do-re-mi-fa-sol-la-si. That was my whole existence. I did nothing but play the cornet.

" Ramón and I escaped at last, and made our way to France. There I made our living by means of my cornet. The cornet was myself, my whole soul. When I played I seemed to be singing, to be expressing myself, my ideas, through the instrument. I grew so familiar with it that I could make it do anything—laugh, weep, sigh, sing, growl. I could make it imitate any bird, any animal. People came to hear us. We gave public performances, and even the greatest musicians came to hear me and my wonderful cornet.

" Two years passed in this way. And then I lost my friend. Ramón died, Ramón who had cared for me in our wanderings so that I might be free to devote myself to my music.

" As I looked at his corpse my madness fell away from me. I became like other men once more. But when I next took up my cornet I had forgotten how to play a single note!

" Now, will you ask me to play the cornet so that you may dance to it? "

PEDRO A. DE ALARCÓN

THE ACCOUNT-BOOK

GAFFER BUSCABEATAS was already beginning to stoop at the time when the events occurred which I am going to relate; for he was now sixty years, and had spent forty cultivating a garden bordering on the shore of La Costilla.

In the year in question he had cultivated in this garden some wonderful pumpkins, as large as the ornamental globes on the breast-work of some massive bridge, and these at the time of our story were beginning to turn yellow, inside and out, which is the same as saying that it was the middle of June. Old Buscabeatas knew by heart the particular form and the stage of maturity at which it had arrived of every one of these pumpkins, to each of which he had given a name, and especially of the forty largest and finest specimens, which were already crying out, " Cook me! " and he spent the days contemplating them affectionately, and saying in melancholy accents:

" Soon we shall have to part! "

At last, one evening, he made up his mind to the sacrifice, and marking out the best fruits of those beloved vines which had cost him so many anxieties, he pronounced the dreadful sentence:

" To-morrow," he said, " I shall cut from their stalks these forty pumpkins and take them to the market at Cadiz. Happy the man who shall eat of them! "

And he returned to his home with slow step and spent the night in such anguish as a father may be supposed to feel on the eve of his daughter's wedding-day.

" What a pity to have to part from my dear pumpkins! " he would sigh from time to time in his restless vigil. But presently he would reason with himself and end his reflections by saying, " And what else can I do but sell them? That is what I have raised them for. The least they will bring me is fifteen dollars! "

Judge, then, what was his consternation, what his rage and despair, on going into the garden on the following morning, to find that during the night he had been robbed of his forty pumpkins! Not to weary the reader, I will only say that his emotion, like that of Shakespeare's Jew, so admirably represented, it is said,

104

by the actor Kemble, reached the sublimity of tragedy as he frantically cried:

"Oh, if I could but find the thief! If I could but find the thief!"

Poor old Buscabeatas presently began to reflect upon the matter with calmness, and comprehended that his beloved treasures could not be in Rota, where it would be impossible to expose them for sale without risk of their being recognised, and where, besides, vegetables bring a very low price.

"I know as well as if I saw them that they are in Cadiz!" he ended. "The scoundrel! the villain! the thief must have stolen them between nine and ten o'clock last night, and got off with them at midnight on the freight-boat. I shall go to Cadiz this morning on the hour-boat, and it will surprise me greatly if I do not catch the thief there, and recover the children of my toil."

After he had thus spoken he remained for some twenty minutes longer on the scene of the catastrophe, to caress the mutilated vines, to calculate the number of pumpkins that were missing, or to formulate a declaration of the loss sustained, for a possible suit; then, at about eight o'clock, he bent his steps in the direction of the wharf.

The hour-boat was just going to sail. This was a modest coaster which leaves Cadiz every morning at nine o'clock precisely, carrying passengers, as the freight-boat leaves Cadiz every night at twelve, laden with fruits and vegetables.

The former is called the hour-boat because in that space of time, and occasionally even in forty minutes, if the wind is favourable, it makes the three leagues which separate the ancient village of the Duke of Arcos from the ancient city of Hercules.

It was, then, half-past ten in the morning, on the before-mentioned day, when old Buscabeatas passed before a vegetable-stand in the market of Cadiz, and said to the bored policeman who was accompanying him:

"Those are my squashes! arrest that man!" and he pointed to the vendor.

"Arrest me!" cried the vendor, astonished and enraged. "These squashes are mine; I bought them!"

"You will have to prove that before the judge!" answered old Buscabeatas.

"I say No!"

"I say Yes!"

"Thief!"

"Vagabond!"

"Speak more civilly, you ill-mannered fellows! Decent men ought not to treat one another in that way!" said the policeman tranquilly, giving a blow with his closed fist to each of the disputants.

By this time a crowd had gathered, and there soon arrived also on the scene the inspector of public markets.

The policeman resigned his jurisdiction in the case to his Honour, and when this worthy official had learned all the circumstances relating to the affair, he said to the vendor majestically:

" From whom did you purchase those squashes? "

" From Gossip Fulano, a native of Rota," answered the person thus interrogated.

" It could be no one else! " cried old Buscabeatas. " He is just the one to do it! When his own garden, which is a very poor one, produces little, he takes to robbing the gardens of his neighbours! "

" But, admitting the supposition that forty pumpkins were stolen from you last night," said the inspector, turning to the old gardener and proceeding with his examination, " how do you know that these are precisely your pumpkins? "

" How? " replied old Buscabeatas. " Because I know them as well as you know your daughters, if you have any! Don't you see that they have grown up under my care? Look here: this one is called Roly-poly, this one Fat-cheeks, this one Big-belly, this one Ruddy-face, this Manuela, because it reminded me of my youngest daughter."

And the poor old man began to cry bitterly.

" That may be all very well," replied the inspector; " but it is not enough for the law that you should recognise your pumpkins. It is necessary also that the authorities be convinced of the pre-existence of the article in dispute, and that you identify it with incontrovertible proofs; gentlemen, there is no occasion for you to smile—I know the law! "

" You shall see, then, that I will very soon prove to the satisfaction of everybody present, without stirring from this spot, that these pumpkins have grown in my garden! " said old Buscabeatas, to the no little surprise of the spectators of this scene. And laying down on the ground a bundle which he had been carrying in his hand, he bent his knees until he sat upon his heels, and quietly began to untie the knotted corners of the handkerchief.

The curiosity of the inspector, the vendor, and the chorus was now at its height.

" What is he going to take out of that handkerchief? " they said to themselves.

At this moment a new spectator joined the crowd, curious to see what was going on, whom the vendor had no sooner perceived than he exclaimed:

" I am very glad that you have come, Gossip Fulano! This

man declares that the squashes which you sold me last night, and which are now here present, listening to what we are saying about them, were stolen. Answer, you! "

The newcomer turned as yellow as wax, and made a movement as if to escape, but the bystanders detained him by force, and the inspector himself ordered him to remain. As for Gaffer Busca- beatas, he had already confronted the supposed thief, saying to him:

" Now you are going to see something good."

Gossip Fulano, recovering his self-possession, answered:

" It is you who ought to see what you are talking about, for if you do not prove, as prove you cannot, your accusation, I shall have you put in prison for libel. These pumpkins were mine. I cultivated them, like all the others that I brought this year to Cadiz, in my garden, the Egido, and no one can prove to the contrary! "

" Now you shall see! " repeated old Buscabeatas, loosening the knots of the handkerchief and spreading out its contents on the ground.

And there were scattered over the floor a number of fragments of pumpkin stalks, still fresh and dripping sap, while the old gardener, seated on his heels and unable to control his laughter, addressed the following discourse to the inspector and the wonder- ing bystanders.

" Gentlemen, have any of you ever paid taxes? If you have, you must have seen the big green box of the collector, from which he tears off your receipt, leaving the stub or end, so as to be able to prove afterward whether the receipt is genuine or not."

" The book you mean is called the account-book," said the inspector gravely.

" Well, that is what I have here—the account-book of my garden; that is to say, the stalks to which these pumpkins were attached before they were stolen from me. And in proof of what I say, look here! This stalk belongs to this pumpkin; no one can doubt it. This other—you can see for yourselves—belonged to this other. This is thicker—it must belong to this one. This to that one. This to that other."

And as he spoke he went fitting a stub or peduncle to the hole which had been made in each pumpkin as it was pulled from the stalk, and the spectators saw with surprise that the irregular and capricious shaped ends of the peduncles corresponded exactly with the whitish circles and the slight hollows presented by what we might call the cicatrices of the pumpkins.

Every one present, including the policeman, and even the in- spector himself, then got down on their heels and began to help old Buscabeatas in his singular comprobation, crying out with childlike delight:

" He is right! he is right! There is not a doubt of it! Look! This belongs to this one. This to that one. That one there belongs to this. This belongs to that! " And the bursts of laughter of the grown people were mingled with the whistling of the boys, the abuse of the women, the tears of joy and triumph of the old gardener, and the pushes that the policeman gave to the convicted thief, as if they were impatient to carry him off to prison.

Needless to say that the policeman had that pleasure; that Gossip Fulano was immediately compelled to restore to the vendor the fifteen dollars he had received from him, that the vendor handed these over at once to Gaffer Buscabeatas, and that the latter departed for Rota, highly delighted, although he kept repeating all the way home:

" How handsome they looked in the market! I should have brought Manuela back with me to eat at supper to-night, and saved the seeds."

GUSTAVO ADOLFO BÉCQUER

1836–1870

MAESE PÉREZ, THE ORGANIST

I

" Do you see that man with the scarlet cloak, and the white plume in his hat, and the gold-embroidered vest? I mean the one just getting out of his litter and going to greet that lady—the one coming along after those four pages who are carrying torches? Well, that is the Marquis of Mascoso, lover of the widow, the Countess of Villapineda. They say that before he began paying court to her he had sought the hand of a very wealthy man's daughter, but the girl's father, who, they say, is a trifle close-fisted —but hush! Speaking of the devil—do you see that man closely wrapped in his cloak coming on foot under the arch of San Felipe? Well, he is the father in question. Everybody in Seville knows him on account of his immense fortune.

" Look—look at that group of stately men! They are the twenty-four knights. Aha! there's that Heming, too. They say, that the gentlemen of the green cross have not challenged him yet, thanks to his influence with the great ones at Madrid. All he comes to church for is to hear the music.

" Alas! neighbour, that looks bad. I fear there's going to be a scuffle. I shall take refuge in the church, for, according to my guess, there will be more blows than *Paternosters*. Look, look! the Duke of Alcalá's people are coming round the corner of Saint Peter's Square, and I think I see the Duke of Medina Sidonia's men in Dueñas Alley. Didn't I tell you? There—there! The blows are beginning. Neighbour, neighbour, this way before they close the doors!

" But what's that? They've left off. What's that light? Torches! a litter! It's the bishop himself! God preserve him in his office as many centuries as I desire to live myself! If it were not for him, half Seville would have been burned up by this time with these quarrels of the dukes. Look at them, look at them, the hypocrites, how they both press forward to kiss the bishop's ring!

109

" But come, neighbour—come into the church before it is packed full. Some nights like this it is so crowded that you could not get in if you were no larger than a grain of wheat. The nuns have a prize in their organist. Other sisterhoods have made Maese Pérez magnificent offers; nothing strange about that, though, for the very archbishop has offered him mountains of gold if he would go to the cathedral. But he would not listen to them. He would sooner die than give up his beloved organ. You don't know Maese Pérez? Oh, I forgot you had just come to the neighbourhood. Well, he is a holy man; poor, to be sure, but as charitable as any man that ever lived. With no relative but a daughter, and no friend but his organ, he spends all his time in caring for the one and repairing the other. The organ is an old affair, you must know; but that makes no difference to him. He handles it so that its tone is a wonder. How he does know it! and all by touch, too, for did I tell you that the poor man was born blind?

" Humble, too, as the very stones. He always says that he is only a poor convent organist, when the fact is he could give lessons in *sol-fa* to the very chapel master of the primate. You see, he began before he had teeth. His father had the same position before him, and as the boy showed such talent, it was very natural that he should succeed his father when the latter died. And what a touch he has, God bless him! He always plays well, always; but on a night like this he is wonderful. He has the greatest devotion to this Christmas Eve Mass, and when the host is elevated, precisely at twelve o'clock, which is the time that Our Lord came into the world, his organ sounds like the voices of angels.

" But why need I try to tell you about what you are going to hear to-night? It is enough for you to see that all the elegance of Seville, the very archbishop included, comes to a humble convent to listen to him. And it is not only the learned people who can understand his skill that come; the common people, too, swarm to the church, and are still as the dead when Maese Pérez puts his hand to the organ. And when the host is elevated—when the host is elevated, then you can't hear a fly. Great tears fall from every eye, and when the music is over a long-drawn sigh is heard, showing how the people have been holding their breath all through.

" But come, come, the bells have stopped ringing, and the Mass is going to begin. Hurry in. This is Christmas Eve for every-body, but for no one is it a greater occasion than for us."

So saying, the good woman who had been acting as *cicerone* for her neighbour pressed through the portico of the Convent of Santa Inés, and elbowing this one and pushing the other, succeeded in getting inside the church, forcing her way through the multitude that was crowding about the door.

II

The church was profusely lighted. The flood of light which fell from the altars glanced from the rich jewels of the great ladies, who, kneeling upon velvet cushions placed before them by pages, and taking their prayer-books from the hands of female attendants, formed a brilliant circle around the chancel lattice. Standing next that lattice, wrapped in their richly coloured and embroidered cloaks, letting their green and red orders be seen with studied carelessness, holding in one hand their hats, the plumes sweeping the floor, and letting the other rest upon the polished hilts of rapiers or the jewelled handles of daggers, the twenty-four knights, and a large part of the highest nobility of Seville, seemed to be forming a wall for the purpose of keeping their wives and daughters from contact with the populace. The latter, swaying back and forth at the rear of the nave, with a noise like that of a rising surf, broke out into joyous acclamations as the archbishop was seen to come in. That dignitary seated himself near the high altar under a scarlet canopy, surrounded by his attendants, and three times blessed the people.

It was time for the Mass to begin.

Nevertheless, several minutes passed before the celebrant appeared. The multitude commenced to murmur impatiently; the knights exchanged words with each other in a low tone; and the archbishop sent one of his attendants to the sacristan to inquire why the service did not begin.

"Maese Pérez has fallen sick, very sick, and it will be impossible for him to come to the midnight Mass."

This was the word brought back by the attendant.

The news ran instantly through the crowd. The disturbance caused by it was so great that the chief judge rose to his feet, and the officers came into the church, to enforce silence.

Just then a man of unpleasant face, thin, bony, and cross-eyed, too, pushed up to the place where the archbishop was sitting.

"Maese Pérez is sick," he said; "the service cannot begin. If you see fit, I will play the organ in his absence. Maese Pérez is not the best organist in the world, nor need this instrument be left unused after his death for lack of any one able to play it."

The archbishop nodded his head in assent, although some of the faithful, who had already recognised in that strange person an envious rival of the organist of Santa Inés, were breaking out in cries of displeasure. Suddenly a surprising noise was heard in the portico.

"Maese Pérez is here! Maese Pérez is here!"

At this shout, coming from those jammed in by the door, every one looked around.

Maese Pérez, pale and feeble, was, in fact, entering the church, brought in a chair which all were quarrelling for the honour of carrying upon their shoulders.

The commands of the physicians, the tears of his daughter—nothing had been able to keep him in bed.

" No," he had said; " this is the last one, I know it. I know it, and I do not want to die without visiting my organ again, this night above all, this Christmas Eve. Come, I desire it, I order it; come, to the church! "

His desire had been gratified. The people carried him in their arms to the organ-loft. The Mass began.

Twelve struck on the cathedral clock.

The introit came, then the Gospel, then the offertory, and the moment arrived when the priest, after consecrating the sacred wafer, took it in his hands and began to elevate it. A cloud of incense filled the church in bluish undulations. The little bells rang out in vibrating peals, and Maese Pérez placed his aged fingers upon the organ keys.

The multitudinous voices of the metal tubes gave forth a prolonged and majestic chord, which died away little by little, as if a gentle breeze had borne away its last echoes.

To this opening burst, which seemed like a voice lifted up to heaven from earth, responded a sweet and distant note, which went on swelling and swelling in volume until it became a torrent of overpowering harmony. It was the voice of the angels, traversing space, and reaching the world.

Then distant hymns began to be heard, intoned by the hierarchies of seraphim; a thousand hymns at once, mingling to form a single one, though this one was only an accompaniment to a strange melody which seemed to float above that ocean of mysterious echoes, as a strip of fog above the waves of the sea.

One song after another died away. The movement grew simpler. Now only two voices were heard, whose echoes blended. Then but one remained, and alone sustained a note as brilliant as a thread of light. The priest bowed his face, and above his grey head appeared the host. At that moment the note which Maese Pérez was holding began to swell and swell, and an explosion of unspeakable joy filled the church.

From each of the notes forming that magnificent chord a theme was developed; and some near, others far away, these brilliant, those muffled, one would have said that the waters and the birds, the breezes and the forests, men and angels, earth and heaven, were singing, each in its own language, a hymn in praise of the Saviour's birth.

The people listened, amazed and breathless. The officiating priest felt his hands trembling; for it seemed as if he had seen the heavens opened and the host transfigured.

The organ kept on, but its voice sank away gradually, like a tone going from echo to echo, and dying as it goes. Suddenly a cry was heard in the organ-loft—a piercing, shrill cry, the cry of a woman.

The organ gave a strange, discordant sound, like a sob, and then was silent.

The multitude flocked to the stairs leading up to the organ-loft, towards which the anxious gaze of the faithful was turned.

"What has happened? What is the matter?" one asked the other, and no one knew what to reply. The confusion increased. The excitement threatened to disturb the good order and decorum fitting within a church.

"What was that?" asked the great ladies of the chief judge. He had been one of the first to ascend to the organ-loft. Now, pale and displaying signs of deep grief, he was going to the archbishop, who was anxious, like everybody else, to know the cause of the disturbance.

"What's the matter?"

"Maese Pérez has just expired."

In fact, when the first of the faithful rushed up the stairway, and reached the organ-loft, they saw the poor organist fallen face down upon the keys of his old instrument, which was still vibrating, while his daughter, kneeling at his feet, was vainly calling to him with tears and sobs.

III

"Good-evening, my dear Donna Baltasara. Are you also going to-night to the Christmas Eve Mass? For my part, I was intending to go to the parish church to hear it, but what has happened— where is Vicente going, do you ask? Why, where the crowd goes. And I must say, to tell the truth, that ever since Maese Pérez died, it seems as if a marble slab was on my heart whenever I go to Santa Inés. Poor dear man! He was a saint! I know one thing—I keep a piece of his cloak as a relic, and he deserves it. I solemnly believe that if the archbishop would stir in the matter our grandchildren would see his image among the saints on the altars. But, of course, he won't do that. The dead and absent have no friends, as they say. It's all the latest thing, nowadays; you understand me. What? You do not know what has happened? Well, it's true you are not exactly in our situation. From our house to the church, and from the church to our house—a word here and another one there—on the wing—without any curiosity whatever—I easily find out all the news.

"Well, then, it's a settled thing that the organist of San Roman —that squint-eye, who is always slandering other organists—that

great blunderer, who seems more like a butcher than a master of
sol-fa—is going to play this Christmas Eve in Maese Pérez's old
place. Of course, you know, for everybody knows it, and it is a
public matter in all Seville, that no one dared to try it. His
daughter would not, though she is a professor of music herself.
After her father's death she went into the convent as a novice. Her
unwillingness to play was the most natural thing in the world;
accustomed as she was to those marvellous performances, any other
playing must have appeared bad to her, not to speak of her desire
to avoid comparisons. But when the sisterhood had already decided
that in honour of the dead organist, and as a token of respect to his
memory, the organ should not be played to-night, here comes this
fellow along and says that he is ready to play it.

  " Ignorance is the boldest of all things. It is true, the fault is
not his so much as theirs who have consented to this profanation,
but that is the way of the world. But, I say, there's no small bit
of people coming. Any one would say that nothing had changed
since last year. The same distinguished persons, the same elegant
costumes, the crowding at the door, the same excitement in the
portico, the same throng in the church. Alas! if the dead man
were to rise, he would feel like dying again to hear his organ played
by inferior hands. The fact is, if what the people of the neighbourhood tell me is true, they are getting a fine reception ready for
the intruder. When the time comes for him to touch the keys there
is going to break out a racket made by timbrels, drums, and horse-
fiddles, so that you can't hear anything else. But hush! there's
the hero of the occasion going into the church. Goodness! what
gaudy clothes, what a neckcloth, what a high and mighty air!
Come, hurry up, the archbishop came only a moment ago, and
the Mass is going to begin. Come on; I guess this night will give
us something to talk about for many a day! "

  Saying this, the worthy woman, whom the reader recognises by
her abrupt talkativeness, went into the Church of Santa Inés,
opening for herself a path, in her usual way, by shoving and
elbowing through the crowd.

  The service had already begun. The church was as brilliant as
the year before.

  The new organist, after passing between the rows of the faithful
in the nave, and going to kiss the archbishop's ring, had gone up
to the organ-loft, where he was trying one stop of the organ after
another, with an affected and ridiculous gravity.

  A low, confused noise was heard coming from the common people
clustered at the rear of the church, a sure augury of the coming
storm, which would not be long in breaking.

  " He is a mere clown," said some, " who does not know how
to do anything, not even look straight."

" He is an ignoramus," said others, " who, after having made
a perfect rattle out of the organ in his own church, comes here to
profane Maese Pérez's."

And while one was taking off his cloak so as to be ready to beat
his drum to good advantage, and another was testing his timbrel,
and all were more and more buzzing out in talk, only here and
there could one be found to defend even feebly that curious person,
whose proud and pedantic bearing so strongly contrasted with the
modest appearance and kind affability of Maese Pérez.

At last the looked-for moment arrived, when the priest, after
bowing low and murmuring the sacred words, took the host in his
hands. The bells gave forth a peal, like a rain of crystal notes; the
transparent waves of incense rose, and the organ sounded.

But its first chord was drowned by a horrible clamour which
filled the whole church. Bagpipes, horns, timbrels, drums, every
instrument known to the populace, lifted up their discordant voices
all at once.

The confusion and clangour lasted but a few seconds. As the
noises began, so they ended, all together.

The second chord, full, bold, magnificent, sustained itself, pouring from the organ's metal tubes like a cascade of inexhaustible
and sonorous harmony.

Celestial songs like those that caress the ear in moments of
ecstasy; songs which the soul perceives, but which the lip cannot
repeat; single notes of a distant melody, which sound at intervals,
borne on the breeze; the rustle of leaves kissing each other on
the trees with a murmur like rain; trills of larks which rise with
quivering songs from among the flowers like a flight of arrows to
the sky; nameless sounds, overwhelming as the roar of a tempest;
fluttering hymns, which seemed to be mounting to the throne of
the Lord like a mixture of light and sound—all were expressed by
the organ's hundred voices, with more vigour, more subtle poetry,
more weird colouring, than had ever been known before.

When the organist came down from the loft the crowd which
pressed up to the stairway was so great, and their eagerness to see
and greet him so intense, that the chief judge, fearing, and not
without reason, that he would be suffocated among them all,
ordered some of the officers to open a path for the organist with
their staves of office, so that he could reach the high altar, where
the prelate was waiting for him.

" You perceive," said the archbishop, " that I have come all
the way from my palace to hear you. Now, are you going to be
as cruel as Maese Pérez? He would never save me the journey,
by going to play the Christmas Eve Mass in the cathedral."

" Next year," replied the organist, " I promise to give you the pleasure; since, for all the gold in the world, I would never play this organ again."

" But why not? " interrupted the prelate.

" Because," returned the organist, endeavouring to repress the agitation which revealed itself in the pallor of his face—" because it is so old and poor; one cannot express oneself on it satisfactorily."

The archbishop withdrew, followed by his attendants. One after another the litters of the great folk disappeared in the windings of the neighbouring streets. The group in the portico scattered. The sexton was locking up the doors, when two women were perceived, who had stopped to cross themselves and mutter a prayer, and who were now going on their way into Dueñas Alley.

" What would you have, my dear Donna Baltasara? " one was saying. " That's the way I am. Every crazy person with his whim. The barefooted Capuchins might assure me that it was so, and I would not believe it. That man never played what we have heard. Why, I have heard him a thousand times in San Bartolomé, his parish church; the priest had to send him away, he was so poor a player. You felt like plugging your ears with cotton. Why, all you need is to look at his face, and that is the mirror of the soul, they say. I remember, as if I was seeing him now, poor man—I remember Maese Pérez's face, nights like this, when he came down from the organ-loft, after having entranced the audience with his splendours. What a gracious smile! What a happy glow on his face! Old as he was, he seemed like an angel. But this creature came plunging down as if a dog were barking at him on the landing, and all the colour of a dead man, while his— come, dear Donna Baltasara, believe me, and believe what I say: there is some great mystery about this."

Thus conversing, the two women turned the corner of the alley and disappeared. There is no need of saying who one of them was.

IV

Another year had gone by. The Abbess of the Convent of Santa Inés and Maese Pérez's daughter were talking in a low voice, half hidden in the shadows of the church choir. The penetrating voice of the bell was summoning the faithful. A very few people were passing through the portico, silent and deserted, this year, and after taking holy water at the door, were choosing seats in a corner of the nave, where a handful of residents of the neighbourhood were quietly waiting for the Christmas Eve Mass to begin.

" There, you see," the Mother Superior was saying, " your fear is entirely childish; there is no one in the church. All Seville is trooping to the cathedral to-night. Play the organ, and do it without any distrust whatever. We are only a sisterhood here. But why don't you speak? What has happened? What is the matter with you?"

"I am afraid," replied the girl, in a tone of the deepest agitation.

"Afraid! Of what?"

"I do not know—something supernatural. Listen to what happened last night. I had heard you say that you were anxious for me to play the organ for the Mass. I was proud of the honour, and I thought I would arrange the stops and get the organ in good tune so as to give you a surprise to-day. Alone I went into the choir and opened the door leading to the organ-loft. The cathedral clock was striking just then, I do not know what hour; but the strokes of the bell were very mournful, and they were very numerous—going on sounding for a century, as it seemed to me, while I stood as if nailed to the threshold.

"The church was empty and dark. Far away there gleamed a feeble light, like a faint star in the sky; it was the lamp burning on the high altar. By its flickering light, which only helped to make the deep horror of the shadows the more intense, I saw—I saw—mother, do not disbelieve it—a man. In perfect silence, and with his back turned towards me, he was running over the organ-keys with one hand while managing the stops with the other. And the organ sounded, but in an indescribable manner. It seemed as if each note were a sob smothered in the metal tube, which vibrated under the pressure of the air compressed within it, and gave forth a low, almost imperceptible tone, yet exact and true.

"The cathedral clock kept on striking, and that man kept on running over the keys. I could hear his very breathing.

"Fright had frozen the blood in my veins. My body was as cold as ice, except my head, and that was burning. I tried to cry out, but I could not. That man turned his face and looked at me—no, he did not look at me, for he was blind. It was my father!"

"Nonsense, sister! Banish these fancies with which the adversary endeavours to overturn weak imaginations. Address a *Paternoster* and an *Ave Maria* to the archangel, Saint Michael, the captain of the celestial hosts, that he may aid you in opposing evil spirits. Wear on your neck a scapulary which has been pressed to the relics of Saint Pacomio, the counsellor against temptations, and go, go quickly, and sit at the organ. The Mass is going to begin, and the faithful are growing impatient. Your father is in heaven, and thence, instead of giving you a fright, will descend to inspire his daughter in the solemn service."

The prioress went to occupy her seat in the choir in the midst of the sisterhood. Maese Pérez's daughter opened the door of the organ-loft with trembling hand, sat down at the organ, and the Mass began.

The Mass began, and went on without anything unusual happening until the time of consecration came. Then the organ sounded. At the same time came a scream from Maese Pérez's daughter.

The Mother Superior, the nuns, and some of the faithful rushed up to the organ-loft.

"Look at him!—look at him!" cried the girl, fixing her eyes, starting from their sockets, upon the seat, from which she had risen in terror. She was clinging with convulsed hands to the railing of the organ-loft.

Everybody looked intently at the spot to which she directed her gaze. No one was at the organ, yet it went on sounding—sounding like the songs of the archangels in their bursts of mystic ecstasy.

"Didn't I tell you a thousand times, if I did once, dear Donna Baltasara—didn't I tell you? There is some great mystery about this. What! didn't you go last night to the Christmas Eve Mass? Well, you must know, anyhow, what happened. Nothing else is talked about in the whole city. The archbishop is furious, and no wonder. Not to have gone to Santa Inés, not to have been present at the miracle—and all to hear a wretched clatter! That's all the inspired organist of San Bartolomé made in the cathedral, so persons who heard him tell me. Yes, I said so all the time. The squint-eye never could have played that. It was all a lie. There is some great mystery here. What do I think it was? Why, it was the soul of Maese Pérez."

EUSEBIO BLASCO
1844–1903

MODERN LIFE

I

WELL, sir, this is about a father who had four sons. The eldest was twenty-four, the second twenty-three, the third twenty-two, and the fourth twenty-one. And the father was a widower, a banker, and very, very rich.

As the four sons had already taken their B.A. (which is of no practical use in modern life), he called them together one day and said to them:

" Now, my sons, you must choose your careers. What do you want to be? "

The eldest, who was called Manuel, replied:

" Father, I want to be a lawyer."

" Right," said the father, " a lawyer you shall be."

The second, who was called Antonio, replied:

" I want to be a doctor."

" You shall be a doctor, I have no objection."

The third, who was called José, replied:

" I, father, want to be a merchant like yourself, and a banker, and make money quickly."

" I shall help you to be what you want."

The youngest brother, after a long pause, said meekly:

" Papa, I want to be a robber."

Then there was a scene! The father jumped in his chair, and nearly struck the ceiling with his head. His brothers called him a vagabond, an idler, a loafer, a cheat, a bad son, a bad brother, and a future bad citizen. Even the servants and neighbours were scandalised on hearing of his perverse instincts. However, the boy kept on repeating:

" I want to be a robber, and a robber I shall be, and if you don't let me, I'll leave home! "

And from home his father threw him, and cursed him, and indeed it was a real family drama.

And that night, Dimas, for such was the name of this rich man's son, packed his bag and said to the oldest servant in the house,

119

who knew nothing of the matter and thought the boy was going to see one of the many relatives his master had in Castile or in Andalusia :

" Ramon, I don't want to trouble father and am in a difficulty : will you lend me one thousand pesetas and I will pay you back next week? "

Ramon, who had saved up some money, counted out two hundred dollars and handed them to him.

" Good," said Dimas, as he left without intending to return, " a debt is a debt; so now I have something to start with."

II

And twenty-five years went by.

Twenty-five years! It is a long time; and nothing was heard of that wicked young man. . . .

And the father was now over seventy, and was getting very old and very feeble, for during that time he had lost his fortune in unlucky speculations. . . . The bank of the Upper Lands failed, and with it went his money and his credit; two or three friends disappeared, owing him thousands of dollars. . . . And he who once had carriages and houses of his own, and shooting-boxes and country villas, was now living, after having paid his debts little by little like a just man, in a small room in the Costanilla de los Desamparados at twelve dollars a month. Poor man!

His sons had no luck either.

Manuel, the lawyer, only received two briefs in the twenty-five years; he lost both cases, although they said his clients were in the right; but the other side had *influence*; the lawyer for the bad people knew ministers, deputies, senators; he won both cases " like winking." And Manuel, in despair, had to be satisfied with employment in a private firm, at two thousand pesetas a year, less what was needed to keep his wife and five children. The only thing he received for his unfortunate campaigns at the bar was the Cross of Isabel the Catholic, given him by a deputy he knew; but he never wore it, as it is not the custom.

Antonio, the doctor, did not do any better. Soon after he started practising, two or three of his patients died, because they had to die, because it was so ordained, because there is sickness that nobody can cure. What could have given greater pleasure to all the doctors who knew and envied him? They began to say that he was a *murderer*, that he knew nothing of medicine, that his father was a swindler, a crafty merchant, and that people who were ill ought not to send for the son of such a father.

Thanks to a friend of his childhood, a doctor like himself, and very ignorant, but who had money and kept a luxurious consulting-

room full of stupendous appliances, and advertised in the newspapers a radical cure, at twenty dollars a visit, of an endless
number of things; thanks to this friend, I repeat, he obtained a
position as doctor at a spa, but one that was quite unknown and
not sufficiently advertised.

The first season he had no more than fourteen patients. Two of
them were gamblers from Madrid suffering from stomach trouble,
but instead of following the cure at the Hydro they passed the
night drinking and playing the guitar.

One of them, by mixing the cure with hard drinking, contracted
a kind of deadly cholera and died in three days; his brother, who
did not want to pay for the baths, began to say that the waters
were a fraud and that the doctor did not know what he was doing,
and published statements in the papers and raised the very devil;
our Don Antonio was dismissed, and he returned to Madrid dis-
honoured, out of employment and without a peseta.

He could not get a patient, no matter how hard he tried. He
established himself in two or three towns, one after the other, in
Navarra, Aragon, and Rioja. The country people did not pay
him, and when any one died they started throwing stones at the
doctor. He returned to Madrid disconsolate, and lived on the little
he received from an apothecary, of the kind who pose as doctors
and sell drugs that cure everything.

José, the one that wanted to be a merchant like his father, did
nothing but lose money, time, and health for twenty-five years.
He opened a shop and sold very pretty things—ties, mufflers,
scents, studs, bracelets, pocket-books, hand-bags, sticks, umbrellas,
shirts, watches, statuettes, knick-knacks, objects of art, novelties.
. . . However, owing to commercial treaties, customs duties, rich
clients who pay when they like, or do not pay at all, wars, bad
times, extended payments, drafts that must be paid at once,
protests, stocks, the devil's interference . . . crash! one day he
went bankrupt. Everybody exclaimed:

" Of course! Like father, like son! What else could you
expect! " The tradespeople rejoiced, the debtors were left in
peace, and our Don José with his wife and children were in the
street, and he had to end by being the manager of a weekly paper
at a salary of six reales a day, not always paid.

The three brothers used to go to sit with their poor father who
was ill, with only one servant and no doctor or medicines, and
attended by his son Antonio, who prescribed things that were very
dear. And in that modest room on the third floor of the Costanilla
they often said:

" What could have happened to Dimas? "

" He must be in prison," said the father.

" He must be dead," said Manuel.

" Or he has been killed.''

" Heaven only knows! "

" Fancy not writing one letter in twenty-five years! "

" What a bad son! ''

" What a wretch! ''

" What a bad brother! ''

" Pray for him, my sons,'' said the father.   " May God have compassion on the unhappy fellow! ''

III

And one afternoon (it was Sunday and all the family were gathered together) the servant entered with a card, and said:

" Sir, a groom has brought this, and a carriage is waiting at the door! "

Manuel seized the card and read:

" The Marquis of Sahagun.''

Tremendous excitement. A marquis! They all began to set the chairs in their places, to arrange the bed of the invalid, to put their ties straight, to hide the cards the three brothers had been playing with near the bedside of their father.

A marquis on a third floor! Whoever can he be?   " Marquis of Sahagun " . . . said the old man.   " Sahagun is my native town, in the province of Leon, and there is no such title there.''

" Here is the gentleman,'' said the servant.

And there walked into the room a man of about forty-five or forty-six, very well dressed, with the red ribbon of some order in his buttonhole, and perfumed with a most expensive scent.

With one voice they all exclaimed:

" Dimas! ''

It was he; in spite of his fair beard and his hair flecked with grey, they all recognised him easily. . . .   And Dimas approached the bed, knelt down and said:

" Father, the Prodigal Son returned poor and in rags to his paternal house. That was in other days. I return a millionaire and powerful. Will you forgive me? "

There is an atmosphere about wealth and a wealthy man that always seduces and hypnotises fools. All the family saw in an instant that the return of Dimas boded good for them all. Twenty-five years of terrible maledictions and accusations were forgotten in an instant.

" My son! " exclaimed the father.

" Welcome to you! ''

Manuel, Antonio, and José hugged and kissed him. Dimas in that room was something like a god.

What rejoicings, what questions, what a happy moment, what merriment!

And after the natural display of affection, his father said to him:

" Tell us, my son, tell us how you have attained such a high position."

Dimas moved towards the door; he locked it, and when they were alone, *en famille,* said before starting his narrative:

" Robbery, father! "

IV

The old man sat up in bed, terrified.

" No, don't be alarmed, *I have done nothing bad,* as they say. I return loaded with honours and millions; I command respect; I have led what they call a modern life.

" You will see:

" With the thousand pesetas I got out of Ramon . . . by the way, what has happened to Ramon? "

" He is very old now, and as an old soldier, we got him into the Invalides."

" This very afternoon I shall hand him one or two thousand dollars."

The figure fell like dew on the family.

" And for you, Manuel, I have set aside twenty thousand; for you, Antonio and José, a like amount. And for you, father, I bought a house yesterday in the Castellana, where we will all live together; you shall reign like a king."

They did not hear him now, they gazed at him as at a supernatural being!

" Well, with that thousand pesetas and another thousand from a friend, I sailed for the United States, a country with money and no morals. Until I could start business (what is nowadays called business and consists in taking other people's money) I found work in the house of a big shipowner, a wealthy man, and in six months I stole his wife."

" Heavens! " exclaimed the father.

" An irresistible folly, father! What the press of both hemispheres call a love drama! Everybody was on my side. She was young and full of life; her husband was old and ill, and treated her very badly. The papers published my photograph, and one of her, and one of the old man shooting himself. I was the hero of the country and went off to California with the object of my love. She brought me half a million dollars, and, as the man with the most money is the most esteemed there, I launched one of those businesses that everybody takes to. A gold mine that had no gold and never existed."

" But that was cheating! "

" But that is done every day, and the public, who are fools all the world over, subscribe the money immediately the shares are put on the market. Afterwards comes the failure. . . . And therefore I put a nobody at the head, to take the responsibility; I only appeared as a salaried manager. When the crash came, the other fellow was arrested and I cried, thief! Ah, you laugh, Manuel, eh? As a lawyer, you must have seen a lot of that, no? In fact, for a fee of ten thousand dollars you would have defended me!

"With the money I made out of that *speculation* . . . (nowadays, father, we call such things speculations, although it used to be otherwise) I went to Paris a wealthy man, settled down in great style and became a French citizen."

" French! " shouted his father, sitting up in bed, " my son a Frenchman! Never! impossible! "

" But, papa, don't you know in Spain we have the cleverest and most convenient law in the world? It is the only one that provides for the possibility of repentance and patriotism. According to Article twenty-one of the Civil Code, the Spaniard who loses his nationality by becoming naturalised in a foreign country may recover it by declaring that such is his wish before the Civil Registrar of the district in which he elects domicile. I have done so, and am as much a Spaniard as before, but have meanwhile made my fortune with the French."

" Smart! " said Manuel.

" Marvellous! " said the others.

" Once in Paris, a city enslaved to money and to those who possess it, I started an endless number of companies, all bad for other people and good for me. The French are like children; they let themselves be gulled with incredible ease. Remember what happened about Panama, about the Compagnie des Métaux, about the Transvaal Gold Mines, which are veritable sparrows' nets. . . . And as money and honours are essential to influence in Paris, and as there is a mania for nobility in that republican country, the first year I was there I went to Rome and bought a title. As Marquis de Sahagun and by lavish dinners, which is the modern system of making friends and admirers, I at once got possession of the market. An inventor without a peseta, like all inventors, described his invention to me. I stole his idea and made a fortune out of it."

" For God's sake, child! "

" But don't you know that no one who makes, invents, or creates a thing ever gets the benefit of it? The author is exploited by the publisher, the actor by the impresario, the inventor by the capitalist . . . capital! I am Capital, and all the world bows down before me! All the women worshipped me; I let my wife run away with a poor fellow who fell in love with her; I conquered the most obstinate; the millions streamed in like water. . . . Decorations, crosses, honours, I have received them from all the countries in the world. . . . Besides, there are agencies that sell them! In a word: here I am, forty-six years of age, called ' the wealthy banker,' the ' great financier,' the ' philanthropist,' because I give thousands of francs to the poor, and now I am going to found a hospital and school and anything else they want here. . . . Well, father! To-morrow we move into the mansion; all the lower floor for you, the first for these fellows and their families; each shall have thirty or forty thousand dollars at the Bank, and I am going to set to work to become a deputy, a senator, a minister. . . . I shall make the laws! ''

And they ended by laughing uproariously, and they were so intoxicated by the gold that fell on them as from the sky, that the father, half paralysed, jumped out of bed, and Manuel ran to tell them at home, and Antonio sang, and José began to think of the great stores he would erect in the very centre of Madrid, and Dimas laughed with delight at seeing them happy, and on leaving he said to a poor man who held open the carriage door:

'' Get to work! Get to work! I have worked since I was a boy.''

And all the family said: '' What a very smart fellow. He always showed great talent! ''

Great talent! ! !

EUSEBIO BLASCO

THE RUSTIC COBBLER

What I am going to tell you was told me by Don José Echegaray in four words.

It is a tale of melancholy philosophy and can be applied to many circumstances in life; for all of us in this lower world have formed illusions about certain things, and the reality has usually left us as badly off as Don Quijote.

The tale, or incident, which Don José related in friendly conversation at the Ateneo was applied by him to his one year's presidency of that stormy house, and I in turn applied it, after hearing it, to my unfortunate election as deputy, which left me with no desire to attempt another.

The interested reader can also apply it to many circumstances of his life.

The story is this:

I

There was once a cobbler who lived shut up in his private bootshop, that is, an attic, in an Andalusian town, seeing, while he worked, the sun through the only window by which light came to the unhappy master of shoemaking.

This happened, as I said, in a city of the south, and the sun that bathes the fertile region where the incident occurred only reached the poor cobbler in a single ray for a few hours.

Through the bars of his small window he saw the blue sky limpid and clear, and as he nailed or stretched his leather, the poor man sighed with a certain anticipated home-sickness for some country as yet unknown to him.

" What a lovely day for a walk! " he would often exclaim to himself.

And when some customer brought him a filthy pair of boots belonging to the coachman opposite or to the carrier at the corner, the patcher would ask him:

" Is it fine outside? "

" A splendid day; there has never been a finer April. Neither hot nor cold, and a gorgeous sun."

The man sighed with more pain than ever, seized the boots
and threw them savagely into a corner, saying:

"What luck you people have! Come back on Saturday for
the boots. The repairs will cost six reales."

He tried to console himself by singing. And he repeated till
nightfall:

> "He who would but cannot
> His liberty enjoy,
> Need have no fear of dying
> For he's already dead!"

And longing looks at the heavens, and more sighs, until sunset.
The unhappy man was almost glad to see darkness set in. His sad
condition and hard lot prevented him from taking the air until the
evening.

One day a customer who lived in the same house came into his
attic with a pair of country boots for him to repair. And as the
cobbler with rustic ideas lamented that he could never see the
country he so longed for, the other said to him:

"You are right, Uncle Gaspar: and therefore I say that the
happiest people in the world are the donkey-drivers."

"The donkey-drivers, really?"

"Rather! they come and go, always enjoying the pure air,
smelling the thyme and rosemary, kings of the world; yes, it is the
finest work there is!"

Uncle Gaspar, when the customer had departed, was thoughtful,
very thoughtful.

That night he did not sleep, but by dawn his mind was made up.

"To-morrow I will tell my nephew to look after the shop, and
with the fifty dollars I have saved I shall buy a donkey and become
a driver."

And so he did, and in eight days he was a *cosario*, as they call
the carriers in the south.

"What a lovely day! What healthy air! Now I'm living,
and not wasting the prime of my life in that hole under the roof!
Gee-up, you beauty!" and Uncle Gaspar, on his first journey,
sang as he picked the broom flowers along the roadside.

There was not a soul within a mile; Uncle Gaspar was, as he
had so often wished, in sole possession of the country!

Suddenly, on rounding some prickly-pears to take a path to the
right, three men fell on him, shouting:

"Halt there!"

One seized the donkey and mounted it, and started off hurriedly
down the road; the other held Uncle Gaspar, whilst the third took
what he had on him—money, clothes . . . everything! They left
him naked, and there and then, so that he would not run after
them, they gave him about fifty strokes with an ash stick, till his

ribs were black and blue, and his shouts must have been heard in the capital; but no one heard them.

In broad daylight!

At three in the afternoon in April, an attack so fierce and so unexpected!

Uncle Gaspar emitted terrible yells.

" Help! H—e—l—p! I'm d—y—i—n—g! "

At about five o'clock a farmer passed by in a cart. He picked him up and wrapped him in a rug, turned back to the city, and put him down at the door of his house. . . .

II

Great was the astonishment of his nephew and neighbours. Questions rained on the battered cobbler. But the latter answered none of them. He was not heard to say a word for many days. He seemed to have been struck dumb.

But one day, at about three o'clock, voices were heard on the stairs, speaking of an excursion into the country:

" Let us go out for the afternoon."

" What lovely weather! "

" Tell the cousins to come with us, to enjoy the fine weather! "

And Uncle Gaspar, disdainfully raising his head and looking at the sky, said to himself in the solitude of his attic:

" Lovely weather. . . . What a thrashing those donkey-drivers will be getting! "

CARLOS COELLO

1850-1888

TIERRA-TRAGONA

I

In the early days of May in the year 1601 nothing else was spoken of in the city of Valladolid, where the Court of Philip III. was then fixed, but the Royal Decree ordering an inventory to be taken of all the wrought silver existing in the Kingdom. This was the celebrated device by means of which the Duke of Lerma hoped to find a remedy for the poverty of Spain. Perhaps one other thing was talked of—the scandalous adventures of Don Guillen Calleja.

Don Guillen was a young man of about twenty-four years of age, good-looking and self-willed, the son of a powerful nabob, who, after having brought the lad up on the principle of a tight rein and a close purse, committed the imprudence of dying, leaving him heir to an immense fortune, and absolutely his own master. Calleja plunged into a life of pleasure just as a young high-mettled colt plunges into a mad race across the fields, when, tired of champing the bit, he has the joy of seeing it fall broken into fragments at his feet. His life was one constant round of amusements, and he had time only for one love affair after another, for gambling and for duelling. No thought ever came to him of the uncertainty of life, the danger of losing his fortune, or that of losing his soul, the greatest and most irremediable danger of all.

At that time, which dramatists depict to us as having been so full of romance, very little account was taken of a stab or so (that is, of course, if it was given to a humble individual), and whilst Don Guillen, a swashbuckler who could give long odds even to Don Francisco de Quevedo himself, was content to stab bullies and gamesters, he could rely on the careful lack of attention on the part of what passed for Justice, who was always disposed to keep her eyes shut whenever she was invited to hold out her hands and not withdraw them empty.

But it so happened that the devil, who never sleeps (and is indeed always on the watch), set going a rivalry in a love affair between our hero and a certain nephew of Don Pedro Martin de Andueza, private physician to His Majesty; and this brought about a duel between the two rivals, the result of which was that the nephew in question lost his life.

Now the doctor loved his sister's son like the apple of his eye, the Duke of Lerma had for Don Martin that respectful friendship which is only due to a doctor of high authority; and the King, who approved of everything done by his favourite physician (to whom he did not give the smallest trouble professionally), signed an order in which, with due regard to the spiritual welfare of the nabob's son, he commanded Don Guillen to be arrested, his confession to be heard, and his execution to be carried out—all within the exact period of three hours.

The Mayor of the city was charged with the fulfilment of this order, so graciously conceived, and as he was told to take very great pains for the apprehension of the unfortunate Calleja, he went to find the latter and said to him: "The King orders me to arrest you and have you hanged: I am in a difficulty, for you are a good friend of mine, and at the same time I am a loyal and faithful subject of my Sovereign. Take to your heels and get out of danger if you can in the five minutes' grace which I am going to give you: when that interval is over I will have you hanged wherever I catch you."

Don Guillen was of such a modest disposition that he did not want to attract the attention of the whole of Valladolid, so he filled his pockets with gold, mounted his best horse, and left the city at a pace which I leave to the imagination of my reader.

II

The aristocratic rake rode on all night without knowing where he was or whither he was going, and when dawn broke and he was beginning to feel a little relieved by the thought that his friend the Mayor was not going to try to catch him, his horse, covered with foam and sweat, gave clear indications of not being able to continue his career. His anxious rider struck the spurs once more into his side, and the noble animal made one last effort and then fell dead, throwing Don Guillen to the ground, where he lay bruised and aching for a long time. At last he got up and looked around him, most agreeably surprised at not seeing even the shadow of a Mayor or the least sign of a sheriff's officer.

The day was so fine that Don Guillen, although not exactly in the mood to admire the beauties of nature, could not help perceiving, when the sun's beams illuminated the landscape, that this place had nothing in common with the arid plains of Old Castile. But still, in two or three hours he could not have got very far from the town of Pisuerga, even riding at break-neck pace. Calleja found himself in the midst of a fresh and pretty vale, in which all

sorts of trees and flowers flourished, and away in the distance, but
not so far as not to be reached without much fatigue, he saw a fine
town which he did not remember ever having seen before, although
he had frequently ridden all over the neighbourhood, shooting hares
and partridges in the fields and wild birds over the lakes.

" What town is that? " he asked a passing peasant.

" Tierra-Tragona," was the reply.

The name, which Don Guillen had never heard, surprised him
even more than the appearance of the town; but he was in need
of rest, and at the same time he hoped to be able to find there
some place in which he could hide from the attentions of his friend
the Mayor. So he went on boldly to Tierra-Tragona, and soon
arrived in the town.

III

If Tierra-Tragona looked attractive from a distance, the eyes and
the mind of Don Guillen were enchanted with a nearer view of it,
for he had never seen anything like it in his life. The splendour of
the city, the richness of its buildings, the width of its streets, and
the sumptuousness of its monuments exceeded anything of which
we can dream in our wildest visions of an enchanted city. And
this charm was added to by the circumstance that the greater
number of the people in the streets wore magnificent clothes and
went about with gay laughter and happy faces; even those who
appeared to be members of the working-classes seemed to share
the animation of the others.

" Is there any popular celebration going on here to-day? Is it
the festival of the patron saint of the town? "

The girl to whom Don Guillen addressed this question, and who
had in her hand a ring, the splendour of which contrasted oddly
with the poverty of her attire, looked at him with some surprise and
replied :

" No, sir. To-day is like any other day to us. This is the land
of cheerfulness, no one has any trouble here, nor is there any
reason why people should be sad."

And shutting the ring up in her closed hand and looking slyly at
Don Guillen, the girl ran off singing and dancing gaily.

IV

Calleja walked through the streets and squares admiring everything that he saw and wondering why such a charming town should
have such an ugly name (for Tierra-Tragona means the Gluttonous
Land), when stepping aside to make room for some person who
was advancing in an opposite direction, he stared in amazement,

uttered a cry, an awful cry of fear, and shrank back into the shadow of a doorway, where he remained as if glued to the spot and incapable of motion.

What had Calleja seen?

A handsome, healthy-looking young man, radiating happiness from his countenance, but dressed in a strange manner, had suddenly staggered, the ground had opened under his feet and had completely swallowed him up.

Some of the people passing in the street had observed the incident, had stopped to talk about it, and then the animation of the people, which had only been interrupted for a moment, began again over the very spot where the event had taken place.

This indifference horrified Don Guillen just as much as the occurrence itself, and he had not the strength to move from the spot where he remained fixed and hidden, almost invisible to the sight of every one.

When he had recovered himself a little, he began to listen to a conversation which was being carried on in a neighbouring balcony between a very beautiful woman and a gay cavalier. The meaning of what he heard was that the lady gave the gentleman the information that her husband would soon be going away for a time; and then both made an appointment for a meeting on the night of his absence, taking undue advantage of his confidence in them. They were still talking and exchanging endearing words, mingling tender expressions with jests against the deceived husband, when all at once the ground opened again and engulfed the lover who was standing under the balcony. The lady uttered a scream, but was soon calm again, and did not even leave the window, and the few curious passers-by who had stopped on hearing her cry, only shrugged their shoulders and continued their way in various directions.

Don Guillen decided to escape from his hiding-place and flee from the town at full speed, but he could not stir; and in a few moments he overheard another conversation which was taking place near him between two men of unpleasant appearance. They asked each other, like two friends who had not met for a long time, how they were getting on in life. One of them kept a gaming-house, and made good profits out of the unfortunate pigeons who came to be plucked under his roof by means of various cheating devices. The other lent money to the sons of rich men, at interest amounting to ten times the sum lent; the money to be repaid when the father died —thus demoralising and impoverishing the younger generation at the same time. They were about to separate after gaily calculating their ill-gotten gains for the day, when the very same thing happened to the usurer as had happened to the unknown passer-by and to the would-be seducer of the wife; but the other man continued on his way without concerning himself about the fate of his friend and comrade.

And what Don Guillen saw in the cases related above continued to be repeated in the cases of others, which he saw again and again as he remained crouching in his corner. The same fate overtook the woman of evil life, who with brazen painted-face and gaudy dress walked the street in calm indifference to modesty, thinking of anything rather than of her sins; the paid bravo who with his unworthy courage took the place of those who were too cowardly to revenge themselves on their enemies in person; the dissolute and foolish youth who shrinks from no course which he thinks will lead to pleasure; even the wretched pickpocket on the watch to profit by the unsuspiciousness of others.

All happened in the presence of the stranger overwhelmed with anxiety and horror, and at last his intelligence and his heart, wounded by so many impressions, so different but all so terrible, permitted him to collect his wits and to form the following reflections which crowded on him tumultuously:

" These people never seem to have any security in their lives; these people appear to be faced with death at any moment, from what I have seen happen here at every step. How can they remain in such awful indifference to death? Why do they not repent of their sins and amend their evil lives? "

A light touch on his shoulder caused him to turn, and he found himself face to face with an old monk, who issued from the door against which Don Guillen was leaning, and which was the entrance to a Dominican monastery.

" Tell me, my brother," said the monk to our hero; " in what country may your honour have been born? "

" I, sir? I was born in Seville, and now I have come here from Valladolid," murmured Calleja, quite surprised that his reflections should have been overheard by any one.

The monk continued:

" And those cities? Are they free from the dangers which cause you so much fear in this town? Does the earth never open there for any one? Is any one certain of the continuance of his existence there? Is there no one there who, given up to vice, spends his life without suspecting that death may assail him when he least expects it, without giving him time to repent and amend his mode of conduct? "

The words of the monk snatched from the thoughtless young man the veil of ignorance which had blinded the eyes of his reason, and he could now see and judge of everything with a clearness unknown before.

Kneeling at the feet of the monk and covering his face with his hands, through which rolled tears of noble shame and penitence, he implored confession of his sins and peace for his soul.

Both entered the monastery, and Don Guillen's prayer was acceded to. Being given a refuge in the holy place, his thoughts dwelt on the possibility of spending the remainder of his days with those good monks, fearing to be once more launched on the stormy sea in which such terrible dangers were to be encountered.

After having his vocation tested by a year's novitiate, Calleja assumed the monk's habit, and it is said that as he passed through the streets of the dissolute town which he sought to save, wrapped in his gown of coarse sackcloth, he enjoyed the greatest of pleasures in the peace of his conscience; and the former sinner awaited with calmness, without the slightest fear, but rather with joyful anticipation, the opening of the unstable ground of Tierra-Tragona beneath his feet.

EMILIA PARDO BAZÁN

1851–1921

THE SOUTHERN EXPRESS

Across the level fields cultivated like gardens, sprinkled with white houses, their red roofs gleaming under a bright warm sun, the train of first-class carriages ran on, on towards Paris. The country people, the market gardeners, who led their mule-carts full of garden stuff, looked at the swiftly-passing train with that peculiar impression of respectful envy which is inspired by the sight of what is inaccessible in our ordinary social life.

Through the lofty, clear glass windows a glimpse could be caught for a moment of the tables in the dining-car, and of people sitting at them, able to eat and drink what they liked. It was like a cinematographic picture, disappearing at the moment of greatest interest behind the wide trail of smoke, and lost in the distance, and the mere ordinary action of having something to eat, attended by waiters in correct style, acquired in the eyes of the spectators, owing to the speed of the train, and the instantaneous nature of the picture, an aristocratic and romantic splendour.

When we crossed the frontier I had huddled myself up in a corner of the saloon carriage, leaving my bag and my yellow-covered novel on the table fixed to the floor, and watching through my grey gauze veil my companions of a few hours' travel with the keen curiosity of one who finds himself in an unknown but fruitful country. They were South American families, with their dark-complexioned children, dressed in the latest English fashions; ladies travelling alone, perfumed, and loudly dressed; elderly ladies attired in a manner which suggested wealth; stiff, reserved English ladies, who sat upright and escaped in some perfectly unaccountable way the invasion of the coal-dust, always keeping their dainty pink cheeks clean and their hair, like spun gold, immaculately smooth. And finally, there were young couples quite wrapped up in each other, who did not care a straw for the lookers-on, and who lived apart in a murmur of honeymoon confidences.

One of these couples sat so near me that their chatter kept my attention off what I was reading, so that I closed the novel by

135

Danilewsky and preferred to turn to the page of real life close at my
side—without suspecting that in it I would find, instead of an
idyll, the elements of a gloomy drama.   However, it was the idyll
which first appeared, and even forced itself on my notice, with all
the insistence of legitimate happiness and with the nonsense which
is for ever the right of happy lovers.

My honeymoon couple—for such I deemed them to be—did not
want to breakfast in the dining-car.   Neither did I, for the shaking
of the train tired me.   The reasons which led them to seek solitude
were no doubt very different from mine; they wanted to be alone to
be refreshed by each other's company only.   I gathered this when
I heard them utter an exclamation of joy as nearly everybody left
the carriage, and noted a gesture of impatience, so pronounced as
to amount to a display of temper, on the part of the woman when
she saw that I did not leave my seat.   As they could not get me
out of my place, they finally appeared to resign themselves to
the inevitable, and to forget that I was there.   They took the
little square hamper down from the rack, and prepared to lunch
together.

She was young, fair, tall, and slim, with that graceful slimness
which appears to have no angles, and which is the special attribute of Parisian women.   She wore a soft, grey cloth travelling
dress, and her little grey cloth toque had as its sole trimming two
white pigeon's wings, quivering as if ready for flight.   She sat close
to her companion and spread a single napkin over his knees.   He
was young too, dark, thin, and sallow, but attractive in that
moment in his evident delight in his bride's attentiveness and in his
anticipation of their little picnic together.   She took parcel after
parcel out of the little hamper, and as each parcel was opened,
some special delicacy appeared.   Sandwiches of paté de foie gras,
pink and white slices of York ham, little square pieces of chicken,
tiny patties, each containing a mouthful of some tit-bit; oysters
embedded separately in jellied white sauce.   And the opening of
each parcel was greeted with cries of delighted surprise from the
husband, and proud and happy giggles from the wife.

" Why, you think of everything!   What forethought!   This is
a real feast."   She played at secrets all the time.

" Just wait a bit.   You haven't seen all yet."

From the little hamper she took a small bottle of Burgundy, a
siphon of soda-water, some silver drinking-cups, and a corkscrew.
Nothing was lacking.   They sat with their knees pressed close
together, so as to be able to accommodate the single napkin, and
no doubt also to feel that they were alone together in this their first
honeymoon meal, which they proceeded to despatch.   Despatch,
did I say?   No, there was no despatch about it.   They lingered
over the opening of each little white paper parcel, whispering,

touching the tips of their fingers daintily, each most anxious for the other to enjoy the feast to the full.

"Another bit? Do you like the ham? Now I am going to give you some wine."

All the time tender glances and happy laughter over every trifle —the rattling of the little china plates, the spilling of the wine gleaming in the silver cups as the train hastened in its onward march.

I could not help watching them covertly, as they played thus like two happy children, but my attention was aroused by something which struck me as strange in the bride's behaviour. Two or three times she made excuses to leave her husband's side, and to manage to pass the door of communication with the next carriage, into which she threw a rapid glance. The only occupant of the carriage next to ours was a man, who sat huddled in a corner, with a checked cloth cap pulled down over his face, and either asleep or pretending to sleep. Only the lower part of his face was visible, a well-formed, strong young mouth and chin, with a small fair moustache partly shading the red upper lip. Each time the bride passed the door opposite to where he sat, the stranger, as I must call him for want of a better name, moved his cap slightly, and a gleam appeared to dart from the eyes half-covered by the peak of the cap. Was this really the case, or did I fancy it? Was I dreaming, or was my sight deceived by the jolting of the train? I could swear that what I saw was a real fact.

But if it was real fact, what was the meaning of the idyll of the little feast? And now, when the dessert was being brought out, the idyll grew still prettier and more interesting. I kept watch under the cover of my veil, and noted the solitary traveller crouching in his corner and the happy young couple giggling over a gleaming bunch of grapes which the bride dangled in the air. Their fingers touched as they picked off the grapes, their lips touched as they nibbled them like rabbits, laughing, chattering, uttering the broken words of endearment used by honeymoon couples all the world over. When the yellow grapes were all gone, a cardboard box came out of the wonderful hamper, and the lid came off, revealing rows on rows of chestnuts coated with snowy icing, like soldiers of the Middle Ages in their gleaming coats of mail. The little play went on—nibbling a chestnut until their lips met, giggling, pretending to quarrel as to who should be the next to pick out the biggest and best chestnut. I must admit that when I had noticed them first they sat so quietly together that I did not imagine they were a honeymoon couple; I thought they might be brother and sister. But now no doubt remained—they were behaving as honeymoon couples behave everywhere in the intoxication of their new companionship, wrapped up in each other and heeding no one

else. This was no brother-and-sister affection, but a real, romantic
love-match, and though I was amused by their childishness, I
blessed them in my heart.

.   .   .   .

She rose to take another little parcel out of the hamper, no doubt
containing fruit or something sweet to crown the little feast.   All at
once she looked about the carriage, and uttered a piercing cry of
dismay: " My bag!   My Russia leather bag!   Oh, where is it?
Where could I have put it? "
" Shall I go and look for it? " he asked anxiously.
" Oh. I should be so glad if you would, dear.   I think I must
have left it in the rack of the sleeping-car."
He went off to look for the bag, and I shivered with a sort of
instinctive horror at what I felt was happening.   For when the
bride was undoing the hamper containing the parcels of dainties,
I had noted her taking her Russia leather bag with shining silver
fittings and carefully concealing it under the seat.   But almost
before I had time to remember this, and even before her husband
had crossed the corridor separating the carriages from one another,
she had rushed into the next carriage, swift as a bird to its nest,
to be met in her flight half-way by the lonely traveller in the cap.
He had risen as if at a signal and run to clasp her in his arms.
No word was spoken, no sound of any kind was uttered.   They
clung silently to each other in a mad embrace in which the two
seemed to be as one, like a statue which can only be broken
asunder by a knife or a hatchet.
How long did this strange, dangerous embrace last?   Perhaps
a second, perhaps five minutes or more.   I sat with my eyes fixed
on them, hardly believing what I saw.   They did not move; they
did not seem even to breathe or to concern themselves about any
one or anything, whilst I, on the contrary, was quivering with
nervous terror.   My heart throbbed, I could scarcely breathe, and
the perspiration gathered on my forehead and rolled down in drops
that blinded me.   I felt that I ought to do something, to say
something, and yet I sat chained to my corner like the victim of a
terrible nightmare.   I looked helplessly for the coming of the only
person who had any right to intrude on the strange drama—the
betrayed young husband, who was engaged in a fruitless search for
the Russia leather bag whose gleaming silver fittings shone from
under the seat, where it had been so carefully and craftily placed.
At last they separated and I could breathe again.   She came
back to her place in my compartment, her fair head drooping as
she passed me.   When she took her place opposite to me, she gave
me such a look!   Agony and entreaty were combined in that one
desperate appeal.   The stranger had returned to his corner and

was again crouching under the shelter of his cap, apparently dozing as before. And while I was still asking myself if I, too, was asleep and dreaming, the young husband came back. He had searched everywhere for the missing Russia leather bag—he had roused all the train officials, but no trace of it could be found. The bride listened to what he had to say, and then laughed happily and kissed him for his trouble on her behalf, holding out the bag at arm's length.

"Forgive all the trouble I have given you, darling. I *am* a silly little thing. I found it where I dropped it behind the seat when I was taking down the hamper!" He was not in the least annoyed or cross with her. They sat down together as before, and she took a last white paper parcel out of the little square hamper. Rosy peaches, warmed by the southern sun, crowned the honeymoon feast, and they nibbled them together as before.

. . . .

All the rest of the way nothing happened—absolutely nothing. They sat together, whispered, petted each other, read newspapers and talked over what they read, cheek pressed against cheek, slept, holding each other's hands, she with her head on his shoulder, and later in the evening, they went off to the dining-car for their meal together.

When the train drew up at the platform of the great station, and the travellers went their different ways, I caught a last glimpse of the couple going arm-in-arm to a cab, followed by a porter carrying the rugs, the little empty hamper, and the Russia leather bag. I wondered again if I had only been dreaming. . . .

EMILIA PARDO BAZÁN

THE PINK PEARL

This is what an unfortunate friend of mine said to me:

" It is only the man who shuts himself up all day and works long hours in the night in order to earn money enough to satisfy the caprices of the woman loved who can comprehend the pleasure of saving up little by little a fixed sum of money to be used to gratify even her vainest and most trifling whim. What she thought of only as a hopeless dream, what even in her wildest imagination seemed an impossible wish, spurred me on to make the efforts which were to render that wish an accomplished fact. The idea that my work and my affection could place what she longed for in her hands was so delightful to me that I dwelt on the thought of her surprise, her admiration, and the clasp of her soft arms round my neck in her transport of coming gratitude.

" My only fear, as I sallied forth with my well-filled pocket-book in my hand and my mind full of joyful anticipation, was that the jeweller might have already found another customer. I wanted to see Lucilla's delight when I placed in her hands the two exquisite pink pearls for which she had longed so much as she hung on my arm and gazed into the shop window. It is so difficult to find two such perfect pearls, alike in shape and colour, gleaming with such an admirable tint, so entirely matched in roundness and size, that I thought it impossible that some rich woman should not have already secured them and locked them safely up in her jewel case. If this had happened, I should have been so miserable that the bare idea of it set my heart throbbing, and I felt a choking sense of relief when I saw the two beautiful pearls in their diamond setting still lying in their white velvet case, flanked on one side by a magnificent diamond necklace, and on the other by a bunch of gold bracelets.

" I fully expected to be asked to pay dearly for my fancy, but still the price asked by the jeweller took me aback when I inquired what he was prepared to take for the pearls. All that I had saved, and even something more, would have to be invested in those tiny things, no bigger than a couple of peas. I hesitated—for buying jewels is not an everyday occupation for a man of my means—and wondered if the jeweller was not taking advantage of my ignorance and asking me for a ridiculous sum in the belief that I was no judge of the value of such things. And while I was considering the matter, I looked out of the shop window and saw my old friend and fellow-student and my best friend of that day, Gonzaga Llorente. To see his familiar face and to run out to call him were one and the same idea. Who could advise me in the matter of the pink pearls so well as the elegant Gonzaga, who was so well up in all relating to fashions, to what was done in the world by people of wealth and refinement, among whom he was so popular, so much sought after, that I could never feel sufficiently grateful to him for coming, as he did come so often, to my modest home? It was so good of a man like him to take any notice of us at all!

" Gonzaga appeared surprised and delighted when I ran out to call him, and he came with me to the jeweller's shop, whilst I told him what I wanted him to do. He admired the lovely pink pearls, and said that several rich ladies of his acquaintance in society would pay any price asked for such rare things to wear as earrings, which was just the purpose for which they had been set in a tiny frame of brilliants. He took me aside and assured me that the price asked by the jeweller was not excessive in view of the marvellous beauty of the pearls; I felt reassured by his words, and was only held back from completing the bargain by my shame at having to confess that I had not money enough. At last I admitted to Gonzaga that much as I wished to make my wife a present of the pink pearl earrings, I was not really able to pay for them. Gonzaga did what any friend would do in such circumstances; he opened his pocket-book and handed me some bank notes, and at the same time he laughed and swore that if I would not accept such a trifling service at his hands he would cut me dead whenever he met me in future. How I suffered! I did not dare to accept the loan, fearing that I might not be able to repay it, and yet I could not take such valuable earrings home unless the full price was paid. At last my wish to please my wife conquered, and I felt so happy that I could have knelt down and kissed the hand which enabled me to make her such a gift. I invited Gonzaga to lunch with us next day and to see me give the pink pearl earrings to my wife; and we separated with this understanding. I went home with the little case in my pocket, and felt as if I had wings on my shoulders.

" Lucilla was dusting and arranging the drawing-room when I came back. She looked at me, and when I said, ' Search my pockets to see what I have in them,' she jumped, clapped her hands in her lively and childish way, and cried, ' Oh, a present for me. Let me find it! ' She turned all my pockets inside out and tickled me all the time, until at last she got hold of the little case. I shall never forget the cry of joy which she uttered when she saw the pearls. Then she pulled my face down and covered it with kisses, saying that I was the best and kindest husband a woman ever had.

I cannot help thinking that she really did love me in that moment.
I had let her think that it was quite impossible for me to buy the
pink pearls, and this little surprise was quite unexpected by her.
In my pleasure at her happiness I could not wait to let her wear the
earrings next day; I made her take the little gold rings out of her
ears, and as I was not disposed to make any mystery, I fastened in
the little pink pearls which she had longed for so much that her ears
were rosy with the delight which radiated from her whole being. It
hurts me bitterly now to think of all these loving follies—and alas,
I shall never be able to cease remembering them.

.　　　.　　　.　　　.　　　.　　　.　　　.　　　.

Next day was Sunday, and Gonzaga kept his appointment to
come and lunch with us. We were all happy and even noisy in
our gaiety. Lucilla had put on her best dress—a grey silk, which
suited her so well, and she had pinned a pink rose in her bodice,
of the very same shade as the pink pearls in her ears. Gonzaga
brought us tickets for the theatre, and we all spent a merry and
very joyous evening. Next day I had to go back to work, and
even to work overtime, to try to make up what I owed my good
friend for what he had paid for the pearls. When I got home and
sat down to dinner with Lucilla, my first glance was at her pretty
little ears. I sprang up and uttered a cry as I saw that one of the
little rings of diamonds was empty. The pink pearl was missing.

" ' You have lost a pearl,' I exclaimed.

" ' You don't say so! ' replied my wife, passing her finger over
her ears and feeling the jewels in them. When she found that the
pearl was really gone, she seemed so terrified that I was alarmed
too, not because of the pearl, but at the sight of Lucilla's anguish
of mind.

" ' Don't worry so much,' I said to her at last. ' It must be
somewhere about. Let us look for it, and it will surely turn up.'

" We searched everywhere. We shook the carpet, turned up all
the rugs, examined the folds of the curtains, moved out all the
furniture, and even opened boxes which Lucilla declared she had
not touched for months previously. When all our search was vain,
Lucilla sat down and wept bitterly. I asked her:

" ' Were you out anywhere to-day? '

" ' Yes. Oh, yes, I did go out,' she replied as if considering.

" ' Where did you go, dear? '

" ' Oh, I went to several places. I went out to . . . to buy
things.'

" ' What shops did you go to? '

" ' I forget now. Oh, yes, I went to the Post Office and to some
places in the same street. I went to the draper's shop in the Square
—to the Parade, and . . .'

" ' Did you walk or go in a cab or bus? '

" ' I walked at first. Then I took a cab.'

" ' Where did you take it? Did you notice the number? '

" ' No, I don't think I did. Oh, no, how should I notice it?
It was just a cab which was passing, and I was so tired,' said
Lucilla, beginning to sob again.

" ' Well, but, my dear, be reasonable.' She was quite hysterical.
' You must surely remember what shops you were in. I will go
round and ask in each of them, if you will give me a list. I will
have an advertisement printed.'

" ' Oh, I can't remember. Do leave me in peace! ' she cried
pettishly. And pitying her evident grief for the loss of my gift, I
said no more just then.

" We spent a very unhappy night. I could not sleep, and I
watched Lucilla too, turning and weeping furtively, pretending to
sleep so as not to disturb me, but not succeeding in being able to
keep quiet, whilst I went on thinking what to do to get on the track
of the lost pearl. I rose early, and decided to let Lucilla sleep, as
she was doing uneasily, and to go and ask advice from my good
and sensible friend, Gonzaga Llorente. I had an idea that the
police in the case of lost treasures might be able to find out where
they were, and I hoped that Gonzaga with his wide influence and
experience might assist me in this very serious and important
inquiry.

" ' My master is asleep,' said the servant. ' But come in, sir.
If you will wait in the study for a little while, I will let you know
when he can see you. In ten minutes' time I will take him in his
chocolate, and then I will tell him that you are here.' The man
could not help remarking my anxiety and impatience.

" I had to make up my mind to wait, so the servant opened the
shutters in the study and invited me to enter. The place had an
odour of cigarette smoke and of perfumes. What would have happened, I wonder, if I had been able to go straight into my friend's
room without having to wait?

" What did happen was that as soon as the first ray of light
entered the shutters which the man was opening, and even before
he had time to request me to take a seat, I saw something gleam
from amid the fur of the white bearskin rug mounted on blue cloth
which was spread at the foot of the luxurious Turkish couch. It
was the lost pink pearl!

" If what passed through my mind at the sight of it had passed
through yours, and if you had asked me what you ought to do in
such a case, I would certainly have said with the greatest sincerity,
' You should have taken down a sword from the trophy displayed
above the couch, rushed into the room of the sleeping traitor, and
made sure that he would never wake again.'

" But do you know what I did do? I stooped down, picked up

the pearl and slipped it into my pocket, left the house quietly and
went home. My wife was up and was dressing, but looking very
uneasy. I stood looking at her, and I did not strangle her, but in
a calm voice I told her to put in her earrings. Then I took the
pearl out of my pocket, held it out between my fingers and said:
' Here is what you have lost; and you see it did not take me long
to find it.'

  " Then a sudden blind fury took possession of me, and I felt as
if mad with the desire for revenge. I rushed at her, tore the earrings from her ears, and trampled them under foot. I did not
murder her; I do not know why, but I ran downstairs and into the
nearest bar, where I asked for a glass of brandy.

  " Did I ever see Lucilla again? Yes, once. She was leaning on
the arm of a man who was *not* Gonzaga. And I noticed that the
lobe of her left ear was disfigured by a scar as if it had been torn
down the middle. No doubt that was my doing, though I did not
remember doing it."

EMILIA PARDO BAZÁN

THE GREEN FLY

WE were enjoying or rather trying to enjoy the fresh air, on the great terrace of Alborada, on a broiling and enervating August afternoon—one of the very few which in that mild climate burn with the rage of the dog-star. The air was saturated, not only with the warm, resinous, pungent scent of the neighbouring pine woods, but also with other peculiar odours; the musky smell of ants and beetles, honey and sweet honeycomb wax; and in the warm atmosphere there was a swarm of dancing insects of all kinds—butterflies of every hue, flies glowing like precious stones and tiny atoms of enamel, " St. Anthony's cows "—those tiny black scarabs gleaming as if newly gone into mourning, ephemeral flies like scraps of transparent gauze, coral-hued ladybirds with black dots on their dainty wing-cases, gnats and mosquitoes like brown silk; and in the sand there was a constant turmoil of sandhoppers like riders practising steeplechasing; and the dainty, bright-hued, and graceful creeping insects of the country made their little slow pilgrimages, looking so much more attractive than their town cousins—the creeping insects of our houses!

We leaned back in our seats, talking at intervals only, feeling lazy, and anxiously awaiting the first breath of the cool evening which would come to fan our temples. The subject of our conversation was the enervating effect which heat produces on our strength, and we discussed the strange psychological influence exercised by different climates, a fact which is now being seriously recognised by historians.

One of us, a scientific physician, said:

" There is no doubt that firmness of character is an excellent thing, and we ought to use all our efforts to develop it. The man was not far from the mark who said that every one could shape his own destiny. And yet, this wealth of Nature which surrounds us and even oppresses us produces on me an impression of fatality which is so profound that I can hardly bring myself to struggle against it. What are we human creatures against the forces of Nature? "

" Why, we are everything! " exclaimed another of us who was a philosopher. " We have conquered the forces of Nature; we have laid them at our feet and obliged them to serve us. Each day finds us more and more in a position of victory in our struggle against them, and our ability to dominate them.''

'' On the contrary they are recovering lost ground. And after all, we cannot conquer ourselves,'' replied the doctor pensively. And as the sun sank behind the chestnut trees in all its golden splendour, and a gust of wind laden with fresh water-drops came to us from the neighbouring mill-wheel as it stopped in its course, and roused our flagging energies by its coolness, the doctor decided to relate to us an episode which had occurred in the course of his professional experience.

'' I was spending my summer holiday in the quiet country village of Caldasrojas,'' said he, '' and there I came across a very pleasant young acquaintance. He was the only son of a widow, and every evening we went for walks together through the sweet country lanes and the quiet hill-paths. By degrees he told me of his hopes, his aspirations, and his hard struggles for life. The death of his father had left the boy and his mother in very narrow circumstances, and the efforts of the widow to keep her head above water and to put her son forward in the world had left their effect on the mind of the lad. Torcuato—that was his name—was a man before other boys are thinking of leaving school, and, above all things, he developed in consequence of his seriousness of disposition a very great and persevering strength of will. Nothing dismayed him, nothing discouraged him, and he acquired a specially brilliant understanding of life, which appeared in his behaviour as well as in his artistic creative faculties. At the early age of eleven Torcuato kept the books of a tradesman in the ancient University city in which he lived; when he was thirteen he obtained the same work for several different employers, and succeeded in earning in this way sufficient to maintain his mother and himself; and at the same time he studied hard, working at his books late into the night, thus depriving himself of sleep, which is so necessary to youth at the critical period of development. It would be more like the truth to say that the lad passed from boyhood to manhood without being himself conscious of the change, and he had no ' troublesome age ' which so often causes anxiety to parents and schoolmasters. No follies, no idle objects of curiosity or pleasure ever attracted Torcuato, or diverted him from his onward progress towards the object of his life. His existence was regulated like that of a fine chronometer, not a fraction of a second was ever lost. Every instant was marked out in which he was to rise, wash, and dress, to sleep, to take his meals; and he kept most rigorously to the programme which he had set for himself. Or it would perhaps be more correct of me to say that he even robbed himself of some of the time appointed for his requirements as a human being, and he effected work of an almost

superhuman perfection of regularity, so as to earn enough for his
entrance into the University and the expenses which were absolutely
inevitable. No task was too mean for his pride to undertake; he
would even have worked as a bootblack if he could have earned
any money or sufficient money by doing so. He wrote essays and
lectures for the older students, sermons for the ecclesiastics in the
University, prospectuses for manufacturers, reports for company
secretaries; everything which might bring him in a little money and
an acquaintance likely to be of use to him. Finally, he passed all
his examinations brilliantly, and obtained a position in the University itself, modestly remunerated it is true, but still affording him
the means to hope on and to continue working, so as to be able to
embark on the career of which he dreamed.

" I asked Torcuato if he had never been ill; for an illness is just
the thing which ruins the hopes of those who have barely sufficient
to make ends meet without any lapping over. He replied:

" ' Ill? I have never had the time to be ill. The only thing
which ever troubled me a little was my digestion, and that is why
I have come to take a little rest in Caldasrojas, without my mother,
and just for a little change—the very first bit of idleness I have ever
had in my life. I am quite delighted with it all; it is a sort of
intoxication to me after my long toil to be able to enjoy the free
open air and the perfume of the flowers and trees! But you must
not think that I am not keeping to my rule all the same. Although
I am young and my youthful inclinations mount to my head and
even to my heart also with an imperious insistence, yet my will
reigns supreme. I am fully master of myself; and I will allow
nothing in this world to interfere with my intention to assure the
future of my mother, to give her a restful and happy old age, and
to make a way in the world for myself. I know that I have some
intelligence and some ability: another man might perhaps waste
this important capital, but I will on the contrary make it bring
me in returns which will go on increasing. Where there's a will
there's a way. Why the Bible itself shows us that this is
true.'

" Torcuato told me this one evening as we were coming back
from the direction of the sea-shore along the road traversed by the
carts carrying produce for export. Our conversation was punctuated by the shrill creaking of the cart-wheels as they toiled along
slowly, not raising any dust, in the sombre calm of the evening sun
sinking to its rest. I shall never forget the scene. Two heavy carts
passed us in an opposite direction to ours, and they were loaded
with partly tanned ox-hides, such as are sent to the coast steamers
for export to England. The setting sun's last rays were reflected in
the copper-coloured skins spotted with yellowish white. Torcuato
raised his right hand to shade his eyes, and I saw something alight

on it, something with a metallic shimmer like a green spark. He
shook his hand to get rid of the tiny insect.

" ' The little wretch. It has stung me! '

" I felt a shiver of uneasiness, for which there was no apparent
reason, and suddenly I caught hold of Torcuato's hand. There was
no sign of the sting. We continued our walk, but I did not feel
inclined to talk now, and I looked furtively at my young friend
from time to time. I noticed that he rubbed his hand mechanically
where the sting had been planted, and presently I saw that a tiny
red blister rose and presently disappeared, giving place to a dis-
coloured depression which grew blackish as I watched it. I *felt*
myself grow pale; we were still about three miles distant from the
little village.

" ' Let us make haste,' I said. ' The sting is of no importance,
but I would like to touch the spot with caustic all the same.'

" ' Why, my hand is swelling,' remarked Torcuato, more in surprise than alarm. I saw that he was unaware of the terrible consequences which may result from the sting of those beautiful little
emerald-tinted flies which have settled on the hides of animals
afflicted with the virulent poison of red pustule.

" ' Red pustule,' I thought, trembling with horror and pity.
' Red pustule. The most malignant plague which exists as a means
of blood-poisoning.'

" I must shorten this tragic tale. When we undressed Torcuato
in the back room of the little chemist's shop to treat the sting, we
found that not merely his hand but his entire arm rapidly showed
signs of inflammation. No doubt remained; the arm must be ampu-
tated. It was the one chance. . . . But how? We had no chloro-
form and scarcely any instruments. I sent to my lodging for what
I had, and with horror freezing my veins and shudders of pity
tearing at my heart, I was obliged to tell the unfortunate young
man the truth. What a look he gave me! What a world of horror,
of protest, and of grief in his eyes!

" ' My right arm! But what about my mother? What will she
say when she hears it? '

" ' Summon all your fortitude, all your strong will now,' I said,
if possible more horrified even than the victim himself. ' It must
be done! There is absolutely no help for it.'

" How acutely I felt the torture which I had to inflict on the
poor fellow. And whether on account of the delay in the operation,
the hesitation to do what should be done at the first moment, or
because the poison of the infection was introduced by a sheathed
sting, the poor young hero could not be saved after all. I prefer
not to give the details of his death, the horrifying symptoms which
appeared, the rending convulsions which preceded the end. If
doctors were to describe some of their cases humanity would detest

itself, as Solomon said, for ever having been born. . . . I have related to you this cruel case to show you what a tiny green fly, a beautiful little object, can do, and how powerless against the work of such an infinitesimal creature is all the force of a strong will, firm, resolute, trained, and seasoned by self-denial and hard work. No, we human beings are creatures of nothingness."

The night fell, and the glow-worms came out in all the charm of their mysterious little lanterns.

EMILIA PARDO BAZÁN

THE WELL OF LIFE

THE caravan went on, leaving the sick camel-driver at the brink of the well. All caravans stop there on account of the reputation of the water, about which so many things are said. Some say that it restores flagging energies at a draught, others that its properties are strange, terrible, and even fatal.

The followers of Ali, the son-in-law of Mohammed and the man who had the task of continuing the religious and political work of the Prophet, profess a special respect for that well. They say that the generous and unfortunate Prince, who was victorious over the army of his declared foe, Aixa or Aja, the widow of the Prophet, slaked his thirst in it on the day of his decisive victory. As all the faithful know, the Prophet's widow fell from her camel during the battle and was respectfully raised and pardoned by Ali, who had sent her back in safety to Mecca. It is said that it was from this period that the discussion as to the qualities of the water of the Well of Life arose. It is reported that when the celebrated Aixa, who was one of the only four incomparable women who ever lived in this world, touched the water with her lips after having been defeated and made prisoner, she declared that its taste was unendurable.

The camel-driver was not thinking of the taste of the water. He watched the disappearance of the cloud of dust raised by the departing caravan and considered himself shipwrecked in the sea of sand of the desert.

It is true that the well was surrounded by what is called an oasis; ten or a dozen palm trees, and a small construction of brick and plaster intended as a drinking-trough for the camels and a resting-place for a short time for the pilgrims on their way to the distant mosque—that was all that the solitary oasis contained. Devoured by the heat, which dried up the blood in his veins, the camel-driver, who had always been sober and frugal, hardly gave a thought to food now, to the bread and dates which formed his usual meal. His sustenance was only spring water.

" They do well to call it the Well of Life. In a few days I shall feel better. I will go on drinking it."

Two or three days went by. The deserted man kept dipping his

earthenware bowl in the skin of water, which his companions had
taken care to fill and place beside him in pitying forethought before
they went on their onward way.   And as he drank he thought:
" My illness must be turning my brain. Just now this water was
quite delicious, and now it tastes as if there were a bitter infusion
in it."

On the third day some maidens from the tribe of the Beni-Said,
who had encamped a short distance away on the slope of a dry
valley, came to replenish their water-skins at the well.   The sick
man begged them to fill his water-skin also, for he was too weak to
lift it up and plunge it in the well.   A young girl about fifteen
years of age, slim as a gazelle, made the chain revolve, and the
bucket came up full of water, cold and clear as crystal. The sick
man stretched out his arms in trembling anticipation of the reviving
draught, and he smiled with pleasure when the maiden gave him
her bowl painted with gay colours and brimming over with the
sparkling water.   But no sooner had he swallowed a few drops than
he made a grimace of disappointment.

" The taste is even bitterer than that of the water in the skin,"
he murmured in consternation.

The girl poured some more water into the bowl and drank it
with evident delight, tasting it slowly as she emptied the vessel.

" What do you say about bitterness? " asked she laughingly.
" Why it is fresher than the snow on the mountain's crest and
sweeter than the milk of our ewes.   It has revived me and done me
good. I have never tasted better water. Try it, girls, and see if I
am not right."

And the group of young water-seekers, before putting their re-
plenished water-skins in the net bags slung across their asses, drank
long draughts of water from the well. They laughed and jested
gaily, pretending to snatch the bowls away from one another and
spilling the water over their red and white striped tunics; their
olive-tinted shoulders, smooth as fresh green dates, gleaming in
the sun, which gilded the outline of their young bosoms and their
slim rounded arms.   Their oval black eyes shone as they played,
and they showed their teeth, like pomegranate seeds, still whiter
through the red lips refreshed by the water. Then they mounted
their donkeys, perching themselves lightly among the laden water-
skins, and set off back to their encampment laughing with the sheer
joy of life and youth.

The camel-driver was alone once more. Just as before he had
seen the dust-cloud of the caravan disappear in the distance, so
now he saw another cloud of the sandy dust gather behind the heels
of the trotting donkeys, urged on by their laughing riders to hasten
home with the water-skins, and disperse in the far distance, not of
the road—for the desert is but one immense road—but of the

illimitable sandy plain. He was consumed by fever, and in despair
he drank again. The taste of the water was still more bitter than
before.

The slow days dragged by. The sick man counted their passing
on the large beads of the rosary which, like every pious Mohamme-
dan, he wore fastened to his girdle. He could only count them thus,
for all the days were alike. Every morning the sun's rays beat
from a sky of brass; every blinding noonday was like the one that
had gone before, gorgeous in wealth of light from the intensely blue
pitiless heavens; every evening the same hot breath came reflected
from the parched sand as the sun sank behind the distant horizon,
and wild animals came from their dens and caves afar in the sandy
plain. Every night the same magnificent background of the sky,
studded with the brilliance of the Eastern stars: and never a cooling
breeze sprang from the earth or descended from the sky. From
what seemed to be a canopy of copper with a deep blue lining, the
stars looked out pitilessly, as if they were the indifferent eyes of a
sovereign grown careless of the sufferings of his creatures.

And the sick man, unable to resist the thirst which consumed
him, drank, drank ever of the water from the well, which daily grew
more bitter and repulsive to the taste; and not only daily but even
with each succeeding draught. It was as though the evil spirits, to
torment mankind, were dropping into the well bags of gall, hand-
fuls of salt, every bitter drug which could make the water unpleasant to a parched palate. There came a moment when the
camel-driver's strength failed him, when the mere sight of the
water made him tremble, and lying down beside the well he resolved
to wait for death, patient and resigned to what could not be avoided,
anxious even for the release from his long suffering.

A voice which called him, a serious and authoritative voice, made
him open his eyes. Before him stood a man of venerable appearance, with a long silver-white beard, and clad in a patched garment
denoting poverty. He leaned on a shepherd's crook, and over
his shoulder he carried the pouch which indicates the mendicant.
His visage, browned by the sun, was distinguished-looking, with
aristocratic features; and his eyes, fixed on the sick man, did not
express pity but serene meditation; the condition of a mind familiar
with the Holy Books and able to penetrate to the heart of all Life.
In his right hand the venerable stranger held the bowl, as if about
to drink from it.

" Do not drink, holy man," said the camel-driver. " It is as
bitter as wormwood. It will only harm you. I cannot bear to
drink it any more."

Without appearing to hear him, the stranger drank, but did not
show any sign either of disgust or of pleasure.

" This water," said he, after he had passed across his mouth the

back of his hand baked by the blazing sun, " is neither bitter nor
sweet. Its bitterness and its sweetness are contributed to it by the
palate which drinks of it. Whilst you have been lying here, have
you not seen others besides yourself? Have not healthy young
people come to drink the water? "

" Yes," replied the camel-driver, " some young maidens came
here, very happy and gay, to fetch water for their encampment.
And they praised the refreshing qualities of the water."

" You see now," said the venerable stranger calmly. " May the
Angel of Death take pity on you and at least permit you to be able
to drink the water of the well. I would take you with me, but my
ass is already too heavily loaded to be able to carry you out of
this plight, and I must hasten on to join some caravan, because if
I go alone the wild beasts will overtake and devour me."

And the venerable stranger went off repeating a verse of the
Koran. When his dark outline disappeared against the glowing
horizon the camel-driver felt that his last hope was gone. In an
access of fever he approached the stonework surrounding the
well, clutched it with both hands, and in his despair, but not without great efforts for his strength was not even sufficient to enable
him to seek for death, he fell head foremost into the well.

.   .   .   .

After the camel-driver had thrown himself into the Well of Life,
the water drawn from it continued to taste sweet to some and
bitter to many others. Only it must be added that when those
with discriminating palates tasted it, they made the reflection
that though it came from the Well of Life, its taste brought to their
minds an irresistible thought of death.

EMILIA PARDO BAZÁN

A PAIR OF SCISSORS

" A MARRIED couple," said Father Baltar, interposing in the most natural manner in the world in the discussion of so mundane a nature, " a married couple resembles a pair of scissors."

" A pair of scissors, Father," exclaimed one of those present in some surprise. " Do you know that your comparison is an original one? "

" More than original; it is just," declared the priest, refusing by a sign the second liqueur glass of Riga kummel. " A pair of scissors, as you know, is an instrument composed of two parts which are alike or very similar, united by an axis, and fastened together by a tiny stud of the same metal. Although each half of the pair of scissors may be fine and well tempered, still if the axis is not there the scissors cannot work. But united by this central piece they can do first-rate work, and shape the web of life to perfection."

" I agree with you there," said another of those who were listening to the priest—a man of a good deal of experience of life and rather sceptical in his ideas of human nature. " But please tell us if you really believe that there are many excellent pairs of scissors to be had? "

" What is really excellent is very rare anywhere, or at least we are so readily inclined to be dissatisfied that it appears rare to us," replied with a smile the man who was both a priest and at the same time (delightful combination!) a person of admirable education. " Although the key of marriage consists in the axis, still the quality of the two blades is of a good deal of importance. Let any of you go into a shop and ask for a pair of scissors. You will be shown a couple of dozen of them, all apparently alike, and all at the same price. It is only by taking the couple of dozen home and using them that you can find out the quality of each. Dressmakers are so well aware of this that when they find a pair of scissors which suits them exactly, they will not part with it for any consideration. I have found scissors which were truly of gold! What was their peculiar attribute? Natural affection refined by the Divine Law. I will relate to you a case which I have experienced and which moved me, although it was only an ordinary romance, and the actors in it were simple commonplace people.

" I was staying in the monastery of S—— to recover from a fever which I had caught in Tangiers, and which stuck to me like a limpet, when I happened to make the acquaintance among that of many other families of a married couple who kept a draper's shop under the colonnade of the Old Square, not far from the Cathedral. They did not come to confession to me, but to their own parish priest: however, they liked to consult me in a friendly way. Her name was Donna Consuelo and the husband's Don Andrés. As they were comfortably off and on good terms with each other, they would have been happy if they had not had a son cut out of the same piece as the wicked Barabbas, who provided them with a fresh annoyance every morning and a reason to blush for him every evening. Quarrelsome, depraved, and prodigal, neither the tears of his mother, nor the reproaches of his father, nor the exhortations which at the request of both I addressed to him from time to time, succeeded in inducing him to abandon a single one of his bad habits; and as it seemed that the young fellow was incorrigible, I advised them to send him off to some other country, where necessity and the lack of resources would oblige him to look out for himself.

" The father approved of the idea, and even the mother herself saw that it was the only thing to be done; and having found that the exile himself preferred Manilla as his place of banishment, to Manilla he was sent, with many urgent recommendations to the Rector of a monastery of our order.

" In about six months' time I began to receive good reports of the conduct of the subject of my recommendation, with praises of his abilities and of his industry; he was improving in his behaviour. When the parents heard this, they jumped for joy. It was the Rector who sent me the news which was so agreeable, because the young fellow was not much of a correspondent.

" Some time passed, until one day the Rector's letter instead of being pleasant reading conveyed terrible news. The son of Don Andrés had been stabbed to death in a quarrel when coming out of a house of ill-repute. I was asked to tell this bad news to the parents.

" It was a sad task, but we are always surrounded by sadness, and thinking that in the first moment the father would have more fortitude than the mother, I sent for Don Andrés to come to my cell, and breaking the news as gently as possible, I told him my sad tidings. He did not hesitate to understand; it seemed as though he had already guessed what was coming. As soon as I said ' wounds,' he understood ' death.' He did not weep, but the expression of his countenance was similar to that of the con-

demned man who issues from his prison door to find himself at
the foot of the scaffold. I use this comparison advisedly, because
I have attended some unfortunate wretches in this bitter experience.

" As soon as Don Andrés could breathe, he folded his hands,
saying, ' Father, I am going to ask you a great favour. Between
us both, let us manage that Consuelo does not know anything of
what has happened. A few years ago my wife was plump and
robust, but the misconduct of our son has ruined her health, and
besides, she will soon be sixty years of age. She has a very
serious internal complaint—a sort of consumption. If she heard
of this misfortune, it would kill her at once. If we can hide from
her what has happened to our child '—he called him this, although
he was more than twenty-seven years of age—' she may live for
some time yet. I will meet all the expenses which may have been
incurred over there, funeral, trial, I will freely forgive my son's
murderer—but Consuelo must not know anything of it all.'

" Did I do well or ill in agreeing? I do not know; but my
heart bled for the unhappy man. Every fortnight or three weeks I
went to the shop with fictitious letters which I was supposed to have
received from Manilla, speaking of the absent young man and
praising his progress in work, education, and good conduct.

" Donna Consuelo, who grew daily weaker in health and who
had an incessant cough and a cruel wasting debility, always roused
herself when I read these letters to her; she listened to them with
a joy which was almost childish, and called Don Andrés to share
her pleasure. ' You see, Andrés, what favours we receive from
St. Anthony,' she would exclaim, with eyes glistening with tears
called into them by joy. ' Oh, how well we are treated by Heaven.
The boy has reformed; he is behaving creditably. In a short time
he will be able to come back here and we will put him at the
head of our business. Father Baltar, I am going to give you
some money to send to him through your friends over there; you
know that young men need some. I don't want my son to be
deprived of anything.'

" And her husband, stifling his sorrow, choking down his sobs,
would say: ' All right, my dear. Give the Father these thirty
dollars, but don't agitate yourself so much. Be a sensible woman.'

" One more pathetic item. When the mother had given me a
sum of money as a present for her son, the father would secretly
request me to use the money for masses for the repose of the dead
boy's soul.

" I played my part conscientiously, for I could see that Donna
Consuelo was growing weaker in health; the shock of the news
would have been more dangerous every day. Don Andrés, either
because he feared some inadvertence on my part or because he

did not wish to leave the invalid, was always present when I went to pay a visit to the house. They always sat together like a pair of birds perched side by side on a branch, pressed close together to keep away the cold: she coughing and saying that her illness was ' nothing at all '; he livid, asthmatic, half-suffocated, but bracing himself up to jest with his wife and even to pay her compliments, a thing which in other circumstances would have seemed amusing to me, but which, as things were, seemed most pitiful to me.

" And still the little comedy of the letters went on, producing such an effect on the poor mother that I even fancied I saw her making signs to me when her husband was not looking at us, signals of approbation, of entreaty, of gratitude. I thought they meant: ' Even though the boy may not be always doing so well, go on telling Andrés that he is behaving like an angel.' I could only suppose this to be the case, because, as I said before, I was never an instant alone with Donna Consuelo.

" One evening I was called late to their house. Don Andrés came to tell me that his wife was dying or very near it, and that she had taken a fancy to make her confession to me. It was absolutely indispensable to invent a letter with the news that ' the child ' was on his way home. ' Let us try to make her last a few days longer by making her believe that,' said he, trembling so much and so anxious that I could not refuse him that last favour. As soon as I entered the sick-room of Donna Consuelo, she looked at her husband and he went out, secretly making me an expressive sign, both warning and imploring.

" I approached the invalid's bed; she was moving her lips rapidly as if she was praying. I sat at the head of the bed and addressed to her those words of hope and consolation which are as drops of balm to a thirsty soul, and with which we clergy are accustomed to smooth the passage to the grave; but to my great surprise, she turned her face to me with an expression of profound gratitude, and seizing my hand to kiss it, said to me:

" ' Father Baltar, may God reward you for all this long long time in which you have been deceiving my husband. Promise me that after I am dead you will not undeceive him.'

" ' What do you mean? Deceive him? ' I asked, thinking that her weakness and fever rendered her delirious.

" ' If it had not been for you,' she went on without listening to me, ' it would be such a misery to Andrés if he knew about " the child." Never let him know it! '

" ' About the boy,' I exclaimed, suddenly remembering my promise to Don Andrés. ' Oh, the boy is quite well, and he is coming over here—he will be able to embrace you soon! '

" ' Yes, indeed, I shall embrace him . . . in the other world.

Do not trouble about me, for I knew it all along, and even my heart told me of it. Do you think that I had not some one over there whom I asked to give me news of my son? The letters came in the name of a friend of mine, so that if there were anything unpleasant to be heard, Andrés should not know of it. And as I had already written to the Father Rector begging him only to let you have good news to tell my husband, when you came with the fictitious letters saying that the child was alive and working well . . . I helped you then to deceive poor Andrés—his health is not very good and any bad news would be so dangerous for him to hear now. It has been a terrible strain for me to keep up the pretence, Father, because in all these years that we have been married I never had a secret from him before.' "

.   .   .   .

Here the priest stopped his narrative, and looking round the company, he saw our faces animated by the most lively sympathy.

" So that both knew it and each concealed it from the other. What a drama of feeling! " exclaimed the one of us who had spoken first.

" You may well say, Father," said the cynic, " that those scissors were of pure gold, encrusted with the finest precious stones."

" I can also say that I have seen them extended in the form of a cross," replied the priest with deep meaning.

EMILIA PARDO BAZÁN

FIRST LOVE

How old was I then? Eleven or twelve years? More probably thirteen, for before then is too early to be seriously in love; but I won't venture to be certain, considering that in Southern countries the heart matures early, if that organ is to blame for such perturbations.

If I do not remember well *when*, I can at least say exactly *how* my love first revealed itself. I was very fond—as soon as my aunt had gone to church to perform her evening devotions—of slipping into her bedroom and rummaging her chest of drawers, which she kept in admirable order. Those drawers were to me a museum; in them I always came across something rare or antique, which exhaled an archaic and mysterious scent, the aroma of the sandalwood fans which perfumed her white linen.

Pincushions of satin now faded; knitted mittens, carefully wrapped in tissue paper; prints of saints; sewing materials; a reticule of blue velvet embroidered with bugles; an amber and silver rosary would appear from the corners: I used to ponder over them, and return them to their place. But one day—I remember as well as if it were to-day—in the corner of the top drawer, and lying on some collars of old lace, I saw something gold glittering. I put in my hand, unwittingly crumpled the lace, and drew out a portrait, an ivory miniature about three inches long in a frame of gold.

I was struck at first sight. A sunbeam streamed through the window and fell upon the alluring form, which seemed to wish to step out of its dark background and come towards me. It was a most lovely creature, such as I had never seen except in the dreams of my adolescence. The lady of the portrait must have been some twenty odd years: she was no simple maiden, no half-opened rosebud, but a woman in the full resplendency of her beauty. Her face was oval, but not too long; her lips were full, half-open, and smiling; her eyes cast a languishing side-glance; and she had a dimple in her chin as if formed by the tip of Cupid's playful finger.

Her head-dress was strange but elegant; a compact group of curls plastered conewise one over the other covered her temples, and a

159

basket of braided hair rose on the top of her head. This old-fashioned head-dress, which was trussed up from the nape of her neck, disclosed all the softness of her fresh young throat, on which the dimple of her chin was reduplicated more vaguely and delicately. As for the dress . . . I do not venture to consider whether our grandmothers were less modest than our wives are, or if the confessors of past times were more indulgent than those of the present; I am inclined to think the latter, for seventy years ago women prided themselves upon being Christianlike and devout, and would not have disobeyed the director of their conscience in so grave and important a matter.

What is undeniable is, that if in the present day any lady were to present herself in the garb of the lady of the portrait there would be a scandal, for from her waist (which began at her arm-pits) upwards she was only veiled by light folds of diaphanous gauze, which marked out, rather than covered, two mountains of snow, between which meandered a thread of pearls. With further lack of modesty she stretched out two rounded arms worthy of Juno, ending in finely-moulded hands . . . when I say *hands* I am not exact, for, strictly speaking, only one hand could be seen, and that held a richly embroidered handkerchief.

Even to-day I am astonished at the startling effect which the contemplation of that miniature produced upon me, and how I remained in ecstasy, scarcely breathing, devouring the portrait with my eyes. I had already seen here and there prints representing beautiful women: it often happened that in the illustrated papers, in the mythological engravings of our dining-room, or in a shop-window a beautiful face or a harmonious and graceful figure attracted my precociously artistic gaze; but the miniature encountered in my aunt's drawer, apart from its great beauty, appeared to me as if animated by a subtle and vital breath; you could see it was not the caprice of a painter, but the image of a real and actual person of flesh and blood. The warm and rich tone of the tints made you surmise that the blood was tepid beneath that mother-of-pearl skin. The lips were slightly parted to disclose the enamelled teeth; and to complete the illusion there ran round the frame a border of natural hair, chestnut in colour, wavy and silky, which had grown on the temples of the original.

As I have said, it was more than a copy, it was the reflection of a living person from whom I was only separated by a wall of glass. . . . I seized it, breathed upon it, and it seemed to me that the warmth of the mysterious deity communicated itself to my lips and circulated through my veins. At this moment I heard footsteps in the corridor. It was my aunt returning from her prayers. I heard her asthmatic cough and the dragging of her gouty feet. I had only just time to put the miniature into the drawer, shut it, and approach the window, adopting an innocent and indifferent attitude.

My aunt entered noisily, for the cold of the church had exasperated her catarrh, now chronic. Upon seeing me, her wrinkled little eyes brightened, and giving me a friendly tap with her withered hand, she asked me if I had been turning over her drawers as usual.

Then, with a chuckle: " Wait a bit, wait a bit," she added, " I have something for you, something you will like."

And she pulled out of her vast pocket a paper bag, and out of the bag three or four gum lozenges, sticking together in a cake, which gave me a feeling of nausea.

My aunt's appearance did not invite one to open one's mouth and devour these sweets: the course of years, her loss of teeth, her eyes dimmed to an unusual degree, the sprouting of a moustache or bristles on her sunken-in mouth, which was three inches wide, dull grey locks fluttering above her sallow temples, a neck flaccid and livid as the crest of the turkey when in a good temper. . . In short, I did not take the lozenges. Ugh! A feeling of indignation, a manly protest rose in me, and I said forcibly:

" I don't want it, I don't want it."

" You don't want it? What a wonder! You who are greedier than a cat! "

" I am not a little boy," I exclaimed, drawing myself up, and standing on tip-toes; " I don't care for sweets."

My aunt looked at me half good-humouredly and half ironically, and at last, giving way to the feeling of amusement I caused her, burst out laughing, by which she disfigured herself, and exposed the horrible anatomy of her jaws. She laughed so heartily that her chin and nose met, hiding her lips, and emphasising two wrinkles, or rather two deep furrows, and more than a dozen lines on her cheeks and eyelids; at the same time her head and body shook with the laughter, until at last her cough began to interrupt the bursts, and between laughing and coughing the old lady involuntarily spluttered all over my face. . . . Humiliated, and full of disgust, I escaped rapidly thence to my mother's room, where I washed myself with soap and water, and began to muse on the lady of the portrait.

And from that day and hour I could not keep my thoughts from her. As soon as my aunt went out, to slip into the room, open the drawer, bring out the miniature, and lose myself in contemplation, was the work of a minute. By dint of looking at it, I fancied that her languishing eyes, through the voluptuous veiling of her eyelashes, were fixed in mine, and that her white bosom heaved. I became ashamed to kiss her, imagining she would be annoyed at my audacity, and only pressed her to my heart or held her against my cheek. All my actions and thoughts referred to the lady; I behaved towards her with the most extraordinary refinement and super-delicacy.

Before entering my aunt's room and opening the longed-for drawer, I washed, combed my hair, and tidied myself, as I have seen since is usually done before repairing to a love appointment. I often happened to meet in the street other boys of my age, very proud of their slip of a sweetheart, who would exultingly show me love-letters, photographs, and flowers, and who asked me if I hadn't a sweetheart with whom to correspond. A feeling of inexplicable bashfulness tied my tongue, and I only replied with an enigmatic and haughty smile. And when they questioned me as to what I thought of the beauty of their little maidens, I would shrug my shoulders and disdainfully call them *ugly mugs*. One Sunday I went to play in the house of some little girl-cousins, really very pretty, and the elder of whom was not yet fifteen.

We were amusing ourselves looking into a stereoscope, when suddenly one of the little girls, the youngest, who counted twelve summers at most, secretly seized my hand, and in some confusion and blushing as red as a brazier, whispered in my ear: " Take this." At the same time I felt in the palm of my hand something soft and fresh, and saw that it was a rosebud with its green foliage.

The little girl ran away smiling and casting a side-glance at me; but I, with a Puritanism worthy of Joseph, cried out in my turn: " Take this! " And I threw the rosebud at her nose, a rebuff which made her pettish with me the whole afternoon, and which she has not pardoned me even now, though she is married and has three children.

The two or three hours which my aunt spent morning and evening together at church being too short for my admiration of the entrancing portrait, I resolved at last to keep the miniature in my pocket, and went about all day hiding myself from people just as if I had committed a crime. I fancied that the portrait from the depth of its prison of cloth could see all my actions, and I arrived at such a ridiculous extremity, that if I wanted to scratch myself, pull up my sock, or do anything else not in keeping with the idealism of my chaste love, I first drew out the miniature, put it in a safe place, and then considered myself free to do whatever I wanted.

In fact, since I had accomplished the theft, there was no limit to my vagaries; at night I hid it under the pillow, and slept in an attitude of defence; the portrait remained near the wall, I outside, and I awoke a thousand times, fearing somebody would come to bereave me of my treasure. At last I drew it from beneath the pillow and slipped it between my night-shirt and left breast, on which the following day could be seen the imprint of the chasing of the frame.

The contact of the dear miniature gave me delicious dreams. The lady of the portrait, not in effigy, but in her natural size and proportions, alive, graceful, affable, beautiful, would come towards me to conduct me to her palace by a rapid and flying train. With sweet authority she would make me sit on a stool at her feet, and would pass her beautifully moulded hand over my head, caressing my brow, my eyes, and loose curls. I read to her out of a big missal, or played the lute, and she deigned to smile, thanking me for the pleasure which my reading and songs gave her. At last romantic reminiscences overflowed in my brain, and sometimes I was a page, and sometimes a troubadour. With all these fanciful ideas, the fact is, that I began to grow thin quite perceptibly, which was observed with great disquietude by my parents and my aunt.

" In this dangerous and critical age of development, everything is alarming," said my father, who used to read books of medicine, and anxiously studied my dark eyelids, my dull eyes, my contracted and pale lips, and above all, the complete lack of appetite which had taken possession of me.

" Play, boy, eat, boy," he would say to me, and I replied to him dejectedly: " I don't feel inclined."

They began to talk of distractions, offered to take me to the theatre; stopped my studies, and gave me foaming new milk to drink. Afterwards they poured cold water over my head and back to fortify my nerves; and I noticed that my father at table or in the morning when I went to his bedroom to bid him good-morning, would gaze at me fixedly for some little time, and would sometimes pass his hand down my spine, feeling the vertebræ. I hypocritically lowered my eyes, resolved to die rather than confess my crime.

As soon as I was free from the affectionate solicitude of my family, I found myself alone with my lady of the portrait. At last, to get nearer to her, I thought I would do away with the cold crystal. I trembled upon putting this into execution; but at last my love prevailed over the vague fear with which such a profanation filled me, and with skilful cunning I succeeded in pulling away the glass and exposing the ivory plate. As I pressed my lips to the painting and could scent the slight fragrance of the border of hair, I imagined to myself even more realistically that it was a living person whom I was grasping with my trembling hands. A feeling of faintness overpowered me, and I fell unconscious on the sofa, tightly holding the miniature.

When I came to my senses I saw my father, my mother, and my aunt, all bending anxiously over me; I read their alarm in their faces: my father was feeling my pulse, shaking his head, and murmuring: " His pulse is nothing but a flutter, you can scarcely feel it."

My aunt, with her claw-like fingers, was trying to take the portrait from me, and I was mechanically hiding it and grasping it more firmly.

" But, my dear boy. . . . Let go, you are spoiling it! " she exclaimed. " Don't you see you are smudging it? I am not scolding you, my dear . . . I will show it to you as often as you like, but don't destroy it; let go, you are injuring it."

" Let him have it," begged my mother, " the boy is not well."

" Of all things to ask! " replied the old maid. " Let him have it! And who will paint another like this . . . or make me as I was then? To-day nobody paints miniatures . . . it is a thing of the past, and I also am a thing of the past, and I am not what is represented there! "

My eyes dilated with horror; my fingers released their hold on the picture. I don't know how I was able to articulate:

" You . . . the portrait . . . is you . . .? "

" Don't you think I am as pretty now, boy? Bah! one is better-looking at twenty-three than at . . . than at . . . I don't know what, for I have forgotten how old I am! " My head drooped and I almost fainted again; anyway, my father lifted me in his arms on to the bed, and made me swallow some tablespoonfuls of port.

I recovered very quickly, and never wished to enter my aunt's room again.

"CLARÍN"
(LEOPOLDO ALÁS)
1852–1905

DOCTOR PERTINAX

St. Peter was polishing the large knocker of the Gate of Heaven, leaving it as bright as the sun—which is not to be wondered at since the knocker St. Peter was cleaning *is* the sun we see appearing every morning in the east.

The holy porter, merrier than his colleagues at Madrid, was humming some little air not unlike *Ça ira* of the French.

"Hola! You get up very early," said he, bending his head and staring at a person who had stopped before the threshold of the gate.

The unknown did not reply, but bit his lips, which were thin, pale, and dry.

"No doubt," continued St. Peter, "you are the savant who was dying last night? . . . What a night you made me pass, friend! . . . I never closed my eyes once, thinking you might be likely to knock; my last orders were not to let you wait a moment, a piece of respect paid to your sort in heaven. Well, welcome, and come in; I can't leave the gate. Go through, and then straight on. . . . There is no entresol."

The stranger did not stir from the threshold, but fixed his little blue eyes on the venerable bald head of St. Peter, who had turned his back to go on rubbing up the sun.

The new-comer was thin, short, and sallow, with somewhat feminine movements, neat in his attire, and without a hair on his face. He wore his shroud elegantly and nicely adjusted, and he measured his gestures with academic severity.

After gazing for some time at St. Peter working, he wheeled round and was about to return on the journey he had come he knew not how; but he found he was standing above a gloomy abyss, in which the darkness almost seemed palpable, and a horrisonous tempest was roaring with flashes of livid light at intervals like lightning. There was not a trace of any stairs, and the machine by which he dimly remembered he had mounted was not in sight either.

"Sir," exclaimed he, in a vibrating and acrid voice; "may I

165

know what this means? Where am I? Why was I brought here? "

" Ah, you haven't gone yet; I am very glad, for I had forgotten something." And pulling his memorandum-book out of his pocket, the saint moistened the point of the pencil between his lips and asked:

" Your name? "

" I am Doctor Pertinax, author of the book stereotyped in its twentieth edition, called *Philosophia Ultima.* . . ."

St. Peter was not a quick writer, and of all this had only put down Pertinax. . . .

" Well, Pertinax of what? "

" Of what? Oh, I see, you mean from where? just as they say: Thales of Miletus, Parmenides of Elea——"

" Exactly, Quixote of la Mancha. . . ."

" Write down, Pertinax of Torrelodones. And now, may I know what this farce means? "

" This farce? "

" Yes, sir. I am the victim of a farce, this is a comedy: my enemies, my colleagues, with the help of subtle artifices and theatrical machinery, exalting my mind with some beverage, have doubtless prepared all this. But the deception is useless. My power of reasoning is above all these appearances, and protests with a mighty voice against this low trickery; neither masks nor limelights are of any avail, for I am not taken in by such palpable effrontery, and I say what I always said, and which is enframed on page 315 of my *Philosophia Ultima,* note *b.* of the sub-note Alpha, *i.e.* that after death the deception of appearances will not exist, and there will no longer be any desire for life, *nolite vivere,* which is only a chain of shadows linked with desires, etc., etc. . . . Therefore, one of the two: either I have died, or I have not died; if I have died, it cannot possibly be I as I was when alive half an hour ago, and all that I see around me, as it can only be a representation, is not, for I am not; but if I have not died, and am myself, what I was and am, it is clear that although what I see around me exists in me by representation, it is not what my enemies wish me to believe, but an unworthy farce designed to frighten me; but 'tis in vain, for . . ."

And the philosopher swore like a coal-heaver. And the swearing was not the worst, for he lifted up his voice towards Heaven, the inhabitants of which were beginning to awake at the noise, while some of the blest were already descending by the staircase of clouds, tinged some as with woad, others with a sea-blue.

Meanwhile St. Peter held his sides with both hands to keep from bursting into the laughter with which he was nearly choking. Pertinax became more irritated at the saint's laughter, and the latter had to stop to try and pacify him by the following words:

"My dear sir, farces are of no avail here, nor is it a question of deceiving you, but of bringing you to Heaven, which it appears you have merited for some good works of which I am ignorant; in any case, calm yourself and go up, for the inhabitants above are already astir, and you will find somebody who will conduct you to where all will be explained to your taste, so that not a shadow of doubt will remain, for doubts all disappear in this region, where the dullest thing is the sun which I am polishing."

"I did not say *you* are deceiving me, for you seem an honest man; the tricksters are others, and you only an instrument, unconscious of what you are doing."

"I am St. Peter. . . ."

"They have persuaded you that you are; but there's no proof that you are."

"Dear sir, I have been porter here for more than eighteen hundred years——"

"Apprehension, preconception——"

"Preconception fiddlesticks!" cried the saint, now somewhat angry; "I am St. Peter, and you are a savant, and like all that come to us, an ignorant fool, with more than one bee in your bonnet. . . ."

The gateway was now crowded with angels and cherubim, saints, male and female, and a number of the blest, who all formed a circle round the stranger and smilingly surveyed him.

.   .   .   .

From amongst them there stepped forth St. Job. "I think," said he, "that this gentleman would be convinced that he had lived in error if he could see the Universe as it actually is. Why not appoint a commission from amongst us to accompany Doctor Pertinax and show him the construction of the immense piece of architecture as Lope de Vega says, whom I am sorry not to see among us?"

Great was the respect for St. Job, and they immediately proceeded to a nominal vote, which took up a good deal of time, as more than half the martyrology had repaired to the gate. The following were by the results appointed members of the commission: St. Job, by acclamation; Diogenes, by a majority; and St. Thomas the Apostle, by a majority. St. Thomas of Aquinas and Duns Scotus had votes.

Doctor Pertinax gave way to the supplication of the commission, and consented to survey all the machinery and magic with which they might deceive his eyes, said he, but not his mind.

"My dear fellow, don't be downhearted," said St. Thomas, as he sewed some wings on to the Doctor's shoulder-blades. "Look at me, I was an unbeliever, and . . ."

"Sir," replied Pertinax, "you lived in very different times, the

world was then in its theological age as Comte said, and I have
passed through all those ages and have lived side by side with the
Critique of Pure Reason and the *Philosophia Ultima;* so that I
believe in nothing, not even in the mother who bore me; I only
believe in this, inasmuch as I know that I am, I am conscious,
but without falling into the preconception of confounding representation with essence, which is unattainable, that is to say, excepting the being conscious, putting aside all that is not myself
(and all being in myself) I *know,* by knowing that everything
is represented (and I as everything else) by simply appearing
to be what it is, and the reality of which is only investigated by
another volitive and effective representation, a harmful representation, being irrational and the original sin of the Fall; therefore, this
apparent desire undone, nothing remains to explore, since not even
the will for knowledge remains."

Only St. Job heard the last word of this discourse, and, scratching his bald crown with his potsherd, he replied:

" The truth is, you savants are the very devil for talking nonsense, and don't be offended, but those things, whether in your
head or imagination, as you please, will give you warm work to
see them in reality as they are."

" Forward! forward! " shouted Diogenes at this moment; " the
sophists denied me motion, and you know how I proved it; forward! "

And they began their flight through boundless space. Boundless?
Pertinax thought it so, and said:

" Do you expect to show me all the Universe? "

" Certainly," replied St. Thomas.

" But since the Universe—seemingly, of course—is infinite . . .
how can you conceive the limit of space? "

" Conceive it, with difficulty; but see it, easily. Aristoteles sees
it every day, for he takes the most terrible walks with his disciples,
and certainly he complained that the space for walking ended
before the disputes of his peripatetics."

" But how can space have an end? If there is a limit, it will
have to be nothing; but as nothing does not exist, it cannot form
a boundary; for a boundary is something, and something apart
from what is bounded."

St. Job, who was already growing impatient, cut him short:

" Enough, enough of conversation! but you had better bend
your head so as not to knock it, for we have arrived at that limit
of space which cannot be conceived, and if you take a step
more, you will break your head against that nothing you are
denying."

And effectually; Pertinax saw there was nothing more beyond;
wished to feel it, and bumped his head.

" But this can't be! " he exclaimed, while St. Thomas applied to the bump one of those pieces of money which pagans take with them on their journey to the other world.

There was no help for it, they had to turn back, the Universe had come to an end. But ended or not, how beautiful shone the firmament with its millions and millions of stars!

" What is that dazzling light shining above there, higher than all the constellations? Is it some nebula unknown to the astronomers of the earth? "

" A pretty nebula! " replied St. Thomas! " that is the celestial Jerusalem, from which we have just descended, and what is shining so are the diamond walls round the city of God."

" So that those marvels related by Chateaubriand, and which I thought unworthy of a serious man—? "

" Are perfectly true, my friend. And now let us go and rest on that star passing below there, for i' faith I am tired of so much going backwards and forwards."

"Gentlemen, I am not presentable," said Pertinax; " I have not yet doffed my shroud, and the inhabitants of this star will laugh at such indecorous garb. . . ."

The three Ciceroni of Heaven all burst out laughing together. Diogenes was the first to exclaim:

" Though I should lend you my lantern, you would not meet a living soul in that star, nor in any other star."

" Of course," added Job, very seriously, " there are no inhabitants except on the Earth; don't talk such nonsense."

" This I cannot believe! "

" Well, let us go and show him," said St. Thomas, who was already growing angry. And they journeyed from star to star, and in a few minutes had traversed all the Milky Way and the most distant starry systems. Nothing, not a sign of life. They did not even encounter a flea, for all the numerous globes they surveyed. Pertinax was horrified.

" This is the Creation! " he exclaimed; " what solitude! Come, show me the Earth; I want to see that privileged region; by what I conjecture, all modern cosmography is a lie, the Earth is still, and the centre of all the celestial vault; and round her revolve the suns and planets, and she is the largest of all the spheres——"

" Not at all," replied St. Thomas; " astronomy is not mistaken; the earth revolves round the sun, and you will soon see how insignificant she appears. Let us see if we can find her amongst all that crowd of stars. *You* look for her, St. Job; *you* have plenty of patience."

" I will! " exclaimed the Saint of the potsherd, as he hooked his spectacles round his ears.

" It is like looking for a needle in a bottle of hay! . . . I see

her! there she goes! look! look how small! she looks like a
microbe! ''

Pertinax looked at the Earth and sighed.

" And are there no inhabitants except on that mote? ''

" Nowhere else.''

" And the rest of the Universe is empty? ''

" Empty.''

" Then of what use are such millions and millions of stars? ''

" As lamps. They are the public illumination of the Earth. And
they are also useful for singing praises to the Almighty. And they
serve as eke-outs in poetry, and you can't deny they are very
pretty.''

" But all empty? ''

" Every one! ''

Pertinax remained in the air for a good time sad and thoughtful.
He felt ill. The edifice of his *Philosophia Ultima* was threatening
ruin. Upon seeing that the Universe was so different from what
reason demanded, he began to believe in the Universe. That
brusque lesson of reality was the rude and cold contact with
material which his spirit needed in order to believe. " It is all
so badly arranged, but perhaps it is true! '' thus thought the
philosopher. Suddenly he turned to his companions, and asked
them, " Does Hell exist? ''

The three sighed, made gestures of compassion, and replied:

" Yes, it exists.''

" And condemnation is eternal? ''

" Eternal.''

" A solemn injustice? ''

" A terrible reality! '' replied the three in chorus.

Pertinax wiped his brow with his shroud. He was perspiring
philosophy. He began to believe that he was in the other world.
The injustice of everything convinced him. " Then the cosmogony
and the theogony of my infancy was the truth? ''

" Yes; the first and only philosophy.''

" Then I am not dreaming? ''

" No.''

" Confession! confession! '' groaned the philosopher; and he
swooned into the arms of Diogenes.

When he awoke, he found himself in his bed. His old servant
and the priest were by his side.

" Here is the confessor, sir, for whom you asked . . .''

Pertinax sat up, stretched out both his hands, and looking at
the confessor with frightened eyes, cried:

" I say and repeat, that all is pure representation, and that I am
the victim of an unworthy farce.'' And he expired really.

"CLARÍN"
(LEOPOLDO ALÁS)

MY BURIAL
THE DISCOURSE OF A MADMAN

ONE night I played chess longer than prudence dictates, with my friend Roque Tuyo in the café San Benito. When I started home all the street lamps were out except the guide lights. It was spring-time, approaching June. The weather was warm, and the mind rather than the body was refreshed by the pleasant splash of the water as it rushed freely from the hydrants, turning the pavements into rivers. I arrived home with my feet soaking wet. My head was like a furnace, and wet feet might do me much harm; I might go mad, for instance. What with chess and the damp I was suffering greatly. To begin with, the policemen who slept at the corner with folded arms, leaning against the coach-house door of some mansion, seemed to me like *black castles*. So much so, that on passing near San Ginés one of the policemen stepped off the pavement to let me pass, and I, instead of saying " thank you," exclaimed, " I castle the king," and walked on. On reaching my house I saw that the balcony of my room was open and from it came a glare as of wax torches. I rapped on the door the regulation three knocks. A harsh voice, as though its owner was half asleep, asked, " Who is it? " " Black King! " I answered, but no one opened. " Check! " I cried three times in one minute, but nobody opened. I called to the night watchman, who was coming from pavement to pavement opening doors and leaving his squares at every move. " Here! " I said, when I could have taken him with my pawn. " Not even if you're a knight; what a way of taking you have! " " It is you who are the horse and the sweep, you ought to be ashamed. . . . And don't make so much noise, for some one is dead on the third floor and is lying in state." " A victim of the damp! " said I compassionately, with my own boots full of water.

" Yes, sir, a victim of the damp; they say he died in a drinking bout; he had all the vices, but gave good tips; well, his widow will get over it, for she is still young and good-looking, and everything can now be done openly and according to the law instead of in the dark." "And what do you know about it, gossip?" "Don't you call people names, young man; I am the watchman and so far have kept as silent as the night, but now the dog is dead. . . . I will say what I like!" shouted that Pyrenean bear, and he lurched off to open another door. A servant came down to let me in. It was Perico, my faithful Perico. "What a time you have been, you idiot!" "Hush! Do not shout, the master is dead." "Whose master?" "My master." "What from?" "He had a stroke, I think. He got his feet wet after playing chess with Sr. Roque . . . and naturally, it happened as Don Clemente told the mistress, ' Don't worry, your brute of a husband will remove himself some day.' " "Look here, if your master is dead, who am I?" "Well, you're the man sent to lay him out, as Don Clemente said he would send some one at this hour, so as not to attract attention. . . . Come up, come up." I reached my room. In the middle of the floor there was a bed surrounded by large candles, as are the coffins of the guests in *Lucrezia Borgia*. The balcony window was open. Stretched out on the bed was a corpse. I looked. Yes, it was I. I was wearing a shirt, no pants, and a pair of socks. I started to dress myself—to lay myself out, I mean. I took out my frock-coat, the one I wore for the first time at the meeting of the Price Club, when Martos made that remark about " traitors like Sagasta," and the late Mata spoke of the tub of the Danaides! I never knew what tub that was. Well, I wanted to change my socks, because the damp was very annoying, and also because I wanted to be clean for the cemetery. Impossible! They had stuck to the skin. Those socks were like the garment of I don't remember whom, but instead of burning, they wetted. That sensation of dampness was sometimes cold and sometimes hot. At times I thought my feet were on my neck, and my ears were setting me on fire. . . . Lastly I dressed in mourning as became a dead man attending the funeral of his best friend. One of the wax candles bent over and drops of burning liquid began to fall on my nose. Perico, who was there alone, because the man who laid me out had disappeared, Perico was asleep on a chair near by. He woke up and saw the havoc the wax was making on my face; he attempted to straighten the candle without getting up, but his hand could not reach the candlestick . . . and yawning, he went off to sleep again peacefully. The cat came in, jumped on my bed and curling himself up went to sleep on my feet. So we passed the night.

At dawn the cold in my feet became more intense. I dreamt that one of them was the Mississippi and the other a very large river in North Asia, but I could not remember its name. What torment I suffered trying to remember the name of that foot of mine! When daylight came through the crevices, to mingle with the yellow light of the candles, Perico woke up; he opened his mouth, yawned loudly, and bringing out a big green purse, began to count out money on the death-bed. A large black fly alighted on my nose still covered with wax. Perico looked absent-mindedly at the fly while he counted on his fingers, but made no move to free me from the annoyance. My wife came into the room about seven o'clock. She had already put on black clothes, just as actors put on mourning in readiness for something sad to happen in the third act. Her face was pale, repentant, but the expression of pain seemed to be more a sign of bad temper than anything else. Those wrinkles and contortions of pain seemed tied by an invisible cord. And such in fact was the case! The will, dominating the muscles, held them drawn by force. . . . In the presence of my wife I felt an extraordinary faculty of my consciousness as a dead man; my thoughts communicated direct with external thoughts; through the body I saw the innermost soul. I had not noticed this miraculous faculty before, as Perico was my only companion, and Perico had no thoughts in which I could read anything. " Go away," said my wife to the servant; and kneeling down at my feet remained alone with me. Her face cleared suddenly; the signs of the vigil remained, but not of the pain. And she prayed mentally after this style: " Our Father (what a time the other is taking!) which art in Heaven (Is there another life and can *he* see me from up there?), hallowed (I will buy cheap mourning as I don't want to spend much on black clothes) be Thy name (The funeral is going to cost me a lot unless his friends undertake it), Thy kingdom come (And if I marry the other, I will do as I like without interference from any one) on earth as in Heaven (I wonder if this creature is in Purgatory?) . . ."

At eight o'clock another personage arrived, Clemente Cerrojos, member of our political committee for the district of Latina. Cerrojos had been my friend politically and privately, although I did not know he was so interested in my affairs as he was. He used to play chess. but finding that he cheated, and moved the pieces surreptitiously, I broke off with him, as a player, and sought a nobler adversary in the café. Clemente remained in my house every evening as company for my wife. He was dressed in that shopkeeper style which consists of a large ample frock-coat of smooth shiny black cloth, and trousers, waistcoat, and tie of the same colour. Clemente Cerrojos squinted with the right eye; the pupil of that eye glistened motionless, without expression, just like a stud one sees on trunks and doors. My wife did not raise her head. Cerrojos sat down on the death-bed, making it creak from head to foot. For five minutes there was silence. But, oh! I saw their thoughts. My wife suddenly thought how horrible it would be to kiss that man or be kissed by him there, before my supposed corpse. Cerrojos thought the same. I could not move; but he imagined I had. He leant over and looked into my eyes, open like frameless windows, and started back. Then he came and closed the loopholes through which my poor corpse was menacing him. People began to arrive.

They carried the coffin to the porch and there left me near the door, one leaf of which was closed. Part of the coffin, the foot, became wet with the fine rain that was falling; always the damp! I saw, that is, I felt by the supernatural means at my disposal, that the mourners were descending. They filled the porch, which was large. All were dressed in black; some wore frock-coats of the previous century. The whole of the district committee was there and many of the rank and file of the party, those who only appear when the hat is passed round for any calamity to some political friend and the subscription lists are published. Among them I saw my barman, who was anxious to devote a tear and a melancholy thought to the memory of the deceased; but his frock-coat was giving him trouble, its skirts got between his legs, and as to his tie it was tickling and choking him; and so he did not think of me for a single moment. The procession lined up. They put me in the hearse and the people started getting into the carriages. There were two sections, one for the family, which, as I had no relatives, was represented by my friends, those to whom my house was open; Clemente Cerrojos presided, on his right was Roque Tuyo, on his left my landlord, who used to come into the house to see if we ill-treated his property. The other section was political. In the centre was Mateo Gomez, an upright, consistent man, who professed this dogma: " My friends are the members of my party." And he swore that Madoz had robbed him of that famous phrase: " I will follow my party even in its errors." One of the titles to glory of Don Mateo was that not a single political friend had died without his attendance at the funeral. Don Mateo esteemed me, but to tell the truth, whilst he walked along to my final abode—an expression he thought of using in the speech it was his turn to make —he kept changing from one colour to another; something mysterious was happening in his throat, and inwardly he was cursing the day I was born and still more the day I died. I was penetrating Don Mateo's thoughts from my hearse, thanks to the double sight already mentioned. The good patrician had, in fact, learnt his speech by heart: it was more or less the funeral oration, as published in the papers, of a certain politician much more famous than myself, delivered by a celebrated orator of our party. But the good Gomez had forgotten more, much more than half the flowery harangue, and hence the difficulties. Whilst his companions in the procession talked with great peace of mind about the vicissitudes of the grain market, to which both devoted their time, Don Mateo endeavoured in vain to rebuild the ruined structure of his prepared speech. Finally, he saw it would be necessary to improvise, since he could not rely on his memory. " The best way for me to get ideas," thought he, " would be to feel truly sorry with all my heart at the death of Ronzuelos " (my name). And he endeavoured to feel sad, but in vain; in spite of his compunctious face, he did not care a fig for the death of Ronzuelos (Don Agapito), that is, my death.

" It is a loss, a real loss," he said aloud so that the others could help him to lament my disappearance from the great book of the living, as Perez Escrich says. " A great loss! " he repeated.

" Yes, but the grain was damaged, and it was lucky he could sell it in that condition," replied one of the people in that section.

" What do you mean by selling? Ronzuelos was incapable . . . he was most upright . . . yes, most upright."

" But, man, who mentiond Ronzuelos? We are talking of the grain sold by Perez Pinto. . . ."

" Well I am talking of the deceased."

" Ah, yes. He was a character."

" Just so, a character, and that is what we want in this country, without——"

" Without *characters*," added another, finishing the phrase and accenting the word on the penultimate syllable.

. . . .

Don Mateo doubted whether *characters* could be so accented or not, but after that he knew what to expect.

We reached the cemetery. Then the mourners, for the first time, remembered me. Round the coffin stood the party which Don Mateo followed even in its errors. There was a silence which I will not call solemn, because it was not. All present awaited with spiteful curiosity the speech Gomez was to make. " He is a fool, you will see," said some. " He cannot speak, but he is a strong man." " And that is what we need," interrupted another. " Fewer words and more deeds is what the country wants."

" Yes! . . . Yes! . . . Yes! . . ." said many. " Y-e-e-s! . . ." repeated the echo in the distance.

" Gentlemen," exclaimed Don Mateo, after coughing twice and unbuttoning and buttoning a glove. " Gentlemen, another champion has fallen, struck as though by lightning (he did not know I had been killed by the damp) in the struggle of progress with obscurantism. Model of citizens, of husbands, and of liberals, among his virtues shone like a star the great virtue of consistency. Upright as few are, his heart was an open book. Model of citizens, of husbands, and of liberals . . ." Don Mateo suddenly remem-

bered he had said this already; he became agitated, felt all thought
and memory sink in a hole darker than the tomb which was to
swallow me, and in that instant envied me; he would have changed
places with the corpse. The cemetery began to revolve, the mauso-
leums danced and the earth sank. I, lying in state, in view of all,
had to make a great effort to keep from laughing and preserve
the gravity proper to the corpse in such a funereal ceremony.
Once more reigned the silence of the tombs. Don Mateo
sought the rebel word, the people kept silent, with a
silence that equalled a storm of hisses; the only sounds were
the spluttering of the candles and the rustling of the wind in the
cypress trees. Don Mateo, while searching for the thread, cursed
his luck, cursed the deceased, the party, and the rotten habit of
speaking, which leads to nothing, for the country wants deeds.
" Of what use to me is my life of sacrifice on the altars of liberty? "
thought he; " because I am no Cicero, I am now ridiculous in the
eyes of many less consistent and less patriotic than myself." At
last he succeeded in finding what he called the thread of his discourse, and continued: " Ah, gentlemen, Ronzuelos, Agapito Ronzuelos was a martyr to the idea (to the damp, my dear sir, to the
damp), to the holy idea, to the pure idea, to the idea of progress,
of undefined progress! He was not a wordy man—I mean, he
was not an orator, for in this unhappy country we have too many
orators, we need character, deeds, and great consistency." There
was a murmur of approval and Don Mateo took advantage of it to
finish his speech. The cortège broke up. Then they talked of me a
little, in order to criticise the funeral oration of the president of the
committee.

" The truth is," said one, striking a match on the lid of my
coffin, " the fact is that Don Mateo has said nothing but common-
places."

" Obviously, man," said another, " the usual thing; besides,
poor Ronzuelos was a good fellow and nothing more. Fancy him
having character! "

" Or consistency."

" He was a great chess player, nothing more."

" On that point much could be said," remarked a third. " He
won because he cheated. He kept the chessmen in his pocket."

The one who said this was Roque Tuyo, my rival, the scoundrel
who castled after moving his king!

I could not restrain myself. " You lie! " I shouted, jumping
from the coffin. But I saw no one; they had all disappeared.
Night was coming on; the moon was rising behind the walls of the
cemetery. The cypress trees bent their pointed tops in melancholy
sway, the wind moaned through the branches, as the people did
when Don Mateo stopped a while ago. A grave-digger arrived.

" What are you doing there? " he asked me, rather frightened.
" I am the deceased," I replied. " Yes, the deceased, do not be
afraid. Listen! I will rent this niche; I will pay to live in it more
than if a dead man occupied it. I do not want to return to the city
of the living. . . . My wife, Perico, Clemente, the party, Don
Mateo . . . and especially Roque Tuyo, disgust me." The grave-
digger said Amen! to it all. It was settled that the cemetery should
be my inn, that niche my bedroom. But, ah! the grave-digger was
a man also. He sold me. The following day they came to fetch
me. Clemente, Perico, my wife, and a commission from the bosom
of my party, with Don Mateo at its head or at its heels. I resisted
to the best of my ability, defending myself with a thigh-bone; but
numbers conquered; they seized me, dressed me in the clothes of a
white pawn, stood me in on a black check, and here I am, where
no one can move me, threatened by a knight that does not take me
and only bores holes in me with his lance. And my feet are soaked,
as though I were rice.

ARMANDO PALACIO VALDÉS

B. 1853

THE BIRD IN THE SNOW

HE was born blind. They taught him the only thing the blind usually learn, music; and in this art he excelled. His mother had died a few years after his birth; his father, a musician in a regimental band, only a year ago. He had a brother in América who never wrote home: nevertheless, he heard indirectly that he was married, had two children, and was in a good position. The father, indignant at the ingratitude of his son, would not hear his name mentioned; but the blind boy still had a great affection for him. He could not forget that this brother, older than himself, had helped him in his childhood, had defended him against the attacks of big boys, and had always spoken to him kindly. The voice of Santiago, as he came to his room in the morning, saying, "Hello, Juanito! Jump up, man, you sleep too long," rang in his ear more pleasantly than the notes of the piano and the strings of the violin. How could such a good heart have turned hard? Juan could not believe it, and tried to find a million excuses for him. At times he blamed the post; at others he imagined that his brother did not want to write until he could send a large sum of money; or again, he imagined that he would give them a surprise some day by appearing loaded with millions at the modest flat they occupied; but none of these thoughts he ventured to tell his father. Only when the latter, in exasperation, declaimed bitterly against his absent son, would he venture to say, "Do not despair, father, Santiago is good; my heart tells me that he will write one of these days."

His father died without ever seeing a letter from his elder son, attended by a priest, who exhorted him, and the poor blind son who clutched his hand convulsively as though trying by force to keep him in this world. When they wanted to carry the body from the house Juan fought frantically, terribly, with the undertakers. Finally he was left alone; but what a loneliness! Without father, mother, relations, or friends: he was even without the sun, the friend of all created beings. For two days he remained in his room, walking up and down like a caged wolf, without touching food.

178

The servant, with the help of a kindly neighbour, finally succeeded in preventing the suicide. He consented to eat again, and thenceforth passed his time in prayer or playing the piano.

His father, some time before his death, had obtained for him the position of organist at a church in Madrid, for which he was paid three pesetas a day. It was not sufficient, naturally, to keep up a house, however modest; and so, after a fortnight, our blind friend sold, for very little, the modest furniture of his home, dismissed the servant, and went into lodgings, paying two pesetas. The money left over was sufficient for his other wants. For some months he lived without going out except to his work; from the house to the church, and from the church to the house. Sorrow so overwhelmed him that he hardly opened his lips. He spent his time composing a great Requiem Mass which he thought the parish priest would let him play for the soul of his dead father. And although it cannot be said that he had all five senses in his work, since one was wanting, we can say that he devoted his life and soul to it.

A change of Government surprised him before he had finished it. I do not know whether the Radicals came in, or the Conservatives, or the Constitutionalists; but some one new came in. Juan only heard of it too late and then to his cost. The new cabinet, after a few days, decided that Juan as an organist was dangerous to the public safety, and that from high up in the choir-loft, at Vespers and High Mass, roaring and humming on all organ stops, he was making a really scandalous opposition to it. As the new ministry was not disposed, so it had affirmed in congress, through one of its most prominent members, '' to tolerate the dictation of any one,'' they at once proceeded with commendable energy to dismiss Juan and find a substitute who in his musical evolutions offered more guarantees and was more in favour of the institutions. When they gave him notice, our blind friend did not experience any greater emotion than surprise; in his heart he was almost glad, as it left him more spare time to finish his Mass. He only realised his position when at the end of the month the landlady came to his room and asked for money. He had not got it, because he no longer earned it at the church; he had to pawn his father's watch to pay her. Then he was quite happy and went on working without worrying about the future. But again the landlady came for money, and again he had to pawn something from his very meagre paternal inheritance; it was a diamond ring. In the end he had nothing left to pawn. Then, in consideration for his affliction, they kept him a few days out of courtesy, but very few, and then they turned him into the street, satisfied with themselves for letting him take his trunk and clothes, the value of which would have paid for the few reales still owing.

He went to another house but could not hire a piano, and this

caused him immense sorrow; he would be unable to finish his Mass.
But for some time he went to the house of a friendly grocer and
played the piano occasionally. Before long, however, he noticed
they were less friendly every time he went there and he gave up
his visits.

They soon turned him out of the new house, but this time keeping his trunk. Then began for the blind man a period of such
misery and anguish that few can have any idea of the sorrows, or
rather of the martyrdom, which fate inflicted on him. Without
friends, without clothes, without money, there is no doubt that one
is very badly off in this world; but if to this we add blindness and
consequently absolute helplessness we can hardly see the limit of
his suffering and misery. From inn to inn, thrown out of each
soon after entering, going to bed in order that his only shirt could
be washed, his boots split, his trousers frayed, his hair uncut, and
his face unshaved, Juan wandered round Madrid for I do not know
how long. He tried to obtain through an innkeeper, more com-
passionate than the rest, the post of pianist in a café, and in the
end they gave it to him, but he was dismissed in a few days. Juan's
music did not please the habitués of the Café de la Cebada. He
did not play *jotas*, *polos*, *sevillanas*, nor anything Andalusian, not
even polkas; he spent the night interpreting Beethoven's sonatas
and Chopin's concertos. The customers were in despair, for they
could not beat time with their spoons.

Once again he went wandering in the poorest parts of the city.
A charitable soul, hearing casually of his condition, helped him indirectly, because Juan shrank from the idea of begging. He ate
just enough to keep himself from dying of starvation in some tavern
in the low quarters, and for fifteen centimes slept among beggars
and thieves in a garret kept for this purpose. On one occasion
whilst he slept they stole his trousers and left him a patched pair
made of drill. It was in November.

Poor Juan, who had always kept in mind the chimera of his
brother's return, now overwhelmed with misfortune, began to
nourish it with fervour. He asked some one to write to Havana,
although no address could be put on the letter as none was known;
he endeavoured to find out if he had been seen, but without result;
and everyday he spent some time on his knees praying for him to
be sent to his help. The only happy moments of this unhappy
youth were those passed in prayer in the corner of some deserted
church. Hidden behind a pillar, breathing the acrid odours of the
wax and the damp, listening to the spluttering of the tapers and the
faint sound of the prayers of the few faithful dotted about the
church, his innocent soul left this world that was so cruelly ill-
treating him and flew to commune with God and His Holy Mother.
Devotion to the Virgin had been deeply fixed in his heart since his

childhood. As he had hardly known his mother, he sought instinctively from the Mother of God the tender and loving protection which only a woman can give to a child: he had composed in her honour some hymns and prayers, and he never went to sleep without touching with his lips the scapular he wore round his neck.

But a day came, however, when heaven and earth deserted him. Refused on all sides, without a piece of bread to put into his mouth, without clothes to keep out the cold, our unfortunate friend saw with terror that the time for begging was close at hand. A desperate struggle took place in the depths of his soul. Pain and shame fought hand to hand with necessity: the darkness surrounding him increased the anguish of this battle. In the end, as was to be expected, hunger triumphed. After passing many hours sobbing, and praying God for strength to bear his misfortune, he resolved to appeal to charity; but yet the unhappy man wanted to mask his humiliation, and decided to sing in the streets at night-time only. He possessed a fair voice, and knew how to sing well; but he was faced with the difficulty of having no instrument on which to accompany himself. Finally, another miserable wretch, slightly better off than himself, let him have a damaged old guitar, and after mending it as best he could and shedding copious tears, he went out on a December night into the street. His heart beat violently; his legs shook. When he tried to sing in one of the main streets he could not; pain and shame brought a lump to his throat. He leant against the wall of a house, rested for a few moments, and when he felt better, began singing the romance of the first act of *La Favorita*. The attention of the passers-by was at once attracted to a blind man who was not singing *peteneras* or *malagueñas*, and many formed a circle round him, and not a few, on seeing how he mastered the difficulties of the work, murmured their surprise and dropped a few coppers into the hat, which was hanging from his arm. When the romance was finished he began the solo in the fourth act of *L'Africaine*. But too many people had collected round him and the authorities feared that this would create disorder, for it was recognised by the guardians of the peace that persons who gather in the streets to listen to a blind man show by so doing dangerous instincts of rebellion and hostility to the institutions, an attitude, in fine, incompatible with public order and the safety of the State. Therefore a policeman seized Juan roughly by the arm and said to him:

" Here, go home at once, and don't stop on the way."

" But I am not harming any one."

" You are obstructing the footway; move on, move on, if you don't want to be locked up."

It is really consoling to see with what care the governing authorities try to keep the public streets always free from singing beggars.

And I believe, in spite of opinions to the contrary, that if they could keep them equally free from thieves and murderers, they would be heartily glad to do so.

Poor Juan retired to his pig-sty very distressed, because he was good at heart, at having for an instant endangered internal peace and caused the intervention of the executive power. He had earned five reales and ten centimes. With that money he bought food the next day, and paid for the use of the miserable straw mattress on which he slept. At night-time he again went out and sang selections from operas and songs. Again people collected round him and again the authorities intervened, shouting roughly:

" Move on, move."

But if he moved on he did not earn a sou, because the passers-by could not hear him! Nevertheless Juan walked on and on, because he shrank, more than from death itself, from the idea of breaking the commands of the authorities, and disturbing, even for a moment, the peace of his country.

Every night his earnings grew less. On the one hand the necessity of always moving on, and on the other, the absence of novelty, which costs one very dear in Spain, were depriving him every day of a few centimes. What he took home was hardly enough to keep him from dying of hunger. His position was now desperate. Only one bright spot did the poor fellow still see in the blackness of his distressing situation. This bright spot was the return of his brother Santiago. Every night on leaving the house with the guitar swinging from his neck the same thought occurred to him: " If Santiago were in Madrid and heard me sing he would recognise my voice." And this hope, or rather this chimera, was the only thing that gave him strength to bear his burden.

Another day came, however, when his anguish and pain knew no bounds. The previous evening he had not earned more than twenty centimes. It had been so cold! For Madrid had awakened under a blanket of snow four inches thick. And all the day it snowed incessantly, which did not trouble most people, and was a source of joy to many admirers of the æsthetic. In particular, poets enjoying comfortable positions spent the greater part of the day watching through their windows the flakes as they fell, and thinking out pretty and ingenious similes such as make the audience in the theatre shout, " Bravo! bravo! " or make one exclaim, on reading them in a book of verses, " What a clever young man this is! "

Juan had not taken more than a cup of bad coffee and a roll of bread. He could not satisfy his hunger by contemplating the beauty of the snow, firstly, because he could not see; and secondly, even were he not blind, it was difficult to see it through the dirty window in his garret. He spent the day doubled up on the mattress, thinking of the days of his childhood and mentally fondling the idea of his brother's return. When night came on, driven by necessity, fainting, he went down into the street to implore alms. He had no guitar now; he had sold it for three pesetas on a previous occasion of great need.

The snow fell with the same steadiness, we may say with the same cruelty. The legs of the poor blind man trembled as they did on the first day he went out to sing, but this time not with shame but with hunger. He passed along the streets as best he could with the mud above his ankles. His ears told him that few pedestrians were about; the carriages made no sound, and he was nearly knocked down by one. In one of the central streets he at last began to sing the first selection of opera that came to his lips. His voice issued from his throat, weak and hoarse; no one approached him even out of curiosity. " Let us try elsewhere," he muttered, and went along the Carrera de San Jerónimo, walking slowly through the snow, covered already by a white layer and with his feet splashing in the wet. The cold was getting into his bones; hunger gave him a sharp pain in his stomach. There came a moment when the cold and pain were so intense that he felt himself swooning; he thought he was dying, and lifting his thoughts to the Virgin, his protectress, he exclaimed in a strangled voice, " Mother, help me! " and after pronouncing these words he felt a little better and walked, or rather dragged himself, to the square of Las Cortes. There he leant against a lamp-post, and still thinking of the help of the Virgin, began to sing Gounod's " Ave Maria," of which he had always been very fond. But still no one approached. The townspeople were all gathered in the cafés and theatres, or else in their homes amusing their children by the fireside. The snow continued falling slowly and heavily, determined to provide the newspaper reporters next day with something to tell their readers in a dozen pretty phrases. The pedestrians who casually passed him did so hastily, muffled in their capes and hidden under their umbrellas. The street lamps had put on their white night-caps and gave out a melancholy light. Not a sound was heard but the vague and distant murmur of the traffic, and the ceaseless fall of the snowflakes like a light and prolonged rustling of silk. Only the voice of Juan quavered in the silence of the night saluting the Mother of Outcasts. At times his song seemed more like a cry of anguish than a hymn of salutation; at others, a sad and resigned moan which froze the heart more than the cold of the snow. In vain did the blind man cry to Heaven for help; in vain did he repeat the sweet name of Mary numberless times, suiting it to the different tones of the melody. Seemingly, Heaven and the Virgin were far off and did not hear him: the neighbours in the square were near, but they did not want to hear him. No one came out to take him in; no balcony window was opened even to throw him a copper. The passers-by, as though pursued closely by pneumonia, did not dare to stop.

Finally he could sing no more: his voice died in his throat; his legs were giving way under him and his hands becoming numbed. He took a few steps and sat down on the pavement at the foot of the railing round a garden. He rested his elbows on his knees and sunk his head between his hands. He thought vaguely that the last moments of his life had come; and he again started praying feverishly, imploring divine mercy.

After a time he thought he noticed that a passer-by stopped in front of him and he felt himself seized by the arm. He raised his head, and suspecting that it would be the usual, asked timidly:

" Are you a policeman? "

" I am not a policeman," replied the man, " but come, get up! "

" I am afraid I can't, sir."

" Are you very cold, then? "

" Yes, sir . . . and besides I have had nothing to eat to-day."

" Well, I will help you. . . . Come on . . . up! "

The gentleman caught Juan by the arms and put him on his feet: he was a strong man.

" Now lean on me and we will try to find a cab."

" But where are you taking me? "

' Not to any bad place; are you afraid? "

" Oh no, my heart tells me that you are a kind person."

" Come along . . . let us get home quickly so that you can dry your clothes and have something hot."

" God will repay you, sir . . . the Virgin will repay you. . . . I thought I was going to die there."

" Nonsense . . . don't talk about that now. . . . The thing is to find a cab quickly. . . . Come along. . . . What is the matter? Did you stumble? "

" Yes, sir; I think my foot struck a lamp-post . . . you see I am blind! "

" Blind! " asked the unknown sharply.

" Yes, sir."

" Since when? "

" Since I was born."

Juan felt the arm of his protector tremble; and they went on walking in silence. Finally the man stopped a moment and asked him in a changed voice:

" What is your name? "

" Juan."

" Juan what? "

" Juan Martinez."

" And your father's name was Manuel, eh? Bandsman in the third artillery? "

" Yes, sir."

At the same instant the blind man felt himself seized vigorously by two strong arms that nearly crushed him, and in his ear he heard a shaking voice exclaim:

" Thank God! I've found you! How awful! . . . how wonderful! Oh! what a blackguard I am; I am your brother Santiago."

And the two brothers sobbed in each other's arms for several minutes in the middle of the street. The snow was falling on them gently.

Santiago suddenly freed himself from his brother's arms and began to shout angrily:

" A cab, a cab! Isn't there a cab over there? . . . Curse my luck! Come along, Juanillo, make an effort; we shall soon be there. . . . But, where have the cabs got to? . . . Not a single one about. . . . There is one in the distance. . . . Thank God! . . . The idiot is going away! Here is another . . . this is ours. Here, driver, . . . five dollars if you fly like the wind to No. 10 Castellana. . . ."

And lifting his brother in his arms as though he were a child, he put him into the cab and got in after him. The driver started the horses and the cab sped quickly and noiselessly over the snow. As they drove along, Santiago, still tightly holding the blind man, rapidly told him his story. He had not been in Cuba but in Costa Rica, where he made a respectable fortune; but he had lived many years in the country with scarcely any communication with Europe. He wrote three or four times by the boats trading with England, but obtained no reply. And always intending to return to Spain in the following year, he ceased making inquiries, planning to give them an agreeable surprise. Then he married, and this event considerably delayed his return. But for four months he had been in Madrid, where he learned from the parish register that his father was dead. Of Juan they gave him vague and contradictory information: some said that he also had died; others, that reduced to utter poverty, he had started wandering through the country singing and playing the guitar. All efforts to discover his whereabouts were fruitless. Fortunately, Providence guided his steps. Santiago laughed and cried alternately, always showing the frank, generous, and jovial spirit of his boyhood.

The cab stopped at last. A servant came out to open the door. They practically carried Juan into the house. On entering he noticed a warm temperature, the aroma of comfort that pervades wealth; his feet sank in soft carpets. Under Santiago's directions, two servants immediately removed his sodden rags and dressed him in clean warm clothes. At once, in the study itself, where a pleasant fire was burning, they brought him a basin of comforting soup and then meat of different kinds, to which they helped him with due discretion considering his weak state. They also brought up from the cellars the most matured and exquisite wines. Santiago kept moving about, giving the necessary orders, every moment asking the blind man anxiously:

" How do you feel now, Juan? Are you better? Do you want some more wine? Are you warm enough? "

When the supper was finished they both remained by the fire for a few minutes. Santiago asked a servant if his wife and the children had retired, and receiving an affirmative reply, said to his brother excitedly:

" Don't you play the piano? "

" Yes."

" Well, come and give my wife and the children a fright. Come into the drawing-room."

And he led him in and sat him down before the piano. Then he raised the lid to increase the sound, carefully opened all the doors and arranged everything so as to give the family a surprise; but doing so with such care, walking on tip-toe, speaking in a comical voice, and generally behaving so funnily that Juan on noticing it could not help laughing and exclaiming:

" Just the same Santiago! "

" Now play, Juanillo, play as hard as you can."

The blind man began to play a warlike march. The silent house suddenly shook like a musical-box when it is wound up. The notes tumbled over each other as they left the piano, but always in bellicose rhythm. Santiago exclaimed from time to time:

" Harder, Juanillo, harder! "

And the blind man went on striking the keyboard with increasing vigour.

" I can see my wife behind the curtains. . . . Go on, Juanillo, go on! . . . The poor girl is in her night-dress . . . he . . . he . . . I am pretending not to see her. . . . She will think I am mad . . . he, he. . . . Go on, Juanillo, go on! "

Juan obeyed his brother, although without relish now, because he wanted to know his sister-in-law and her children.

" Now I can see my daughter Manolita, who is also in her night-dress. . . . Hush, we have also wakened Paquito! . . . Didn't I say they would all get a fright! . . . But they will catch cold if they walk about like that much longer. . . . Stop playing, Juan, stop playing." The infernal din ceased.

" Here, Adela, Manolita, Paquito, put some clothes on and come and meet my brother Juan. This is Juan I have told you so much about, and I have just found him in the street within an ace of being frozen to death in the snow. . . . Hurry up, get dressed quickly! "

Santiago's kind-hearted family immediately came forward to

embrace the poor blind man. The voice of his wife was sweet and musical: to Juan it seemed that the Virgin spoke to him: he noticed that she wept when her husband narrated how he found him. And she even wanted to add more comforts to those Santiago had given him: she sent for a foot-warmer and herself placed it under his feet: then she wrapped a rug round his legs and put a soft cap on his head. The children hovered round the chair caressing their uncle and letting him caress them. In silence they listened, tongue-tied by emotion, to the brief story he gave them of his misfortune. Santiago called himself names: his wife cried: the children, wide-eyed, held his hand and said: " You won't be hungry any more, or go out into the street without an umbrella, will you, uncle? . . . I don't want you to, Manolita doesn't want you to, either . . . nor papa, nor mamma."

" I dare you to give him your bed, Paquito! " said Santiago, becoming merry again immediately.

" But it is too small, papa! Upstairs there is a huge great big one he can have——"

" I don't want a bed now," interjected Juan. " I am so comfortable here! "

" Does your stomach hurt you as it did before? " asked Manolita, hugging him and kissing him.

" No, my child, no, bless you! . . . It does not hurt at all. . . . I am very happy. . . . The only thing is, I feel sleepy. . . . I can hardly keep my eyes open . . ."

" Well, don't keep awake for us, Juan," said Santiago.

" Yes, uncle, go to sleep, go to sleep," said Manolita and Paquito in the same breath, putting their arms round his neck and covering him with kisses.

.   .   .   .

And he went to sleep. And he woke up in Heaven.

At dawn on the following day, a policeman stumbled over his body in the snow. The ambulance doctor certified that death was caused by exposure to the cold.

" Look, Jiménez," said one of the policemen who had carried him, to his comrade, " look at the smile on his face."

ARMANDO PALACIO VALDÉS

THE CURATE'S COLT

MANY of you must have known my friend the Curé of Arbin, and have had occasion to admire his noble and generous character, the simplicity of his nature, and a certain innocence of soul that God only gives to those He has chosen for Himself: qualities which made him esteemed and loved by all. He lived in the rectory within a stone's-throw of the town, waited upon by a very old woman and her husband no less ancient. There was also a bull-dog which nobody could remember as a puppy, and a horse that had come into his possession more than twenty years ago, and then it was not young. As Don Pedro, for so the curé was called, was well over seventy, it was quite correct to say that the house was a museum of fossils. We will first have the story of the horse, leaving the history of the bull-dog for another time, as it is less interesting.

In the town it was simply known as " Don Pedro's colt." But as the reader will understand, this was only a nickname they had given it for fun. The author of the jest must have been Xuan de Manolín, at that time the most humorous and free-thinking soul in the parish. The beast's real name was Pichón, and it was so called by its owner and by the servants. It had once been grey; but when I saw it, all the black hair had fallen out or turned white. It was not bad to look at; peaceful by nature; its gait moderately racking. For this reason the curate had not dared to make him trot for years and preferred to leave half an hour earlier on his excursion to the neighbouring parishes. Patient, noble, sure, knowing those roads better than any, Pichón had enough qualities to make him prized by his master as a jewel. The outstanding virtue of this animal, however, was its frugality. As the little grass that grew in the meadow was nearly all eaten by a milch-cow owned by the curate, the unfortunate Pichón was compelled to wander for nine months in the year through paths and lanes, watching the grass spring up to nibble it long before it reached full growth. No hack, ancient or modern, ever digested his food to greater advantage; for his hindquarters were always rounded and glossy, as though he boarded in the house of a marquis. So much so that more than once Don Pedro was asked if he fed him on hay

188

and barley. Barley, for Pichón! He had heard of it sometimes; but seen it, never.

As though these qualities were not sufficient, Pichón possessed another very valuable one: a prodigious memory. Whenever the curate of Arbin had once stopped at any house in the neighbourhood, Pichón always stopped dead on passing there again, as though inviting him to dismount. Naturally, when it came to the house of the curate's sister in Felechosa, or to the rectory at Pino, where for many years Don Pedro had been playing a never-ending game of cards with the reverend brother, the horse not only stopped, but went straight to the stable.

But Pichón, without any reasonable cause, had many enemies in the town, some open, others hidden. Finding no means of combating him in open fight, they carried on a secret and insidious campaign: they assailed him through his old age. As though all of us were not to reach old age under penalty of death! thought the quadruped very reasonably. They began by giving him the derisive nickname of "colt." Well did Pichón know that he was not and did not pretend to be a colt. When had any one seen him frisking about, trying to look young before a mare, however giddy? To live honourably, avoid all foolishness, eat whatever one could get, and not meddle in the elections—these were the fundamental axioms he had learned from his long experience.

Not satisfied with nicknaming him, his adversaries adduced false evidence against him. They said that once on the way from Lena to Cabanaquinta he went to sleep with Don Pedro on his back, and a mule-driver had to wake him up with a stick. Pure calumny. What had happened was, that at the rectory at Llanolatabla, where his master stopped nearly seven hours, they had not given him a single blade of grass; and naturally he dropped from sheer weakness. In the same way the jocular neighbours, and many that were not, invented unkind stories about him, and ceaselessly teased the curate on the subject. At times this made Don Pedro very irritable in spite of his recognised patience. "Cáscaras! What has the poor animal done to those fools to make them so nasty about him?"

The most merciless of them was Xuan de Manolín. The curate never passed his tavern on horseback but he came to the door to shout one of his jibes; sometimes he even seized the horse by the bridle and, behaving very politely at first, ended by drawing down its lip and asking with apparent innocence:

"Have the marks disappeared from his teeth?"

The customers, who also came out to the door, shrieked with laughter at this and similar jibes, and Don Pedro rode away annoyed, muttering indignantly.

Finally, so harassed was he by the chaffing of his parishioners,

who were joined by his fellow-clerics of the neighbouring places
when he met them on some feast day, that he resolved to get rid
of the horse, although it would cause him genuine regret.   Nevertheless when the fair came at Ascension time, when he proposed to
sell it, he hesitated and very nearly turned back.   But he had
already told some of the neighbours what he was going to do.   All
the parish knew of his decision and applauded it.   What would
they say if he still kept Pichón after all?

Melancholy and miserable Don Pedro straddled him one morning, and step by step reached Oviedo.   As he neared the town,
his conscience pricked him more and more.   Whichever way he
looked at the matter, and although he thought of numerous examples of the case, the fact remained that it was nothing but ingratitude to sell poor Pichón after twenty years of faithful service.
What would happen to him?   Perhaps he would draw a coach:
perhaps die shamefully in a bull-ring.   In any event, martyrdom.   The innocent way the horse walked along without misgiving or suspicion made its master feel a shame he could not
hide.

At the fair, animals were very cheap.   Pichón was old, nobody
wanted him.   Only one horse-dealer offered fifteen dollars for him.
The curate finally let him go at that price for fear of the chaff of
the neighbourhood if he appeared again with the silver-grey beast
in Arbin.   As soon as he lost sight of it he felt better, as the presence of the quadruped had been very painful.   He took the train
to the town, and when he arrived had the unhappiness to receive
congratulations for what he secretly considered a misdeed.   In a
few days, however, the horse was entirely forgotten.   But he certainly required another.   Although he enjoyed good health, and,
thanks to God, his legs were still strong, some of the parishes were
very far, and it was impossible to borrow a horse from Xuan de
Manolín every day or from Cosme, the miller.   On the advice of
these two and other well-informed parishioners, he decided not to
wait for the fair of All Saints at Oviedo, but hoped to find a mount
at the fair of San Pedro de Boñar, where nearly all the horses of
the province of Leon were taken.

No sooner said than done.   When the time came, availing himself of the mule of a friendly driver who was going to Leon with
his drove, he took the road leading to Boñar by the Puerto de San
Isidro.   There it was just the contrary to Oviedo.   Animals were
dear.   Under forty dollars it was impossible to buy a serviceable
horse.   For forty-three and the usual drink on completion of the
bargain, our curate became the owner of a dark sorrel horse, not
very spirited, but safe and steady, without its equal on that side of
the Esla, or even in the valley of the Orbigo, according to the
dealers who sold it to him.   And so it ought to have been; because

Don Pedro remembered the Spanish proverb: "Sooner than tire, a sorrel horse will die."

On its back he turned once more towards his town, riding through Lillo and Isoba and crossing the abrupt passes of San Isidro. He journeyed along happily, satisfied with his purchase, as the animal took those steep hills well, and above all did not take fright, a possibility he had dreaded more than anything. But on arriving at Felechosa a thing happened which astonished him greatly. As he was going to dismount for a moment a his sister's house, the horse of its own accord went straight to the stable.

"What a nose that animal has!" exclaimed Don Pedro going into the house. And he swelled with pride.

He stopped there longer than he intended, and calculating how much time he had he saw it was impossible to stop at Pino for a game of cards with the curate. But on arriving at this place he received a fresh and still greater surprise. The horse, ignoring the pulls at the bridle and the blows from the stick, refused to follow the main road and, turning off slightly, went towards the priest's house and entered the stable.

"Wonderful! wonderful!" murmured Don Pedro, opening his eyes wide. And in gratitude for such marvellous instinct he stopped lashing it and got down to greet his friend.

When he reached the town, night had fallen, and so the neighbours were unable to see and admire the splendid and intelligent beast. But next day some of them came to the stable and, after inspection, said that it was a good horse, and heartily congratulated its owner on the purchase. "It's a *beauty* of a horse, Don Pedro! Now you have a mount that will last you till you die."

"What a blessing you got rid of that old thing, it might have died on the road any day!"

The curate pretended to be pleased with their congratulations; but that reminder of Pichón still impressed him unpleasantly.

Five or six days passed without occasion arising for Don Pedro to use his new horse, at the end of which time he told the servant to clean it and bridle it, as he intended going to Mieres. The man appeared in a few moments and said:

"Do you know, Father, that Leon (this being the name of the new horse) has some white marks that won't come off?"

"Rub hard, silly, rub hard; he has probably brushed against the wall."

In spite of his efforts the spots would not disappear. Then Don Pedro, annoyed, said to him: "Give it up, Manuel, you have no strength left. Watch me and see how I get them off at once."

And taking off his soutane and rolling up his shirt-sleeves he seized the brush and currycomb and started to clean it himself. But his hopes proved ill-founded. The marks not only would not disappear but began to get larger and larger. " Here, bring some soap and warm water," said he finally, hot and angry.

And then there was trouble! The water was at once stained red, and the white marks on the horse spread till they nearly covered his body.

To sum up, so much did they rub him that in half an hour the sorrel horse had disappeared and in his place stood a white one.

Manuel took a few steps backwards, and with consternation written on his face, exclaimed: " God help me, if it isn't Pichón! "

The priest stood rooted to the root. And in truth, under the coating of red ochre, or some other dirty mixture they had used to disguise him, was the old, patient, much-abused Pichón.

The news spread like a flash through the town. In a short time a crowd of people were assembled in front of the rectory, guffawing and making witty remarks, as they looked at " the curate's colt " which the servant had brought out to the stable. When the fun was at its height, Don Pedro appeared in the passage, his face grim and angry, and said:

" It serves me right, Cáscaras, for having listened to such fools as you! . . . If anybody says a word to me about him again I shall break his bones. Cáscaras! Recáscaras! "

Understanding that he had good reason to be annoyed, the onlookers stopped joking and returned slowly to the town.

JACINTO OCTAVIO PICÓN

1853–1923

AFTER THE BATTLE

I

ALMOST hidden between trees of great age and surrounded by thick walls, there stood in one of the eastern departments of France a few years ago a superb mansion, sufficiently distant from highways and roads to show that whoever lived there loved solitude and calm. Round it was a garden uncultivated and neglected, which had grown to resemble in its wildness a virgin forest. The branches of the trees stretched out beyond the enclosure; the roots, well nourished with sap, had made the pathways uneven by their growth; the shoots of the shrubs were entwined one with the other in the thick grass and made passage difficult; a stream, winding among the thick trunks, lent its monotonous voice to the park; a pond, converted into a lake by the crumbling of the stones that once confined it, reflected like a black mirror the dark masses of the leafy groves; and at one end, aground in the mud, lay an abandoned and rotting gondola, burying itself by its own weight in the greenish tangle of the stagnant water. Clinging to the bricks and stones, climbing the roughened surface, the tenacious ivy had covered the walls of the house, and from the frieze of the first floor it hung in long wavy fringes, swayed by the wind. The grasses carpeted with green the spaces intended for flower-beds, the cultivated rose-bushes had been replaced by wild brambles, the amaranth gave way to the thistles, and where once grew the mignonette, nothing showed now but the mint. A narrow path, beaten by constant passage, led from the gate of the park to the house, and between the steps leading to the entrance, in the crevices of the stones, grew strips of thick green moss like broad bands of silky felt. Of two marble angels which formerly stood at the ends of the balustrade, only one remained on its pedestal; the other, fallen and half-buried in the earth, showed its torso covered with grey or gold stains, according as the sun or the damp had affected it. In the interior of the house was a large patio and in the centre of it a well, its iron bars climbed by the weeds which grew round the base; the stone flags on the ground were framed in green; and

193

at the corners of the shelters overhanging the balconies, the gutters were being widened by the continuous trickle of the rain.

The rooms preserved traces of the luxury with which they were furnished. The satin, the brocade, the velvet, and the damask lavished on furniture and walls were worth a fortune; the passe-menterie, lambrequin, curtains, and carpets made a rich ensemble; but everything was old, faded by the light, and impaired by time. At the edges of the hangings, the warm-toned satins had paled; the seats of the chairs were threadbare; the gilt on the frames was chipped; the doors hung badly on their hinges; and the marble tiles moved under worn carpets. The dust, spread over canopies, silks, and mouldings, softened the tints and dulled the brightness; and in the candles of the chandeliers and candelabra time had changed the dull whiteness of the sperm to the dirty yellow of beeswax.

Within those old walls, impregnated with the character and colour of another century, there lived in seclusion a most beautiful woman called Hortensia.

II

No one knew who she was: voluntarily separated from the bustle of the world and waited on by half-a-dozen servants, her existence was, so it seemed, purposely arranged to excite the curiosity of others.

There everything was sad: in the parterre were no flowers now, or poultry in the stockyard: even the birds fled from the neigh-bourhood of the house, preferring the pleasant shades of the adjacent wood to the slopes of the roof, covered with dark slate.

Doubtless there existed great analogies between that woman and her residence, similarities on which, perhaps, was founded her affection for the old mansion and the gloomy park. The rooms and the walks formed, by their sadness, a proper and adequate setting for that calm and melancholy beauty. The languid movements of Hortensia and the slow swaying of the half-fallen branches, as though tired of living, were very similar: between the paleness of her face and that ever whitish sky was a mysterious resemblance, in which blended the poetic melancholy of the country and the placid serenity of the woman: her look and the light of those places were alike; vague, undecided, as though continually bathed, one in a mist suspended in the atmosphere, and the other in a moisture of tears that brightened her eyes.

Repentant Magdalen to some, inconsolable widow to others, lover waiting hopelessly for the advent of one who never came, Hortensia was a living enigma to the people of the district. If her heart held secrets, no one succeeded in learning them. Like a trunk that hides 'neath rough bark the wood-borer which corrodes its heart, so did she disguise her troubles under the impassive calm of her counten-ance.

III

Came the year 1870, and when hostilities broke out between
Germany and France, the country people fled in terror. The
Empire lost four successive battles, and the struggle ceased to be
called *the war* and became *the invasion*. The roads were blocked
with escaping peasants driving their live stock before them;
harassed beasts scattered, destroying the crops; carts upset, over-
loaded with the furniture of the fleeing country-folk; and columns
of smoke from the fires filled the atmosphere with threatening
clouds, in which danced the sparks from the burning roofs.

The property belonging to Hortensia was situate on a plain not
far from which rose two hills, separated by a gorge that the French
had fortified, and behind the house was a hamlet, considered to be
a strategic point.

The Prussians wished to force back the outposts who occupied
the plain, and hardly had the battle started when Hortensia, from
the top of her house, saw great masses of troops which spread themselves in close formation over the meadows, and extending later
into dark lines, were hidden in the little clouds of white smoke torn
at intervals by the flashes of the artillery. For three days the boom
of the guns was heard, on the fourth the Prussians assailed the
French position with increased energy, and shortly afterwards fugitives began to pass the garden wall, soldiers with the terror of
defeat stamped on their faces, and ruined farmers leaving their
wrecked dwellings behind them and their fields laid waste by the
hostile fire.

As the day drew to a close, when all the vanquished who could
escape had passed, Hortensia saw on the grey stretch of a path-
way leading to the house a group enveloped in the whirling dust
raised above the bushes by the wind. It was like a dark horizontal
line between two vertical ones, which advanced with slow and
measured movements. Its shape stood out at last, clear and distinct,
so that the eyes could make out the figures. They were two soldiers
who were carrying a wounded comrade on a stretcher.

Hortensia guessed they were coming to her house, and, descending from the roof, ordered her own bed to be got ready; and so
speedily did she act that when they reached the door of the park
she was there to receive them, saying as she indicated the path
they were to follow:

" Along there."

IV

Following that wounded man came others, and then others, and
afterwards many more. The first were placed in the best apartments; finally, all the rooms were occupied. It was necessary to
accommodate them in the servants' quarters, in the corridors, even in

the attics and stables. The house was converted into a field hospital; a section of the army medical corps established itself there; and as the distant roar of the artillery died down, within the walls of the mansion could be heard the moans and groans of the wounded.

Hortensia took from her wardrobe a superb dress of red satin, divided it into four with her scissors, and, sewing two broad strips crosswise on a white sheet, ordered this improvised flag to he hoisted on the highest point of the house.

V

The Germans had routed the French, but the latter re-formed a short distance from the mansion and resolved to defend the gorge. From the positions gained the Prussians could shell the hollow, and between the latter and the victorious batteries stood the house of Hortensia, on the roof of which waved the Red Cross Flag. Then the Commander-in-Chief of the Germans ordered the property to be evacuated, and to effect this an officer at once set out, dismounting half an hour later before the railings of the park.

The aide-de-camp, who expected to see some frightened and submissive villager, was received by Hortensia with a blank refusal and a resistance impossible to overcome with the two orderlies attending him; but he was smitten by the charms of the woman who showed him all the rooms of her house full of men mangled by grape-shot, and accompanying him to the gate of the park declared that she would not leave the place, and that if they bombarded it she would suffer the same fate as those who had placed themselves under her protection.

The officer returned, annoyed at receiving such a vigorous reply, but so struck with her beauty that when reporting what had happened to his chief, although he told him a great deal about the large number of wounded he had just seen and of the refusal he had listened to, he told him much more about that fascinating woman. So much did he praise her that the General, a young man who was evidently no fool, decided to settle the difficulty himself, and mounting his horse, with two soldiers as escort, set out for the mansion.

Night had fallen when the chief of the German forces, vanquishers of France in that region, reached the railing surrounding the house. The branches hung over the walks, converting each path into an archway; on the horizon some orange clouds were darkening gradually, until they remained as stains of deep purple on the azure sky; the trees reflected on the ponds their shapeless masses, which trembled slightly in the wind; the ivy hanging from the tops of the walls let its loose shoots sway; the abandoned flower-beds exhaled the fresh penetrating smell of damp earth; the darkness of the night was beginning to envelop the square mass of the house; and a few bats flew round, attracted by the light of the windows, which threw their yellowish rays on to the gravel in the garden.

At the foot of the door, as though thrown down before the entrance to a precinct of peace, were two piles of weapons; side by side in the grass could be seen the rifles of the conquered and of the conquerors.

Hortensia received the General in the vestibule, leaning on the handrail of the balustrade. The Prussian was still young. His high rank was based on his nobility: his elegant and manly beauty, his chivalrous and martial appearance would have captivated any other woman. He forgot when he saw her that he was a soldier, remembering only that he was a man, and uncovering his head courteously, advanced towards her with his helmet under his arm, as he would have carried his gibus in a salon.

" I receive you here," said Hortensia, " because my house is a pool of blood: inside you may trample on French uniforms, but you would risk trampling on German ones as well."

The discussion was lengthy, but the General was not violent or rude; he even heard with calm the same resolute refusal which his aide-de-camp had transmitted to him. Hortensia, leaning slightly on the balustrade, looked like some fantastic image. Her white dress absorbed the little brightness there was in the vestibule, everything was becoming black around her, and the outline of her figure showed up against the murky background, while the light reflected from a round window on the ground floor seemed to place behind her head a golden halo, cut across by the lines of lead which secured the panes of glass. . . . The frogs started a discordant chorus in the adjacent pond, and at intervals could be heard the calling of the German bugles in the distance.

But the Prussian only heard the sweet voice of Hortensia. He forgot the Fatherland and the King, the hatred for France, the victory and the war. The barbarian from the north fell at the feet of the Latin woman, and she raised him unruffled, without anger, comprehending that her beauty was an excuse for such audacity.

" Go," said she to him. " To-morrow, no doubt, you will attack the gorge that lies behind this house . . . now understand me clearly: If not a single one of your shells falls here, if the bullets of your battalions do not strike against these walls, if those who are suffering here are not further injured through any fault of yours . . . then come in the evening and your triumph will be double."

.   .   .   .

A moment later the German was on his way back to the camp, intending to demonstrate to his companions that there was no need to evacuate that house; and in the mansion reigned an imposing silence, which was only broken by the lament of some wounded soldier or the wild caw of the birds hidden in the hollow tree-trunks of the adjoining wood.

Next day the invaders attacked the French position, silencing
their fire after several hours of horrible cannonade. History will
never tell what commands were given for that fight, nor who
ordered the assault; but the fact remains that not a single bullet
flattened itself against the walls of the house; not a shell burst in
the park; no fragment of grape-shot fell within the boundaries of
Hortensia's domain; the projectiles described their trajectories passing over the roof without grazing it, whistling above the branches
without scratching them; and at the conclusion of the skirmish
there was not a stone chipped nor a tree-trunk scored by the lead
on the whole of the estate.

VI

After the battle of the day, the silence and calm of the night
descended over the fields. On the distant horizon, as though issuing
from the ground red with the blood poured out, the moon was
rising slowly and majestically, like a great ball of fire: first it illuminated, with the reflected light of flames, the farm-houses and the
woods; then, as it ascended the heavens, it seemed less yellow,
more brilliant, as though the higher it rose from the ground the
purer it became; finally, from its immense height it dominated the
vast extent of the country.

Hortensia, serene as that summer night which enveloped her in
its mist of silver light, awaited the Prussian at the same spot as on
the previous evening, her elbows resting on the marble balustrade,
her gaze fixed on the garden, thinking every moment that she heard
the gallop of the horses. Suddenly came the sound of the iron-shod
hoofs on the road. Soon afterwards the German handed the reins
to the orderly who followed him, and advanced towards the
steps.

Hortensia received him graciously, gave him her hand to kiss,
and then turning round, went into a spacious room from which two
lateral doors gave access to the other apartments on the ground
floor. She at once picked up a little lamp she had previously placed
on an iron seat, and by pushing lightly with her foot against one
of these doors, opened one of its leaves: raising the lamp as high
above her head as she could, and letting the light fall within, she
showed the German three wounded soldiers lying upon the ground
on mattresses and rugs. One of them, sitting up against the wall,
had his forehead bound round with cloths, and from between the
folds of the bandage a little stream of blood trickled down in a thin
line, till it was lost in his beard; another was breathing heavily in
his sleep, as though an enormous weight lay upon his chest; and
the third, his face buried under the folds of the cloak which served
him as a pillow, sobbed as he tried to stifle his moans between the
double thickness of the cloth.

Hortensia allowed the German to contemplate that picture, and then, pushing him outside, opened the door of the room opposite. There a French officer was lying on a yellow divan of old damask. His legs were stretched out on a heap of cushions, and his face, contracted by the pain, showed the grim tenacity of one determined not to complain. A small lamp, burning low, shed its subdued light over the room, the shadows of the hangings blackened the light carpet which covered the floor, and on a small lamp-stand lay forgotten a case of surgical instruments and a roll of lint.

The Prussian scarcely had time to take in what he saw before Hortensia led him to the upper rooms. The marble staircase was stained with mud; in some places blood had left a trail of large drops; and on one of the landings, seated on a stool, was a man with his right hand bandaged, trying to fill his pipe with his left. They reached the first floor. The most luxurious salon of the house, once reserved for festivities and entertainments, was transformed into a hospital ward. In the centre, upon a jasper table, were several small pots, and on the marvellously sculptured mantelpiece a basin of common earthenware, full of dirty and blood-stained water, on which floated a few pieces of rag. On a background of white pillows stood out the heads of many wounded, one of them beginning to show in his face the proximity of death. From a couch near the door rose an acrid and repugnant smell. Two large mirrors, placed opposite one another at each end of the room, reproduced the beds in a long row, multiplying their reflections endlessly; and that perspective, deceptive but no less sad than the reality, gave the salon an appearance which inspired gloom and consternation.

They went over the whole house from the attics to the kitchen, which had been converted into a dispensary. Not a door was left unopened. Finally, coming to her own room, Hortensia drew back the curtains round the bed, and, half hidden on pillows of finest linen, appeared the almost infantile face of a soldier who perhaps, in the delirium of fever, thought he felt the last kiss they gave him as he left his village. The German looked impassively at that victim of his victory, and then, turning to the lady, seemed to ask with his eyes when the annoying pilgrimage would end.

Hortensia made him pass through yet more rooms and more apartments full of wounded, until, going out into the vestibule, they arrived at the stairway whence they had started. There, raising the lamp to the level of her face, which was illuminated by the last glare of the dying flame, as though it had now fulfilled its mission, she stretched out her arm towards the park gate, and dismissing the Prussian with a charming smile, said to him serenely with the calmness of the night:

" You have seen for yourself; there is no room for us."

JACINTO OCTAVIO PICÓN

GASPARON'S REVENGE

THE brazen throats of the bells boomed out the mellow noon hour, the gates opened, and before the last clang of the clappers had died away the first surges of the human sea inside began to pour out resistlessly—the silent, weary multitude that formed the personnel of the factories. No one spoke; neither man sought woman, nor the girl the young man's flattery and wooing, nor the child its customary games and idleness. The strong appeared fagged out, the young old and feeble, and the old half-dead. They were a breed twice oppressed, these factory hands, by ignorance and selfishness. The crowd was quickly dispersed, like a cloud the winds tear into ribbons and then shred to atoms; it poured out first in a turgid stream, split up into groups, and quickly drifted off in silent pairs, pairs which seemed to divide without audible farewells or salutes, some taking the roads to their houses, others entering the near-by inns and taverns, disseminating and losing themselves, merged and absorbed by the agitated circulations of the busy neighbourhood.

One of the last to come out was Gaspar Santiagos, also known as Gasparon, or Big Gaspar, because of his tremendous strength, great height, and massive build. These characteristics dominated his whole appearance, giving him a sympathetic, kindly, slow manner and visage; but his face, for all that, was bright and quick of expression, his glance frank and sincere. He was so robust, he looked like Hercules in a blouse.

He walked rapidly along in the shadow of the mud wall, crossed two or three streets, traversed a plaza, and passing on by covered alleyways and vacant lots to save himself needless steps, debouched upon a wide street whose gigantic elms knit overhead, their delicate lacework of foliage forming a coolly inviting arched vault of shadow, under which sat awaiting him on the fallen trunk of one of the giant trees a pretty and graceful young woman, with a neat basket before her, a dog beside her knee, and a clean, fresh baby in her lap. The delighted beast rushed toward him, the little one stretched out its tiny fists, and while the man drew up the basket and broke apart the sixteen-ounce golden loaf, his wife, never taking her eyes from his face, laid out to one side on the tree-trunk the salad, uncorked the bottle of red wine, gave him his napkin and wooden spoon, and poured out the well-cooked, steaming stew into the thick but clean white plate edged with a blue stripe.

When the bell sounding the recall from the luncheon hour began ringing in the distance, Gasparon hastily tilted the last drops of stew and wine down his capacious throat, lighted a cigarette, gave the child a kiss, threw the dog the broken remnants of his lunch, and, affectionately squeezing the wife as a miser embraces his treasure-chest, was off on the road to the factory at a rapid pace.

He entered the gate, crossed a yard full of pig-iron in piles, and entered a long, wide shop, lighted by windows through whose blackened panes could be seen grimy walls, great piles of coal, spark-spitting, crackling forges, and tall chimneys that vomited forth in dense clouds great bubbles of the heavy coal smoke and pulverised dust. High overhead and lengthwise of the shop ran in complicated lines an incalculable number of shining steel and burnished iron levers, columns, and wheels, united by leather belts which surged up, swung low, and gyrated dizzily like crazy members of some living mechanical organism, in which nothing could falter without paralysing the whole machine. The planked floor trembled with the pulsations of the steam, whose stertorous sighing could be heard all about; and from other shops, weakened by the uproar and the distance, came the clangour of metal being beaten and the droning hum of whirring machines mixed with the bench-songs of women.

At the end of the first shop stood another exactly like it, and spanning the court between the two was a narrow little bridge, beside which a colossal flywheel revolved at high speed.

When Gasparon reached the middle of the little structure, he saw an apprentice come running out of the second shop at such speed and having such impetus that he could not check his wild career. There was no time to go back, and, perceiving that both could not pass the great wheel at the same time, Gasparon bent his huge bulk far outward over the rail, flattening himself as much as he could. The lad came on like a streak of lightning, turned badly as he violently collided with the big fellow, and fell face downward, barely remaining upon the single, wide, heavy timber that formed the floor of the bridge, hanging suspended over the oily abyss of the deep wheel-pit, not daring to let go his hold and fall, unable long to remain where he lay. Gasparon, more fearful of the distant than of the nearer danger, stretched out his hand to the child, who, blinded by fear, snatched at it with such force and anxiety that the powerful workman was well-nigh overbalanced. As he lost his equilibrium, Gasparon instinctively threw out his free arm wildly as a counterpoise. His fingers came into sudden contact with something—he gripped a spoke of the whirling fly-wheel, and the mighty arm splintered just above the hand. The

lad said afterwards that, to add to his terror, he heard it break
with such a noise as one hears when the wood-chopper's axe rives
apart a splintered timber. But, even hurt as he was, the fellow
retained his presence of mind well enough to step back coolly a
pace or two, raise the frightened boy in his sound arm, and carry
him to safety on the shop floor before he collapsed, struck down
silently by the severity of his pain.

There was shouting and running, and his comrades picked him
up gently, taking him in a chair to the near-by hospital, where
the surgeons took off the hopelessly maimed arm at the elbow.

Gasparon's convalescence was slow; in it disappeared first all
his little savings, then the pawnbroker's loans upon his Sunday
clothes, his cloak, and his wife's mantle; after that a collection
taken up for him by friends and charitable neighbours vanished
speedily; and last of all a donation from the treasury of the
Strikers' Aid Fund. There was no use thinking of any new sort
of manual labour; for the arm he had lost was his right, and he
had been right-handed.

Forty days or so after the accident his wife presented herself at
the cashier's window at the factory office. It was a small room,
divided by a wooden partition, surmounted by a metal screenwork
pierced here and there with small openings like windows, through
which she could see a well-dressed old gentleman in a freshly
laundered shirt reading a paper, seated close beside the cash-drawer.
About him, well within his vision, stood two men posting endless
figures industriously in great books, over whose little pine pulpits
they bent.

" What is it you want? " asked one of the clerks as she approached.

" How is Gasparon getting along? " queried the other kindly.

" Well! As if he could 'get along' at all—a one-handed
man! "

" And you have come——? "

" To get his pay," she replied nervously.

One of the clerks opened a large book and began turning the
leaves, mumbling " Gasparon—Gasparon."

" His name is Santiago—boring-mill gang, second section,"
volunteered the woman dully.

" Ah, yes; of course—Gaspar Santiagos! Here he is! "

" And he gets——" She sighed, and her eyes were troubled.

The clerk figured rapidly for a moment on a scrap of paper, and
without looking up, asked, " Was he paid the week before? "

" Yes, sir."

" H'm—then there are—there must be——"

The old gentleman in the clean shirt dropped his paper and
looked up, but not at the anxious woman.

" What day was it he hurt himself? " he demanded.

" The twentieth of last month—Wednesday, about two o'clock,''
she replied sadly.

" Then there is no trouble in finding out what is due the man,"
remarked the old gentleman suavely. " Monday, one; Tuesday,
two; Wednesday—two days and a half, at four and a half the day,
makes eleven pesetas and twenty-five centimos: two dollars and a
quarter altogether. Pay her, Luis.'' He shrugged his shoulders
and picked up his paper.

The clerk took a small wicker basket full of silver from one of
the drawers of the desk and counted out the pitiful sum, making
the payment without a word. The young woman, mechanically
taking what was proffered, went out, weeping softly. When the
noise of her footsteps had died away, the clean-looking old gentleman remarked severely: " Don't forget that Gasparon is discharged! Make a note of it on your books.''

When the workmen learned, as they speedily did, that Gasparon
had been given only his bare two and one-half days' pay, their
wrath boiled over and their indignation knew no bounds. Delegates
were appointed quickly from the various shops and mills of the
great works, and the little convention, meeting one night in the
back room of The Frenchman Tavern to learn the full details of
the case and take action thereon, the big fellow himself was cited
to appear and state his facts.

Gasparon related his misfortune with the greatest good nature,
showed his fellows the cicatrised stump of his arm, scarred deeply,
and afterward during the progress of the meeting seemed
more interested in bothering his neighbours to roll cigarettes for
him than in the business on hand. He had not yet been able
to manage his *cigarillos* with only his left hand, and since comfort is a prime factor in life, he was deeply engrossed in his
tobacco.

A smutty lamp which gave scarcely any light burned feebly
overhead without illuminating the room. The smoke of cigars and
cigarettes and the fumes of the cheap oil and wick filled the chamber
with a stifling haze; it was almost impossible to see faces, while
heads and bodies shaded off indistinguishably into the pungent
gloom.

" I bear on my shoulders the weight of fifty-two years of shop
work,'' growled a heavy voice from somewhere in the rear of the
room. It was the voice of a man who, by virtue of his age, had
spoken first. " And I know more than the rest of you. I've been
in many a factory in my time, and I ought to. I started when I
was twelve. I've always said it would be far better for every one
if the proprietors could be obliged to make some provision for
those of their men who can no longer work. You all know already

what happens when there is no compulsion—disabled, knotted hands and an empty belly."

" I, with fewer years," rumbled another voice, " have still more experience. Let us take unanimous action, keep our secret and spoil their material, their tools, their everything and anything, what you will. We can, without danger to ourselves, make them lose time; we can found their metals badly, weave their materials worse. In a single year there won't be a factory in Spain with a peseta's credit——"

" No! " shouted a third voice in a raw tone. " Nor a work-man with bread! " " The eight-hour day! Give us the eight-hour day! " roared a brawny chorus.

" Good counsel—to be dogs eight hours instead of nine, eh! "

" Raise the pay! Make 'em come up wi' the union scale! "

" And have them also raise the cost of clothes, bread, houses, if they can—until they tax the air we breathe! "

The bootless squabble might have gone on until dawn had not a voice, until then silent, broken sharply into the discussion. It was a huge voice, a roar that impeached the little, wizened body from which it poured full-throated, a voice that thundered an indomit-able will in spite of its owner's size.

" We haven't come here to squabble, but to avenge a cruel wrong! " it bellowed. " Have you nerve enough? Yes or no? —answer me! I know where there are three dynamite cartridges, weighing from five to six pounds apiece. One we can use on the model shop, which is what they value most; another on the owner's house—in the rear, where the family generally is; the last one we can hold in reserve, in case one of the others should not explode properly. We can draw lots for the chance, and whoever pulls the black straw does the job! "

A prolonged silence greeted the cold-blooded, horrible proposi-tion of wholesale murder and arson. Some were held back by the pure horror of the proposal, others by the fear of punishment. In the spirit all were accomplices before the fact, but the flesh was very weak; no one said: " I will dare it."

Gasparon was quickly on his feet, took a couple of pulls at his cigarette, walked over to stand under the lamp, so that they could read in his face the firmness of his resolution, and spoke plainly to the plotters.

" This is either all nonsense or all infamy. A ' Widows and Orphans' Fund ' or pensions for them, with money? You are dreaming! A strike? What for?—to stumble and fall upon your faces for weakness when there is nothing left in the house to eat? To stay in pawn to your very last rag until obliged by hunger to return to work, at the owner's terms? The proposition of the dynamite is the savagery of a coward!—for my part I will not assassinate anybody! Leave the vengeance to me. I will see that it is ample and not easily to be forgotten."

Some of the men murmured in surly disapproval, and others accepted the big fellow's proposal with good grace. The pusillanimous for fear, and the more exalted because they all saw in Gasparon's eyes something tremendous and mysterious, agreed to his undivulged plan, and the meeting was dissolved like one of those passing summer thunder showers whose bolt is not shot.

The day following Gasparon posted himself on the street to beg, directly in front of the palatial residence of the factory-owner. Supplications, threats, offers of all sorts to get him to go away were in vain. There he remained. He was there when the rich man, new lord of the modern feudality, came out to go to his work, to the exchange, to his varied amusements; when the señora, his lady wife, returned to pray; and when the children, the fair daughters of the house, went out to balls and parties, dressed in their daintiest shimmering frocks. There he stayed, close to the grating of gilded ironwork tracery about a window through which the ample silk curtains blew in soft folds. There he could be seen from dawn to dusk, showing his mutilated stump of an arm, resting the ragged bulk of his great body against the marble façade of the building, and always wearing about his neck, fastened by a cord, a neat little printed sign, bearing this inscription: *Crippled and Rendered Useless in the Factory of Don Martin Peñalva.*

VICENTE BLASCO IBÁÑEZ

1867–1928

THE CONDEMNED

FOURTEEN months had Rafael spent in his narrow cell.

For his world he had those four walls of dismal bone white, all the cracks and crannies of which he knew by heart; his sun was the little window high up, crossed by bars that cut the blue strip of sky; and as to the floor of scarce eight paces, barely half was his, due to that clanking and degrading.chain, the ring of which, biting into his ankle, had almost become part of his flesh.

He was condemned to death, and whilst the documents of his case were being examined in Madrid for the last time, he lay there for months and months buried alive, decaying like a living corpse in that coffin of mortar, desiring, as a momentary evil which would put an end to other greater ones, that the hour would speedily come for the garrote to close round his neck and finish everything once and for all.

What troubled him most was the cleanliness; that floor swept every day and well scrubbed, so that the damp, rising through the folding bed, got into his bones; those walls, on which not a speck of dust was allowed. Even the companionship of the dirt was denied the prisoner. Complete solitude. If rats could get in there, he would have the consolation of sharing with them his scanty meal and talking to them like good companions; if he had found a spider in a corner he would have amused himself by taming it.

In that sepulchre they did not want any other life but his. One day, how well Rafael remembered it! a sparrow peeped in at the window like a naughty child. The bohemian of light and space chirped as though expressing the surprise it felt to look down upon that yellow and emaciated being, shivering with cold in the height of summer, a few handkerchiefs knotted round his brow and a ragged blanket girt about his loins. It must have been shocked by that sunken and pallid face, with the whiteness of papier mâché; it was frightened by that strange Red-Indian dress, and fled, shaking its feathers as though to free itself from the tomb-like stench rising from the grating.

The only sound of life came from his companions in gaol as they

206

exercised in the yard. They at least saw the open sky over their heads, and did not breathe the air through a loophole; their legs were free and they had some one to talk to. Even in prison there are degrees of misfortune. Rafael did not understand man's eternal discontent. He envied the prisoners in the yard, considering their situation most desirable; they envied those outside, enjoying liberty; and those then walking in the streets were perhaps discontented, yearning for the unattainable! . . . How sweet is liberty! . . . They deserved to be in prison.

He was on the last rung of misfortune. He had tried to escape by tunnelling the ground in a fit of desperation, and the vigilance of the guards weighed on him, incessant and oppressive. If he sang, they imposed silence. He tried to amuse himself by reciting in a monotonous chant the parts he remembered of the prayers his mother taught him, and they made him stop. " Are you pretending to be mad? Well, then, keep quiet! " They wanted to keep him whole, sound in body and mind, so that the executioner would not have to operate on damaged flesh.

Mad! he did not want to be; but the confinement, the inability to move, and the bad and scanty rations were finishing him. He had hallucinations; some nights when he closed his eyes, wearied by the regulation light to which he could not become accustomed even after fourteen months, he was tormented by the extravagant idea that while he slept his enemies, those people who wanted to kill him but were quite unknown to him, had turned his stomach inside out, and were tormenting him with cruel stabs.

In the daytime he was constantly thinking of his past, but his mind wandered and it seemed he was reviewing the story of another.

He remembered his return to the little town of his birth, after his first spell in prison for wounding; his fame throughout the district, the people at the tavern in the plaza admiring him enthusiastically: *What a great Brute Rafael is!* The best girl in the town decided to become his wife, more from fear and respect than from love; the people at the Town Hall flattered him, giving him a rural guard's rifle, and inciting his brutality as a weapon at the elections; he reigned unopposed throughout the parish; he held *the others*, those of the fallen band, in his grip, until they, becoming tired, took shelter behind a certain bully who just then came out of prison, and pitted him against Rafael.

Heavens! his professional honour was in danger: he must settle that bully who was robbing him of his bread. And, as an inevitable consequence, came the ambush, the deadly shot and the finishing blows with the butt to stop his cries and kicks.

In fact . . . the usual thing! And in the end came the gaol, where he met some old companions; the trial, at which all who

formerly feared him took vengeance for the dread they had felt by
giving evidence against him; the terrible sentence and those cursed
fourteen months waiting the arrival from Madrid of the death
which, judging by the time it was taking, was doubtless coming
by cart.

He was not without courage. He thought of Juan Portela, of
the handsome Francisco Esteban, of all those valiant outlaws whose
escapades, narrated in verse, he had always listened to with enthusiasm, and he recognised that he possessed as much grit as they
to face the final moment.

But some nights he sprang from the bed as though discharged
by a hidden spring, making his chains sound with a dismal clang.
He cried out like a child and immediately regretted it, endeavouring vainly to stifle his sobs. It was another being that shrieked
within him; another being he had not known before, which was
afraid and cried out constantly, calm only coming when he had
swallowed half-a-dozen cups of that burning beverage of chicory
which in prison they called coffee.

Of the old Rafael who wanted death to finish matters quickly,
there only remained the outer shell. The new Rafael, born in that
sepulchre, thought with terror how fourteen months had now gone
by and the end must inevitably be near. Willingly would he agree
to pass another fourteen months in that misery.

He became suspicious; he had a presentiment that destruction
was approaching; he saw it on all sides: in the curious faces which
looked through the grating in the door; in the chaplain of the
prison, who now came every afternoon as though that fetid cell
were the best place in which to chat and smoke a cigarette. Bad,
very bad!

The questions could not be more disquieting. Was he a good
Christian? Yes, Father. He respected the clergy, had never been
wanting on that point; and as to the family, there was nothing to
be said; all his people had gone to fight for the King, because the
priest in the town told them to. And to show his Christianity, he
drew from the rags that covered his chest a dirty greasy bundle of
scapulars and medals.

Then the chaplain spoke to him of Christ, Who, although the
Son of God, had found Himself in a position similar to his, and this
comparison immensely pleased the poor devil. What an honour!
. . . But although flattered by such a similarity, he wanted it to
happen as late as possible.

The day came when the terrible news burst on him like a
thunder-clap. In Madrid they had finished. Death was coming;
and speedily, by telegraph.

When he was told by a warder that his wife, with the child born
while he was in prison, had come to the gaol asking to see him,

he doubted no more. When *she* left home then the *thing* was upon him.

They talked to him of a reprieve and he clutched feverishly at this last hope of all unfortunates. Did not others get it? Why should not he? Moreover, it was no trouble to that good lady in Madrid to give him his life; it was simply a case of signing her name.

And to all the official grave-diggers who from curiosity or duty visited him—lawyers, chaplains, and reporters—he asked, with piteous entreaty, as though they could save him:

" What do you think, will she sign? "

Next day they would take him to his town, bound and guarded like a wild beast going to the slaughter-house. The executioner was already there with his tools. And at the door of the prison, waiting to see him as he left, was his wife, a buxom brunette, with full lips and meeting eyebrows, her spreading skirts emitting, as she moved, a pungent barn-like smell.

She seemed terrified at being there; in her stupefied look was numbness rather than pain, and only when remembering the baby at her breast did she shed a few tears.

" Sir! What a disgrace for the family! She knew he would end in that way. If only the child had not been born! "

The prison chaplain endeavoured to console her. Resignation: she could still find, when widowed, a man who would make her happier. This seemed to fire her, and she even spoke of her first lover, a good boy, who withdrew in fear of Rafael and now often approached her in the town and in the fields as though he had something to tell her.

" No, there are plenty of men," she said quietly with an attempt at a smile. " But I am very Christian; and if I take another man, I want it to be as God wills."

And noticing the astonished look on the faces of the priest and doorkeepers, she came back to reality, and continued her difficult weeping.

As night fell the news came. Yes, she had signed. That lady, whom Rafael pictured in Madrid with all the splendours and adornments of the eternal Father's altars, yielding to telegrams and prayers, had prolonged the life of the condemned man.

The reprieve caused a tremendous commotion in the gaol, as though each of the prisoners had received a free pardon.

" Rejoice, woman," said the chaplain at the doorway, to the wife of the reprieved man. " They are not going to kill your husband: you will not be widowed."

The girl remained silent, as though struggling with ideas which developed slowly in her brain.

" Very well," she said at last with calmness, " and when will he come out? "

"Come out! . . . Are you mad? Never! He must be satisfied that his life has been spared. They will send him to Africa, and as he is young and strong, he may live for another twenty years."

For the first time the woman really cried with all her heart; and she did not shed tears of sorrow, but of desperation and rage.

"Come, woman," said the chaplain, irritated. "You are tempting Providence. They have spared his life, do you understand? He is no longer condemned to death. . . . And still you complain?"

The girl stopped crying. Her eyes shone with an expression of hate.

"Very well: let him live. . . . I'm glad. *He* is saved, but . . . what about me? . . ."

And after a long pause she added between sobs that shook her dusky body, ardent and of such brutal fragrance:

"And now . . . I am condemned."

VICENTE BLASCO IBÁÑEZ

EVE AND THE POOR

WITH hungry gaze fixed on the rice boiling for the evening meal, the reapers sat listening to old Correchola, their shaggy, raw-boned leader. Their ruddy faces, bronzed by the sun, shone in the fire-light, and the air of the kitchen was heavy with the scent of bodies weary with the toil of the fields; while through the open door of the farm-house, beneath a sky of violet hue, in which the stars were just beginning to peep forth, could be seen the fields, dim and in-distinct in the gathering darkness, some already harvested, the hard surface cracked by the heat of the day, others with waving mantles of grain trembling beneath the first sighs of the evening breeze.

Groaning over his aching bones and the hard lot of those who toil, the old fellow finally exclaimed:

" But it is all the fault of Eve, the first woman. My grand-mother told me that long ago, and it is too late to mend matters now. The poor will always be the victims of the rich, and we can only submit to our fate."

Then, seeing that his fellow-labourers indicated a desire to know more of this new charge against Mother Eve, old Correchola began, in his picturesque Valencian dialect, to tell of the shabby trick played on the poor of the world by the first of womankind.

" The story goes back to a time not long after the expulsion of the erring pair from Paradise, condemned to earn their bread by the toil of their hands. Adam's days were given up to the digging of the soil and worrying about his crops; Eve spent her time pluming herself in the door of their hut, and with every year came more mouths to feed until the poor father was in despair.

" From time to time there flitted by one seraph or another, who had come to take a glance at the world that he might tell his Lord how things were going here below since the first sin.

" ' Child! Little one! ' Eve would then cry with her sweetest smile. ' Dost thou come from above? How is it with our Lord? When thou returnest, tell Him that I have repented of my disobedi-ence. Ah, how happily we lived in Paradise! Tell Him that we toil diligently and that our one desire is again to see His face and to know that He is no longer angry.'

211

" ' What thou askest shall be done,' answered the seraph, and spreading his wings he was soon lost to sight among the clouds.

" Messages of this sort were repeated at intervals, but brought forth no response. The Lord remained invisible, engrossed in the mighty affairs of the universe. But one day a gossip from the heavenly regions—for even in those days there were such things—stopped before the cottage, and seeing Eve, called out:

" ' Listen, Eve, if it is pleasant this afternoon, it is possible that the Lord may descend for a brief time. Last night as He was talking to the Archangel Michael I heard Him say, " What has become of the banished ones? " '

" Eve was overwhelmed at the possibility of this great honour. She cried loudly to Adam, who, as usual, was bending over his work in an adjacent field. Then what a commotion arose! Eve swept the house from top to bottom, put a brand new coverlet on the bed, scrubbed the chairs with soap and sand, and then, bethinking herself of personal neatness, donned her best skirt and decked Adam out in a fig-leaf jacket that she had made for his Sunday wear. She was just thinking that everything was ready when her attention was attracted by the crying of her twenty or thirty children. And what an unkempt brood to receive the Omnipotent, with their tangled hair and dirty faces!

" ' How can I let this rabble be seen! ' she cried. ' The Lord will say that I am a careless woman, a bad mother. Men do not know what it is to struggle with such a family! ' After much hesitation she selected her favourites, washed the three prettiest, and drove the rest of the squalid troop off to the stable, where she locked them in despite their cries.

" And it was high time that all was ready. A gleaming white cloud was descending on the horizon and the air was filled with the sound of wings and the melody of a chorus which lost itself in the infinite distance, repeating in mystic monotone, ' Hosannah! Hosannah! ' Soon the heavenly band reached the ground and advanced along the way in such resplendent glory that it seemed as if all the stars of Heaven had come down to pass between those fields of grain. First came a group of archangels as a guard of honour. These, sheathing their fiery swords, quickly passed the house, with courteous greetings to Eve, and then with soldierly freedom dispersed among the fig trees, while Adam muttered curses under his breath and gave up his crop for lost. Then came the Lord, His beard of shining silver, and on His head a flashing diadem brilliant as the sun, followed by St. Michael and all the attendants and dignitaries of the celestial court.

" The Lord greeted Adam with a kindly smile and spoke graciously to Eve, while the abashed pair, quite melted at His gentleness, offered Him their best arm-chair. And what a chair that was for comfort! With its heavy frame and braided seat of the finest grass! Such a chair as the village priest might have! So now the Lord, sitting thus at ease, questioned Adam about his affairs, the state of his family, his daily labour, and other things.

" 'That is well,' He said to them. 'That is well. That will teach thee not to take thy wife's advice. Didst thou hope to have for ever the easy life of Paradise? Gnash thy teeth, My son, and toil and gain thy bread by the sweat of thy brow. Thus thou wilt learn not to rebel against thine elders.'

" But then, regretting His severity, He added in gentle tones:

" ' What is done is done, and My curse must be fulfilled. My word cannot be changed. But as I have entered this house, I will not leave it without some token of kindness. Eve, bring thou those little ones to Me.'

" The three little ragamuffins arranged themselves in line before the Omnipotent, who looked at them fixedly for a time.

" ' Thou,' He said to the first one, a solemn, pudgy youth, who listened scowlingly, with his chin resting on his hand, ' thou shalt be charged with judging thy fellow-man. Thou shalt make the laws and shalt say what is right and what is crime, changing thine opinion whenever thou wilt, and thou shalt subject all evil-doers to the same rule, which is even as a physician doth cure all ills by the one medicament.'

" Then He pointed to the next, a lively, dark-skinned lad, always with club in hand, ready to beat his brothers.

" ' Thou shalt be a warrior, a chieftain. Thou shalt lead men like sheep to the slaughter, and yet they shall sing thy praises. The people, when they see thee covered with thy fellows' blood, shall gaze upon thee in admiration as at a demi-god. If others kill, they shall be murderers: if thou killest, thou shalt be proclaimed as a hero; cause the fields to run red with blood; lay waste the towns with fire and sword; destroy and kill; and poets shall sing of thee and historians shall record thy deeds. Others than thou who do these things shall be cast into chains.'

" Reflecting for a moment, He turned to the third: ' Thou shalt gather the wealth of the world. Thou shalt loan money to kings and princes and shalt treat them as thine equals; and if thou ruinest an entire people, the world shall wonder at thy genius.'

" Poor Adam was weeping for joy and gratitude, while Eve, anxious and trembling, strove to speak but could not, for in her mother's heart remorse was busy and she was thinking of the poor little ones locked in the stable who were to be for ever debarred from these mercies.

" ' I am going to bring them to Him,' she said in an undertone to Adam, but Adam, ever timid, objected, murmuring: ' It would be too great a presumption. The Lord will be displeased.'

" Just at this moment the Archangel Michael, who had come much against his will to the abode of the outcasts, ventured to remind his Master of the passing time and the need of haste. The Lord arose and the archangel escort came hurrying back to attend Him on His way. But Eve, impelled by her remorse, ran quickly to the stable and threw open the door. ' Lord,' she cried, ' behold, here are yet others. Some gift, I pray thee, for these poor ones! '

" The Almighty looked with surprise at the filthy crowd playing in the dirt of the stable.

" ' There is nothing left to give,' He said. ' Their brothers have taken all. However, woman, I will reflect and later we shall see.'

" St. Michael pushed Eve aside, urging her to importune the Master no further, but she pursued Him with her supplications:

" ' Something, O Lord, something for these poor ones, I pray! Else what shall they do in the world? '

" The Lord, already on the threshold, turned for a moment.

" ' They have their destiny,' He said. ' They shall be charged with serving and supporting the others.'

" And from those unhappy creatures whom our first mother hid in the stable," concluded the old harvester, " are we descended —we who, with bended back, wrest our scanty living from the soil—we, the poor of the earth."

VICENTE BLASCO IBÁÑEZ

THE TOMB OF ALI-BELLUS

At that time (said the sculptor Garcia), in order to pay for my daily bread, I passed a good part of my time restoring images in the churches and gilding altars, and in pursuit of this work I travelled over the entire province.

Once I received an important commission: to restore the great altar in the church of Bellus, which work was to be paid for by a legacy left by an old lady, and thither I betook myself with my two apprentices, who were not much younger than I was.

We boarded in the house of the priest, a gentleman who was absolutely incapable of remaining quiet for any length of time; hardly had he finished saying mass when he would saddle his mule and go off to visit the priest of some neighbouring parish, or he would take his shot-gun and game-bag and attempt to depopulate the country of birds. While he was thus vagabonding, I and my two companions were perched upon the scaffolding erected in front of the altar, touching up and regilding this complicated piece of work of the seventeenth century and putting new wings and noses on the whole group of angels.

In the morning, when mass had been said, we were left absolutely alone. The church was an ancient one, a huge building, with white-washed walls and small chapels under arches extending along the sides. It had that peculiar atmosphere of silence and beauty combined which we find in all buildings constructed in the Arabic style of architecture. Through the open door we could get a glimpse of the solitary square in front of the church, flooded with sunlight; we could hear the cries of people calling to each other in the fields beyond; sometimes a lot of chickens would very irreverently enter the temple, walking around the altar with a look of solemn admiration, until they were frightened away by our songs. I must tell you that, familiar with this kind of work, we acted in the church as we would in the studio, and I gratified all this crowd of Saints, virgins, and angels, covered with the dust of centuries, with all the songs I had learned at the theatres, when I occupied a seat in the top gallery. Sometimes I gave them *Aïda*, and again I favoured them with some voluptuous refrains from *Faust*.

Possibly on this account some of the neighbours drifted into the

215

church every afternoon, a lot of gossiping old women who had nothing better to do than watch our work; and sometimes they went so far as to dare criticise because I didn't put enough vermillion on the cheek of some lost angel. The best-looking and doubtless the richest of the lot, to judge by the authority she seemed to exercise over the others, would sometimes come up on the scaffold, doubtless to impress me with her superiority, standing in such a way that I couldn't move without almost falling over her.

The floor of the church was composed of large slabs of stone, and in the middle of it was a large circular stone in the centre of which was a rusty iron ring. One afternoon I was standing on this stone and wondering what there might be beneath it. As I was stooping down and trying to lift the ring from its socket, the same woman—whose name, by the way, was Pascuala—came in and seemed to be extraordinarily astonished at seeing me in this position.

That whole afternoon she passed on the scaffold, paying no attention to her companions below, but looking at me sharply in a way which indicated that she wished to ask me a question. Finally the question came. She desired to know what I was doing on that stone, which had never been known to have been lifted within the memory of man. I denied having lifted it, but my denials seemed only to excite her curiosity the more, and feeling a boyish desire to hoax her, I managed to arrange it so that every afternoon when she entered the church she found me standing on that stone and examining it closely. The work came to an end, and we took down the scaffolding; the altar shone like a sun of gold, and just as I was about to leave the church the woman, devoured by curiosity, made another attempt to get at what she called my secret.

" If you only tell me, Mr. Painter," she said supplicatingly, " I will keep the secret."

And the painter—for this is what they called me—as he was young and of a somewhat mischievous disposition, and especially as he was going to leave that part of the country within an hour, forthwith whispered to the lady the most absurd fairy tale. I made her promise at least twenty-five times not to whisper a word of what I was about to say, and then I told her a series of lies as quickly as I could manufacture them, drawing from the most interesting novels I had ever read. I told her that I had lifted the stone by means of a mysterious force of which I alone knew the secret, and that beneath it I had seen the most extraordinary things. First I had encountered a long, steep staircase leading into the bowels of the earth; then I had come upon a number of passages leading in all directions. From one of them there came a faint light, and following this I came to a large room in which burned a lamp of antique form, which had been burning for a thousand years. In the centre of this room, lying upon a couch of marble, was a large man. He had a long grey beard, his eyes were closed, and beside him there was an enormous sword; on his head was a turban in which glittered the Moorish half-moon of gold and diamonds.

" It is a Moor! " she interrupted.

Yes, a Moor. How wonderfully bright she was to have discovered it! I went on to say that he was wrapped in a mantle that shone like gold, and on the marble were certain inscriptions in a strange language which even the priest himself could not read; but I, being a painter, and painters know everything, I had deciphered it without the slightest difficulty. The meaning was—was— ahem, " Here lies Ali-Bellus: this tomb is dedicated to him by Sarah, his wife, and Macael, his son."

One month later when I was in the city of Valencia I found out what had occurred in that good little town after I left it. Pascuala at once informed her husband, who the next day repeated the entire story at the tavern. General stupefaction! To think they had lived all their lives in that town, had been to that church every Sunday and did not know that just beneath their feet there lay the man with the long beard, the great sword, and the turban! And then to think that it was the great Ali-Bellus, who had a wife by the name of Sarah and a son by the name of Macael, and who had undoubtedly founded the town! And all this had been seen by a stranger, who had been there but a few days, while not one of them had even suspected it!

The following Sunday, after the priest had left the little town to go and dine with one of his friends, a large part of the population rushed back to the church. The husband of Pascuala succeeded in getting the sexton to surrender the key, and all, even the mayor and the secretary, entered the church, armed with pickaxes, crowbars, and ropes. How they did sweat! That stone had certainly not been moved in three centuries. The strongest of them used every effort, but for an hour the stone did not move the fraction of an inch.

" Courage, courage! " yelled Pascuala. " Remember that beneath that stone is the Moor! "

Encouraged by her, they redoubled their efforts, and after another hour's work they managed to pull up not only the stone but the greater part of the floor of the church. One would have thought that the whole edifice was coming down, but little they cared about that! All looks were fixed upon the yawning hole before them. The boldest scratched their heads with evident indecision; but one, more courageous than the others, finally caused a rope to be tied around his waist, and, murmuring a prayer, they lowered him down while all held their breaths. That lowering didn't tire them very much, for the man's feet were on bottom even while his head was outside.

"What do you see?" they yelled in chorus.

He was moving all around that pit, feeling with his hands, without finding anything but four solid walls and a few heaps of rotten straw.

"Look around! Search!" screamed those who were gathered closely about the edge of the hole. But the investigator could find nothing but the four walls of this narrow pit and the rotten straw. He climbed out and others took his place, accusing the first one of being stupid, but finally all were convinced that there was nothing there but a hole about six feet square. To say that they were angry would be to put it very mildly. They simply raved. The women took occasion to revenge themselves upon Pascuala, who had lorded it over them for so many years. Their misfortunes reached their climax, however, when the priest returned. Seeing the floor of the church and hearing the story of what had happened, he declared that he would excommunicate all the inhabitants of the town and close the church, and was only calmed when the daring discoverers of Ali-Bellus promised to construct a better floor at their own expense.

"Did you ever go back there again?" one of those present asked the sculptor.

"You couldn't hire me to. More than once I have met some of the inhabitants of this town in the city of Valencia, and, strange to say, when they spoke to me about the hoax they laughed and thought it a wonderfully good joke. They all assured me that they were not among those who had gone into the church, for they had suspected the trick from the beginning. They always terminated the conversation by inviting me to come down and visit them and have a good time. They smiled angelically when they gave me this invitation, but there was a certain gleam in their eyes that gave me to understand that the town would probably be the unhealthiest place for me on earth."

RUBÉN DARÍO
1867–1916

THE BOURGEOIS KING

FRIEND! The sky is dark, the air cold, the day sad. A merry story. . . . Just to brush aside grey and misty melancholy. Here it is:

There was once in an immense and brilliant city a very powerful King, who had rich and fanciful garments, naked slaves both black and white, long-maned horses, glittering weapons, fleet greyhounds, and beaters with brass horns, that filled the air with their fanfaronade. Was he a Poet King? No, my friend: he was the Bourgeois King.

This sovereign was very fond of art and gave largess freely to his musicians, to his composers of dithyrambs, painters, sculptors, apothecaries, barbers and fencing masters.

When he used to go to the forest, beside, a wounded and bleeding deer or wild-boar, he would make his rhetoricians improvise allusive verses, while the servants filled the goblets with the golden wine that sparkles, and the women clapped their hands with elegant and rhythmic motion. He was the king of all, in his Babylon of music, of laughter and the noise of feasting. When he tired of the madding city, he went to the chase, deafening the wood with his throng; and the frightened birds flew from their nests and the babel echoed through the deepest caves. The fleet-footed dogs broke through the brush in wild career, and the huntsmen, bending over the necks of their horses, let their purple cloaks wave in the air, their faces flushed and their hair flying.

The King possessed a superb palace where he had accumulated riches and marvellous works of art. He reached it through masses of lilies and extensive ponds, saluted first by the white-necked swans, then by the haughty flunkeys. Good taste! He went up steps flanked by columns of alabaster and smaragdine, guarded on either side by marble lions, like the thrones of Solomon. Refinement! Besides the swans, he had a vast aviary, as became a lover

219

of the music of cooing and singing birds; and next to it he broadened
his mind, reading novels by M. Ohnet, or beautiful books on gram-
matical questions, or Hermosillan criticisms. Yes; he was a staunch
defender of academic correctness in letters, and of the furniture
style in art; a sublime mind, a lover of polish and orthography.

　　　．　　　　　．　　　　　．　　　　　．　　　　　．

Eastern fancies! for ostentation and nothing more. It was an
easy thing for him to have a salon worthy of the taste of a Gon-
court and of the millions of a Croesus; chimeric creatures of bronze
with open maws and twisted tails, in wondrous and fantastic groups;
lacquers from Kioto inlaid with the leaves and branches of a
monstrous flora, and animals of an unknown fauna; butterflies
with strange-coloured wings on the walls; coloured roosters and
fishes; masks with horrible expressions and eyes that seemed to
see; halberds with blades of great antiquity, and handles carved
with dragons devouring the lotus; in egg-shells, cloaks of yellow
silk, as of woven spiders' thread, ornamented with red herons and
green rice plants; vases and porcelains centuries old, of the kind
painted with warriors of Tartary, half-clad in a single skin, holding
stretched bows and quivers of arrows.

For the rest there was the Greek room, filled with marbles;
goddesses, muses, nymphs, and satyrs; the room of the gallant
period, with paintings by the great Watteau and by Chardin; two,
three, four, how many more rooms!

And Maecenas walked through them all, his face reflecting a
certain majesty, his stomach happy and the crown on his head, like
a king of diamonds.

　　．　　　　　．　　　　　．　　　　　．　　　　　．

One day as he was seated on his throne, surrounded by courtiers,
rhetoricians, and masters of riding and dancing, they brought him
a queer specimen of a man.

" What is that? " he asked. " Sire, it is a poet."

The King had swans on his pond, canaries, sparrows, not to say
many rare birds, in his aviary: a poet was something new and
strange. " Bring him here."

And the poet: " Sire, I am starving."

And the King:

" Speak, and you shall eat."

He began: " Sire, long have I sung of the things that are to be.
I have spread my wings to the hurricane, I came to the world in
the dawn: I seek for the chosen race that is to wait, a hymn on the
lips and a lyre in the hand, for the rising of the great sun. I have
abandoned the inspirations of the corrupt city, of the perfumed
chamber, of the muse of the flesh that belittles the soul and powders
the face. I have broken the flattering harps of the weak against
the goblets of Bohemia and the jars where foams the wine that in-

toxicates but strengthens not; I have cast aside the cloak that made me seem an actor, or a woman, and I have dressed myself in a savage and splendid style: my rags are regal. I have gone to the virgin forest, where I have been strengthened and fed with the milk of nutriment and the liquor of a new life; and by the edge of the angry sea, tossing my head in the black and mighty tempest, like a commanding angel, or an Olympian demigod, I have given myself to iambics and deserted the madrigal.

" I have embraced Nature in her grandeur, and have sought in the warmth of the Ideal, the verse in the star in heaven on high, and the verse in the pearl in the ocean below. I have desired strength! Because the time of great upheavals is at hand, with a Messiah all light, all energy and power, and it becomes us to receive His spirit with a triumphal arch of poetry, with stanzas of steel, with stanzas of gold, with stanzas of love.

" Sire! Art is not in the cold casings of marble, nor in the highly finished painting, nor in the great M. Ohnet! Sire! Art does not clothe itself in trousers, or talk in bourgeois, or dot all its i's. Art is magnificent, it has cloaks of gold, or of fire, or it goes naked; it mixes the clay with inspiration, and paints with light; it is powerful, and strikes with its wings like the eagle, or with its paw like the lion. Sire, between an Apollo and a goose, choose the Apollo, although one be made of baked clay and the other of ivory."

" Oh! Poetry! "

" Well! Rhymes are prostituted, verses are made to the beauty spots of women, and poetic syrups are manufactured. And, sire, the bootmaker criticises my hendecasyllables, and the master of chemistry corrects my inspiration. Sire, it is you who authorise all this. . . . The ideal, the ideal. . . ."

The King interrupted:

" You have heard him. What is to be done? "

And a philosopher of that mode:

" If you will permit, sire, he can earn his bread by playing an organ; we can put him in the gardens, near the swans, and he can play when you are walking there."

" Yes," said the King; and addressing the poet: " You shall turn a handle. You shall keep silent. You shall play an organ that will give out valses, quadrilles, and two-steps, unless you prefer to die of hunger. A piece of music for a piece of bread. No gibberish about ideals. " Go! " And from that day onwards, by the edge of the pond where lived the swans, the starving poet could be seen turning the handle; tiriririn; tiriririn . . . ashamed in the sight of the great sun! Did the King pass by? Tiriririn, tiriririn! . . . Did his stomach feel empty? Tiriririn! And this, amid the mocking of the free birds that came to drink the dew from the lilies; amid the buzzing of the bees that stung his face and filled his eyes with tears . . . bitter tears than ran down his cheeks and fell on the hardened ground!

And winter came, and the poor poet felt numbed with cold in body and soul. His brain seemed petrified, and he thought no more of his grand verses; the poet of the mountain crowned with eagles was now nothing but a poor devil turning the handle of an organ: tiriririn!

And when the snow fell he was forgotten by the King and his subjects; the birds were sheltered, but he was left in the icy air that gripped his body and lashed his face.

And one night when the snow from above was falling in crystallised flakes, there was a feast in the palace, and the light from the sconces danced merrily on the marble, on the gold, and on the robes of the mandarins in the old porcelains. And frenzied applause was given to the toast of the professor of rhetoric, teeming with dactyls, anapæsts and pyrrhics, while the champagne sparkled in the crystal glasses, with its clear and fleeting bubbles. A winter's night, a night of festivity! And the poor devil, covered by the snow, near the pond, turned the handle of the organ to warm himself, shivering and stiff from the cold, reviled by the north wind on the frozen and merciless mantle of snow, in the darkness of night, the mad music of two-step and quadrille floating among the leafless trees; and he died, thinking that the sun would rise next day and with it the Ideal . . . and that Art would not be dressed in trousers, but in a cloak of fire, or of gold. . . . Until the King and his courtiers found him next day, the poor luckless poet, like a sparrow killed by the frost, with a bitter smile on his lips, and his hand still holding the handle.

.   .   .   .

Oh, my friend! The sky is dark, the air is cold, the day sad. There is grey and misty melancholy about. . . . But, how the soul is comforted by a timely word or a hand-shake! Au revoir.

RUBÉN DARÍO

THE WATER NYMPH

WE were seated round the table, just six of us, in the Château newly bought by Lesbia, the capricious and untamable little actress whose extravagances were then on every lip. Our Aspasia presided, and at the moment held between her pink fingers a moist lump of sugar, which she was sucking with childish pleasure. We had reached the liqueurs. The table glittered like a lake of precious stones, and the light of the flickering candles merged in the half-empty glasses, changing colour in the ruby Burgundy, the burning gold of the champagne, and the emerald depths of the crême de menthe.

We talked with the enthusiasm of respectable artists after a good dinner. We were all artists of varying degrees of importance, and there was also a fat scientist whose immaculate shirt-front was decorated by a monstrous cravat, tied in a large knot.

Some one said, " Yes, Fremiet! " And from Fremiet we passed to his animals, to his masterly chisel, to two bronze dogs that stood near by, one nosing the scent of the quarry, and the other gazing upwards, his thin tail rigid and erect, as though looking at the hunter. Who mentioned Myron? The scientist who recited Anacreon's epigram in Greek. " Drover, take your herd to graze afar, lest thinking Myron's cow alive, you want to take it with you."

Lesbia finished sucking the lump of sugar, and with a silvery laugh:

" Bah! I prefer the satyrs. I would like to give my bronzes life, and if possible, my lover should be one of those shaggy demi-gods. But even more than satyrs, I adore centaurs; and I would let myself be stolen by one of those monsters if only to hear my lover wail at my deceit, sadly playing on his flute."

The scientist interrupted: " Satyrs and fauns, hippocentaurs and syrens have existed like the salamanders and the Phoenix."

We all laughed; but above the chorus rose the voice, irresistible, charming, of Lesbia, her face flushed with the flush of beauty, radiant with happiness.

" Yes," continued the scientist, " what right have we to deny facts affirmed by the ancients? The gigantic dog, high as a man,

223

seen by Alexander, is as real as the kraken spider that lives in the depths of the sea. St. Anthony the Abbot, at the age of ninety, went in search of the old hermit Paul who lived in a cave. Lesbia, don't laugh. The saint was walking through the desert, leaning on his staff, and wondering where he would find the man he sought. After walking for a long time, do you know who told him the direction he was to take? A centaur, ' half man and half horse,' says the author. He spoke as though annoyed, and fled so rapidly that the saint soon lost sight of him; he galloped away with his hair flowing and his body nearly grazing the ground. During the same journey St. Anthony saw a satyr, a little man of strange appearance, standing near a streamlet; he had a hook nose, a rough and wrinkled forehead, and the lower part of his ill-formed body terminated with the hoofs of a goat.''

'' In fact,'' said Lesbia, '' M. Cocureau, future member of the Institute! ''

The scientist continued:

'' It is affirmed by St. Jerome that in the time of Constantine the Great a live satyr was taken to Alexandria, and his body was preserved when he died. Moreover, he was seen by the Emperor in Antioch.''

Lesbia had refilled her glass of crême de menthe, and was moistening her tongue in the green liqueur, like a kitten.

'' It is said by Albertus Magnus that in his time two satyrs were captured in the mountains of Saxony. Enrico Zormano assures us that in Tartary there were men with only one leg, and one arm only on the chest. Vincencio in his time saw a monster that was brought to the King of France; it had a dog's head (Lesbia laughed). The thighs, arms, and hands were as hairless as ours (Lesbia wriggled in her chair like a ticklish child); it ate cooked meat, and drank wine willingly.''

'' Colombine! '' called Lesbia. And Colombine came, a little lap-dog like a bundle of wool. Its mistress took it up, and amidst shouts of laughter from all:

'' Take that! The monster was like you! '' And she kissed it on the mouth, while the animal trembled and distended its little nostrils with excitement.

'' And Filegon Traliano ''—concluded the scientist finely— '' asserts the existence of two kinds of hippocentaurs: one of them eats elephants.''

'' Enough of this wisdom,'' said Lesbia. And she finished her liqueur.

I was happy. I had not opened my lips. '' Oh! '' I exclaimed, '' I prefer nymphs! I would like to watch those nudities of the woods and fountains, although, like Actæon, my dogs devoured me afterwards. But nymphs don't exist! ''

That merry gathering broke up amid laughter and farewells.

" Well," said Lesbia, burning me with her fawn-like eyes, and lowering her voice as though speaking only to me, " nymphs do exist, and you shall see them."

. . . .

It was a spring day. I was wandering in the gardens of the castle, with the air of a confirmed dreamer. The sparrows were twittering on the fresh lilies and pecking at the beetles protected by their shells of emerald, by their breast-plates of gold and steel. Among the roses, carmine-coloured and vermilion, the penetrating odour of sweet perfumes; farther on, the violets, in large masses, with their soft colour and virgin odour. Beyond, the tall trees, the leafy branches harbouring a thousand bees, the statues in the half-shades, the bronze discobolus, the muscular gladiators in their superb gymnastic attitudes, the perfumed bowers hung with ivy, the porticoes, beautiful Ionic reproductions, caryatides all white and inviting, and vigorous telamones of the atlantean order, with broad backs and giant thighs. I was wandering in the labyrinth of these charms when I heard a noise, over there in the darkness of the wood, in the pond where live the swans— some so white that they seem carved in alabaster, others with half the neck as black as ebony, suggesting a black stocking on a white leg.

I moved nearer. Was I dreaming? No, never! I felt as you did when you first saw Egeria in her grotto.

In the centre of the pond, amongst the frightened swans, was a nymph, a real nymph, submerging her rose-coloured form in the crystal waters. Her hips above the water seemed at times gilded by the gentle light filtering through the leaves. It was a vision of lilies, roses, snow, and gold; I saw an ideal with life and form, and I heard above the gentle splashing of the broken waters a mocking and harmonious laugh that fired my blood.

Suddenly the vision fled, the nymph rose from the pond, like Cytherea on her wave, and gathering her hair, that shed diamonds in her path, she ran between the rose-bushes, beyond the lilies and violets, beyond the leafy trees, until she disappeared, alas, round a bend. and I was left: a lyric poet, a cheated faun, looking at the large alabaster swans which seemed to mock me as they stretched towards me their long necks, at the end of which glistened the agate green of their bills.

. . . .

Later, we were lunching together, the same friends of the previous evening, and among us, resplendent in his shirt-front and large black bow, the fat scientist, future member of the Institute.

And suddenly, whilst we were all talking of Fremiet's latest work in the Salon, Lesbia exclaimed in her merry Parisian voice: " Té! as Tartarin says, the poet has seen nymphs! . . ." All looked at her astonished, and she gazed at me, gazed at me like a cat, and laughed like a ticklish child.

THE BLUE BIRD

PARIS is a gay yet terrible place. Among the frequenters of the Café Plombier, painters, sculptors, authors, poets, yes, all aspiring to the old green laurel—good and plucky boys—no one was more beloved than poor Garcin; nearly always sad, a good absinthe drinker, a dreamer who was never drunk, and, like a true Bohemian, a fine improviser.

Among the drawings and sketches of future Delacroix that decorated the walls of the untidy little room where we had our merry meetings were verses, complete stanzas in the heavy sloping writing of our blue bird.

The blue bird was poor Garcin. You don't know why he was called by that name? Well, it was we who christened him.

It was not a mere whim. He was a sad drinker, and when we asked him why he frowned and stared at the ceiling, whilst we were all laughing like lunatics or like silly children, he replied with a rather bitter smile: " Comrades, it is because I have a blue bird in my head, and therefore . . ."

It also happened that he was very fond of visiting the country in the spring-time. The air of the woods was good for his lungs, so the poet used to tell us. When he returned from his excursions he always brought bunches of violets and sheaves of paper covered with madrigals, written to the rustling of the leaves under the cloudless sky. The violets were for Nini, his neighbour, a girl with fresh and rosy cheeks and eyes of the deepest blue. The verses were for us. We read them and applauded them. We all admired Garcin. He was a genius that would shine. His time would come. Oh, the blue bird would fly very high! Bravo! Good! Here, waiter, more absinthe.

* * * * * * * *

Garcin's principles:
Of flowers, the pretty bell-flower.
Of precious stones, the sapphire.
Of the immensities, the sky and love; that is to say, Nini's eyes.

And the poet often said: " I think neurosis is always better than dulness."

.   .   .   .

At times Garcin was sadder than usual.

He would walk along the boulevards indifferent to the luxurious carriages, the well-dressed men, the beautiful women. When passing a jeweller's shop he would smile; but when he came to a book-shop, he approached the window and examined the contents eagerly; at the sight of the beautiful volumes he said he felt decidedly envious, and frowned; to relieve his feeling he would look at the sky and sigh. And then he would hurry to the café in search of us, nervous, excited; he would order his absinthe and say:

" Yes, caged in my head is a blue bird that wants its freedom. . . ."

.   .   .   .

Some began to think his mind unhinged.

A brain specialist, on being consulted, said it was a case of special monomania. His pathological experience left no room for doubt.

Decidedly, poor Garcin was mad.

One day he received a letter from his father, an old cloth merchant in Normandy, which ran somewhat like this:

" I have heard about your mad behaviour in Paris. So long as you continue, you shan't have a *sou* from me. Come and keep my books in the shop, and when you have burnt your stupid writings, you lazy scamp, you can have my money."

This letter was read out in the Café Plombier.

" Will you go? " " Won't you go? " " Will you agree? " " Will you take any notice? "

Bravo, Garcin! He tore up the letter, and leaning out of the window, laughed loudly and improvised a few stanzas, which ended, if I remember rightly:

.

'Tis true I'm doomed to idleness,
    Yet at my fate I do not gird,
So long as, caged within my brain,
    Safe and secure is the Blue Bird!

.   .   .   .

After that, Garcin's character underwent a change. He became talkative, took a dose of merriment, bought a new coat, and began a poem in terzets, entitled, naturally, " The Blue Bird."

Every evening at our meeting a fresh part of the work was read. It was excellent, sublime, extravagant. It pictured a very beautiful sky, a very fresh landscape, a country conjured up as by the magic brush of Corot, children's faces showing among the flowers, Nini's eyes moist and large; and added to all, the good God who sends, flying over it all, a blue bird that, without knowing how or when, nests in the poet's head, where it remains a prisoner. When the bird wants to fly and spreads its wings and strikes the walls of his head, he casts his eyes heavenwards, puckers his forehead, and drinks absinthe with a little water, drawing the while at a cigarette. That is the poem.

One night Garcin came, laughing loudly, but yet very sad.

. . . .

His pretty neighbour had been carried to the graveyard.

"I have news for you! News! The last canto of my poem. Nini is dead. Spring comes and Nini goes. The violets can remain in the country. Now for the epilogue of my poem. The publishers do not even condescend to read my verses. You will very soon have to separate. The law of time. The epilogue must be entitled: *How the blue bird took wing to the blue skies.*

The middle of spring! The trees in bloom, the clouds pink in the morn and pale at eve; the gentle breeze that shakes the leaves and flutters the ribbons of the straw hats. Garcin did not go into the country. Here he comes, dressed in a new suit, to our beloved Café Plombier, pale, and smiling sadly.

"My friends, embrace me. Embrace me, all of you; bid me good-bye, with all your hearts . . . the blue bird is taking wing. . . ."

And poor Garcin wept, and wrung our hands hard and went away.

We all said: Garcin, the prodigal son, is going to his father in Normandy. Muses, farewell; farewell, Graces. Our poet has decided to measure cloth! Here! A glass to Garcin!

Pale, frightened, sorrowful, on the following day all the frequenters of the Café Plombier, who made such a noise in the untidy little room, stood in Garcin's lodgings. He was lying on the bed, on the blood-stained sheets, his head shattered by a bullet. On the pillow lay fragments of his brain. . . . Horrible!

When we had recovered from the shock, and were weeping over the body of our friend, we found on him the famous poem. On the last page he had written these words:

To-day, in the middle of spring, I have opened the door of the cage for the poor blue bird.

. . . .

Ah! Garcin, how many people are afflicted as you were.

JOSÉ FERNANDEZ BREMÓN

19TH CENTURY

THE CURSE OF TONGUES

I

NEVER shall I forget my old schoolmate and eccentric friend, Juan Claro.

He was a good student, laborious and painstaking, but exceedingly quarrelsome and taciturn, even to the extent of avoiding his class-mates. Later he became barbarously and offensively outspoken on all occasions. Since his hands were always ready and eager to back up his tongue, he had sooner or later measured strength with every student in college who believed himself capable of avenging Juan's stinging remarks by an appeal to fisticuffs.

His predilection for me was due to my toleration of what he called his " frankness." Juan really had many good qualities, and my enjoyment of his sagacity and the conviction that he was his own worst enemy and morally incapable of living in ordinary society made me seek his company and esteem him highly. His character was as opposite to most men's as it was possible to imagine. At last, after a more than usually stormy college career, he became involved during the last few weeks of his fourth year in a fight, which brought him before the disciplinary committee, and he was summarily dismissed from the university.

" Well, anyway," Juan said to me when it was all over, " I had the great satisfaction of telling the old bears how the professors' wives flirt with us and everybody else! "

Some years later we chanced to be riding together in the stage-coach to San Isidro, when another and a more curious phase of his trouble-making nature asserted itself in a most startling and unexpected manner. Just in front of us on the outside of the coach was a very pretty young woman accompanied by a rather grim-looking, old moustached fellow. Juan eyed first one and then the other, and finally managed in some way to attract the young woman's attention. For a few moments they cast sheep's eyes at each other, when Juan suddenly spoke to her escort.

" Pardon me, stranger, but is the young lady your wife? "

" What's that to you? " growled the old moustache fiercely.

" Nothing at all," retorted Juan, with a slow and dangerous smile, " but I cannot resist the pleasure of informing you that for some time now she has been eyeing me with a good deal of interest."

Everybody on top of the lumbering old vehicle gasped. We expected nothing less than a fight on the spot. Had the stranger thrown himself upon Juan there and then we could not have said a word, for the insult was so uncalled-for; but to our amazement he merely shouted vociferously to the driver to stop, clambered down himself, and took the young woman, now very pale and trembling, down after him, and handed Juan his card. Claro glanced at the pasteboard, laughed in the face of the old gentleman, and tore the card into bits. It was the business card of a dry-goods house, and the old fellow was a miserable shopkeeper instead of the soldier or man of the world we had thought him. Juan said afterward he was almost sorry he had said anything to him; it was a pity to waste powder, even in words, on a man beneath one's own station.

It was this same Juan, the incorrigible, who cried out in a loud, clear voice, before a roomful of friends, when told that his father was dead: " It's high time! "

The people about, of course, withdrew from him in horror, not-withstanding the old man's death had left Juan many times a millionaire. I was the only one left in the room to hear his better self express the genuine sorrow I knew he felt. After that it was long before I saw him again, only hearing occasionally that his old and unchecked habit of giving his thoughts a reckless tongue had grown into a positive infirmity. I had almost entirely forgotten the man, with his queer ways and his inexhaustible wealth, when one day I got a note from him. It ran as follows:

" DEAR LUIS—I give you two proofs of my confidence. The first is to ask you to do me a favour. I wish you to send me a servant. I must have one of good antecedents, and with the indispensable quality of being stone-deaf. The person with whom I have to live is a deaf-mute, so it would be well for the servant to be able to converse in the sign-manual, thus saving me the nuisance of teaching it. The essential thing is that he must be as deaf as a mud wall—I have two excellent dogs to guard the house, and their ears are all that can be desired.

" The second proof is that I save you the annoyance of a fruitless trip out here. Since my servants cannot hear nor know when any one calls, they open to nobody, and merely bring me in the letters and cards left by the postman under the gate. I shall read your reply with satisfaction.

" Your old friend and fellow-student,   JUAN CLARO."

After attending to Juan's request, I heard no more from him for so long a time that I had again forgotten that my old friend was alive. Then one afternoon a stoutish man in deep black entered my office and made queer signs to me with his hands. For a moment I could not remember him, but at last I recollected that this must be the man I had sent out to the provinces in accordance with Juan's instructions in that curious letter. The poor fellow gesticulated quite uselessly at me, with his sprawling fingers wriggling in all directions like so many worms. My equally futile words pattered vainly against his granite tympanum, and we were as far apart as though walls separated us. At last, with a quick gesture which I took to mean patience, and a profound bow, he drew a folded paper from his coat pocket and laid it upon my table. It was another letter from Juan, and I read it with interest, the mute watching me narrowly as I took it up. The script was fine and close-written, and the sheets of manuscript were so numerous as to promise a longish bout at deciphering my friend's none too distinct hieroglyphics; so I settled back in my chair to read in comfort, little guessing what was coming.

II

" DEAR LUIS," the letter began, " you have been and are my only friend. You have many friendships, but I can do no less than make you my confidant, though I suppose I now occupy but a very small place in your affections. Nevertheless, I must recover what space I formerly held, and in order to do that satisfactorily, must, in some measure at least, explain away my former and more recent offences.

" Though you have, indeed, always remained my friend, your visits to me gradually became more and more irregular until they finally ceased altogether. All my other acquaintances had dropped me, and when you no longer came to me I began to wonder what it was that kept me friendless and alone, no matter where I was. I thought the matter over carefully and became convinced that since I had not mastered my old foolish habit of thinking aloud, it was mastering me, nay, had mastered me, to the extent that I found myself powerless to correct the fault. Well, to make a long story short, I bought a place out here in the country and shut myself up with a servant, thinking to become, like Descartes, an ascetic and lonely philosopher. But my man turned out a thief, and one day when we were talking about it he attempted to justify himself. He declared he had robbed the merchant who was his employer because the latter had entrusted him with all his secrets, though paying him a beggarly pittance as wages. ' As you think out loud, sir,' he finished up brazenly, ' I think you had better have only mutes for your servants in future.' I did not fully understand what he meant, and forced the rascal to explain, which he did with the greatest reluctance.

" ' Well, sir, if you must know,' he said, ' you think out loud all day long, on every subject. You speak of the interest you get from the bankers, of how long it is since you had a bath, and whether you are clean enough to go one day more without taking one. You see I know all your most secret thoughts. I could tell you the names of your former mistresses, and the circumstances under which your mother died; just how much your father left you, and where and how it is invested and kept. I know that at the present moment you have right here in your pocket fifty thousand pesetas that came in this morning's mail from the bank; and you don't know what to do with such a sum in notes. My advice, respectfully offered, would be to put it in the bank at once.'

" The fellow's talk and his confession shook me up considerably, and I resolved to act on his advice. I saw at last that what had been a mere mannerism in my early youth had become a vice I could not control even in the most favourable circumstances. I was always making a noise wherever I went; it was the buzzing of my inmost thoughts, expressed verbally, though without my realising it. You can see how impossible it would be for me to live in society in close touch with my fellow-men. Every whimsical or serious notion or idea that popped into my head would just as surely pop out again in words. The more effort I made to suppress this grotesque yet dangerous failing the worse it became. It was as if the very fact of dwelling on it aggravated my disease. At last I gave up trying, and permitted myself full swing. Crimes, vice, the defects of beauties, the miseries of the rich and powerful, the evil qualities of any and all; noble, lewd, scientific, foolish, whimsical or serious thoughts dripped in words from my tongue like the slaver of a panting dog at noon.

" Of course, the first thing I did was to get rid of Francisco; the next, I wrote to an agency, and the following afternoon a mute presented himself, a white-haired and moustached old fellow who appeared very vigorous in spite of his years, and who proved active and serviceable. I thought he would do very well, but he had the grave fault of extreme curiosity, and many a time I caught him spying on me through the gate or window. Since the man could not talk, and it was too much of a nuisance to write out conversations with him on any ordinary and trivial subject, I purchased a number of good parrots and magpies to make my speechless life less burdensome. You may be sure they very soon developed an astonishing flow of conversation. One of them, my favourite because of his talkative powers and ability to carry on a genuine conversation, I called Nuño. You remember Nuño, don't you?

—the chap at college who was the wonder of the professors and the despair of dullards like myself for his ability to read a thing once and then reel it off by rote without the slightest effort?

" I could not, however, depend entirely upon my birds for amusement, so I used to sit out on my second-storey balcony every fine afternoon, watching the farmers in the distance and the people who occasionally passed by on the road. By twisting my neck a little I could see between the trees to the shoulder of the near-by cemetery. I had been sitting there for several weeks when I noticed a young woman, clad in deep mourning, come out of the postern gate of the cemetery and pass down the road to some point beyond my house. Her dress was modest and her face pretty enough. In Madrid, or any good-sized city, she would not have attracted the slightest attention; but here, on a lonely road, away in the country, she completely captivated me. ' Who can this unknown be? ' I wondered to myself every afternoon, as I sat hidden on the balcony, watching her pass. ' Can it be that a veteran like myself is to fall a victim to this simple country girl? ' I asked myself one afternoon as I was walking mechanically along the road down which she always disappeared. I turned to see if I could locate the exact spot where she vanished each day, and to my annoyance saw my servant trailing along a few paces in the rear.

" ' Idler! ' I said in the sign-manual, ' you were spying on me! '

" ' No, sir! ' he answered out loud and without repressing an evil smile. It annoyed me the more to feel that he could talk to me as he pleased, while I, because he was stone-deaf, had to use the slow and difficult signs. ' I wished to speak to you of the young lady who passes this way every afternoon.'

" ' Who is she? ' I asked, forgetting to reprimand him.

" ' Her name is Sofia,' he responded humbly. ' I saw you watched her with interest, so I ventured to set myself the task of finding out who and what she is. Her family is excellent and honourable, but now very poor. The girl herself is unmarried and virtuous; she lives with a sister of her father, who is employed in the country some miles away, but is too poor to support her properly. The girl has, however, one insurmountable defect—she is absolutely deaf and dumb, a perfect mute.'

" You can imagine how I felt when I heard that! I dismissed my man with a wave of the hand and walked on alone to think it over. Next day my decision was formed. I waited for her at the corner of the cemetery, with a blessed sense of security and confidence I had never known in my affairs with other women. For Sofia the mute I was a man without a fault. My hands would not stutter nor betray my secret thoughts; they could express sensible ideas of love in a rational way. And my lips, talking their loudest, could never be hurtful to her. We should live together happily, and she need never know my miserable secret.

" The tongue of my fingers was laconic. A declaration in the usual roundabout terms of love would have been interminable and ridiculous, spelled out, so I simply signed to her with my hands: ' I love you. Will you make me happy—can we not be friends? I know your name and position. I live alone in that big house. Will you share it with me? '

" Anxiously I waited for her reply, which was some time in coming. At last she looked up at me with a faint smile and replied on her fingers:

" ' Friendship comes little by little. Love comes later, and sometimes never. I can only say to you that, deprived of all chance to mingle with the world, it is very pleasant to talk to you.'

" That was all I could get from her in the way of a promise that afternoon, though we talked rapidly in silence for an hour or more. She promised to come back every day. Eventually she accepted me, although I confessed my besetting weakness. I will not weary you, old friend, with the details of how I took every possible precaution to prevent myself from interrupting the ceremony by letting slip verbally what I thought of the fat priest, nor yet of how successfully I got through the ordeal. For once I managed without any bad mistakes, but the strain was terrible.

" Of course, we lived in Paradise for a while; but the sneaking, spying habits of my servant soon came to be worse than ever. I attributed the perpetual eye at the keyhole to the poor wretch's isolation, and bore with his fault as I could. But there came a day when I lost my temper completely. I found him peeping into the room where Sofia was dressing. I seized the wretch by the hair and shook him vigorously.

" To my horror the whole of the top of his head came off and dangled idly from my nerveless fingers. I shut my eyes, sick with fright. You know how powerful I am—I thought that in my rage I must have scalped him, without realising I was pulling so hard. It was some moments before I could pull myself together enough to look down at him, for I fully expected to see a raw and bloody skull. You can imagine my astonishment, and then my anger, when I tell you that I found myself looking at the closely-shaven black head of my former servant—Francisco, the thief.

" ' Pardon, master! ' he shrieked, falling on his knees, thoroughly frightened. ' Fidelity to you and yours made me adopt this deception. I could not bear to leave your service! '

" It was some moments before I got the better of my temper.

I did nothing rash, but, turning a deaf ear to Sofia, who had interceded for him, I ordered the sneaking scamp out of the house instantly, throwing his stuff after him. When he had at last cleared out, Sofia threw herself into my arms, weak and pale, with a terror I did not then understand, supposing it to be what any good woman would feel, and signed to me: ' You did well to get rid of him! He is dangerous—look out for him all the time! '

" This, contradicting her intercession for him, and Francisco's own interference in my love affair, filled me with horrible doubts. I began to watch her narrowly, without her suspecting it. I thought the thing over out loud, as usual, speculating on what he and she had done, how far each was culpable, to what extent I had been deceived, and so on. I saw that she wept almost all the time when I was not with her. When we were together she tried to be as bright and cheerful as ever, but under the strain her health, always delicate, began rapidly to fail, so rapidly, in fact, that I thought I could see a daily change for the worse. At last Blas, our baby, turned from the breast and beat upon it furiously with his tiny hands. It seemed to me symbolic that even her own child turned against her. I felt there could no longer be any doubt; but when, after convincing herself that she could no longer feed the little fellow, she crushed him feverishly to her heart and cried *out loud* in agonized tones, ' My son! Oh, my son! ' my own heart almost stopped beating.

" My wife able to talk! To hear! Not a mute at all! But even while I was wondering over it, she paled and swayed and slipped from her chair, white and silent, into my arms. She had been able to keep her deception without a single false step or slip through all the unusual vicissitudes of our five years of married life, until maternal love had wrenched her secret from her. I had been spied upon by a vile stratagem, an iniquitous deception. I had no doubt it was the work of Francisco, who had certainly profited in some way by the contemptible deceit. While these thoughts were surging through my brain and finding their echo on my running tongue, I turned to Sofia, who was regaining consciousness, ' They were after my money,' I concluded bitterly and aloud. ' She certainly had this man Francisco for a lover! God knows —Blas may not even be my child! '

" Sofia raised herself wearily on one arm and stared at me in a peculiar fashion for a full minute, silently, and I felt an uneasy sense of something about to happen.

" ' That man, Francisco,' she whispered unsteadily and with a groan, ' is my father! ' and she fainted again.

" I cannot begin to tell you how I felt at that moment, nor how strange, how impossible it seemed that I should be my own body-servant's son-in-law. I was too much dazed to realise anything except that my suspicions of poor, consumptive Sofia had been unjust, and that my father-in-law, Don Francisco Lopez y Vivo, and my ex-body servant, Francisco Lopez, were one and the same person.

" ' I have had no designs upon your wretched money," ventured Sofia, when she had recovered her senses. ' On the contrary, I have saved you endless rage and worry regarding it. My father told me of your sad situation, and I quickly learned to pity you. It pained me deeply to see you walking past the house almost every day, talking incessantly to yourself in a clear, bold voice, pitched in a high, resonant key, passing from one thought to another with the greatest rapidity and inconsistency, and always alone, in spite of your youth, good looks, and money. From that first day when I learned your story—your habit had told the story thousands of times, so that my father knew it by heart—I did not cease to question my father about you unreservedly and with the most imprudent interest, as I now see.

" ' " It lies easily in your hands to be rich and the mistress of that great house," he said to me one day in a very mysterious manner. I had not an idea of what he meant at first, but when at last I did understand, the plan, which should have been repugnant to me, which ought to have disgusted and repelled me, seemed perfectly justifiable and right, and I accepted the opportunity by no means unwillingly. I saw myself at your side, able to comfort you, to help you to enjoy life—I fell in with my father's plans without reserve. You may not believe me, Juan, but I honestly believed I was doing right. I thought I realised what it would mean to you if I made my small sacrifice and gave up speech, the privilege of crying out in fear or joy, even my very voice itself, to bring a little temporary joy into your bleak and uncomfortable life. Perhaps I was wrong. God knows—I thought I was doing well, doing my very best, for you.

" ' Afterward I had to protect you from my father's covetousness, for he never could forget your money, and he craved it with an unholy lust. Yet I was able to control him by the threat of exposure. That was why I wept when you dismissed him; that was why I told you he was dangerous and would bear watching —but oh, he was and is my father just the same, and it nearly broke my heart to say it!

" ' I loved you at first, dearly. I love you yet. But you are only mortal, and you were far more yourself in thinking I could hear nothing than a man who knows his wife is his real other half. You never felt that way regarding me. Believing that my ears and tongue were both dead you gave your thoughts free rein, realising to the full your infirmity, and thinking aloud all day long, and sometimes far into the night. Not a day has gone by but I have heard you talking to yourself, suspecting my dis-interestedness, attributing to me the most odious of motives in marrying you. I have heard you roar with laughter as you joked to yourself over my simple ways. I have heard you recount your previous love affairs minutely in the most revolting terms, pass my various defects and faults in merciless review, complain of being tired of me, and dream eagerly of another and less monoton-ous life.   Yet in spite of all this I managed to hold my peace.'

" I could not let her conclude her story. The gentle arraign-ment was more than I could bear. I endured torments during her brief recital. I saw myself pitifully unworthy such an unheard-of sacrifice. I remembered the many cruel, wicked things I would to God I had never said; and, ashamed before the woman who had so smilingly endured these five long and bitter years of hell for my sake, immured in a living death, I dropped on my knees before her, kissing that dear face with the profoundest pity, and even as I kissed her I heard myself crying out, to my own horror and disgust:

" ' Francisco has married me to his daughter, who is an angel! I am my servant's son-in-law!   But she will be dead of consump-tion by autumn! '

" It makes me sick to think of that even now, but it was said and I could not unsay it. Shortly after that, realising that it was not right for little Blas to be with me and hear all my wild talk, we sent him away to remain until he had attained years and knowledge of the world enough to come back to us without being permanently injured by being near me. With his departure Sofia's illness made terrible strides. One afternoon, when it cost me more effort than usual to carry her to her invalid's chair on the balcony, I capped all my previous crimes of cruelty by exclaiming fever-ishly: ' How heavy she is still! Will she take many days more to die? '

" I cannot recall without the bitterest remorse the glance she gave me, full of melancholy, though with the love-light shining through it. Did she hear and understand my insensate words? Did she hear them in heaven or on earth? Was it the shock of hearing them that killed her? I never knew, for when I knelt and took her hands between mine, kissing them passionately and plead-ing with her to pardon me, she was dead. I verily believe my many cruel words, all of which were absolutely impossible for me to suppress or even to control, did more, really, to kill her than the fatal disease itself.

" I am alone. I cannot bear to stay in this house, where every-thing reminds me of Sofia, constantly and continually accusing me for my criminal brutality. I am dying, almost literally, for want of the society of my fellow-men, yet I dare not intrude my hateful presence upon even you. My company either offends or horrifies. Happiest and most blessed of creatures are men able to conceal their thoughts! Am I really a monster in soul, and a being exceptional among my fellow-creatures of like appearance? Worse! Am I not a murderer?

"Your unfortunate friend,   Juan Claro."

III

Juan's letter left me sick and dazed for weeks after I had read it, but being a busy man full of professional cares and duties to the rest of the world, I had with the lapse of time completely forgotten it. One day, however, the door of my private office opened, and, pallid, his strong face greatly altered, seamed, and aged, Juan Claro entered. I was struck dumb for a moment, for I had no idea he was coming. Naturally I expected to be greeted with violent abuse and reproaches—I had never replied to that horrible letter. It was simply impossible; I could not do it, though I had tried faithfully to do so promptly. Juan, however, remained perfectly silent, and his expressive lips curled slightly in a faint, sad smile. He opened his arms, breaking the spell, and I threw myself into them, crying:

"Thank God, you are cured! Now you can come back into the world again!"

But Juan, though nodding assent, made not the slightest attempt to reply, and I asked him with an uneasy, nervous feeling if anything was the matter—if he had a sore throat.

The man's eyes opened wide as I asked the question, and a curious expression came over his face as he stared at me dumbly; but I felt relieved when he touched his throat on both sides near his tonsils and nodded affirmatively. With one foot he drew a chair up to my desk, seated himself, motioned me to sit down, took up a pen, and invited me to read over his shoulder while he wrote.

"If *you* want to think out loud," he began, "go ahead! I can see already that you have formed an unfavourable opinion." I confessed I could not understand him.

"I can explain my silence in a few words," he continued. "A few days after Sofia died I learned that my precious father-in-law had applied judicially for a commission to examine and report upon my mental condition, assuring the court that I had lost my faculties entirely and was not in my right mind. My excellent relative told the judges I had a vast estate which would fall to my son at my death, and he, of course, wished to administer the property for his grandson, should I be proven incapable, until the child attained his majority.

" The exigency was pressing, and it worried me greatly to think what might happen to Blas if by any ill chance the doctors should pronounce against me. I felt certain his scoundrelly grandfather would take care that the child either should never grow up or never get more than a tithe of the estate. In the condition in which I found myself no ordinary doctor would have certified to my sanity, for Sofia's death had left me more eccentric than ever. The danger that I would be shut up for ever in an asylum rendered me desperate and almost maddened me. I was willing to take any chance, to go to any length to attain my purpose. At last, seeing no other way out of my predicament, I hunted up a directory, wrote a note to a surgeon I knew, and awaited his arrival with impatience. Eventually he came, carrying under his arm a neat medical case.

" ' You have everything that will be required? ' I asked him.

" ' Oh yes,' he replied. ' Are you the companion or a relative of the sick man? '

" ' I am the sick man myself,' I smiled back at him, and stated just what I wanted in a few terse words.

" ' My God, no! I can't do that! ' he exclaimed. ' What you propose is a crime for which I should be responsible to the law! '

" ' Don't be a fool, now! ' I retorted sharply, covering him with a heavy revolver I had secreted in my pocket in case he should prove obstinate. ' Don't get nervous, but do as I tell you. My case is unusual. It demands an unusual remedy, and I purpose to have it, whether you like it or not. Do as I wish, or—the rose-bushes there by the fence would cover a new grave very neatly; no one would ever guess it was there! '

" ' But—explain yourself,' he stammered, pale and scared. ' Tell me the reason for your amazing request! '

" I told him briefly, and he replied doggedly that I might kill him before he would permit so heinous a crime. I laughed in his face, and waved the pistol. I had to have my joke. I was talking to a live man at last, and the fright I gave him was thoroughly enjoyable. It did me good to make him squirm.

" ' I know you, you doctor! ' I cried. ' You are my old school-mate, Nuño. You are still a very wise old monkey! Do as I tell you, or I'll drop something new into that skull of yours that never let anything go once it got hold of it! '

" ' Very well, then,' he returned, flushing hotly as he recognised me. ' But remember—it is the insulted man, not the doctor under compulsion, who treats you! '

" ' Oh, anything you like,' I laughed jovially, ' so long as you do it, and do it right.'

" Now I am a highly esteemed person, a man greatly respected and admired," Juan scribbled on with another of those queer smiles I was unable to understand, but which I already recognised as having in them something sinister, something to be dreaded. " The doctors have declared me perfectly sane, my former friends all appreciate me, and even Nuño, who is at heart really not a half-bad fellow, dines with me once a week. So must you."

" But what did you do—what medicine did Nuño give you to work this marvellous change? " I demanded, somewhat annoyed by his ignoring the very fact he knew I most wanted to learn. " And why don't you talk out loud? Surely your throat is not so sore you cannot speak except in whispers! "

Another of those bitter smiles answered my query before Juan bent to his scribbling again.

" Here is the *corpus delicti*," he wrote on, taking out a package from his coat pocket with one hand while his pen was kept busily scratching with the other. It was a bottle. " That is the instrument with which I killed Sofia," he added, his powerful shoulders quivering with emotion. " Before, I could not live among men; now, I am beloved and respected. Everybody seeks me out and makes much of me. Yet I am the same man. I am delivered of the curse of tongues, the bane of humanity! I am the same, yet another person, the old, yet a new Juan. But I am all here! " he added, and his empty mouth opened in a ghastly laugh as he dropped the bottle into my startled hands.

I glanced at it hastily, to look up at him horrified, aghast. He looked at me curiously for a moment, reached over, shook my hand, dropped the bottle back into his pocket, and was gone.

JOSÉ FERNANDEZ BREMÓN

A SILKEN CORD

A CHINESE STORY

I

THE noble Chao-sé was extremely unfortunate. Yet his rice crop had been abundant; the white flower of the tea-plant almost hid the dark branches in his leafy orchards; the cocoons of his silkworms could not have been finer; he had an autograph from the Emperor in which figured the word *cheon,* a credential for long life; and finally, he had seen hacked into ten thousand pieces the body of his enemy, Pe-Kong, who had insulted him by cutting off his pig-tail.

Why, therefore, had the noble Chinaman ordered a beating to be given to the idol of Fó, so that its bulky porcelain body now lay in pieces on the ground?

But the fact remains that Chao-sé had scolded his old cook when presented with a stewed dog that his guests had found exquisite; he had disdained a cup of tea although it was genuine Hyson; and he took no notice of the monkey in spite of its caresses.

"My dear relatives," said Chao-sé with gravity, after the meal, to the three respectable Chinamen who listened to him, squatted in the drawing-room. "You already know that I intended to present my son at the court of our Celestial Sovereign."

The speaker and his hearers bowed their heads until their pig-tails touched the ground, and the monkey had to be removed because he imitated the action of those grave personages.

Chao-sé continued:

"My son Te-kú has not taken advantage of my teaching: he does not know how to bow his body eighteen times, nor does he know the unalterable formulas of our wise etiquette; he has repudiated the virtuous daughter of Ling, whose feet will fit into nut-shells; and you will, no doubt, be astonished to hear, my beloved relatives, that he was challenged by Chung, whose honoured body lies in the tomb, and refused to cut open his stomach whilst his adversary expired in triumph with his abdomen ripped open, in due and proper form. In this ignominy I want to ask your advice, and I submit myself to what you may decide to save the honour of my family."

242

" You ought, in the first place, to disinherit Te-kú," said the
eldest relative.

" And distribute the property amongst us," said the second
relative.

" And as our reputation is lost, a victim is required; you ought
to strangle yourself to save the honour of the family," said the most
distant relative.

These were the decisions of his advisers. Chao-sé felt a tardy
remorse at having called them together.

II

" What present do you bring me in that box? " said the wife of
Chao-sé that same evening, as her husband deposited on a lacquered
table an ivory box carved with figures representing the revolution
of the Yellow Caps.

" Beautiful and beloved Tian, I am preparing a surprise for
you," said the noble Chinaman, gallantly.

Tian sat up in bed, showing her husband two little feet of but
two inches each.

" You have been a model wife and I want history to speak of
you as a model of virtues. Well, the family council demands a
victim to save the honour of my family; as I have a certificate of
long life written by my sovereign, it would be ungrateful and dis-
respectful if I cut short my life. Therefore I have selected you,
my beloved Tian, to save our honour by means of the silken cord
you will find in this box. I think you will be grateful to me for
this proof of distinction and affection."

" Master! " said Tian, very much frightened, " I dare not kill
myself, I am as timid as a chicken."

" Do not fear, my beloved; if you cannot kill yourself, since you
are as timid as a chicken, get the cook to help you."

And the noble Chao-sé went out of the room after affectionately
kissing his wife.

III

Tian seemed calm; the cook Kin was terrified.

" Kin, you require rest," said the former.

" I sleep little, madam," replied he, rubbing his eyes.

" You must be anxious to obtain the rewards that are reserved
for you in the next life."

" I do not know what the great Buddha intends for me."

" Will you fly with me? " said Tian, looking tenderly at the
poor cook.

" Madam . . ." tremblingly answered the unfortunate man.

" Fly from a house where your stews are not appreciated, be
with me and be master of my magnificent jewels."

Kin kissed the ground to express his gratitude.

" Avoiding the vengeance of Chao-sé. . . ."

" Oh yes," exclaimed the cook terrified.

" There is a way. Your master Chao-sé, protected by an order of the Emperor, will live for many years yet; during that time we can fly from the earth and lose ourselves in space."

" I do not understand."

" It is very simple: I want you to accompany me on this last journey. Take the silken cord and hang yourself outside here, while I get together my jewels and kill myself; my resuscitated body will go in a short time to meet yours."

Kin opened his slanting eyes with terror: Tian smiled at him very sweetly.

" Good-bye," she said, " do not fail to meet me "; and she pushed him gently through the doorway, after having put the noose round his neck.

As Kin left the chamber of Tian, he heard a noise in the corridors. " That must be the monkey," he said, as he walked along very troubled, but taking the soft silk cord from his neck. " I must not commit suicide for two reasons: first, because I am not certain of coming to life in another world. Second, because if I come to life, the powerful Fó might take vengeance on me and beat me to pieces as I beat his idol."

The noise was repeated. It was not the monkey but Te-kú who made the noise, as he robbed the treasures of his father; the garden window was open; the jewels shone in a sack.

Kin, indignant, could not but reproach him for his action, and told him the position in which he had placed his family.

Te-kú kept on asking him to keep quiet, but Kin's replies grew louder and louder.

Finally, much moved and frightened, the former exclaimed, " Give me the silken cord: I am the guilty one, and it is I who must make the sacrifice."

And putting on the fatal necktie he fastened one end to the iron bar of the window, flung the sack on his back for his travelling expenses, and affectionately embraced the cook, saying:

" Go away and close the door, I do not want you to witness my agony."

Kin had no great confidence in him, but dared not annoy him. As he descended into the garden, he heard a loud knock and a cry of pain.

" Can he have fled . . .? " exclaimed Kin with suspicion.

The garden was very dark, but a struggling body hung suspended from the window and another darker shadow swung below.

" He has kept an appointment for me," said Kin, breathing freely and rubbing his neck. " The guilty one no longer lives."

He then went to his room, filled his pipe with opium, and fell asleep on his mat.

IV

At dawn on the following day the relations of Chao-sé, dressed in white—strict mourning in China—went to his house to offer him their last tributes; but to their great surprise they found him dressed in white also, and looking very solemn.

" So you are alive! " said his relatives indignantly.

Chao-sé then explained his scruples, the terror of his wife and the substitution of the cook and the voluntary expiation of his son. The relatives, after an animated discussion, expressed their agreement.

" Let us go into the garden, where no one has yet entered," said Chao-sé to his relatives. " We will take down the body of my unfortunate son."

The procession followed him, and on reaching the scene of the catastrophe they all received a great shock.

Hanging by the silken cord and swinging like a pendulum was the stiff body of a monkey.

" It is not my son," said Chao-sé, astonished.

" Master, I saw him tie the cord round his neck," said the cook. " Without doubt the monkey has taken the form of your son and left his own in the window. There is some magic here and the divine Fó is avenging himself."

" It is not so," replied the heirs: " it is Te-kú hanging by the cord. Do you not recognise his features? It is a perfect likeness."

" But," exclaimed Chao-sé in self-defence, " look at that mouth. . . ."

" It is just like yours, noble Chao-sé," said his relatives.

" Look, gentlemen, at those ears."

" They are just like yours."

" Remember that a victim is required," they whispered into his ear.

The noble Chinaman confessed, in the end, that it was his son, although somewhat disfigured.

The death of Te-kú was certified; they gave the monkey a magnificent funeral, and the council of relatives declared the honour of the family to be unstained.

EPILOGUE

In spite of his Sovereign's certificate Chao-sé lived only a few years. To claim his property a youth presented himself, saying that he was his son, that his name was Te-kú, and that he had fled from the paternal house by jumping from the garden window on a dark night.

When the matter was submitted to the courts a learned mandarin delivered the following verdict, which now serves in China to settle all similar cases:

" The death of Te-kú being legally proven:

" No one having disappeared from the house of Chao-sé on the day mentioned but a monkey whose whereabouts are unknown.

" I declare that if the plaintiff is right in saying that he fled, he can be no one but the monkey;

" And if he has not spoken the truth, he deserves to be hanged with the silken cord preserved by the relatives of the deceased."

In face of such an alternative, Te-kú chose to declare himself a monkey and was handed over to an organ-grinder.

JOSÉ FRANCÉS
19TH CENTURY

THE EXPRESSION

A FEW moments before the voice of the prompter sounded through the corridors of the theatre, the manager knocked at the door of Pablo Heredia's dressing-room.

" May I come in? "

" Come in, Don Luis."

Heredia, the star actor, turned his gaze from the looking-glass to the face of the manager.

" You look very glum, Don Luis. . . . Small audience, eh? "

" So small, that we cannot go on like this, friend Heredia. We must put on *Fuerza rota* as soon as possible. Otherwise I think there will be no salaries next Monday."

He dropped into one of the arm-chairs near the wardrobe.

Heredia did not answer, but turned again to the glass and painted his eyes lightly.

There was a long silence. Neither of the two men wanted to speak first, fearful of saying anything hasty. The manager put his trust in *La Fuerza rota,* a rough, brutal drama dealing with crime-hardened men and women, suiting Heredia's temperament down to the ground. The great actor had welcomed the work with enthusiasm, and predicted that it would be his greatest triumph. Nevertheless, the final scene worried him very much. The principal character receives a knife-wound and lies dying from loss of blood, unconscious, in the misty throes of death, at the feet of a woman.

During the rehearsals he merely suggested the expression without accentuating it, with that monotonous indifference he always exhibited away from the public.

But the manager and the author of the work saw in the weak and undefined expression all the tragic intensity which the great actor would impart at the culminating moment. They talked of it, and the hope ran from one lip to another and appeared in the theatre gossip of the critics.

Heredia was proud of it at first; then he shrugged his shoulders; and finally began to experience an unreasoning dread, an almost

animal fear, of the third act, of that expression of supreme con-
vulsion in which would be portrayed everything: rage, pain, love
for life, love for woman, shame at defeat.

But above all, the violent facial tension with which death clothes
pain whilst still in life. . . . What must the eyes be like? What
colour ought the lips to acquire? And how should the voice sound?
Ought the hands to tremble? Should they claw the air? Should
they have that weakness, that sickly softness that seems to stretch
the fingers?

Cruel, terrible questions, to which he could find no answer before
the looking-glass; they absorbed his thoughts during the day and
kept him awake at night.

The rehearsals went on and on. The author and the management
fixed two or three dates and Heredia always postponed them. The
others all knew their parts. Some afternoons they boasted of re-
hearsing without the prompter. The news of Heredia's fear spread
among the players. They made biting and sarcastic jokes about
the actor and the title of the piece. His companions spoke of him
with that malicious jealousy so common among people on the
boards.

And nevertheless, in spite of the empty theatre, the author's
despair, the manager's protests, despite the fact that he saw his
fame in peril, Heredia delayed the production.

. . . .

" May we start, Don Pablo? "
It was the prompter looking in through the half-open door.
" Come in," said Don Luis.
" Yes, sir? "
" Bad, eh? "
". Yes, sir. . . . Besides, nearly all of them are deadheads. . . .
But don't worry: we can manage them. There are more of us on
the stage."

Heredia bit his lips.
" All right. . . . Go on, start; call the scene before."
The prompter rushed off. A bell sounded sharply, three long
rings. Afterwards came the usual orders.
" We are going to begin! Lights on! "
The sound of hurried steps on the floor above, the opening of
doors, and the frou-frou of skirts. Then a deep silence: the curtain
had gone up.
" Well, friend Heredia, what are we going to do? I for one can-
not go on like this. The author talks of withdrawing the piece. . . .
Think of it . . .! There is no alternative but to fix a date."

Heredia resigned himself.
" All right . . . say . . . Monday."

" Monday? No, Heredia, certainly not. Friday. That will give us four full houses for certain; the first night, the Saturday evening, and the two performances on Sunday."

" But . . ."

" No, no. To-day is Tuesday; now then, in three days, the day after to-morrow, you arrange a dress rehearsal and I will advise the photographers. I am going now to tell them in the box-office to get the notices out and to order the posters from the printers. Do you agree? "

" Very well, I agree."

The manager fled, and in the passage ran into the prompter, who arrived shouting:

" Come along! your cue, Don Pablo! You will be late for your entry. . . ."

II

About two o'clock in the morning he left the theatre after settling details and answering questions about the new piece.

He went alone, refusing to be accompanied. The night was damp and misty. November was drawing to a close, and the keenness of the air made him turn up the collar of his coat.

He started walking aimlessly, anxious for solitude, for reflection, away from the stifling air of the theatre, free from that sudden fever awakened in him by the proximity of the first night which was to ensure the salaries.

He was dazed, dubious, frightened, in that cruel emotion of uneasiness and hostility that racks body and mind when final decisions have been made after long hesitation.

How must he express that moment? How ought the eyes to look? What should the voice sound like . . . ?

He walked along unconscious, deaf, insensible to the steady drizzle, unheeding the slippery ground.

Gradually he left behind him the broad central streets and came to the poorer quarters, which on that November night were wrapped in tragic darkness. Streets of crime and poverty, with lamps that shone yellow, and at intervals the red glow of a tavern. . . .

Since the first rehearsals of *La Fuerza rota* he had acquired that custom of walking about the plebeian quarters, searching in the dens, in the coffee-houses, and in the taverns, for the type imagined by the author.

But always with companions, like a merry party on the spree. Not as now, alone and full of anxiety, muffled up in his fur coat.

Suddenly he stopped and looked round him. He had lost his way. He was at the far end of a narrow street. To the left, the blackness of some vacant land. To the right, the squalid hostility of tall houses with narrow doorways.

Not a voice nor the sound of footsteps. Through the mist showed
the dark yellow stains of distant street lamps.

He started walking back quickly, with heavy resounding steps,
telling himself he was not afraid. For a moment the dreadful silence
of the spot chilled his heart.

Where could he be? Perhaps in——

He turned a corner and stopped to look from end to end of the
new street. He did not recognise it either. . . . Opposite to him
three women were wrangling in filthy language. . . .

He continued walking through other streets, all similar and un-
familiar, more than ever lost and with growing uneasiness.

His mouth felt dry, his temples throbbed. . . .

By chance he found himself outside a tavern. The memory of
his obsession came back to him, the search for the type, that fierce,
cynical figure of a hooligan which he had to create on the following
Friday.

He put his hand on the latch and opened the door. A heavy,
evil-smelling vapour struck upon his face.

The room was small and squalid. There were three tables
occupied and one vacant. Behind the counter a fat man with a
red moustache reading *The Radical*.

His entry created considerable surprise. Then, on seeing him sit
down and unbutton his fur coat, there were whispers.

At one table sat a ragged old woman, taking short sips at a large
glass of brandy.

At the other table a woman and a man conversed in low tones.
And at the last table, the one in the corner, two men.

The barman approached Heredia.

" What's it going to be? "

" Anything . . . Beer. . . .''

He saw how foolish he had been to enter there, to take off his
gloves and let them see the jewels on his hands. But there was no
help for it, and, as on other occasions in times of danger, he put
a bold front on his rashness. He stared fixedly, impudently, at the
two men in the corner.

The men avoided his gaze. They were poorly dressed and appeared to be gaol-birds.

Little by little the instinctive fear of the actor changed to
curiosity, almost to joy. Either of those two men could serve him
as his model. Their foreheads were narrow, their eyes sunken
under the double darkness of the eyebrows. The hairy hands
with their short fingers and bitten nails looked like claws. The
lower jaws protruded with a primitive expression of beasts.

But in a short time, seeing they were watched, the two men
exchanged a few words in a low tone and left the tavern.

Time passed. The old hag had fallen asleep on the table. The man and the woman continued their whispering. The barman went on reading *The Radical*.

Heredia got up, paid, and went out into the street.

The cold and the mist awaited him outside as before. He looked up and down, wondering which direction to take.

After all, it mattered nothing. He would come to a stop somewhere. The street was silent and deserted. His steps echoed on the pavement. He lit a cigar.

Long and narrow streets. Short and narrow streets.

Suddenly, unexpectedly, a broad avenue with leafless trees. At the end, black factory-buildings. He was in the Rondas.

He stopped and looked in vain for the two lights of a cab.

He heard footsteps behind him. He turned his head and thought he saw two men in the mist.

Could they be . . . ?

He continued walking, and suddenly two arms seized him from behind, a leg was thrust between his, and he fell sideways. . . .

Then a blow in the chest, a sensation of acute cold, and he lost consciousness. . . .

III

When he opened his eyes, they were laying him on a bed in the ambulance station. He felt a penetrating pain in his left side. His throat was dry, his chest panting, his forehead damp, and a strange coldness in the nose. . . . An extreme languidness and lassitude crept up his limbs.

He vaguely recalled a knife-thrust, perhaps death., . . .

And he also remembered the other thing—the expression, that expression which he had never expected to find.

And suddenly, as if demented, he sat up in bed shouting:

" Here! Here! Quick! A mirror! A mirror! I want to see my face! "

ARTURO REYES
1864–1913

FROM BULTO TO CORACHA

At twelve o'clock sharp I shall be at your window; just think that if you decide to like me. in less than fifteen days you will not be Lola ' the Carnation ' but the queen of women.''

And after saying this Don Luis moved slowly away from the window, at which Lola stood until he had disappeared.

Lola's thoughts were in a whirl, and well they might be: on one side Don Luis, a handsome fellow with more gold than was ever found in Peru; on the other, Joseito, a lazy, happy-go-lucky but lovable lad, who only had clothes on his back by divine mercy.

When Don Luis had gone, the little gipsy sat down at a table, placed one elbow on it, and rested her pretty face on the palm of her hand. Heaven knows how long she would have remained buried in her weighty thoughts, if she had not been disturbed by the entry of Uncle Bitoque, a gipsy older than a palm-tree, more bent than a pot-hook, clothed in a ragged Marseillaise jacket, the *faja* or waistband extending from the armpit to the hip, a pair of trousers extensively mended, shoes well ventilated, shirt without the slightest trace of its primitive whiteness, and a hat which, so its owner swore, had been called a *catite* in the very remote days of his youth.

The old man came into the room with all the freedom permitted him by his distant relationship to '' the Carnation,'' and with all the slowness necessitated by his years and rheumatism; taking a seat opposite the girl he asked her in a slightly thick voice:

'' May we know why the finest girl in Bulto has her dark little face so sad to-day? ''

'' It's nothing, grandfather; I seem to ache all over.''

'' A very pleasant ache, caused by a welcome silver dart! And the old woman? Where is the ugly bird? ''

'' Where is she? By her stall! ''

'' Listen, Lola, have you any more of that rascally Farajan which is better than elixir? A few drops would do me nicely! ''

Dolores got up, and taking a bottle from a little cupboard

emptied its contents into a glass, which she offered to the old man.

He swallowed it with relish, and after licking his lips and passing the back of his hand across his mouth, exclaimed:

" What splendid stuff it is! There never was a finer drink! Every glass of it makes me feel a year younger. Now I am going to smoke like a chimney, while you tell me what is the matter with the prettiest little gipsy in the world; for you know quite well that this *puri* (old man) has a lamp in each eye, and he will tell you which is the best path in the wood and the gentlest wave in the sea."

" And what do you want me to tell you? "

" I want to know whether after all you are going from Bulto to Limonar or from Bulto to Coracha."

" And how can I tell? Do you know what has happened to the daughter of my mother? "

" I am sure I do, my winsome one, I am sure I do. The trouble with you is that you are in the middle of a field with two paths before you, and you don't know which of them will lead you to the land of your dreams. Am I not right? "

" When you have finished, I'll tell you."

" Well, then: one of them seems smoother than the palm of your hand, but you are a little frightened of that path, because you fear, and rightly so, that if you go along there you may stumble and fall over a precipice; the other path is steeper than the hill to Golgotha, and to climb it you need strength and will, but at the end of that difficult little path is the fountain with the clearest water of life. Isn't that gospel truth? "

" Go on, grandfather, I like to hear you."

" Good: you are at the beginning of the two paths, unable to decide which to take, when a *gachi* (old woman) uglier than the Oritgoza and as good as can be, loving you with all the trunk and all the branches, tries to push you along the path she thinks the best: but in your heart you have a boat loaded with dreams, and each time you think of taking that path it casts anchor and you cannot move. Isn't that right? "

" Yes, you are right, grandfather."

" That just shows Bitoque knows a thing or two! "

" Since you are almost a wizard, tell me which path the daughter of my mother should take? "

" There are more thorns in that question than on a bramble-bush; but there is no need for me to tell you, for you have examples to look at. Remember what happened to Cloto ' the Mendru-guita.' "

" And what happened to her? "

" Oh, nothing! She disdained a *calé* (boy) better than the gold in a ring I had, for a Castilian more treacherous than Judas Is-

cariot. Within a year she had lost everything, and with a
churumbel (baby) in her arms, had to earn her living as a fortune-
teller, looked down on by all the gipsies, and no one willing to
give her a crumb."

" The man who threw her into the ditch must have had a bad
heart and no money."

" Neither good nor bad; neither much nor little; just an ordinary man: but we are all like that, we deserve to be punished."

" Yes, but Don Luis——"

" Heaven defend us, Lola! I did not mention any names;
don't be silly, Don Luis is a good fellow, has plenty of coin in
his pocket, and is spick and span to look at."

" That is on the surface; but what about inside? "

" Who can tell what the man is like inside! He might be sweet
as syrup or bitter as gall. If you ask me about Joseito, that is
another matter, because I have known him since he was born;
of course, the poor gipsy is just pining for you. The lad looks
as fine as a statue, as handsome as a painting, and is good beyond
a doubt, and as to singing, there is no one in all Coracha who
can beat him and no one who would dare sing in front of him;
besides all that, for you, and you alone, he has scorned a good
chance."

" How and when did he do that? I have heard nothing
about it."

" Because you are in Limbo and have only an ugly old bird by
your side croaking to you what suits her best; what I tell you is
as true as the sun that shines on us: Joseito, unwilling to play you
a trick and because he loves you from head to foot, has taken no
notice of Batatero's grand-daughter, Tonita ' the Lunares,' who
would give the eyes in her head for what you are going to throw
away."

A few moments later Uncle Bitoque left the room, and as he
went off Lola murmured quietly:

" That *gachi* Lunares is looking for trouble, and she will get the
marks of my fingers on her face! "

II

It was eleven o'clock in the evening, and the cold night dew had
forced the neighbours to go indoors, thus preventing them from
turning the street of Miraflores into a spacious dormitory, as is
their custom in summer.

Lola, with a frown on her pretty brow, was seated on one of
the best chairs in her room, listening to her aunt, who was saying:

" It is settled that you give Don Luis notice to quit, that you
throw away your good luck; let that be quite settled; and now, tell

me what you are going to do with your Joseito, with that tramp whose mouth must be rusty from eating so little, and his suit stuck to his back with gum to prevent the wind blowing it away; tell me what you are going to do: are you going to feed him on *polos* (Andalusian songs) and gipsy dances? "

" But all times are not alike."

" Come, come, child, somebody has bewitched you; you have been caught with bird-lime and nets."

" For God's sake, don't torment me any more, you have nearly driven me mad already; for you, to get you out of this miserable place, I would stifle my heart, I would destroy this love which springs from the depths of my soul; but what would happen if, after three days, after throwing all I love into the street, Don Luis should change his mind? What is going to happen to us? Our people will throw ashes on our heads; poor José would give me what I deserved, he would spit in my face; and I would have to throw myself into the Gualmeina. Is that what you wish for me? Are those your plans for me? "

" I only desire to do the best for you! I see things through other glasses; when I gave you that advice I was thinking only of you; I may die any day when least expected, and before going I would like to put you where you deserve to be. Now, you think it is a bad road; you prefer poverty with José to wealth with Don Luis. Very well, do as you like, for I don't want to go against your wishes; and when Don Luis comes later on, tell him to put spurs to his horse, for rather than see you unhappy I am ready to do anything."

And saying this, the old woman bent her wrinkled face to Lola's, who kissed her on the forehead, exclaiming:

" People are right when they say you are an angel."

When the old woman had retired to bed, Lola seated herself at the window-sill; through the half-open shutter, from which the whole street could be seen, came the light of the moon, its rays lighting up Lola's beauty, her fawn-like eyes, her dark complexion, her red lips, her white teeth, her oval profile, the graceful shoulders covered with a shawl of red crepon, the black ribbon which encircled her throat, and the printed muslin of her dress.

When Dolores was completely lost in thought, a figure appeared round the corner of the street: it was Joseito, who came forward somewhat unsteadily, dressed in his far from brand-new clothes, but lively, youthful, with his beautiful eyes saddened, and a drawn expression on his usually cheerful and roguish face.

Joseito had heard that Don Luis had spoken to " the Carnation " that morning; he had been told by Narizotas his best friend; when he heard it he felt cold, a sudden pain gripped him, and " I am going to find out what that young man wanted; it is probably nothing urgent," he murmured in a threatening tone, trying to escape from his friend.

" Get that idea out of your head, my boy," said Narizotas, taking hold of him by the arm. " Men are stronger, more wilful, and think more; naturally, when Don Luis approached Lola, he obtained her consent; so give her as good as she has given you, and quit this silly fooling, and come with me. To-day I have had some luck in business and we are going to get drunk; one cannot sell a horse profitably every day, nor get full of wine every night."

And making the best of things, Joseito went with Narizotas. It was eleven o'clock at night when the former, after leaving his friend at the tavern to sleep off the effects of the wine as comfortably as he could, started off, if not completely in the dark like his friend, at least more than in the twilight, towards the house of the girl of his thoughts.

Joseito, on arriving opposite the house, with his hat pushed back, and his large, black, curly locks over his temples, remained silent for some moments leaning against the wall; he could not go away without speaking to " the Carnation "; the thorn in his heart was very painful, and she must be the one to take it out.

He remembered, while thinking of this, the best weapons with which he had formerly captured that fair fortress, and throwing back his head he sang in a sweet voice, in a plaintive voice, in a voice full of caressing harmonies :

> Dicen que me has orviao
> por otro, gitana mía;
> el que tu querer me quite
> pena tiene de la vía.[1]

That rhythmic voice, ardent and full of tenderness and tears, that couplet, at once a lament and a terrible sentence, moved the innermost soul of Dolores, and throwing the window wide open and leaning on the window-sill, she exclaimed in trembling accents :

" What are you doing, Jocelillo? "

" Singing, lest I die of pain through your deceit."

" Come here, my Lilac, and tell me what ails the boy I love most."

And José approached the window slowly, reached her, seized the iron bars with both hands, and looking at Lola with very mournful eyes, moist and shining, exclaimed in a melting voice :

> [1] They tell me you've forgotten
> me for another, gipsy mine;
> he who robs me of your love
> must pay me with his life.

" They told me you were going to leave me, because I was poor, because I was miserable, and because I was badly dressed."

.   .   .   .

And it is related that when Don Luis came that evening to the corner of the street of Miraflores and saw José below the window of Lola " the Carnation " he turned pale, frowned angrily, and after a few moments of hesitation continued his way, murmuring in a grieved and choking voice:

" Yes, it is best as it is; it is the only time I have approached a woman with my heart in my hand."

ARTURO REYES

WHAT A TEAR CAN DO
A TALE OF ANDALUSIA

I

DOLORES " the Little Miracle " knew not what to do nor which
path to take at the cross-roads where she found herself, owing to
the unexpected wooing of Joseito " the Caramel," and after a
night of sleeplessness, of tossing and more tossing on her couch, and
of sighs and more sighs, she jumped out of bed : with her hair still
in disorder and, perhaps for the first time in her twenty years,
without looking at herself in the mirror, she went out to the patio,
eager to inhale deeply the early morning breeze.

The day, like all or nearly all summer days in Andalusia, was
fresh and fragrant, and a soft wind gently shook the green leaves
of the fig-trees ; the clothes hanging out to dry on cords and bass
ropes looked like pennants and snow-white streamers.

Dolores filled her lungs with the fresh and fragrant air, and
seating herself in the chair in which Señá Pepa " the Tulip "
generally took her *siesta,* she again became absorbed in her sad
meditations.

And so buried in her thoughts was our gentle heroine, that she
did not at first hear a door opened and some one come out of one
of the rooms round the patio. It was Señá Pepa, a little old
woman, not only thin, but bent, with her chin on her chest, the
tip of her nose on her chin, and a mouth stretching almost from
ear to ear, dressed in a clean, much-mended skirt, and a jacket of
the same cloth, a dark kerchief covering her hair, thin and white
as snow.

Señá Pepa came forward slowly and silently, leaning on a stick,
and stopped in front of Dolores to gaze at her young and graceful
figure, her face with its regular features, full dark eyes, and the
mouth purple-lipped and somewhat large ; the soft red glow of her
complexion darkening near the ears, between the eyebrows, and
on the upper lip into velvet-like shades, as dark, almost, as her
heavy eyebrows and her curly abundant hair.

Señá Pepa, after contemplating her in silence for several

moments, tapped the ground with her stick and exclaimed in a cracked and discordant voice:

" Good-morning, my sleepless one, God bless you this day."

Dolores raised her head and replied with a melancholy smile:

" Good-morning, Señá Pepa, I hope He will, for we certainly need it very much."

The old woman came forward until she was close to Dolores, who had got up to give her the seat, and after sitting down without having the politeness to thank her, exclaimed:

" And how is it you are up so early? What has prevented you from sleeping? Mosquitoes or your thoughts? "

" Mosquitoes! It was not the wicked mosquitoes that robbed me of my sleep, Señá Pepa! "

" Well, if it is not mosquitoes, it must be love; for at your age, Lola, when sleep will not come and you lie awake, it is the penalty of love."

" I can't say whether it's love; but I do know that I have not closed my eyes all night, and that my head is split with so much thinking, and my body aches with so much turning and tossing on my mattress."

" But what is happening to a child prettier than the morning star? "

" Well, what is happening to me is this. . . . I am going to explode, if God does not help me."

" Going to explode? "

" Yes, señora, I am going to explode."

" And why is that? "

" Well, because . . . you know I have been almost betrothed to Toñico ' the Cartameño ' for a long long time, you know that, don't you, Señá Pepa? "

" Why, of course, it is known all over the province! "

" And do you know also that yesterday Joseito ' the Cartujano ' came to me, with his heart almost quaking? "

" I didn't know that; I had no idea that fine young man had spoken to you."

" And you know who Joseito ' the Cartujano ' is? "

" Of course! . . . most certainly I know . . . the son of Caña-maque . . . a handsome fellow, who looks as though he were made of pasteboard and decked with tinsel."

" And you know Toño very well, don't you? "

" Of course. . . . I have often sung him to sleep. . . . Why, when he was born I was living next door to his mother—who has gone to glory, poor Catalina—a good woman with a heart larger than a tower, and a wonderful voice for singing *jaberas* and *polos* that nearly drove us frantic with delight! "

" Well, then; the trouble with me, Señá Pepa, is, that Toño is very fond of me; Toño has been following me about almost since I could walk, and although Toño is not all I could wish for, the truth is that I am fond of him; but Toño . . . Toño . . . Toño——"

" Toño . . . what? "

" Well, Toño has nothing more than the night and the day and——"

" There I think you are wrong," interrupted " the Tulip " sharply, " because Toño earns money, not for driving in carriages or for gambling but certainly enough to keep his palate from fainting and to avoid walking about with nothing on."

" That also is true, he earns . . . earns . . . but he does not benefit by it . . . he does not know how to spend it; surely the man must owe some money . . . have some expenses, for money was made to spend."

" Well, he has no vices and does not get into trouble, and as to being nice, he is almost more than need be."

" But I don't say he is not: let us talk about what interests me most; and it is, as I have already told you, that Joseito ' the Cartujano ' has approached me and has asked me to marry him, and at once; and you know quite well that ' Cartujano ' has plenty of *parneses* (money), and as well as having many *parneses* he is not a bad fellow, and besides . . . as my mother says: ' Don't you be silly, Dolores, love won't feed you; sorrow follows happiness, and necessity is like a bramble-bush, all thorns; now give up your silly ideas, and if " the Cartujano " comes as God wills, go on with " the Cartujano " until Toñico gets jealous, and if Toñico becomes bitter, let him stand it or not stand it, or let him jump off the Morro or emigrate to Argentina.' "

" Your mother always looked at things in that way; she never had any other god but money; that is why her hair was always so well arranged, and she always lived like the very angels, wore only kid boots, dressed only in silk frocks, and adorned her fingers with nothing but rings set with rubies."

And with so much irony did Señá Pepa say this, that Dolores exclaimed in a pleading voice, and looking at her entreatingly:

" But what I want, grandmother, why I have come out so early to the patio, is simply to get your advice."

" Look here, Dolores," replied the old woman with an expression of annoyance, " don't you ask me for advice, because I'm not going to give it you, do you understand?   I am not going to give it to you because I have had enough of not minding my own business, and being torn to bits in every dispute.

" But listen, what I am going to tell you is this . . . that although it may not seem true, I was twenty myself once, and if I was not beautiful, at least I was not a fright, and in my early flights two birds came after me, as in your case, and wanted to

carry me off, one Juan ' the Frog,' and the other my Paco, to-day
my Seño Frasquito, and ' the Frog ' had more notes than cells in
a honeycomb or nuts on a nut-tree, and my Seño Frasquito had
nothing but a rag in front and another behind and two pairs of
socks; and I married my Seño Frasquito because my heart told
me to.   Now, though it is true that I have had to work hard and
have had many troubles, it is also true that whilst the crust is
always hard, the crumbs are soft and at times more than soft.''

II

What Señá Pepa said to Lola that morning seemed to have confused her altogether, and when the hour arrived for Toñico to come
to her house, to be driven to distraction by merely looking at her,
she went out, as usual, to the patio, and sat down by the kerbstone
of the well, where she and her faithful lover were accustomed to
hold their pleasant conversations.

'' But listen, Lola,'' said Señá Rasolfa, the landlady, in a
sarcastic voice, '' surely there is better work for your pretty figure
at the window to-night.''

'' That depends on what my own wishes are,'' replied she, with
a show of ill-temper.

'' Well, it is Joseito ' the Cartujano ' who says so; he is telling
everybody who cares to hear him that he is coming to-night at ten
o'clock to your window to talk to you about the first banns.''

'' That will depend; eh, Dolores? '' asked Uncle Paco, the
basket-maker, and seeing that she did not reply, he continued:

'' The truth is, I myself would not know which road to choose,
and if I were in ' the Cartameño's ' skin I would make more noise
than the loudest tattoo.''

Soon the conversation became general between the neighbours,
and Dolores was already beginning to feel tired when Toñico ' the
Cartameño ' came into the patio, looking sad and disconsolate.
After saluting the gathering in a stifled voice he went up to Dolores,
seized her roughly by the hand, gazed at her with questioning
anxiety, with a look of pain, of supplication, of love, and asked
her in a trembling, almost frightened voice, in a voice so low that
he could only be heard by Dolores:

'' Is it true, Dolores, what I have just heard? is it true that
you are going to leave me for a fellow called Joseito ' the Cartujano '? ''

Dolores glanced at Antonio with a timid look, and answered in
an unsteady voice, but trying to smile:

'' And who on earth told you such bad news? ''

'' What does it matter who it was! . . . some one . . . and,
upon my word, I felt tempted to kill the man who told me!   But

then I began to think, and realising that I do not deserve to have
you, I said to myself: ' Perhaps it is true . . . perhaps she does
not care for me . . . perhaps she cares for that other fellow, and
if she cares for him, to ask her to give him up would be as if they
told me, even if the King himself told me, to stop liking the one
who is even more to me than the water I drink and the air I
breathe.' "

" Well, can't I like you, Toño! can't I like you, my Toño! "
exclaimed Dolores; his low and quivering, almost sobbing voice,
rather than his words, beginning to wound her heart and to arouse
her conscience.

" But . . . but I do not say you can't like me! . . . I do not say
that . . . you will like me, but as one likes a friend . . . a friend
. . . how terrible! Dolores, how terrible! For a long time, a very
long time, I have thought of no one but you; you have always
been the rose-bush that has filled my soul and mind with flowers;
whenever I had a sorrow, any great doubt, I thought of you and
my doubts vanished; when my body ached from so much working,
day and night, I said to myself: ' Go on and suffer and break
yourself if need be, body of mine, for it is through her and for
her that you are suffering and enduring, it is to save so much money
that she shall want for nothing, so that she may have everything
she wishes '; and I worked and worked, and fled from my friends,
and never entered a tavern, and at the cost of sweat and toil, I
had already got, without the world knowing it, all the feathers for
making my nest, and when I thought of saying to you, ' Listen,
Dolores, here is my heart and my nest, both are for you, if you
want them; when I was trembling with joy . . . when I thought
I had already won paradise, when——"

And Toño " the Cartameño " had to pause, and a tear, only one,
wavered between his long black lashes.

Dolores saw that tear, saw Toño dash it away roughly and angrily
with his clenched fist, and something noble and tender rose in her
soul and:

" But who on earth told you that I do not want your nest and
your heart for myself? Who has invented that story against me? "

.   .   .   .

And an hour later, when Toño " the Cartameño," radiant with
joy, saw himself portrayed in the large pupils of Dolores, and " the
Cartujano," weary and desperate, withdrew from the street, tired
of exhibiting the grace of his figure before the closed window of the
woman he sought in vain, the neighbours continued their animated
whispers in picturesque groups, and Señá Pepa and Señó Frasquito,
seated in the doorway of their room and bathed in the moonlight,
doubtless thought with melancholy vagueness, as they watched
Toño and Dolores, of their own long-distant youth and its dead joys.

RAMÓN DEL VALLE-INCLÁN

B. 1869

FEAR

THE slow and terrifying chill that seems the herald of death, the real chill of fear, I have felt but once. That was many years ago in the time of entailed estates, when rank and title were to be obtained by military service.

I had just been awarded the cordon of chevalier in the grenadiers. A post with the royal guards would have been my preference, but my mother objected, so, following the tradition of the family, I became a grenadier in the regiment of the King. I cannot remember how many years ago that was, but the down had hardly sprouted upon my lips, and to-day I am almost a white-haired old man.

Before I joined my regiment my mother wished to bestow her benediction. The poor lady was living in retirement, within the precincts of a village where stood our ancestral home, and in those days I was submissive and obedient.

On the afternoon of my arrival she sent for the Prior of Brandeso to come to hear my confession in the family chapel. My sisters, Maria Isabel and Maria Fernanda, who were little girls, went to the garden to gather roses, and with these flowers my mother filled the vases on the altar. Then she called me gently to give me her prayer-book and to exhort me to examine my conscience.

" Go to the pulpit, my son," said she. " That is the best place for you."

The castle pulpit was in the centre of the platform, contiguous to which was the library. The chapel was dark, damp, and full of echoes. In the background appeared the armorial bearings granted by Ferdinand and Isabella to the Lord of Brandamín, Pedro Aguiar de Tor, known also as El Chivo (the Ram) and El Viejo (the old man). That famous warrior was buried at the right of the altar, and above him was the statue of a knight in armour, kneeling in attitude of prayer. The jewelled holy-lamp, with its dim flame, burned night and day before the platform. The gilded clusters of sacred fruit seemed to present themselves to the worshipper. The patron saint was that pious Oriental King, the one of the three wise men who offered myrrh to the child Jesus. His tunic of silk bordered in gold shimmered with the mystic splendour of an Oriental miracle. The light of the lamp, hung on silver chains, fluttered like some timid bird, eager to fly upward to the saint's shoulders.

My mother desired that hers should be the hands which that afternoon would place the baskets of flowers at the saint's feet as an offering from her devout soul. When that had been done she kneeled before the altar with my sisters at her side. I, from above, heard only the murmur of her voice as it brokenly repeated the *Ave Marias*, but when it was the children's turn to make responses, I heard every word of the ritual.

The afternoon dragged on dismally and the prayers rumbled through the silent darkness of the chapel, hollow, sad, and sublime, like an echo of the Passion. My eyes grew heavy. The girls moved to one side and seated themselves upon the steps of the platform. Their dresses were as white as the linen of priestly vestments. I could perceive only the dim shadow of my mother as she prayed under the presbytery. In her hands was an open book, and she read with bowed head.

As it grew later, the wind stirred the drapery of a lofty window, and then I could see in the darkened sky the orb of the moon, supernatural and pale, like some goddess who is worshipped in woodlands and marshes.

My mother closed the book with a sigh and called her daughters. I saw their two ghostly forms pass across the presbytery and divined that they were once more kneeling beside her. The light of the lamp cast its feeble rays upon her fair hands as they again opened the book. Her slow, pious voice scarce broke the silence as she read. The girls were listening, and I was dimly conscious of their tresses spreading over the white frocks and falling in identical manner on each side of their faces, endowing them with sad and Christlike expression.

I had fallen asleep when suddenly the shrieks of my sisters aroused me. I looked and saw them in the middle of the presbytery clinging to my mother. They were crying with terror. My mother grasped their hands and all three fled.

I descended in haste. I was about to follow them, but stopped, overcome by fright. In the sepulchre of the ancient warrior his bones were rattling! It made one's hair stand on end. The chapel had become deathly silent, and one could hear distinctly the hollow, awe-inspiring rolling of the skull upon its pillow of stone. A fear came over me such as I have never experienced since, but I did not wish my mother and my sisters to think me a coward, wherefore I remained motionless in the middle of the presbytery, with my eyes glued on the half-open door. The light of the little lamp flickered. On high a window curtain blew back and clouds were seen passing over the moon, while stars were appearing and disappearing like our mortal lives.

Suddenly in the distance resounded the animated barking of dogs and the tinkle of little bells. A grave and churchly voice cried:

" Here, Carabel! Here, Capitán! "

It was the Prior of Brandeso, who had come to receive my confession. Then I heard the tremulous, frightened voice of my mother, and heard distinctly the pattering of the dogs' feet as they ran. The grave, churchly voice rose majestically like a Gregorian chant:

" Now we shall see what it was—certainly nothing supernatural. Here, Carabel! Here, Capitán! "

And the Prior of Brandeso, preceded by his greyhounds, appeared in the door of the chapel.

" Grenadier of the King, what has happened? "

" Señor Prior, I heard the skeleton trembling within its tomb."

The prior slowly crossed the chapel. He was an erect, haughty figure, for in his youthful years he also had been a King's grenadier. He came up to me, walking without lifting the loose folds of his white vestments, and as he placed his hand on my shoulders and looked into my eyes, said solemnly:

" May the Prior of Brandeso never be able to say that he has seen a King's grenadier tremble! "

He did not remove his hand from my shoulders and we remained motionless, looking at each other in silence. At that moment we heard the skull of the warrior turn. The prior's hand did not tremble. Beside us the dogs pricked up their ears, and the hair on their necks bristled. Anew we heard the skull move on its pillow of stone. The prior shook me and said:

" Señor Grenadier, we must see whether these are goblins or witches! "

He approached the sepulchre and laid hold of the two rings of copper embedded in the flagstone which covered the body and bore the epitaph. I stepped forward, trembling. The prior looked at me without opening his lips. I laced my hand over his in one of the rings and pulled. Slowly we raised the stone. The cavity, black and cold, was before us. I could see that the dry and yellowish skull was still moving. The prior put his hand down into the tomb and laid hold of the fearful object, then, without a word, handed it to me. I took it, trembling. I stood in the middle of the presbytery, and the light from the lamp fell upon my hands. As I looked horror overcame me, and I convulsively dropped the skull, for within it was a brood of snakes, which uncoiled, hissing, as it rolled down the steps one at a time. The prior's fierce eyes glared at me from beneath his cowl as from behind the visor of a helmet:

"Señor Grenadier of the King, there is no absolution for you! I do not absolve cowards!"

And he left the chapel, drawing after him his long priestly vestments. The words of the Prior of Brandeso resounded long in my ears. I can hear them yet. It is perhaps from them that I learned afterward to smile at death as at a fair lady.

RAMÓN DEL VALLE-INCLÁN

LUCKY BOY !

THE oldest old woman in the village, holding her grandchild by the hand, walks along a green-bordered path, which looks sad and numbed beneath the cold light of dawn. Her back is bent and she sighs as she walks, giving advice to the child, who is crying quietly.

" Now that you are beginning to earn money you must be humble, for it is the law of God."

" Yes, ma'am, yes. . . ."

" You must pray for your benefactor and for the souls of the departed."

" Yes, ma'am, yes. . . ."

" You must buy a rush cape at the fair of San Gundian, if you have saved enough money, as it rains often."

" Yes, ma'am, yes. . . ."

" When you walk along the paths you must take off your clogs."

" Yes, ma'am, yes. . . ."

And the grandmother and her grandchild go on walking, walking, walking. . . . The loneliness of the road heightens the sadness of that infantile psalmody which seems like a vow of humility, resignation, and poverty taken at the commencement of life. The old woman shuffles along in her clogs, which clatter on the stones in the road, and she sighs under the shawl thrown over her head. The grandchild sobs and shivers with the cold; his clothes are ragged. He is an albino lad, with sunburnt and freckled cheeks; over his forehead, like a slave of another age, his straight fair hair is closely cropped, suggesting fibres of maize.

In the livid sky of the dawning day still glimmer a few fading stars. A fox fleeing from the village dashes across the path. In the distance can be heard the barking of dogs and the crowing of cocks. . . . Slowly the sun begins to gild the crests of the hills; the dew sparkles on the grass; round the trees, in timid flights, circle the young birds that are leaving the nest for the first time; the streams laugh, the branches murmur, and that green-bordered road, sad and deserted, awakens like an old road of many seed-times and vintages. Flocks of sheep climb the slope of the hill; women come singing from the fountain; a white-haired villager goads his oxen as they stop to nibble by the fences. He is a patriarchal old man; from a great distance his voice is heard:

" Are you going to the fair at Barbanzón? "

" We are going to San Amedio to find a master for the lad."

" How old is he? "

" Old enough to earn: he was nine in July."

And the grandmother and her grandchild go on walking, walking, walking. . . . Under the genial sun that shines over the hills the people of the villages pass along the roads. A merry, sunburnt horse-dealer trots along with a joyous clatter of spurs and hoofs; old women from Cela and Lestrove set out for the fair with chickens, flax, and rye. Over there, in the ravine, a rustic waves his arms and shouts to frighten the goats, which are jumping gracefully among the rocks. The grandmother and grandchild stand aside to make way for the rector of Lestrove, who is on his way to preach at a village festival.

" Good-morning and God bless you! "

The rector pulled up his horse, which had a quiet and dignified gait.

" Are you going to the fair? "

" We poor people have nothing to do at the fair. We are going to San Amedio to find a master for the lad."

" Does he know his Catechism? "

" Yes, sir, he knows it. Poverty does not prevent one being a Christian."

And the grandmother and her grandchild go on walking, walking, walking. . . . In the distant blue haze they descry the cypress trees of San Amedio, growing round the church, black and pensive, with their languid tops anointed by the early golden light. In the village every door is already open, and the wavering white smoke which rises from the chimneys vanishes into the air like a greeting of peace. The grandmother and her grandchild reach the porch. Seated in the doorway a blind man implores alms, and raises his whitish agate eyes to Heaven.

" May the blessed Saint Lucy preserve your good sight and health in this world to earn your bread! . . . May God give you to keep and to give! . . . Health and luck in the world to earn your bread! . . . So many good people of the Lord cannot pass without giving a poor man a trifle! . . ."

And the blind man holds out to the roadway his dry and yellow palm. The old woman approaches with her grandchild by the hand and murmurs sadly:

" We are poor people too, brother! . . . They told me you were looking for a servant. . . ."

" Quite true. The one I had before got his head broken at the pilgrimage of Santa Baya de Cela. He is quite silly now. . . ."

" I have brought my grandson."

" You have done well."

The blind man stretches out his arms, groping the air.

" Go nearer, boy."

The grandmother pushes the boy, who trembles like a gentle, timid lamb before that horrible old man, wrapped in a soldier's cape. The importunate yellow hand of the blind man rests on the boy's shoulders, gropes round his back, travels down his legs.

" Will you get tired carrying the packs uphill? "

" No, sir: I am used to it."

" To fill them we must knock at many doors. Do you know the village roads well? "

" Where I do not know, I ask."

" On the pilgrimages, when I sing a verse you have to respond with another. Will you be able to? "

" With practice, yes, sir."

" To be a blind man's servant is what many people would like."

" Yes, sir, yes."

" As you have come, let us go to Pazo de Cela. The people there are charitable. Here there is not a coin to be had."

The blind man rises stiffly and rests his hand on the shoulders of the boy, who looks sadly at the long road and over the green humid country, to where, in the distance, a labourer walks with his back bent as he cuts the grass, whilst a cow grazes quietly, dragging the halter. The blind man and the boy move slowly away, and the grandmother murmurs as she dries her eyes:

" Lucky boy! nine years old and earning the bread he eats! . . . Praised be God! . . ."

ELIAS ZEROLO

D. 1900

HER FATHER'S SLAVE

THE bay of Rio de Janeiro is one of the largest and most beautiful harbours in the world. Spacious enough to give ample anchorage to every fleet that sails, the bay is a veritable sea. Its shores are covered with that vigorous and variegated vegetation to be seen only in America and Asia. Many islands dot its noble bosom like colossal emeralds, and along its numerous little bays, which appear at first insignificant and look like mouths through which the vast interior of Brazil gets its aliment, are scores upon scores of wharves and docks, giving life and movement to the lovely panorama.

One day when I was crossing the bay to Nictheroy on the little steamer that serves as a ferry, I saw my excellent friend Señor Thussel. Thussel was a lawyer, the son of a French immigrant who had married a rich Brazilian heiress, and one of those political liberals who, without provoking any great outward disturbance, determine the real progress of the Brazilian people. Benevolent in his attitude toward the proceedings of the conservatives, he was firm and unyielding only where slavery was concerned, holding that with it there could be no temporising by the law. For him there existed only one solution of the difficulty: slavery's instant abolishment. Everything but that, Thussel would say heatedly, was infamous, an acknowledgment that man had the right to buy and sell his weaker and more unfortunate brothers and sisters.

He, invariably so gentle and kindly, treated every one who dared differ from him on the subject with the sternest reproach and greatest severity. So unyielding would he be that it seemed to his friends as if he must have felt upon his own shoulders, at some former time, the lash of the overseer's cruel whip.

His speech was slow and deliberate, and he chose his words carefully, striving for the utmost precision and elegance of diction, a habit very common among the best people of Rio de Janeiro. Always calm and careful in the debates at the Athenæum and in his favourite clubs, Dr. Thussel was instantly a different man when he discussed slavery. Then his bold features would wrinkle and his flashing eyes lighten ominously. He would clench his hands with a nervous, violently spasmodic action, and pour out with lightning

270

rapidity, in the most eloquent and moving tones, the iron-hard, bitter logic and passionate energy of his irrefragable arguments. His broad, humane ideas fell like hammer-strokes upon his opponent. Those who saw the man in such heated moments could not at all recognise the philanthropist with whom they were acquainted, so great was the change in him.

When I met him on the ferry-boat Thussel's face wore an unusually disturbed and sombre look, far from its customary suave air, and I knew something very serious must be on his mind. His greeting was gloomy, but I answered with a smile, and seating myself beside him, endeavoured as best I might to cheer him up. After a moment or two of silence, I asked what was troubling him.

In answer he rose, and signing me to follow, led to where a little knot of slaves stood huddled together in a detached, miserable group, clinging to each other, as if to find in the contact strength to withstand the misfortune which had overtaken them because of their black skins. Among them was one old fellow, far advanced in years, who held close to his breast a good-looking young girl; his tears were mingling with hers.

Thussel pointed at them with a sweeping gesture of despair, and we stood for a moment watching them silently.

" They are father and daughter, sold to different owners upcountry," my friend said as we returned to our deck-chairs. " In a short time—when we reach Nictheroy—they will be separated. The law that permits such a thing is abominable! "

" Do you know the old man? " I asked, moved by his interest in the pair.

" No," he replied bitterly, " I do not. When I came aboard I heard the noise and inquired the reason for their weeping. After all," he added in ironic accents, " it is merely one of the legitimate consequences of present conditions. The owner of any article has the right to dispose of it as he sees fit. There is nothing wonderful about it." He paused for a moment, and then went on in a sadder tone: " It makes my blood boil to see the misfortunes of these poor creatures, beings who are gifted with minds, nourished like my own, with red blood. The sight of that poor old father and his daughter fairly turned me sick when I saw them first. It recalled to me a bloody drama in which certain members of my own family figured. It was many years ago, but you might recognise many of the characters, even without my naming them."

Thussel was silent for a moment, pressing his hands to his temples, but whether to collect his thoughts or to ease the pain of the hateful memory I did not know.

" Yes? " I said, eager to hear the story.

" Yes, I'll tell you about it, if you care to listen. Everybody knows something about the miseries of slavery, but to hear a personal anecdote may impress the horrors of the traffic upon you for ever. There is time for the tale before we reach Nictheroy.

"My mother's family, with the exception of her elder brother, had always lived in Rio dè Janeiro. The boy, a born adventurer, left the paternal roof when a mere child and made many trips into the wild interior of the empire. He had no particular reason for running away except that he was naturally restless and loved the extraordinary; but he was of a keenly money-making spirit, a most unusual quality in one so young. He had been in turn soldier, sailor, hunter and miner, but always making money. He did no one knows how many other things, until, after years of wandering, he settled down to the life of a steady-going business man in Pernambuco.

"Applying to his new venture his tireless activity and great intelligence, these qualities, with his encyclopædic knowledge of the country, gained at first hand during his wanderings, virtually assured success from the outset, and the house of Señor de Lima, as he chose to call himself, became in the course of a very few years one of the most respected and substantial firms in the metropolis.

"Only on the South American bourses and in the greater cities are fortunes thus built up. Our cities themselves are really nothing but huge exchanges. In both you will see the same vertiginous activity, with one thing in mind, one god at heart: gold—the idea of gain, the cult of the golden calf. On the other hand, however, the very fortunes which appear most solid and enduring not infrequently collapse at the slightest breath, like castles built of gamblers' cards. But you shall see.

"Steeped in this oppressive atmosphere of commerce, my uncle spent the best years of his life. Meditating on the futility of it all, his mind wandered back into the past. He remembered that there was someone in the world who could call him father, and he decided to live alone no longer.

"One day one of his female slaves presented herself to him, bearing a bundle in her arms.

"'Your child, my master!' she said with simple awe.

"My uncle looked at the little creature a moment, and charging the mother to bring her back when six years old, sent both to the Capivara *hacienda*, one of his most distant and inaccessible plantations. The negress reached Capivara safely, carrying a letter to the overseer. My uncle ordered the overseer not to put the woman at any hard work or to abuse her while she should continue to have the child at breast.

"The overseer's wife immediately took the slave and her pretty baby under her protection, and made the infant a Christian by having her baptized Maria in the church nearest the *hacienda*. So fond did she become of the little one that she wished to adopt it for her own, begging her husband to try and have both mother and child freed. The overseer, though not a religious man by any means, was an indulgent husband, and agreed for his wife's sake. He saw nothing out of the way in such a request from his wife, and although a rude, coarse man, ordinarily thinking no more of the slaves than of the animals that did the heavy work about the plantation, he passed so many pleasant hours caressing and playing with the pretty creature that he permitted it to call him father when it at last began to lisp that sweet name.

" The poor slave mother was deeply grateful, but she was a mother first, and she looked upon these demonstrations of affection with some secret alarm and never let fall a single word or hint to indicate its father's identity.

" Four years passed, and she fell sick. Fearing to infect the *hacienda*, she ran away with the child, reaching my uncle at Pernambuco after untold suffering. The wretched woman told him she had come back to die, which proved to be true. My uncle was astonished at the exact likeness of the little girl's features to those of his sister, who afterward became my mother. It seemed as if Providence had given her the resemblance as a safe-conduct to his affections and to ensure his acknowledgment of her paternity.

" A few hours after the child reached his house he took her with him in a boat to Rio de Janeiro, placing her there in the care of some excellent ladies whom he charged with her education and religious training, but to whom he vouchsafed nothing as to her parentage or family.

" In Rio the young girl proved, by her intelligence and aptitude for study, the model of her school. When my uncle learned this later he had Maria come and live with him. She occupied the place of a legitimate daughter in his house, awakening in him sentiments and emotions long dormant and dulled.

" Maria was grateful to her father and showed her appreciation by her careful management of his domestic affairs and the interest she took in the slaves, who found in her—as if she were aware of her true origin—a friend and protectress for whose loving help they gave thanks every hour. She interested her indulgent father, who gratified her every whim, and obtained his permission to have the slaves knock off work an hour every day, during which she gave them instruction in morals as well as taught them their letters. The slaves very soon showed the benefit of this care and could easily be distinguished from other slaves by their cheerful willingness to work and their moderation in life.

" Maria's skin and complexion were so clear and fair that she would have passed in Europe for a white girl. Her large, full eyes, shaded by long, silky lashes, showed their beauty and light modestly; a nose saucily retroussé; a small and gracious mouth which, when she laughed, revealed a perfect set of pearls; an oval head, crowned with a mass of soft black hair, dressed in exquisite taste, all showed Maria to be, not a statuesque beauty, nor yet the perfect type of female loveliness conceived by artists, but one of those ineffably lovely women, one of those peerless creoles who are the torment of half the human race. Added to her beauty and moral qualities there was the practical certainty of her inheriting my uncle's immense fortune, since every one believed her to be his legitimate daughter. She was, accordingly, welcomed heartily by Pernambuco society, and there was always a perfect cloud of those flies of fortune, suitors, hovering over and about her in the hope of winning her hand. Not one of them received the slightest encouragement; but so delicate and insinuating was her tact that she managed to keep them all her friends, who sounded her praises everywhere.

"One of them, however, persisted in his importunities. This was Señor Sousa, counted one of the richest bachelors in Pernambuco. He was one of the most vicious and avaricious of men, with a mind even more dulled than those who had made their money by slave-trading. In the possibility of a marriage with Maria he saw a means of largely increasing, by a single stroke, his own considerable fortune. For the girl he cared nothing, except in a merely sensual, animal way; it was her money and good looks he was after, and both for self-gratification only.

"All the suitors, however, were not like Sousa. Many of them, fairly eligible young fellows, were so entirely ignored that the more disappointed ones began to believe and to hint openly that Maria could not be heart-whole or free. And they were right. Maria loved Luis, a clerk of my uncle's, and Luis loved her with a passion that defied even death. Not a word had either spoken—indeed, that was not necessary, their eyes had spoken for them.

"Sousa was not the kind of man to be thwarted or crossed with impunity by any one. Accustomed always to having people bow before the weight of his gold, Maria's refusal inspired his base mind with a bitter desire for revenge. With a persistence and energy worthy of the Inquisition, he set himself to learn every minor detail of my uncle's past life. He could find nothing exceptionable, and it would seem as if his infamous designs were to be frustrated. But one day, while poring over a mass of papers in which he was eagerly reading a résumé of the life of the man he sought to injure, he was suddenly struck by the fact that no mention was made anywhere of Maria's mother. He began at once to suspect the worst. He started afresh, with renewed hopes, on his investigations. For some time his researches were without results. One night, however, very late, he found himself, while travelling, in Capivara, an estate my uncle had sold ostensibly for the reason that it was profitless, but in reality because of business reverses.

" The overseer, who was much distressed that the new owner did not show him the same consideration which my uncle had always extended, praised the Señor de Lima in the highest terms. The Señor Sousa very artfully led him on and managed to turn the conversation upon the youthful and private life of my uncle, who, he said, was the only one of his friends of whom he knew nothing bad. The overseer then remembered that he had once suspected my uncle of an amorous intrigue, though he had made up his mind that he had been wrong. He told Sousa, omitting no detail, of Maria's strange arrival and of her even more mysterious departure four years later. Since that time he had not heard nor seen anything of either the child or the mother, and no one knew what had become of them.

" That was enough for so crafty a fellow as Sousa. Without allowing the overseer to suspect how valuable had been his information, the wily villain thanked the man and next day left the *hacienda*, changed his plans, and returned at once to Pernambuco.

" Some two weeks after he had arrived home Sousa might have been seen in his office before an enormous pile of books and papers, the examination of which occupied him several days. Had any one been about as he finished each book he would have heard Sousa talking to himself cheerily, expressing the keenest satisfaction. A broker interrupted him once in his labours to tell him regretfully that Señor de Lima's paper was no longer being taken on the Street, that no one would discount it in the market, and that it seemed probable that the present difficulties of the firm were due to their repeated recent heavy losses, which made failure appear inevitable. Sousa heard the news with a diabolical smile, and the broker on leaving heard him chuckle: ' What luck! '

" Fortune, which had hitherto smiled upon my uncle, seemed to have deserted him entirely. He was put to the necessity of suspending payments and calling an immediate meeting of his creditors. He thought that they, realising that his losses were not due to imprudence or lack of experience, and also remembering his personal probity and business intelligence, might accept conditions which would enable him to recoup his losses, tide over his difficulties, and eventually re-establish the credit of his house. He called the meeting and awaited the day on which he should face his creditors with a tranquil mind, having everything in readiness for them, with his plans all prepared.

" The hour of the meeting came, and the other creditors were gathered in the office, when Sousa entered and begged a moment's private conversation before they began the business of the day. He

and my uncle went into the next room. Sousa had called him out
to urge again his suit for the hand of Maria, offering in exchange
for the old man's consent and assistance the exercise of his powerful
influence with the other creditors in order to obtain a favourable
settlement. If the settlement were impossible, the schemer offered
to place his entire fortune and business at my uncle's disposal.
Instead of accepting the apparently generous offer, the old man
reaffirmed briefly his previous reply and Maria's old refusal. Sousa
insisted, begging for a chance to talk to her himself, urging that
she might have changed her mind; but my uncle refused him that
also, fearing that Maria, knowing the low condition of his affairs,
might consent to sacrifice herself to a hateful union in order to save
her father's good name.

" At the meeting my uncle did not succeed in getting his proposi-
tions accepted by the creditors. They seemed at first to be inclined
in his favour and might have dealt leniently with him; but Sousa,
who held three-fourths of the protested notes, opposed this in un-
stinted terms, eventually frightening the other creditors into agreeing with him. Though they could not understand why Sousa should
unnecessarily expose himself to the loss of several *contos* of *reis*
for the satisfaction to be gained by ruining an old man and his
daughter, they followed his lead like sheep and the deed was done.

" A few moments later they adjourned to the Bankruptcy Court
and placed the matter there. My uncle laid before the judge a
complete inventory of his estate and goods. Sousa, at his own
request, was permitted to examine the papers, and, seeing that
among the list of slaves there was no such name as Maria, denounced the omission instantly, presenting the court with incontest-
able evidence and accusing my uncle of fraud in hiding something
which really belonged to his creditors. He went even farther; he
committed the infamy of making the court and the others suspect
that De Lima maintained the fiction of having Maria pose as his
daughter the better to sustain and cover up an illicit relation.

" In consideration of the bankrupt's personal condition and his
estate, the court rendered judgment with the greatest haste and
secrecy. The court's messengers, sent to find the missing slave,
found my uncle with his daughter, who was trying to make light of
the disaster and endeavouring to encourage the broken old man with
hope for a new start. It was at this moment that the agents of the
court appeared to notify him of the judge's decision and to take
away his daughter, who, before the law, was nothing more than a
piece of merchandise, nothing but a female slave, the property of
rapacious creditors. Never had a man been so terribly punished
for an oversight.

" I never knew just what happened at that painful moment; my
uncle's mind became almost unhinged. The blow was terrible,

and, as he might have anticipated had he really known his man, Sousa added the insult of his presence before the sorrowing pair.

" For a long time we physicians and lawyers discussed among ourselves the effect the misfortune might have upon my uncle. At times he was seen to press his hands to his heart and shut his eyes quickly, his head thrown back. But he opened his eyes again and looked upon his persecutors in what seemed to be his normal condition—only he was practically insensible to his surroundings. He showed his usual energy in only one way: not even the law could separate him from his daughter, and he went with her to the pen where the other slaves had been quartered under guard.

" Maria received the fatal news with all a martyr's fortitude. Raising her eyes to heaven she implored the divine aid in a hasty prayer, kissing the hand of her father, who looked at her with the impassive stare of an idiot. The officials noticed that only in the moment when he drew her to him and put his arm about her waist to lead her where the constables indicated, did she weep at all or lose any of her sweet fortitude.

" Disgusting, repellent scenes occurred during the confinement of the slaves. Every day the infamous Sousa came to the pen to see them, and, as he said, to shelter father and daughter with his magnanimous protection, while really exposing them to the most humiliating indignities. And my uncle made not the slightest attempt to throttle the brute! The old man must undoubtedly have been driven into insanity by the inhuman treatment he received. But even the most excruciating agony must have an end, and at last the day of the sale ended—temporarily, at least—the slaves' confinement.

" Nothing more iniquitous can be imagined. Mere words and phrases do not exist to paint in its true reality and brutal cynicism that disgraceful outrage upon humanity called slave-trading.

" The buyer and seller present themselves in the market and submit the slaves to the most scrupulously rigid and searching examination on the stand from which the sale is made. The dealers calculate, with the cold, hard sense of a mechanic studying the condition of a complex and delicate machine, the animal strength and character of each of the poor wretch's members, and his or her more or less robust physical condition. If the merchandise happens to be female, it is pitiful and shameful beyond measure to witness the brutal examination, the poor woman standing practically naked, with quivering body and beating heart, before the prospective buyer, who is an interested and heartless spectator, the while the keen-eyed auctioneer points out the condition and health of those who are virgins and those who have been mothers, and those who, at times, are intended for a far more infamous traffic than mere slavery, each according to her comeliness and the perfection of her body and form.

" My uncle's slaves, sane and robust, educated by her who they knew loved them and who now found herself among them, drew a large throng of buyers to the market. Perhaps, also, the intending buyers were in great measure attracted by a morbid wish to see the unfortunate Maria exposed for sale. She and her father stood a little apart from the black mass of the rest, and inspired a deep sympathy in the blunted consciences of even those who had come to take an active part in the sale. And the sympathy, by reason of its disinterestedness, extended to the other slaves as well, so that none of the buyers exposed them to the usual indignities or annoyances. Sousa alone showed the most callous indifference. He approached Maria and made as if he would feel and examine her body and limbs with his own hands. But the other slaves covered her with their bodies, and an ominous murmur of vengeance went surging up from the solid black bodyguard, causing him to step back hastily with a bitter curse.

" Maria alone failed to sell. No one seemed willing to take the responsibility of separating her from her father. The auctioneer shouted himself hoarse, proclaiming her beauty and virtues in stentorian tones as the ashamed girl stood forth, clad as lightly as possible, before the leering, pitying, curious, sympathetic assembly. But at last the bidding was started.

" Various low offers were made, the girl's price rising rapidly, *peso* by *peso*, and there were many who would really have liked to own her, once their scruples, faint enough at best, had been overcome. But to all these bids there was but one reply, and Sousa made it in golden words. From time to time the auctioneer announced the higher bid until they were almost convinced that they could achieve nothing against so formidable an antagonist as the determined scamp who was doing most of the bidding. His rivals somewhat too quickly abandoned the field to the crafty Sousa, who showed his evident satisfaction at securing his bargain so easily. But a new bidder suddenly stepped out of the crowd, and for the first time the poor girl showed some interest. It was Luis, formerly one of my uncle's best clerks. He began by overbidding the previous price, and once more the contest was in full swing, with the crowd pressing forward and craning necks to enjoy the struggle. Sousa grinned at the youth with an evil, sour grin, and the price rose steadily by leaps and bounds as each named a new figure. The auctioneer rubbed his hands with pleasure and egged on the bidders to greater efforts. The battle of the *pesos* raged until Luis had bid to the limit of his unfortunately too small resources.

" Maria the slave girl brought really an amazing price, and was finally knocked down to the highest bidder, the malevolent Sousa, whose satyr face and working lips told of his hellish intentions even more plainly than had his wild bidding. But he was not destined to defile my uncle's pretty lamb nor to pollute the virgin beauty of her innocence.

" As the auctioneer shouted the result of the sale, Luis, with a broad, long-bladed, heavy knife in his hand, threw himself violently upon her, and the innocent Maria fell, her snowy bosom almost cloven in two by the force of the terrible blow."

I sat breathless, waiting for the rest, but Thussel maintained a moody silence. I knew there must be more to the story, so, after waiting respectfully a moment, I inquired: " What happened to Luis? "

" He got away," replied Thussel sadly, " and managed to escape the vengeance of both the law and Sousa. Under another name he went to Paraguay, entered the army, and began a most distinguished career. Absolutely ignorant of fear, his reckless daring became a byword among officers and men, and he died at last just as his troops were achieving a famous victory."

Thussel stopped again, seemingly unwilling to go on, but I knew he had still something to tell, though I realised that he must do it in his own way. " Ah, well," he said at last, " you can see in this tragedy simply a recurrence of the old Roman story which stirred the Eternal City to its foundations. Virginius assassinated his daughter for the same reason that urged Luis to kill Maria. The centuries pass, but they bring the same tragedies with them over again, and the tragedies bring the same results and cause the same poignant griefs every time. When the tree is the same, does any one idly wonder what the fruits will be like? But perhaps this was a little different. The real murderer, Maria's father, was not punished——"

" Her father! " I cried, amazed beyond expression. " Her father! I thought you said that Luis killed her! "

Thussel smiled wearily.

" Yes—killed by her father, indeed! Luis struck the blow, it is true, but he was simply the weapon, the machine. My uncle had commanded him to do it! His daughter should never be a slave. Should she be sold, Luis was to slay her with one swift, painless stroke! My uncle——"

But the rattle and clamour of the sliding gang-plank, the shouts of the deck-hands, the cries of the slaves, and the roar of escaping steam as the boat drew alongside the Nictheroy wharf, drowned Thussel's words, and I never heard the fate of his uncle.

CARMEN DE BURGOS

B. 1878

FLOWERING HEATHER

Not far from Alcira, in southern Spain, shut off from the high-road, nestling in a delicious bit of ground and sheltered by spreading trees, stands a little white cottage which makes the traveller long from a distance for its graceful vine-arbours, where the leaves of the bindweed interlace with the tendrils of the grape vine. Here the rays of a fiery sun wrap the earth in the glowing embrace which engenders life.

The fields presented all the varied golden tints of harvest time; amongst their green tangles of leaves the vines were beginning to show their closely clustered bunches of grapes; the date-palms bravely shook their fruit-laden branches and in the atmosphere floated aromatic and intoxicating odours of vitality. This vivifying breath of nature penetrated the fragile and fatigued organism of Mercedes, filling her blood with oxygen, giving her renewed life.

Mercedes was the owner of the landed property. She was a charming young orphan girl of eighteen years of age, of a delicate constitution and worn out by the constant excitement of social festivities at court.

Now, her existence had undergone an indefinable change. The surrounding atmosphere of love and fecundity, which enwrapped her and renewed her health, at the same time wrought upon her imagination. The young girl, whom her physicians' prescriptions obliged to remain here, began to dream of some enamoured swain, very distinct indeed from the country louts who surrounded her.

Imagination, however, will perform miracles in the heads of romantic maidens. Mercedes had never loved, and, like all lovely and admired women, she had so far worshipped only at the shrine of her own beauty. One day she found a branch of blooming heather fastened to the iron railing of her window. The newly budded tiny flowers flaunted their pretty pink, and the dewdrops gleamed in their petals like powdered diamonds.

In the evening, when they were all assembled under the grape-arbour, Mercedes asked who had brought her the flowers, and

Manuel, a lad of twenty who worked in the vineyard, confessed with a shaking voice, twisting his old hat in trembling fingers, that it was he who had picked the flowers for the lady, showing his hands all torn by the spikes of the tough little shrub.

A peculiar sympathy awoke in the heart of the young woman, who found herself the mistress of the poor fellow's soul, well pleased with his passion and the secret homage he devoted to her. Henceforward Mercedes kept the lad at her side under all sorts of pretexts, not without causing considerable comment in the observant vicinity.

On each and every day Manuel would bring her branches of blooming heather, with which she contrived strange adornments for herself. Her blue-black hair, interwoven with the tiny pink flowers and small green leaves, gave her a strange aspect and made her eyes shine with greater brilliancy. A necklace of the same flowers increased the delicate pallor of her skin, and bunches of heather scattered capriciously here and there on her floating white garments lent her the looks of a Druid priestess in the depths of her sacred grove.

The kindness of Mercedes, and her smiles, encouraged Manuel; and their friendship assumed the form of an idyll in which the great lady condescended to her rustic swain, making him sweet promises of love, which filled the boy's whole life. She did not reflect seriously upon the situation. With his bronzed skin, his regular energetic features, and his large and expressive eyes, Manuel appeared handsome to her; his ardent and savage wooing, converted into a respectful homage, flattered her vanity. At his side she felt less bored—but that was all.

One day Mercedes went with all the farm-hands on a pilgrimage to a neighbouring shrine. She sat merrily enthroned amongst the girls, waiting with impatience for the moment in which Manuel would join them. But amongst the visitors at the feast there were some friends of hers, who spoke to her of the world she had forgotten in the recesses of her sequestered nook, and the wave of memory rushed over her, brimming with gaiety and pleasure.

In her endeavour to shake off this impression she sought Manuel with her eyes, and at last discovered him, not daring to approach her in his rustic bashfulness. Mercedes would have called him, but she refrained. She felt ashamed of him. What would her friends say? She the sweetheart of one of her menials!

She looked again at Manuel. How homely he was! Buttoned up in a thick cloth jacket, a red handkerchief drawn through a metal ring knotted around his neck, clumsy cow-hide boots which hampered his movements—she wondered how she could ever have thought the fellow good-looking.

The return trip was a gloomy one.   Mercedes appeared absent-minded, and not a single time did her eyes seek those of Manuel. She understood that their relations had gone too far; and that very day, most rapidly and unexpectedly, she completed arrangements for her return to Madrid.

A year has passed; we are in the elegant boudoir of the city house inhabited by Mercedes.   The young woman is reclining in an easy-chair, and before her, pale and trembling, stands Manuel, in whom it is difficult to recognise the light-hearted youth of Alcira.

"How pleased I am to see you!" she said to him with feigned cordiality.   "Tell me how you are and give me the news of the village."

When he made no reply, she added: "Do not worry, my lad; I have sent for you because I am thinking of getting married.   My husband may have to go up there on business, and I do not want him to know—you understand what I mean.   That was a piece of folly, and I could no more have resigned myself to being a farmer's wife than you would ever make a fine gentleman.   But do not get angry—listen to reason—you shall be inspector of the property and manage it in your own way.   You ought to get married yourself.   Above all, never tell any one about that ridiculous child's play!"

"I understand, Señorita Mercedes.   You may be sure that you will not be molested," was all that Manuel managed to say, as he abruptly left the room.

Mercedes, startled by his expression of suffering, murmured uneasily to herself: "How seriously he must have taken it!"   In eternal feminine vanity and selfishness, she added, triumphantly: "He loves me still, and Luis will never know!"

"Yes, beloved Luis," said Mercedes two days later to her fiancé, "I have had a great shock.   The inspector of Alcira has been run over by an electric car—an incredible piece of stupidity —stood gaping in the middle of the street!"

"It is indeed a sad and deplorable accident, but I see no particular reason for you to grieve about it.   What are you holding in your hand there?"

"A bunch of wild flowers which the unfortunate man charged them to deliver to me, when they picked him up dying."

"What a strange gift!"

"He had brought them for me from Alcira, because during my stay there he used to present me with these flowers, knowing my fondness for them."

"And maybe you had been flirting with him, just to keep your hand in?   However, such sins are too trivial to count.   Throw the stuff away and do not let us think any more about the matter! ''

'' How good you are, my Luis, and how much I love you! '' said she, throwing the heather branch into the fire, which crackled noisily, whilst a column of white smoke slowly arose in the air, exhaling a pungent perfume of flowering fields.

JUAN DE DIOS PEZA

19TH CENTURY

LA MULATA

MORE than two hundred years ago there lived in Córdoba—that beautiful, gardenia-scented garden-spot of Vera Cruz, in Mexico— a mysteriously beautiful woman, whose eyes must surely have caught their burning blackness from the rays of the hot African sun. Yet she was fair as a lily, showing that she was also a daughter of the white race. No one knew what her parentage was. People who had looked upon the curling blackness of her magnificent hair, her rounded voluptuous form with its undulating tigerlike grace of movement, and her full red lips, called her La Mulata, suspecting that she was the daughter of Spanish and African parents.

No one knew whence she came, and in those days of the dark and dread Inquisition there were many secret doings and many mysteries. But innumerable rumours were abroad in the village concerning her, some saying in hushed tones that so versed was La Mulata in the occult sciences that even the powers of the air were obedient to her will, and malignant spirits hastened to do her bidding; that during the tranquil hours of the night, when only the voice of the watchful cock broke the silence, the sweeping of heavy wings could be heard over the Mulata's house; demoniacal sights, not meant for the eye of mortal man, could be seen, had one the valour to watch; and that even the devil himself, in the form of a dark, saturnine man of great beauty, took human form to visit her.

Terrible and weird were the tales told of the mysterious Spanish-African beauty. More than one crazed or dying person had been found near the small house in which she lived, retired and alone. One luckless being—a night watchman—was found dying of fright and unable to speak of what he had seen. His screams and convulsions, upon being commanded to tell what had injured him, were awful; and his one coherent plea was that he be allowed to die without speaking.

Other men, who passed too near to the palms and orange-trees which curtained her house entrance, had been found dumb and paralysed afterwards. 'Truly, a terrible and mysterious power had this beauteous Mulata, while her fascination drew to her any man, of whatever station, who once looked upon her.

The people suspected the woman; her every action was watched, and her every word occasioned trepidation. But unless one had the courage to watch her house at midnight (which the Virgin and all the Saints forbid!) there was nothing upon which to base her condemnation. Quiet and tranquil was her behaviour when abroad; no native Mexicana frequented the Church more than did she, and her downcast eyes and modest mien could not but quiet slander, and stop the most malevolent tongue.

Only the Alcalde (mayor), who was of the greatest good-fame and authority in the village, could not still his doubts, but swore to himself that she was indeed a woman of the strongest magic. And yet the village knew that he was no fair judge, nor yet an impartial one; for despite his many years and grey hair, the Alcalde had conceived so violent, so overpowering a passion for this fair woman of mystery that he could not rest, eat, nor sleep for thinking upon it. In vain did he endeavour to suppress, to throttle his love —it could not be done! The more he struggled to forget her, the more did he remember; and at last, driven by an irresistible force, he went to La Mulata, and humbly confessed his love.

It was in vain. Nothing—neither promises nor entreaties, the offer of princely gifts, tears, the oath of constancy—could move this woman, so fair of face and so hard of heart. Utterly in vain were the Alcalde's entreaties, for she would give him not even one ray of hope.

Then the Alcalde vowed that he would ignore her; meet her disdain with disdain. In vain: for even the sight of her in the far distance set his elderly heart aflame. The more he wished to forget her, the more did he remember: he prayed to hate her, and could only idolise! In his moments of calmness he could not explain to himself this consuming passion: not taking into account the human weakness, which is always the slave of reason, he concluded that it was no human love which so inflamed his soul and mind, but that he must be instead in the toils of a witch, an enchantress, who had been sent to him by the devil.

In such a case, thought Don Martin de Ocaña, there was but one remedy—and that the " Holy Office." Only through the Inquisitors could he rid himself of this woman of magic and her infernal wiles.

Once arrived at this terrible decision, the Alcalde did not hesitate: with a steady hand he wrote the denunciation which was to be the death-knell of the beautiful Mulata; with firmness and precision he recounted the rumours which filled the village, and the terrible situation in which he himself was placed, entreating

also—which was unnecessary, for the Holy Office dearly loved a
new victim—that the Señores Inquisitors make speed and haste in
delivering his village of this dread enchantress, the " Mulata of
Córdoba! "

During the calm of the midnight hours, it seemed to the Mulata,
alone in her palm-shaded house, that the quiet night had been
profaned by strange noises: there was the sound of loud tones, the
tramping of many feet.

From her window she heard voices, approaching nearer and
nearer: there were moving torches, and strange shadows cast in
their wake: soon there came into view guards and horsemen,
apparently making toward her solitary house. At their head she
recognised Don Martin, the Alcalde, on his prancing white charger.
She smiled and waited.

Reaching her house, the cortège halted; the place was surrounded by guards: a " Bando " (proclamation) of the " Holy
Office " was read in a loud voice, that all might hear; and a command was then shouted to the Mulata de Córdoba to come forth and
surrender herself to the officers, a prisoner of the Inquisition.

But La Mulata did not obey. Enveloping her form in a white
mantle, she stole through a rear door, past the frightened guards,
and soon gained the open meadow behind the house. Here
awaited her a man whose features were obscured by his large
sombrero, but whose eyes scintillated in the darkness as though
phosphorescent. The ample folds of his mantle did not suffice
to disguise his tall and splendid form. He held the reins of two
chargers.

Upon one of them leaped the Mulata, and with a jeering laugh
the strange man flung himself upon the other as both steeds sprang
forward; their hoofs flashed fire and they whinnied in wild, unearthly fashion. Straight for the Alcalde and his troops they
made. There was wild uproar, the woman laughing loudly as her
charger leaped and pranced in the midst of the bewildered men.

" The witch," they cried. " Sorceress! Stop! Retrace your
steps! After her, men! "

In the wild confusion the guards ran into each other: Don
Martin was jostled in a manner most unbefitting his rank as
Alcalde, and of course the culprit escaped.

Soon the horsemen, with Don Martin leading, were on the enchantress's trail: in the distance they could see the flutter of her
white mantle, and the phosphorescent sparks that were struck
from the horses' feet. The pursuing horsemen crossed themselves
as they watched, and more than one of them entreated Don Martin
not to set them to pursuing demons—for what earthly horse could
so cast fire from his hoofs?

But the Alcalde set his teeth, and merely bade his men gallop

the faster, so that this witch could the sooner grace the
" hogueras " (bonfires) of San Lazaro.

Soon it seemed that the chargers of the fugitives were tiring,
or else their riders. Close in front fluttered the white mantle of
the woman, and the hearts of the pursuers beat with renewed hope.
Fast and faster they spurred, the Alcalde leading; another step,
and he could seize the mantle itself. At that moment the woman's
horse gave a furious leap, and the clouds of dust that arose
momentarily blinded the pursuers.

When they could penetrate the darkness sufficiently to distinguish the two fleeting forms, they were far out of reach, and
jeering laughter floated back—which in no way allayed the dismay
and chagrin of the Alcalde.

Furiously he ordered a halt, and while his men rested and muttered over the uselessness of riding down sorceresses, Don Martin
reflected. He was persuaded that the Mulata and her mysterious
companion were demons in human form, and therefore useless to
chase: the memory of their jeering laughter upset his saner reflections, and then with an oath he ordered his followers to gallop
anew in the pursuit.

Hours later the Alcalde stopped his exhausted horse and gazed
uncertainly about him. One man after another had dropped behind
in the chase, until now he found himself alone, his horse half
dead, in a dense, dark forest from which he could see no egress
—nay, he could not even distinguish the path he had just followed!
There was only one thing to do: travel on, and he forced his tired
horse into the forest.

He had long ago given up all hope of reaching or apprehending
the Mulata. Judge, therefore, of his surprise when he suddenly
beheld the woman herself, on her great horse, not far in front of
him, and evidently awaiting his approach. Both she and her
pawing charger were as fresh as they had been at the beginning
of the chase, whereas the Alcalde was almost worn-out, and his
stout animal in like condition.

Behind the witch, half obscured by dense bushes, was her
sombre companion of the night before, his face still hidden by his
sombrero, and his form shrouded by the heavy cloak.

As the Alcalde gasped and rubbed his eyes, believing that he
was dreaming, the Mulata spoke, and her voice was soft and sweet.

" Enough, Don Martin de Ocaña! Are you now convinced that
you can never reach me? Though you pursued for years, you
could never do so. I would ask your pardon for last night's work
but for your cruel persecution of me. And now, return to Córdoba, where I also go, to be imprisoned."

As she ceased speaking, and before the Don could recover from
the stupor of astonishment into which her words threw him, she

leapt her horse past him, followed by the stranger; there was the
sound of galloping hoofs, and then silence reigned once more
throughout the great forest.

Again rubbing his eyes, Don Martin dropped his tired head upon
his breast and allowed the white charger to take his own way back
to Córdoba.

Great was the sensation in Mexico when it became known that
the " Holy Office," in a late session, had sentenced " La Mulata
de Córdoba " to be burned to death. It was furthermore rumoured
on all sides that on account of the great beauty and wickedness of
the prisoner the occasion would be a very great one, such as to
leave memories to all who witnessed it.

Meanwhile, in a dark dungeon, entered only through dreary
subterranean passages where the light of day never reached, nor
rumour from the outside world, the Mulata paid the penalty of her
" malicious and inhuman heresies," as the Holy Office designated
them. Valiantly did the Inquisitors labour to bring her back to the
straight road and to confess one by one her atrocious crimes. With
this worthy end in view, the good doctors came and went in that
dismal dungeon, without success. For what could they do with the
fair woman whose only confession was, that *in any difficulty or
danger the devil himself aided and abetted her*?

To-morrow was to be the Mulata's last day on earth; and even
now the slaves, under their Spanish task-masters, were driving
the stakes and making ready for the fire which was to reduce to
ashes that lovely body.

Once more it was the midnight hour. La Mulata slept tranquilly; and, forgetting that she was in the cells of the Inquisition,
dreamed that she slept in her palm-shaded house, her body covered
with flowers.

A stealthy noise startled her from her sleep; and she listened, as
slow footsteps crept cautiously down the passage leading to her
miserable cell; nearer and nearer they came: a key grated in the
lock, and the heavy door swung back on its hinges.

Frightened, she cowered against the wall, as the gaoler entered,
bearing a rush-light; and behind him came the youngest of the
Inquisitors—one whom they said would become the next Viceroy.

The old gaoler, putting down the light, went out of the cell; and
the Inquisitor spoke, his eyes burning, his voice hoarse and
tremulous:

" Listen, beautiful one: it has come to this! For more than ten
nights I have sought you, to offer you life and liberty in exchange
for nothing more than your love. Nine times, overcome with
shame, I have gone away. Now, I am here. Know that ever since
you were brought before the Tribunal I have loved you with a love
hardly human, more like a devouring flame. Come with me, to

liberty. I am rich, and we will pass our lives where no one will know your history, not even your name. I love you! When I am with you, and your glorious eyes gaze upon me, I forget even God and my duty, and my soul remembers only you. Give me your love—come with me, and we will exchange this miserable dungeon for the most splendid of palaces. My adored one, come with me."

"Sir, such noble thoughts as yours I do not merit. How can you, an hidalgo of a princely house, condescend to me, the enchantress whom the people hold in horror: a sorceress at whom the children cry out in terror? "

"Because I adore you; and I hold you in my thoughts as high as the Empress is held, whom all delight to honour. You are all in all to me: I pray you, tell me that you love me! "

"No! And though I know that you will be angry, and that my death will be hastened, I will not deceive you. No more words of love, sir, will I hear from your lips. I bid you farewell."

Trembling, pallid as the dead, the youngest Inquisitor arose, his glowing eyes fixed on the enchantress.

"It is well, heartless one," he cried. "You will suffer for this. Why have you bewitched me with your unearthly beauty, why have you led me to such an end? It were unmanly to say more to you, as you are; but when you come to the stake, you will remember this night, and what I offered you! "

Grasping the light, he turned from her, and was about to leave the cell when the Mulata detained him. Softly she said:

"Though it will anger you, sir, answer me one question before you go. If you respond as I wish, then I will listen to your words; aye, will even love you."

"Speak; what is the question? " cried the Inquisitor.

"Do you, sir, see this barque which I have drawn with charcoal on the wall here? What is the one thing it needs? Answer that! "

The youngest Inquisitor studied the picture, which, the more he studied, seemed to grow larger and more perfect. It needed nothing, yet he feared to speak.

"What does it need? Answer me," insisted the Mulata.

"It is perfect: it only seems to need one to direct it," hazarded the unhappy Inquisitor.

"That is not the answer, but now it will have some one to direct it," said the witch; and as she spoke, she stepped to the wall. As in a dream, the Inquisitor saw the wall disappear: the ship grew larger and larger: waves rocked it gently to and fro, and the breezes filled its large sails. As in a dream, the Inquisitor saw the Mulata kiss her hand to him from its deck, and then the barque began to move, slowly at first, then fast, and faster: it was far gone now, gone for ever.

Many years after the Inquisition, an old man, who looked even older than he was, wandered in the streets, hopelessly crazed. No one knew him, and he did not know his own name. He was confined in an asylum for the insane, where he babbled unceasingly of a barque that one night sailed from a prison-cell to a far port, carrying the woman he loved.

It was the youngest Inquisitor, who was to have been the next Viceroy, and whose high-born family mourned him as dead.

As for La Mulata, she was never seen again, nor even heard of, save in the old-world legends that one hears sometimes from the " gente de la calle " (people in the street). So it is supposed that the devil at last took her, and that no more will her wiles enchant and destroy poor mortal men.

PORTUGUESE
Short Stories

Contents

ALEXANDRO HERCULANO

1810–1877

THE VILLAGE PRIEST

THE village was prettily situated on the slope of a mountain, with a stream running through it down to the sea. Almost the highest house in it was the presbytery, but still higher stood the church, as if it were guardian of the parish at its feet. It was built in the mixed style of Moorish and Renaissance, like so many of the churches of Portugal, which furnish a proof that the noble conquerors of India did not return from the East with empty hands. For in those days devotion was a matter of luxury, and to build a church was a proof of wealth equivalent to having a country seat, a yacht, and a racing stable in these less pious times.

But if the church was rich, the village was poor, and the good parish priest led a hard life of solitary work—for he had no curate —and of self-sacrifice. How poor he was, perhaps no one really knew, except his old housekeeper Jeronyma. For many times he dined on bread and coffee when he had given help to some one in the parish in time of sudden need. He had a little field which he tilled himself, and the corn and vegetables from which served for his scanty table.

Down in the valley, in a little cottage by the stream, lived the village laundress, Perpetua Rosa, an industrious creature, who looked after the clean linen of the parish in return for a humble livelihood. She had one daughter, Bernardina, who aided her in her work, and who was said to be the prettiest girl not only in the parish but in a dozen parishes round.

Be that as it may, when Bernardina came along the little path leading from her mother's cottage with her basket of clean clothes balanced on her head, two or three young fellows would mysteriously appear as if they had sprung from the ground, to help her with her burden, and when she was seen to enter the barn where dancing took place on festival days with the goodwill and approval of the parish priest, the hearts of the other girls sank before the prospect of being partnerless, at least until Bernardina had made her choice of all the likely young fellows at the dance. But of all the lads who flocked round her, the one who made her heart beat

most quickly was Manuel da Ventosa. And this was the poor
girl's greatest trouble.

For Manuel da Ventosa was certainly too great a catch to be
seriously dreamed of by the daughter of a poor village washer-
woman. His father, Bartholomeu da Ventosa, was a rich miller,
a decent and honest man, every one agreed, but possessed by ten
thousand devils of avarice. He owned two mills and several farms,
and he looked for a wife for his son who would enable him to add
to his wealth. And much as Manuel admired Bernardina, he feared
his father more.

Not only was Perpetua Rosa very poor, but she had the misfortune to be in the miller's black books for another reason. One
day when she was doing the washing for the mills she had the bad
luck to lose three old torn sacks. The miller almost died of rage.
He told every one that the sacks were new, and swore that Perpetua Rosa would have to replace them. And he took his washing
away from her and sent it to a woman who lived in the next
village. Needless to say, he forbade Manuel to speak to the
daughter of the poor laundress or even to approach her at dances.

So matters stood one afternoon when the parish priest, walking
round the church and reading his breviary, happened to glance in
at the open door, and there, kneeling in the shaft of crimson
light cast by the great rose window, a muslin scarf draping her
fair head, was Bernardina, sobbing as if her heart would break.
And the good priest did not need to be told the reason, for only
that day Jeronyma had mentioned in her morning gossip, as she
served his breakfast, that the miller was about to ask the hand of
a rich farmer's niece in the next parish for his son Manuel.

The priest continued his walk, but the breviary was closed and
his eyes were fixed on the ground. He was so wrapped in his
meditations that, to the horror of Jeronyma, who was watching
him from the presbytery garden, when the Angelus rang, he did
not kneel down or even remove his hat, but continued to walk
round as though the sacristan were not pulling energetically at the
rope in the belfry. Jeronyma made the sign of the cross, and
hoped the priest was not going wrong in his mind by some malice
of the devil. He had seemed rather odd that morning, and had
left his breakfast, which he usually enjoyed, almost uneaten.

It was long past nightfall when the good old man returned to
the presbytery. Never within the memory of man had he been
known to have his supper so late. And after supper, Jeronyma
heard him walking up and down his modest sitting-room, repeating
over and over again:

" Nothing did I bring into this world, and nothing can I take
away from it."

Next morning the old priest rose with the sun, and called to

Jeronyma, who was lighting the fire, that she was to hurry with his breakfast, for he was going out early. When he appeared, she saw that he had some important call to make, for he wore his best hat and carried his silver-headed walking-stick, the one article of luxury which he possessed.

The housekeeper set the coffee to boil and began making some potato cakes to give her reverend master a hot breakfast before his walk. She also put a couple of eggs in the pan to tempt his appetite.

As soon as he entered the sitting-room, the priest opened a locked cabinet and pulled out a drawer. From it he took a thin folded sheet of crisp paper.

" Jeronyma! Come here, Jeronyma! "

" Breakfast is almost ready, sir. If your Reverence will have a moment's patience."

" It isn't that, woman. Here is a note for fifty dollars. Take it to Agostinho's shop and change it into gold for me."

" Yes, sir. But—where did it come from? There was no baptism or funeral yesterday, and you never have such a big fee as this."

" Eve will never be dead while you are alive, most inquisitive of women! " exclaimed the priest, laughing amid his pretended anger.

" Your pardon, sir. I meant no offence. I will do as you tell me."

And still staring at the priest in wonder, she extended her hand covered with the corner of her apron, not to soil the spotless note.

But when the priest had received his fifty dollars in gold and Jeronyma came in with the tray containing the coffee, eggs, and potato cakes, she suffered a still greater shock, which nearly resulted in her dropping the tray and leaving her reverend master breakfastless.

The fifty dollars lay on the table in two rows, and the priest was adding others to them, which he took from a leather pouch. Nor did he stop until a hundred gold pieces gleamed on the table in the morning sunshine.

" Not a word about this, Jeronyma, until I give you leave to speak," he enjoined. And when he put on his hat and left the presbytery after making a good breakfast, his housekeeper heard him repeating to himself:

" Nothing did I bring into this world, and nothing can I take away from it."

The miller stood at the door of one of his mills, superintending the loading of some mules with sacks of flour for the neighbouring town. He was in very bad humour, and he rated his boys soundly for their slowness at work. Suddenly the rap of a stick on his shoulder made him turn round.

" What? Your Reverence here so early! . . . You young

ass, can't you put that sack on top of the other two? . . . Your
Reverence is welcome. Has anything happened? . . . May the
devil fly away with you! Don't you see you will break my rope?
. . . Come in, your Reverence.''

"Yes, Bartholomeu,'' replied the priest. "Something has happened. I have been priest of this parish for forty years, and this
is the first time that such a thing did happen. It is a difficult
thing to settle, and I have come down to ask your advice, because
I know you are a prudent man.''

The priest sat on a stool which stood at the mill desk, and the
miller took his place on a sack of wheat opposite. Both old men
measured each other with their eyes for a moment in silence, as if
each was trying to penetrate the other's thoughts. The priest was
considering how to begin what he had to say, while the miller
was wondering if his pastor was contemplating some festival and
had come to ask him for a money contribution. He began to
invent a dozen falsehoods to avert such a calamity.

"My friend,'' said the priest at last, "I have a good sum of
money here with me; a hundred gold pieces of five dollars each,
which have been entrusted to me by a pious person as a dowry for
a poor girl of this parish. I have undertaken to make the selection, but it is not easy, so I have come to ask the aid of your
judgment. I know you are an honest man, Bartholomeu, though
a trifle niggardly. . . .''

"Don't believe that, your Reverence,'' exclaimed the miller,
red with anger under the flour which powdered his cheeks. "That
is what the evil tongues of the village say because I do not throw
away my hard-earned money on them. May the devil fly
away . . .''

"There, there,'' interrupted the priest. "Never mind what
people say. Let us keep to what we ourselves have to say. Now,
you know every girl in my parish. Which of them do you think
deserves this dowry best? ''

The miller looked up at the ceiling and appeared to reflect,
while the priest watched him with a sly smile.

"Not Genoveva da Silva, at any rate,'' he said at last. "Like
mother, like daughter, and of all the idle, gossiping . . .''

"I was not thinking of her,'' replied the priest. "Talk of the
good girls of the parish.''

"Nor Clara the muleteer's daughter either. You would never
give it to Catharina Carriça, would you? ''

"My good man, she would spend it in six months on laces and
hair ribbons. Think of some one else.''

After a long silence, the miller spoke, nodding gravely.

"I have an idea, but of course I don't know. I would not
venture to advise your Reverence.''

" But, man, I came here to ask your advice. Tell me your idea."

" Well, you know my niece Joanna. There is not a better girl in the parish. Of course her father is not very poor, but his farm has not done very well this year, and he still owes me forty dollars which he borrowed for stock. Joanna is an angel, and the dowry would come in very nicely . . ."

The priest cut short his admiration for his relative by a peal of hearty laughter. " Oh, oh, my friend! What a good idea indeed! My dowry is to pay your forty dollars! That is really excellent. I am so glad I came to ask your advice! " And then becoming suddenly serious, he went on: " Bartholomeu, your avarice will land you in a place in the next world, out of which all your money will not get you. You are trying to get the better of your parish priest when he comes to ask your honest advice. Is that right, Bartholomeu? Is it fair, do you think? "

" But, your Reverence . . ."

" Well says the proverb: ' I went to my neighbour's house and I was saddened; I returned to my own and I was consoled.' The best thing will be to keep to my first idea."

" Oh, well, if your Reverence has already made up your mind? "

" All right," returned the priest; " I just wanted to see if you and I would be of the same mind, but your avarice has blinded you to all sense of justice. Well, we have not settled anything after all."

And the priest rose as if to take his leave.

" Your Reverence will excuse me. Just tell me who you think ought to have the dowry."

" The girl I intend to give it to is Bernardina, the laundress's daughter."

" What! Perpetua Rosa's daughter? Your Reverence is joking. Of all the worthless hussies in the village! And if the mother gets her claws on the money she will make short work of it! "

" Stop, stop, man. That is not what people in the village say, and the women's tongues there are no better than anywhere else. The mother and daughter are very poor, but see how neat and respectable they keep themselves. I hear they owe money to Agostinho at the shop, but if they could pay him they would. Well, they will be able to pay him now, and have plenty left, for it is only a trifle they owe him. I will go and tell them about it at once. Bernardina ought to make a good match now."

Whilst the priest was talking, a brilliant idea seized the miller's imagination. After all, if he could not get the money for his niece, he might get some of it anyhow for himself. Perhaps his three old sacks were not lost; he might get three new ones for them now. And he might take over Perpetua Rosa's debt from Agostinho and charge good interest on it.   Anyhow, it would be odd if he did not reap some advantage from the dowry.

"Well, your Reverence," he said eagerly.   "It is quite true that we must not believe all we hear, and I suppose you know best what to do with the dowry.   I am obliged to you for asking my advice, and I hope Bernardina will make good use of the money."

"Then that is settled," returned the priest.   "Now we have to settle something else; to find a good husband for the girl.   You know all the young fellows about here, and you may be able to advise me about that too.   Think it over.   Perhaps we may be able to agree better this time.   Now that I think of it, you had better let me leave the money in your care.   I am not much good for taking care of money.   You have kept your own so well that I know this will be safe with you.   You will not be troubled with the charge long, for with this money we shall soon have Bernardina married."

The old priest displayed the hundred gold pieces before the miller's avaricious eyes, which danced in his head as he saw the glitter of the gold.   His pastor noted this and smiled to think that he was making use of a wile of the devil to do a work of God.

Taking leave of the miller, who still stood staring at the gold, the priest went out.   The miller came running after him.

"If your Reverence has not breakfasted, you might stop and have some with me.   I have only humble fare, but still . . ."

"Thanks, my friend, but I have breakfasted, and I must go to see Bernardina."   And shaking his stick at the miller's back as he returned to feast his eyes on the gold, the priest muttered:

"A morsel eaten at that old miser's table would choke me."

As he turned the corner of the road he came full on Manuel da Ventosa, gun on shoulder, and dog at heel, off for a morning's shooting.

"You good-for-nothing young scamp, why don't you go in and help your poor old father, who has to work so hard and is so poor?" exclaimed the priest with a grin which belied his stern words.   "Leave the rabbits alone for a bit and come along with me.   I want to talk to you."

And as the young man obeyed, he went on:

"You must go to your father first thing to-morrow morning and ask his leave to marry your sweetheart Bernardina."

"Oh, your Reverence!   He would never give me leave.   He has forbidden me to speak to her, and as you know I am quite dependent on him, I must obey him."

"Then you do not want to marry Bernardina? "

"I want nothing better, sir, but what am I to do? "

"Do as I tell you, Manuel.   Leave the rest to me.   It is your

duty to marry the girl you love, who will make you a good wife.
Don't speak to your father till to-morrow, though, and then come
and tell me what he says. Now go after your rabbits and don't
tell him you met me."

The young fellow stooped and kissed the old priest's hand. He
was trembling with joy and could not express his thanks otherwise.
And as the old man hurried away, the tears stood in his eyes and
he too was unable to say anything.

All that day Jeronyma was more convinced every moment that
something had disordered her master's brain. He kept singing
joyful psalms, the " Te Deum " and the " Tantum Ergo," and he
played for fully half an hour with the presbytery cat. He fully
enjoyed his simple dinner, however, and went out to read his
breviary afterwards, not forgetting to say the Angelus when the
bell rang. But when he took off his shoes for the evening,
Jeronyma, coming in with his slippers, was horrified to see him
skipping about in his stocking feet, throwing his shoes into the air
and catching them like a schoolboy.

Why was the good priest so joyful? Simply because he had
secured the happiness of two of his young parishioners at the cost
of his own savings for forty years, and of a small legacy left to him
by an old college friend. He had intended to leave this money for
the further adornment of his beloved church, and it was the sight
of Bernardina's grief which caused the other idea to dawn on him.
Small wonder that he had forgotten the Angelus and come in late
to supper. A project of forty years is not so lightly dismissed.

He knew his parishioners well, and his plan with the miller was
founded on this knowledge. All day the hundred pieces of gold
lying in his money chest occupied the miser's imagination and at
night they kept him awake, a vision at once celestial and infernal.
He began to calculate what could be done with this money, added
to his own, scraped together for so many years. He could buy the
farm belonging to Ignacio Codeço and put his son Manuel in to
work it and get more money, and so buy other farms. But first
of all, he would go to Agostinho and offer to take over Perpetua
Rosa's debt for a smaller sum. He would persuade the shopkeeper
that it was lost money, and that he was only taking it over out of
charity. But he must make haste, before Agostinho heard of the
dowry. He would go first thing in the morning. Then he would
try to persuade his brother, Joanna's father, to let him have the
farm for the forty dollars he owed him and a little more. Other
ideas occurred to him and still others, until it seemed as if there
were hardly anything he could not do with the aid of those hundred
gold pieces. To a miser, five hundred dollars is a lot of money.
And the money was there, in his own box, in his power. What
should he do to make it all his?

Should he deny having received it from the parish priest? After all, there had been no witnesses present. But no! He was avaricious, and he loved money and money's worth, but he had always been honest, in his own way, which is the way of many men. He had pinched and ground and lent money at interest, but he had never robbed any one. At last, after revolving many plans, he fell into the snare which the good priest had set for him.

There was only one way to get all the money honestly into his power. Bernardina was a pretty girl and well brought up, and he knew his son was fond of her. Why should he not marry her, and then his father would have her dowry? That was certain, for Manuel was afraid of him and married or single would remain under his thumb. There was only one thing to be settled now, and that was which would be the best farm for him to buy. His brother's could be had cheap, but that belonging to Ignacio Codeço would bring in more money. And while the good old priest slept happily because he had left himself penniless, the miller tossed about in wakefulness because of his unexpected wealth.

The result of the conversation which father and son had at breakfast was that both went off in search of the parish priest, whom they found issuing from the church after saying his early Mass. Manuel had not told his father of his meeting with the priest the day before, and the miller feared a snub for proposing his son as a husband for Bernardina, similar to the one he had received for suggesting his niece as the best recipient of the dowry.

The good priest, however, was only too delighted at the success of his scheme, and he readily accompanied the miller and his son to Perpetua Rosa's cottage. He had not gone there the day before, preferring to await the maturing of his plan.

The wedding was fixed for Easter, and the priest had the satisfaction of preaching a sermon after he had pronounced the blessing on the union which had cost him the renunciation of the dream of his life. After exhorting the bridegroom to practise the virtues of industry, sobriety, and honesty, and recommending the bride to be affectionate, modest, and obedient to her husband, adding in the homely phrase common to our land that the husband must provide the dinner and the wife must make it fit to eat, the old priest let himself go and preached a thumping denunciation of the sin of avarice; surely a strange theme for a nuptial sermon, but one which seemed very acceptable to all but one member of the congregation present. For all knew how Bernardina's dowry had changed the miller's view of her as a daughter-in-law, but only the village priest was fully aware of the miracle which had wrought the change.

JOÃO REBELLO DA SILVA

1822–1871

THE LAST BULL-FIGHT IN SALVATERRA

I

THE King José, the first of the name, was spending his holidays
in Salvaterra. The truth is that evil tongues said in strict confidence that in Lisbon His Majesty was always at the lathe, and
the Marquis de Pombal was always on the throne. This saying
was founded on the fact that the King was an excellent amateur
turner, and the Marquis was an excellent amateur ruler.

The season was the middle of spring. The meadows were sweet
with flowers, the woods were in full verdure, the corn and fruit
farms were full of promise, and the fresh breeze ruffled the curls of
the country girls and stole kisses in passing from the perfumed
roses. Everywhere one heard singing and saw signs of happiness,
joy and love under the bright beams of the glorious sun.

A Royal bull-fight called the Court to Salvaterra. The nobles
of the Court were able to breathe more freely on such occasions.
The presence of the Minister who aped the King was less obtrusive
on such days of amusement. The bulls were fierce, the bull-
fighters accomplished, the bull-ring gorgeous, and the ladies present
were, of course, adorable. Every one was ready to be amused,
and not the less so because the Marquis de Pombal had to stay in
Lisbon, where he was engaged in a difficulty of State with the
Spanish Ambassador.

In the by-ways of the Palace whispers were heard of the discussions which had taken place between the Spanish Envoy and
the Portuguese Secretary of State, and some of these whispers
were full of praises of the Minister, uttered aloud so that the very
walls might repeat them; whilst others were full of blame, muttered to satisfy private rancour. Pious people and the nobles were
on the side of the Spaniard, and they prayed to God that the war
which seemed imminent might precipitate the fall of the new
nobility. The magistrates and professional classes took the side of
the Marquis de Pombal and sneered openly at the enthusiasm of

the adherents of the cause of religion and the old order of things. The Marquis de Pombal had firmly refused the requests made by the Spanish Government.

" Very well," said the ambassador; " an army of sixty thousand men will march into Portugal and will . . ."

" Will do what? " asked the Marquis, flourishing his eyeglass and speaking in an indifferent tone.

" Will enforce the will of the King, my master, and will cause your Excellency and your Sovereign to do what is right and just," replied the ambassador.

The Marquis frowned, and putting his eyeglass in its place, looked severely through it at his visitor. Then he said, coldly:

" Sixty thousand men seem a good many guests for a small country like ours, but with the help of God, the King, my sovereign Lord and Master, will find means to accommodate them. Other soldiers of the King of Spain have been safely lodged in Portuguese prisons before now, and your Excellency is at liberty to inform your Royal Master of that fact."

And rising to dismiss the ambassador, he added:

" Your Excellency knows well that every one is free to do as he likes in his own house, but when he is dead, four men can come and carry him away."

The ambassador went away, swearing by God and the Blessed Virgin that he would see the matter through, and the Marquis prepared for war. There was no doubt that, whatever might be his faults, the Marquis de Pombal was a great Minister and did a very important service to his country. In these latter days there are not so very many Ministers of State to be found who deal so promptly with the threats of foreign ambassadors.

II

The Portuguese nation, so powerful after the great discoveries made under the auspices of Henry the Navigator, with their resultant addition of vast and rich colonies to the tiny mother country, so much admired and respected in subsequent days for enterprise and enlightenment, fell on evil times as the consequence of the marriage of the reigning sovereign with a Spanish princess, and the subsequent introduction into Portugal of religious intolerance and the persecution of the more enlightened minds. Up to that time, the rulers of the country had been too much occupied with their profitable and interesting task of national extension to trouble about the religious convictions of their subjects. But the introduction of the Inquisition by Isabella of Castile and Aragon, the decay of heroism under the sinister influence of narrowness and greed, and the discouragement of independence of thought, brought about the first clouds in the fair sky of Lusitania, which were destined to gather into tempests and to overwhelm all the brightness of the early days.

The Minister of State, though deemed to be too anxious to take on his shoulders the mantle of Royal government, was, as even his enemies admitted, an honest man. He dreaded the idea of what would inevitably come to pass if his Royal master spent all his time in amusements, and to save trouble, yielded to the arrogant demands of Spain. He could not endure the thought of his country, after all her splendour, becoming merely a Spanish province, of her ancient nobility being forced to bow the knee before the proud and astute Castilian, and he hoped to be able to rouse both the nobles and the middle classes to a sense of their duty to their country and of the danger which threatened it.

Nations have their seasons like the earth, their periods of fertility and of sterility. And the Minister recognised with unerring vision that when a nation disregards the menace daily held up before it by a powerful neighbour, when its people avoid work and prefer idleness with its attendant evils, when its nobles vie with one another in luxury and display, and above all, when its monarch shirks the duty of attending to affairs of State, then the hour of peril is at hand; the time has come for the ambitious neighbour to rally his forces and swoop down upon his prey.

The Marquis favoured industry and endeavoured to study the welfare of the middle classes. Any progress made by the country was really due to his efforts. If manufacturing industry never reached any high level, it was not his fault but that of the idle Ministers who succeeded him in the Government. Some blame must also be laid on the people themselves, who did not like to work more than they could help.

Thus the Minister cared little for the Royal bull-fights. He preferred to see the working classes at the plough instead of on the seats of the bull-ring, and as for the bull-fighters themselves, who might be of noble family, he said that they would be better employed in serving the State with pen or sword, while those of the middle classes ought to be working honestly, earning a respectable livelihood and so contributing to maintain the general welfare of the nation. Such were the Minister's principles.

But although King José willingly left the affairs of State to his Minister, he would not yield an inch in the matter of bull-fights. In this respect he was a true Braganza. The nobles knew this and they derived two kinds of satisfaction from it: the pleasure of their national sport and the knowledge that they were annoying the Minister. To be able to annoy him without risk to themselves, and under the pretext that they were doing the will of their Sovereign, was a double source of delight to them, and they rejoiced in it openly.

The Royal regulations with respect to these public shows enjoined the utmost splendour. This was another cause of rejoicing.
Their national love of display could be gratified to the utmost,
and the courtiers and their families, especially, of course, the
ladies, tried to outrival one another in fine clothes, costly furs,
and jewellery, and magnificent headgear brought from France and
ornamented with diamonds and pearls of great value. The lovely
wives and daughters of the great nobles sat in their boxes hung
with the finest curtains of Eastern silks, and smiled approval at
the feats of valour and dexterity of the combatants in the arena.

III

The great bull-fight opened like a scene from the Arabian Nights.
The curtains of the Royal box were drawn back; the band began
the strains of the Royal March, and the King entered the box,
accompanied by his suite, all blazing with orders and in jewelled
robes. He stood bowing to the vast crowd, and as he took his
seat the massy doors of the arena were flung apart and the horsemen rode proudly in. They were all members of the noblest families in the kingdom, and they made a gallant show with their rich
costumes, plumed hats, and sword-hilts sparkling with jewels.
Each held his lance aloft in his right hand, while his left controlled
his splendid Arab horse. One of them, the leader of the cavalcade,
advanced beneath the Royal box and swept off his hat in salutation.

This was the Count dos Arcos. His costume was of black
velvet, cut to fit his slender figure tightly. The collar and deep
cuffs were of the finest lace, made by the patient fingers of Spanish
nuns; the doublet opened over a vest of snow-white cambric.

The Count was not above middle height, but he was slight and
well proportioned, and all his movements were graceful. He was
pale, but his face was full of expression, his large dark eyes being
so very bright and speaking that they made him irresistible in
anything he demanded. The son of the Marquis de Marialva, and
a favourite of his father, who trained him in horsemanship and was
himself the best rider in Portugal—perhaps in Europe—when he
was on horseback the nobility and distinction of his bearing
attracted the attention of every one. He and his mount, as if
forming one unit, appeared to realise the idea of the Centaur of
classic myth.

The elegance of his advance through the arena, directing his
magnificent horse without effort, called forth long and repeated
applause, especially when he turned and careered round the ring.
During the third round, making his horse to sink to its knees,
he drew up in front of a box in which a lady was seated. All eyes

were fixed on her, as she put the silken curtains aside and, blushing at the acclamation of the crowd, acknowledged the homage of the noble cavalier.

The glance which she cast revealed the secret of her soul as a flash of lightning makes everything clear for a moment in the darkest night.

When the young man had again reached the space in front of the King, the latter smiled, and said to his companions:

" Why does the Count come to a gay festival dressed almost in mourning? "

Then he gave the signal for the bull-fight to begin.

The bulls were of pure breed, fierce and full of fight. The danger to the men was great, and the sight roused all the enthusiasm of the spectators.

Several bulls had been disposed of after a brisk fight, and now the gate of the arena opened once more and a black bull rushed in at full charge. He was a magnificent creature, with all the points of purest breed. His legs, graceful as those of a deer, were made for great swiftness, and his strong shoulders and long horns marked him as an adversary to be reckoned with. When he reached the very middle of the arena he stopped short, lowered his fine head, pawed impatiently at the sand, and uttered a ferocious bellow. All the spectators were captivated by the sight of such a fine animal, and a dead silence prevailed. Then the bull charged the horsemen and soon three of the finest horses lay dead on the sand.

IV

There was a brief pause. None of the horsemen advanced against the wild beast, for such it certainly was. The bull roared, lashed his tail, and trampled the sand, as if to challenge the oncoming of an enemy. The Count dos Arcos took up the challenge and rode forward, driving the point of his flexible spear into the muscular neck of the animal. A terrible bellow was answered by the cheers of the multitude and the music of the trumpets, and the Count dos Arcos, withdrawing his spear, galloped round the arena. As he passed beneath the box in front of which he had caused his horse to kneel, a small white hand appeared between the curtains and dropped a rose. Without slackening his speed for an instant, the noble youth bent from his saddle, picked up the rose from the sand, kissed it with an upward glance, and placed it in the opening of his vest. Then facing the bull he remained motionless with his spear fixed for a moment, and anon began to describe circles round the furious animal, gradually narrowing in his course until he could almost lay his hand on its head.

The Count raised his eyes to the box in which sat the fair lady of his devotion, touched the rose in his bosom and charged the bull, driving his lance in between its shoulders. The animal responded by a frantic onslaught, causing the horse to rear upright and piercing its body again and again with his strong horns. The horse fell, carrying its rider with it, and before he could disengage himself the bull was upon him.

All happened so quickly that the last echoes of the applause of the spectators had not yet died away when they were changed into cries of horror and anxiety. The red-cloaked attendants of the Count, all nobles of the Court, vainly endeavoured to distract the bull's fury by waving their cloaks before his eyes. He saw nothing, stopped for nothing; all his rage was concentrated on the prostrate form on the sand. It was only when he was satisfied that his vengeance had been fully wreaked that he seated himself on the trampled sand with the air of a conqueror, resting his forepaws on the Count's lifeless body.

A silence more expressive than any sound of lamentation could have been fell like a mantle over the vast arena. The King, the nobles, the ladies, and all the others present leaned forward breathlessly to assure themselves of the terrible thing which had happened, and then raised their eyes with a common impulse to the open sky above them as if to follow the flight of the soul which had just left the mangled bleeding body on the sand.

The silence was broken by a shriek of such anguish of mind that all present shuddered and started. The lady who had thrown the rose to the Count fell back into the arms of the other ladies who had rushed forward to her assistance. She continued to scream as if her agonised heart were breaking from her bosom.

The King covered his face with his hands, and sat as if turned to stone, and his grief was sincerely shared by all who had known and admired the gallant Count.

But there was still another act of the awful drama to come. The Marquis de Marialva, father of the dead youth, had followed his magnificent prowess with pride and happiness, leaning from his box and smiling at the applause of the crowd. Now he rose with a terrible cry:

" My son! my son! My only son, the heir of my house, the consolation of my old age! "

He clapped his hand to his side, as if to seek for his sword, and then remembered that he himself had armed his son with that trusty sword when he embraced him before his entrance into the arena. The old man stood for a moment as if unable to realise what he was about to do, and began to descend the steps leading from his box to the outside of the sanded ring.

" His Majesty commands that the Marquis de Marialva await his orders,'' said one of the Royal chamberlains, laying his hand on the old noble's arm.

The Marquis shook off the detaining hand, looked the chamberlain full in the face with a glance of terrible anguish, and continued to descend the steps without a word.

The chamberlain followed him.

'' His Majesty's orders are that misfortune enough has occurred already, and he does not wish to lose two of his most valued nobles. Will the Marquis disobey the commands of the King? ''

'' The King's commands are issued to the living, and I am already dead,'' replied the old man. '' See that. What is it? Just now it was my only son.'' He pointed to the corpse lying beneath the black hoofs of the victorious bull. '' His Majesty can do all things except this one. He cannot dishonour the grey head of the old man who has served him loyally and well for so many years. Tell him this and let me pass.''

The King half rose, and uttered an exclamation of horror as the Marquis continued to descend to the arena. Well did he know that never in his life had the Marquis spoken anything but the truth, never had he broken a promise. He stood quite still watching his old vassal breathlessly, awaiting with the silence of despair the issue of the moment.

V

The Marquis entered the arena, steadfast and determined as an ancient Roman in the face of certain death. As he approached the body of his son, his features were convulsed with anguish, and tears broke from his eyes. But he dashed them away and stooped to pick up the sword which had become loosened from the torn belt to which it had been attached.

With one of the impulses which sway crowds, the whole assembly of spectators rose to their feet. Their horrified expression and the tears which flowed from many eyes spoke of their anxiety and tension of feeling.

What was going to happen to the unhappy old noble? How could he be saved from apparently certain death?

The bereaved father knelt beside his dead son and pressed a kiss on his forehead. Then rising, sword in hand and cape on arm, he faced the bull, now roused to new fury by the appearance of another enemy.

The silence was profound, and all, even the King, remained standing, watching the strange drama.

The bull charged, but the Marquis parried the charge with sword and cape. The panting animal charged again and again, his red nostrils breathing steam beneath the glossy black of his muzzle.

Still the old man frustrated every onslaught, calculating his distances, and seeking to fatigue the bull with every renewed effort.

The spectators gradually became accustomed to the scene, and began to breathe more freely, though they still remained with their gaze fixed immovably on the two combatants, both animated by the desire for victory, the knowledge that their struggle was a fight for life.

Suddenly the King uttered a sharp cry. The bull charged again, and this time his horns were directly on a level with the breast of the Marquis. All present fell on their knees and began to pray aloud for the soul of the last Marquis de Marialva.

But now something amazing happened. With an agility not to be expected from a man of his years, the old noble leaped on the bull's broad head, and with an unerring hand drove his sword into the animal's neck, fair between the shoulders. The splendid beast sank on his knees, gave one last despairing look at his victorious enemy who stood now before him, and rolled over lifeless.

Tumultuous applause and cries of thankfulness burst forth from all in the great circle. But the Marquis, pale as a ghost, and trembling from head to foot, did not seem to hear the thunders of jubilation; to see anything but one—the body of his son, on which he threw himself in an uncontrollable transport of grief.

VI

A new sensation came into this memorable spectacle now. The door of the Royal box was flung open, and the Marquis de Pombal, pale, agitated and covered with the dust of travel, entered and made obeisance to the King.

" We are at war with Spain, your Majesty. There was no way of preventing it. It is a terrible thing that your Majesty should permit these savage spectacles to waste your time and kill your nobles when the safety of the kingdom is at stake. Continue in this way, your Majesty, and there will soon be no such country as Portugal! "

Stunned for an instant by the news, the King, without comment, said slowly and almost humbly:

" This, your Excellency, is the last bull-fight that will ever take place in Portugal during my reign."

" I hope I may rely on your Majesty's wisdom that such will be the case. There are not so many men in your Majesty's kingdom that you can throw the lives of the best of them away in exchange for that of a bull."

After a moment's pause, during which the King remained silent, the Minister added:

"Will your Majesty permit me to go down and offer my sympathy to the Marquis de Marialva?"

"Go. He is a father. You know what to say to him?"

"The same as he would say to me if my son lay where the Count of Arcos is lying now."

The King left the box, never to return to it, and the Minister, descending the steps with all the dignity conferred by his lofty stature, raised the old nobleman in his arms and respectfully kissing his hand, said:

"My lord, a nobleman of Portugal like you is better able to give great example than to be moved by the example of others. You had a son, and God has taken him from you. Now, listen to me. Spain has declared war on us; the King, my Sovereign Master, has need of the sword of the wisest and bravest of his trusted servitors."

And taking the Marquis by the arm, he led him from the arena.

Dom José I. kept his word, and during his reign there never was another bull-fight in Salvaterra.

BRITO ARANHA

1833–1914

GOOD EXAMPLE

In a modest house in the suburbs of Alfama, near Lisbon, there lived a young married couple, known to their friends as José Maria and Anna Rosa.

Anna was about twenty years of age, not exactly beautiful, but pleasing of features and expression. At twenty years of age great beauty is not necessary to interest and attract. Her intellectual faculties were not so very striking either, nor was her education on a higher level than that of most girls of her station, but she was gentle, modest, and sensible, with a calm dignity which caused her to be respected in her little circle. People who knew her intimately called her affectionately " José's Anninha."

The husband was a little older, being about twenty-two years of age. He, too, was a good-looking and sweet-natured individual, and he did not lack friends who both liked and respected him. In the locksmith's factory, where he worked, he was esteemed by all, from the manager down to the smallest apprentice; he was punctual, obliging, and a skilled worker, and he earned enough to keep the modest home in comfort.

The factory was a small one, doing a good business with regular customers. The proprietors were several gentlemen forming a syndicate, and they were almost unknown to the workmen. They seldom came to the works, and when they did come, they shut themselves up in the office with the manager, examined the books, and received the manager's report as to the progress of the business. They never interfered with his activities or with his management of the workmen, recognising that this was not their province, and that they would only cause trouble and friction by their interference. They were quite satisfied to know that things went on smoothly and that the profits of the syndicate were increasing steadily.

José Maria was foreman in this workshop, and he had the full confidence not only of the manager but of the workmen. He was cheerful and friendly with all of them, but now and then, when they talked politics, as workmen in every country have a habit of doing, he would laugh and say:

" We cannot interfere with the government of the country; we should not know how to do it.   But we can do our own work which we have learned, and so be sure of being able to get our living honestly and with a good conscience.   If we can give a good account of what is entrusted to us, we need not care who rules the State."

" You are right, José," observed a workman.   " Let each of us think of his work here and of his home when he leaves here.   For my part, when I go home after a good day's work and find myself with my children round the supper-table, I am just in a little Paradise, which I would not exchange for all the Governments on earth."

When José Maria's baby was born there was great rejoicing in the little home.

As the workman's pay, though enough for modest comfort, did not permit of much margin for luxuries, Anninha, as a proud mother, resolved to add to the capital of the small family by her own work, and thus obtain little extras for the use of the child, and put by a trifle for the future.   She had good taste and was skilful with her needle, and she soon obtained orders from the wives of some of the shopkeepers in the neighbourhood for clothes to make and mend.   In time she saved enough to buy a sewing-machine, and then the work was done more easily and quickly.

A second and third child came in time to cheer the home of the honest foreman, and peace and happiness continued to bless the happy household.

II

Things were not quite the same in the home of the manager of the little factory.   It was not that his wife was intentionally lacking in her duty, but she was of a restless, irritable, and discontented temperament, always looking at the dark side of things for preference. She really loved her husband, but did not know how to make him happy.

Antonio Diniz and his wife had only one child, a little girl, just old enough to perceive the want of harmony which reigned in her home without being able to do anything to remedy it.   The mother grew into the habit of indulging her nervous agitation to such an extent that she flew into a violent passion on the slightest provocation, and her husband began to dread to return home after his day's work.

The manager became so much worried and distressed by the unhappy state of things at home that he, too, began to grow peevish and irritable.   The workmen under his charge recognised that something was wrong, but they knew that it was no affair of theirs.

They could not comfort him in any way, and they did not dare to concern themselves with his private life.

One evening when Antonio returned from work he found his wife in a state of uncontrollable fury. Something of a trifling nature had annoyed her, and she had worked herself up into such a rage that she had lost all control over herself. The little girl had run into her bedroom in terror, and when the husband asked what was the matter, his wife hurled a torrent of abuse and recriminations at his head. She was laying the table for supper, and in her agitation the vessels fell from her hand and rattled on the floor.

Seeing that she was really beyond herself with rage, the husband decided to keep silence, in the hope that her excitement might die out for lack of encouragement. But she was not disposed to calm herself; in fact, her husband's coolness only seemed to enrage her more. Suddenly she snatched up a sharp knife, which she had placed beside the cheese dish, and hurled it in Antonio's face.

The unhappy husband, with the knife quivering in his cheek, and the blood pouring down on his clothes, endeavoured to overpower the furious woman, and a violent struggle took place. But the shock of the wound and the loss of blood weakened him so much that he reeled and fell heavily to the floor in a fainting condition.

The noise of the fall and the shrieks of the woman brought some of the neighbours to the scene. The wounded man was taken to the hospital, and the half-mad woman was carried off in charge of the police, no one being able to ascertain exactly what had taken place.

III

The bad news of Antonio Diniz's domestic unhappiness soon circulated through the neighbourhood and among the workmen who were under his care. When gossip had run its course, and the evil tongues which abound in every class of society had wagged to their full capacity, the matter came to be more calmly discussed, and all the blame was given to the woman. Antonio had always been known to be a quiet and decent fellow, regular in his hours and not given to quarrelling with any one, whilst his wife's lack of education and of self-control were well known to all who had anything to do with her. The men at the factory could all relate how quiet and sensible the manager had been until lately, and how they had guessed that the change in him was due to some great domestic trouble, which was no business of theirs.

José Maria, as foreman, had to take the manager's place now, and the esteem in which he had always been held was increased by the quiet dignity with which he discharged his new duties, without in the least altering the friendly relations which he had always had with his fellow-workers.

As to the neighbours' gossip, he advised his wife not to join in it or encourage it, and if she were asked any questions about the unhappy manager to reply that her husband never spoke at home of anything which happened at the factory. His work was one part of his life, and his home quite another.

Antonio was still in a very dangerous condition, and his wife had been placed in a convent attached to the prison in the hope that her violence, which was still unabated, might yield to steady treatment by the nuns. A couple of weeks passed in this way.

One morning, José Maria rose earlier than usual, saying that he had to see to a particularly important piece of work, and might be late in returning to dinner, as there was to be a meeting of the syndicate that afternoon, and everything must be in readiness for it. Anninha gave him his breakfast, telling him how she had obtained some new customers for her needlework, and was going to save some money so that the children might go to a good school. The pair laughed and chatted like a couple of sweethearts, and José Maria left for the factory after tenderly kissing his wife and the children. Anninha leaned from the window to watch him and to wave a farewell to him before he turned the corner of the street.

The children went off to school, and the happy wife sat down to her sewing-machine, singing as she worked. How happy she was; what a good husband she had, and what nice children! She was happier now even than when she had married first, for now she had four people to love her instead of one, and by her own efforts she was able to maintain order and comfort in the little home. And she worked and sang until it was time to go and prepare the dinner.

The children came back for the mid-day meal, but their father did not appear. It was the first time such a thing had ever happened, but Anninha told them that no doubt he had been kept at the works to prepare for the meeting of the syndicate, now that he had to act as manager. When they went off to the afternoon school, she went out to buy something specially good for supper, as her man would be sure to come home worn out and hungry after his busy day.

It was not yet six o'clock, and Anninha still worked and sang, whilst the savoury soup bubbled in the large saucepan by the fireside. She had taken special pains with that soup, knowing that it was a favourite dish of José's. A nice fresh fish and a carefully-made salad were to follow it. Her man was worth a little attention from the wife he made so happy. Suddenly there was a knock at the outer door. Anninha ran out in delight at the thought that José Maria had come home so soon. She threw the door open, and saw six of the men from the factory. They stood with uncovered heads, and at their feet lay something shrouded in a dark cloth.

Who can picture the anguish, the incredulity of the poor wife? Impossible to take in the full meaning of what the sympathetic workmen had to tell her. José Maria had worked incessantly all day, refusing the offers of the men to bring him a meal, saying laughingly that the supper his wife would have ready on his return would be worth waiting for. At the close of the meeting of the syndicate, as José Maria was being complimented by the gentlemen on his capable discharge of the duties so unexpectedly thrust upon him, he staggered, threw up his hands, and fell dead, struck by a sudden syncope.

IV

Now a period of struggle began for the poor widow. Her grief at the loss of her faithful and loving partner was increased by the knowledge that poverty stood at the door of the sad little home, and that three helpless young creatures were dependent for life itself on the work of her unaided hands. The Portuguese people have always been noted for their large-hearted charity and kindness to neighbours in trouble, and many of Anninha's acquaintances, wives of workmen like herself, found means to help her to the best of their ability. Clothes for the children, little articles of household use for herself, home-made preserves, bread, potted meat; all these found their way to her, and were pressed on her as a favour to the donors. But she was not the only poor widow in her circle, and although charity knows no limits, the means of bestowing it is often very limited indeed.

Anninha was too honest and high principled not to cast about for every possible chance of earning a livelihood for herself and her family, which had now diminished in number, for the elder boy had been admitted, through the influence of one of the gentlemen forming the syndicate, to the Free School, from which so many men of humble origin have issued on their way to a distinguished career.

One day as she had just returned from a search for work she found a letter from the manager of the factory where José Maria had been employed. He told her that he was better and had left the hospital, and he asked her to call and see him at the factory.

Anninha did not delay responding to the invitation. Next morning she presented herself at the factory, and was received with warm sympathy by her poor husband's chief and friend. He told her that his wife had been found to be insane, and had been sent to an asylum. His little girl was learning to keep house for him, and he was just beginning to know the peace to which, after leaving his work, he had long been a stranger. After making some inquiries into the circumstances in which Anninha found herself, Antonio informed her that out of respect for her late husband the workmen had wished to subscribe for a testimonial to him, and he himself had been authorised to put down a sum on behalf of the members of the syndicate as well as on his own behalf. He thought the best testimonial would be to help the widow, so the sum when complete would be handed to her.

Anninha thanked him with tears, and took leave of him. A few days later she received a visit from a workman, who brought her the sum subscribed and at the same time told her that the manager's wife had just died in the asylum in a fit of raving mania.

V

A year had passed in this way, the widow working hard and bringing up her children with the greatest devotion. Her father, a carpenter who had been a widower for many years, had come to live in her little flat, and by his work, in which he was still skilled, he helped to eke out the sums obtained by his daughter's industry.

Antonio Diniz continued his task as manager of the factory, which prospered as before. One of the best workmen had been appointed foreman in succession to José Maria, and it seemed that the whole of the past relations of the two head workmen had been covered by the waves of time.

One day, at a meeting of the syndicate, mention was made by one of the gentlemen of the tragedy which had happened in that room just a year before, when the honest foreman fell dead at their feet.

" By the way, Antonio," he asked, " what has become of the widow? Has she married again? "

" Oh no, sir," replied the manager. " She will never marry again. She is a good quiet creature, thinking only of her children, and working hard to bring them up honestly. She is a good example to every workman's wife. But then poor José was a good example to every workman."

The gentlemen of the syndicate made some other inquiries, and then said they wished to send the good woman some money, so a subscription was made up. Antonio undertook to see that the sum was sent to Anninha with the compliments of his masters, and he locked it away in the safe until one of the men could take it to her next day. But as he walked home that evening his mind dwelt in a curious way on the question asked by the gentleman. " Had she married again? " Why should she not marry again?

When Antonio took the money out of the safe, and was about to call one of the men to send him with it and a friendly message to Anninha, a sudden idea flashed across his mind, and made him put the money back in the safe again. He had not seen the widow for a long time. How did he know she had no thought of marrying again? He would go himself that evening to where she lived, and see her in her own home, where he had never yet been. The money to be sent to her would give him a good excuse for calling on her. He would not announce his visit, but would just go and chance finding her as she was. He remembered his own unhappy married life,

and thought of how often he had envied the humble joy of his foreman's little home, to which he had always been so glad to return
when his day's work was over.　Yes, he would go and see the excellent woman who had made his poor comrade so happy; he would
have the satisfaction of cheering her by the gift he had to bring,
and he would tell her how well the gentlemen had spoken of poor
José Maria, and how much he was still missed in the factory.

VI

Antonio felt a strange perturbation when he arrived at the house
where Anninha lived with her father and her children.　Would she
be glad to see him or not?　Would she think his visit an intrusion,
bringing her painful reminders of past sorrow?

Anninha opened the door, and on seeing her visitor she coloured
lightly as she asked him to enter.　Could she be of service to him;
had he come about some needlework, perhaps?

The manager found himself strangely embarrassed.　He hardly
liked to explain that he had come to offer her money; he did not
care to say that he had come because he wished to see her.　As a
way out of the difficulty, he said that he was the bearer of a little
present to her children from the gentlemen of the factory.

Anninha politely offered him a seat and introduced him to her
father, who had just come in from work.　The presence of the elder
man put the others at their ease.

After a few minutes' general conversation, Antonio, with an impulse for which he could not account, said to the father, whose name
was Gregorio: " Master Gregorio, will you grant me a word in
private, with your daughter's permission? "

" You will take a glass of wine with my father, sir? " said
Anninha.　" You can talk to him as freely as you like, for I have
some work which I ought to deliver, and I will take it now.　The
children can come with me.　Good-evening, sir, if you are not here
when I return."

And packing up her work, she called the children, and departed
with a blush and a curtsey.

Antonio opened his heart to the old man.　He told him how unhappy his married life had been; how lonely he was now, not knowing exactly how to bring up his little daughter.　He repeated all the
praise of Anninha which he had heard from poor José Maria, whose
domestic happiness he had so often envied.　Could not such happiness be his at last?　Was there any chance that Anninha would
take him for her husband?

" Have you ever said anything of this to her? " asked the old
carpenter.

" This is the first time I have ever been in her house.　It is almost the first time I have seen her since her husband died. Do you think she will have me? "

" You must ask her. Are you in such a hurry, sir? "

" Yes, yes. I cannot wait any longer; I must have some order in my house, some comfort in my life. There is nothing to wait for except Anninha's consent."

" Well, sir, I cannot promise you that, but I can say that if she marries you, it will make me very happy. She has always been a good daughter, a good wife, and a good mother, and she deserves a good home."

" You are right, Master Gregorio. She has always been a good example. I can give her a good home, and there will be a comfortable corner in it for her father. My little girl, too, will be happy to have Anninha's children for her playmates."

The men sat smoking and chatting until Anninha and the children returned. She looked rather surprised to see the manager still there, but was too hospitable to express anything but pleasure. Timidly she asked if he would share their simple evening meal.

" Indeed I will, with pleasure, Anninha," replied the manager; " but first of all, your father has something to tell you." And he signed to the old man to speak of what had passed between them.

Anninha blushed and then grew pale as she listened. When her father stopped speaking, she hesitated and faltered: " But, sir, can I believe that you are asking me to marry you? Asking a woman who is plain and poor, and who has the care of a family on her hands, to share your home? Think well, sir. It is not a thing which once done can be undone! Will you not be sorry later? "

" I shall never be sorry, Anninha. Your children will be safe in my house, they will have a father in me, as my child will have a mother in you. And they cannot fail to be happy when they see that we are happy too. I have been very unhappy in the past; will you not take compassion on me now? "

" Do not speak like that, Master Antonio. Should I not be grateful to you for coming here, in the goodness of your heart, to offer a safe home to my children and a kind companion to myself? I will marry you, Antonio, and with the blessing of God I will make you as good a wife as you deserve to have."

" Anninha, I have only one thing more to ask. Let us be married this day week. I have waited too long for calm and happiness. Do not make me wait much longer."

And kneeling hand in hand before the old man, they asked his blessing for themselves and for their children.

RODRIGO PAGANINO

1835–1863

THE GREATER BURDEN

I

THE sun had set a quarter of an hour before. It was time to leave off work and to go home to the evening meal. All the workmen on the estate lived in the neighbouring village, and all bent their steps thither, some singly, some in groups of two or three, chatting as they went.

André Pimenta, one of the most industrious of the workmen, put on his coat, took up his empty basket, and set off alone, paying no heed to the invitations of some of his comrades to go and have a glass of wine with them at the inn, and not even bidding them good-night.

There was a good deal of talk about this when they assembled in the village inn for their usual evening glass of wine and gossip. Never had they known André to remain aloof or be ungracious until now. What had come to him? Perhaps the poor fellow was ill, or some one had hurt his feelings.

He had always been, not merely a good workman, but as merry as a lark both while he worked and on the way home. Now, he had worked all day in silence, not taking any notice of the jokes and songs of his comrades.

When the group of workmen reached the little bridge over the brook, André was sitting there, moodily gazing at the running water.

" Well, André, thinking of drowning yourself? "

" Hallo, André, too tired to go home? "

" André Pimenta, shall we send Magdalena to fetch you home? "

Not a word did he answer, nor did he move from his sullen position on the low wall, gazing at the fast-running brook. The men went on their way, marvelling at the change in their fellow-workman. They knew him to be a good and honest labourer, fairly well educated for his class, and an excellent husband and father, always sitting at his door in summer playing with his children and chatting to any of his neighbours who might happen to pass; and in winter always to be found at his fireside reading aloud and keeping the happy home in tune.

320

Never was a doctor required in that house, nor even an apothecary, and no visitor who dropped in could ever report the slightest family dissension.

Not that the villagers were too much inclined to speak well of their neighbours. On the contrary, even the parish priest himself was not always free from their criticism. But when it came to André and Magdalena Pimenta, all agreed that they lived as happily as the angels in Heaven.

Magdalena herself could not make out what was the matter with her man when he came in without a word, pushed the children aside as they ran to meet him, and flung himself on a bench by the window.

The good woman did not like to ask any questions, but as she busied herself with the supper she cast many furtive and uneasy glances in the direction of her silent spouse. A basket stood at the end of the bench on which he sat; he pushed it on to the floor, with a muttered oath, and buried his head in his hands.

Magdalena could not hold out any longer. She hurried to him and knelt down beside him, while the frightened children looked on from near the door.

" You are ill, André? Or . . ." and she grew pale. " Has anything gone wrong with the work? You have not lost your place? "

" What the devil, woman? Lost my place? I just wish I had."

" Well, come to supper, anyhow. You will feel better after the nice stew I have made."

" I don't want any supper. I can't eat anything."

Magdalena waited until the children had finished their supper and gone out to play, and then she cleared away the supper things, and sat down with her knitting on a low stool at André's feet.

" Tell me," she said gently. " The children are not here now, and I want to know what is the matter. Surely you have confidence in me, and perhaps I can help you."

" Have you ever thought," returned André after a short pause, " that there are people in this world, yes and a great many of them too, who do not have to work all day long as I do to get bread for their children? "

" Why, yes, of course. What then? Those are matters which do not concern us."

" Don't they concern us? They concern every one. Here am I, a man as good as any other, who never did any harm to any one, who works from morning till night to find food and shelter for you and the children; and if I were to fall ill to-morrow, I might have to go to the poorhouse infirmary; if I were to die, you and the children might have to beg your bread."

" But we were born poor, and the poor must work or starve."

"You are only a woman, and you cannot understand. I must not blame you, though, for I am a man, and I never understood those things until to-day."

After a while, Magdalena got him to tell what had happened. Two gentlemen from Lisbon had come down to see the owner of the estate, and to bargain with him about the purchase of some timber. They went about among the workmen and watched what was being done. Then they sat down near where André was at work and began to talk about the advantage of being a landed proprietor and having poor wretched creatures slaving to make money for the master to enjoy.

"Poor wretches," said one, "toiling all day like that for so little money."

"Well, as to that," replied the other, "if they did not work, we should have nothing to eat, for it is only by their work that we live. The master of this fine property would be in an odd way if he had not these poor men to work for him, and to make money for him to spend."

"Certainly, I suppose we cannot all be equal. For my part I should be dead in a day if I had to work as they do."

And they went on talking in this strain until the master came to take them over the property and show them his woods.

André seemed to have his eyes opened for the first time in his life. He had never thought of such things before, but now he reflected on what he had heard, as he went on working mechanically. He had always worked contentedly, never reflecting on any rights beyond what he had earned. Now a hundred new thoughts crowded into his brain. He could not say anything to his comrades; he must go home, think, digest as it were, the new mental food he had picked up.

"I tell you, Magdalena, the master, Dom Manoel Fernandes, makes all his money out of our work. What does he do for a living? He owns more than a dozen farms, any one of which would keep us in comfort for the rest of our lives."

"André, man, I am ashamed of you. You are envious of the master. It is a great sin. And in any case, you cannot reform the world. We ought to be thankful to have health and work to do, you on the estate and I in the home."

"Envious? No, Magdalena, I am not envious. But I am a man as well as the master, and he ought not to have all the rights while I have all the trouble; I and the others like me."

"For the love of Heaven, man, talk of what you understand," said a voice behind the couple. It was the master, who had come out to take a walk after his guests had gone, and he called at the cottage door to give Magdalena some sweets for the children. He had stopped in the doorway and heard the man's last words. Magdalena started, and there was a moment of silence. Then André, realising that defence was rather difficult in the circumstances, took the offensive.

" Now, sir, it isn't fair to stop and listen to what a man may have to say to his wife, Dom Manoel! " The master laughed.

" Words are but wind, it is true, but yours were loud enough to be called hurricanes. And if you do not want people to hear what you say, you must put your fingers in their ears or speak softly."

" You are right, sir," said Magdalena, desiring to smooth matters over. " Words are but wind, as you say, and I am sure my poor André never meant any harm."

" And there is no harm done, my good woman. Even the king himself is made of flesh and blood, and we are all but human. But let us say a word on that subject. André here would like to be rich and the owner of a farm or even of many farms, I suppose? "

" Oh, sir, don't pay any attention to what he said. He is a good man and a hard worker, as you know."

" That is true, Magdalena. And for that reason I am going to make him an offer. All my estate can be his if he likes to have it."

" You are pleased to jest, sir," said André, staring at the master, while the children gathered round to listen.

" Just listen to me, André. I have bought another estate in another part of the country, and I want to go there for a couple of months, say three months. As you are a steady man and a good worker, and as you have some education, I will make you my agent to look after the property here while I am away. If you are as quick with your arms as with your tongue, at the end of the three months my estate of Chibanta here will be yours if you care to have it."

" Oh, sir . . ."

" Say no more now, but instead of going to work to-morrow morning, come to my office. Leave the rest to me." And Dom Manoel went off smiling after a good-night to the astonished pair.

Magdalena, woman-like, recovered speech first.

" Why were you such a fool, André? He will dismiss you to-morrow, as sure as fate. Then where shall we be? "

" It's hard if a man can't speak a couple of words in his own house after his hard day's work. But I am sure the master is only joking. Even if he dismisses me, I am a good workman and I can go elsewhere, though it will be hard to leave our little home here."

Next morning André set off for Chibanta, looking like a man going to execution. Dom Manoel stood awaiting him at the door of his office. " Well, André, my man, I hope you will look better to-morrow than you do to-day. One would think you had all the sorrows of the world on your shoulders."

" Sir, I know you are going to dismiss me from your service.
You must do as you like, but it is hard that for a few hasty
words . . ."

" Nonsense, man. What you said yesterday has been said. We
have other things to say to-day. We have very much to say,
indeed, for to-day you begin to act as my agent."

And Dom Manoel took André round the estate and introduced
him to the amazed workmen as their new head and agent over the
whole estate. Then he brought him back to the office and explained
everything to him very carefully and thoroughly.

Dom Manoel Fernandes was amused to see the air of grave responsibility and knowledge of business which his former workman
assumed almost unconsciously as the day wore on. Soon he began
to say confidently: " You may leave everything to me, sir. I shall
know how to manage everything. I know all the men, and I shall
be able to see to all the work easily. You can make your mind easy
while you are away."

" Yes, my man. And now, my agent must have a suitable house
to live in, and you had better move in here with your wife and
children. If things go on as we expect, it will be your future home
in any case. But now listen to me before you go home. Envy is
a very ugly thing, and a very foolish thing, but there is something
more foolish still; that is, to judge by appearances only. I have
the name of being very rich, I have a fine house here, I have a
large estate of woodland, farms, and crops, and I employ a great
many men in the village, but I give you my word of honour I often
do not know where to turn for a little ready cash, and I have more
trouble on my mind than the poorest labourer in my employment."

And as André shook his head as though unable to credit this, the
master smiled and said: " Wait till I see you again after three
months, and then you will tell me what you think."

II

André entered on his new duties with all the zeal of the novice.
His wife and children were delighted at the idea of living in a fine
house, and all was bustle and excitement over the prospect of
moving in.

André took his new responsibilities very seriously. All the diligence which he had formerly employed in his daily toil was now
devoted to his task of supervision, which did not end with the day.
No going home to rest at six o'clock now. He never had any break
during the day, and hardly slept at night. Often, when he had
come home late, wearied by the multitude of cares on his shoulders,
and had gone to bed after the supper which he was too tired to eat,
he would drop into a sound sleep, only to be awakened by the bark-

ing of the watch dogs. Then he would go out to see if anything was wrong; if the keepers and night watchmen were at their posts, and if all was right in the stables. When he came back, sleep was gone, and he would lie thinking over the orders to be given to the men next morning. It would never do for him to forget anything; and it was all so new to him.

The more he tried to master his work, the more odd little unknown details seemed to crop up; small in themselves, but important as parts of the whole. The different kinds of land, the qualities of seeds, the proper moment for sowing, weeding, transplanting, pruning, grafting; the various manures and fertilisers to be selected, the thinning and topping of the timber, the care of all the different kinds of live stock; all these had to be decided by him. In obedience to the master's orders, all the men came to him for instructions, and it would never do for him to hesitate or confess ignorance. His dignity would not permit him to consult the workmen or to discuss matters with them. He was too near them in origin for that. Often when he had given an order he felt that he ought to change it for another one, but he was afraid to do so, thinking that would lessen his authority and make the men despise him. When he was asked about anything and had given his answer, unexpected difficulties would present themselves in the way of executing the directions given, and he did not know how to remove them. And with all this, he could not help overhearing the remarks made by the farm-hands and labourers; how they laughed at him behind his back and ridiculed the orders they were carrying out.

André had always been noted for his cheerful and friendly nature. Now he became gradually morose and distrustful of every one.

Even his home life changed for the worse. Magdalena, as the wife of so important a man, wished to dress fashionably and imitate the manners of the ladies whom she saw when she drove into the market town. The children were always asking for something new: dainty food, new toys, new amusements. They were never satisfied, and when they had got one thing, they at once began to think of what they wanted next. André had not always the money to gratify their wishes, and this led to scenes of tears and recriminations.

" I really think, André, you might spend more on me and on the children! "

" I have not got the money to spare, woman. I have to build new barns."

" Barns, indeed. You think more of your barns and your cattle-sheds than of the comfort of your wife and children! "

" I tell you I am really short of ready money now."

" Don't tell lies. I know that yesterday you sold a lot of corn to the miller. His wife told me so. What do you do with all the money you get? ''

And so on. At the end of two months André felt as if he were going mad. One morning he took a sudden resolution. He rose before dawn after a sleepless night, during the greater part of which Magdalena had wept and reproached him because he had refused to buy her a diamond cross like that worn by the wife of a neighbouring squire.

André went to the stable and saddled one of the riding-horses. Then he left a letter for one of the most intelligent of the men, containing some general orders, mounted and rode to the market town, where he breakfasted and took the train for the nearest town to the estate where Dom Manoel Fernandes lived now. He left his horse at the inn, with instructions to send it back to Chibanta at the first opportunity. At the sight of the master standing superintending the loading of a cart of grain, André rushed forward, hat in hand.

'' Take back the estate, sir. Take Chibanta off my shoulders, or I shall put an end to myself. Such a life as I have is quite unbearable! ''

The master smiled. '' Already, André? ''

'' Oh, sir, don't ask me to go on for another month. I cannot do it! '

'' Well, and your poor wife and children, and the prospect of the hospital if you fall ill? ''

'' I shall be in another kind of hospital, sir, if you do not release me. I shall be in a lunatic asylum. Did any one ever think it was so difficult to manage an estate? ''

Dom Manoel Fernandes took pity on the poor man, and invited him to his office. There over a glass of good wine from his own vineyards he heard the whole unhappy story.

'' And as for my wife and children, sir, they are as unhappy as they can be now, because nothing contents them. After all, Magdalena is a sensible woman at heart, and when she has no longer any position to keep up I am sure she will be glad to be a simple labourer's wife once more. And the children are ours and must do as they are told.''

So said, so done. The master accompanied his faithful servant back to Chibanta and took over the reins of government once more. When the position was explained to Magdalena, she fell in with the idea of a return to her former life of simple contentment, as her husband had foreseen. The children were rather dissatisfied at first, but the old golden rule of obedience to parents which prevails in our peasant homes soon conquered. The family returned to the cottage in the village, and André took his place in the ranks of the workers again.

But his master took a special interest in his work, and the experience which he found too burdensome on a large scale was of use to him in small ways. He earned better wages and was able to save money. When a small farm fell vacant, the tenancy was offered to him and accepted gladly. Now he was out of the reach of poverty and care.

But when André heard others speak with envy or admiration of the riches of the master or of his friends, he always said with decision:

" I know more about all that than you do. God has given wealth to some and poverty to others; no one seems to be contented with his own lot. The rich man envies his workman's toil; the poor man wishes for riches and power—but of the two I can tell you which is the greater burden."

JULIO CESAR MACHADO

1835–1890

THE FISHERMAN OF LESSA DA PALMEIRA

I

LESSA DA PALMEIRA is a place worth seeing when the sun is setting behind the purple hills, and the fishermen's wives, in their gay skirts and white caps, are spreading the nets to dry as they join in their country part-songs, with melancholy or passionate cadences.

Most people will tell you that the proper time to see Lessa da Palmeira is in the summer, when the fashionable folk of Oporto repair thither for rest and change, and when they are to be seen in their smart costumes, toned down for country wear, but new and smart still, walking on the sands, bathing in the warm sea, and listening to the string bands of wandering musicians, passing from one town to another. I do not think that this is the best time myself.

What I am going to relate took place in the very early summer, before the season had begun, and when the fashionable folk were still dancing in crowded rooms in the city.

At first sight of Lessa it would be difficult to say if it is a rich seaside place or a poor fishing village. In the midst of streets of humble cottages there are side avenues leading to splendid stone villas, overgrown with jasmine and roses. One would say that the smile of wealth was insulting the tears of poverty, if the very contrast did not add to the mystery and poetry of the place.

This is the secret of it all.

Lessa is in a land of fishermen. Each man who earns his living by the sea has his home in the village, to which he repairs to rest from the struggle with wave and wind and to enjoy the calm happiness of his family circle. Some of these men, weary of constant toil or fired by ambition, sign on as sailors on some ship going from Oporto to Brazil, where they seek riches and ease. But before sailing, each one of them goes to kneel in the little chapel dedicated to the Christ of Mattosinhos, and makes the vow that if he attains fortune he will build a fine house to the glory of the little town.

The Christ of Mattosinhos has a quaint legend attached to the great crucifix which fills the whole space above the altar of the little chapel. One of the fishermen told me the story one day, as I lay on the sand and basked in the early summer sun. I had come over from Oporto for a rest after my new play had been produced at the Theatre Royal.

One day the right arm of the figure on the crucifix was missing. No one knew what had become of it; no one could account for the strange occurrence, least of all the good priest who ministered to the little parish. At night when he locked up the chapel the two arms of the figure were suspended from the cross; next morning when he unlocked the door and went to say his early Mass there was only one. Was it a miracle or a sacrilege?

The crucifix was no less honoured than of old, but all the faithful of the parish lamented constantly that the Christ should be obliged to remain so incomplete. The old women of the village—and there are more old women in Lessa da Palmeira than anywhere else in the world—met every evening to pray and tell their beads for the restoration of the right arm of their Patron.

" I feel sure," said Brazia, one of the oldest of these dames, " that the good God sent His arm off to work a real miracle. He will have given it to replace the arm which some poor man has lost by an accident. Who can say what use He may have made of it? "

" Nonsense, woman! " retorted Paula, almost her rival in years and in the use of her tongue. " Some rascal of a Jew must have stolen the arm and flung it into the river."

" But if it were in the river we would see it."

" It has no doubt floated out to sea."

" If it were in the sea we should have no storms."

" Hold your tongue, woman. The storms are sent for a purpose, and we shall see what we shall see."

Next day a terrible storm arose and none of the fishermen could put out to sea. Instead of attending to their boats, they gathered in the seaweed and broken timber flung on the beach by the fury of the waves, and cart-loads of this timber were stored in the baker's sheds to dry. The baker himself bought a lot of it from the fishermen to heat his oven.

A few days later the baker dismissed his apprentice for lack of respect. The boy had declared that the oven was bewitched.

" You wretched urchin! " cried the baker, purple with rage. " My oven bewitched! My oven, which bakes the best bread in the whole province—yes, and in the whole of Portugal for that matter! "

" I say it is bewitched and I repeat it," maintained the lad obstinately. " I went to put a log of wood on it this very morning, and every time I put the wood on, it jumped off again and the

flames rushed out and scorched me. I had to put the log back in
the timber shed and leave the oven alone. May the good God let
the devil carry me away if I am not speaking the truth! ''

The baker got a new boy and for a couple of days all went well.
But on the third day the boy came weeping, with a burned hand,
and refused to go near the bewitched oven again. He was putting
timber in the furnace and the timber jumped off every time he put
it on; while the flames came out over his hand.

'' Merciful Heaven, what a misfortune! '' exclaimed the enraged
baker. '' If people get to think my oven is bewitched, I shall lose
all my customers. There is only one thing to do. I shall call all
my neighbours, all the fishermen, every one in the village, so that
they may see that there is no foundation for all these silly tales
spread by idle ragamuffins who do not want to work and may
deprive me of my livelihood. Yes, I will ask the parish priest to
come too, and I will feed the furnace under the oven in the face
of them all.''

So the good baker did, and partly to oblige him, partly out of
curiosity, there was a vast multitude, headed by the parish priest,
in and around his bakery. The baker himself took armfuls of wood
from his store and threw it into the furnace. The flames fastened
on the wood, and the oven was briskly heated as usual. The baker
looked smilingly round at his audience, and said to the parish
priest:

'' Your Reverence can witness that there is no truth in the tale
that my oven is bewitched.''

And he took another armful of wood and threw it in.

But suddenly a dark log which lay among the rest flew violently
back, and the flames rushed out and scorched the baker's arms and
the faces of those standing nearest.

The commotion was intense, and every one ran back in a panic.
Only the parish priest came forward and examined the rejected log
more closely. Then he sent to the chapel for holy water, and
sprinkled the smoking log until it was cool enough to lift. And he
began to chant the '' Te Deum '' in thanksgiving for the miracle
vouchsafed to his parish.

The log was indeed the missing arm of the Christ of Mattosinhos.
And the baker's shop became a sort of shrine, visited by all the
faithful not only in Lessa da Palmeira but in many villages and
towns in the province, to the great profit and glory of the excellent
baker.

Pious ladies from Oporto came to be present at the ceremony of
restoring the recovered arm to the figure on the crucifix. And
who could doubt that the whole incident was a miracle performed
purposely to rekindle Christian faith and to rebuke the indifference
of this age of unbelief?

Before starting on their perilous adventures beyond the seas the fishermen of Lessa, turned sailors, repair to the chapel and kneel before the great crucifix, to utter the simple prayer:

" May the arm of the Lord protect me in all the dangers of the sea."

II

Now it was believed in Lessa that the mother of the fisherman Raimâo was forty years of age. If her birth certificate could have made it known that she was fifty-two, no one would have believed it, and indeed no doubt the people were right. A woman may reasonably be considered as old as she looks, and it is pleasanter to be fifty and look forty than to be forty and look fifty.

She had been a very handsome woman and was still well worth looking at, with her clear skin, dark brilliant eyes, and perfect teeth. Her wavy hair was still untouched by grey, and her form was slim and well balanced as she walked. Her name was Anna, but the other women of the place always addressed her as " Madame Anna."

Anna's husband had been one of the most respected fishermen of the village, and during her nine years of widowhood no one had ever had the slightest reason to cast a reflection on her conduct. More than one of the well-to-do fishermen had sought her hand, but no one had succeeded in obtaining a promise from her.

She had two sons. The younger wished to study for a profession, so he was sent to school in Oporto. But after a time a run of bad luck in fishing made it impossible for the widow to keep him at school, and he was obliged to return to the village and take service in the boat of one of the fishermen, who wanted a lad to help him.

Roberto was a serious boy, silent and docile, but ever oppressed by a melancholy regret for the studies which he had been obliged to relinquish—studies which he had now no hope of ever being able to resume. When the sea was too rough for fishing, he would sit with the others mending the nets and watching the great waves dash against the lighthouse on the rocks. Sometimes his comrades rallied him on his seriousness, and then he would smile and say gently:

" I am not really unhappy. I do not know why it is, but the sea, the river, and the sky make me feel so small and lonely."

They laughed at his fancy, but all liked him.

The master of the fishing-boat had a pretty little daughter, and one day he said laughingly to Anna:

" This is your Roberto's future wife."

The mother smiled, but the boy blushed.

" And I am nowhere, I suppose? " said the elder brother, Raimâo, laughing too.

" Oh, my boy, I had forgotten you. Well, Isabel will be a woman one day, I suppose, and she will have a woman's right to choose. I have no doubt she will choose the husband who pleases her most."

The child slipped her little hand on Roberto's arm and murmured:

" I will choose this one."

Every one laughed at the little bit of babyish nonsense. But a few days later, Roberto went to the little chapel of the Christ of Mattosinhos and kneeling before the crucifix promised to build a splendid house for the glory of the town on the spot where his mother's cottage stood if the arm of the Lord would direct him to the way of fortune.

To the boy's excited imagination it seemed as if the right arm of the figure moved from the cross and pointed towards the distant horizon. He was but a child when he knelt down, but he rose up a man! He would be a sailor and seek riches beyond the sea.

That night when he knelt before his mother to ask her blessing, according to the good old custom of the province, he kissed her hand and his tears dropped on it. When she asked what was the matter, he smiled and asked again for blessing. Next morning he had disappeared.

A letter from Oporto told his mother that he had signed on a trading ship bound for Brazil.

III

Ten years had passed without Roberto ever having the chance of returning. One day a letter came from Oporto to the humble cottage in which he had been born, and next morning the handsome bronzed young sailor came to embrace his mother and brother.

He was now twenty-four years of age. Raimâo was twenty-six, and looked at least thirty-six. He had spent his life, so far, in constant struggle with the rough elements of wind and waves, out of doors in all weathers, and toiling to support those dear to him.

For Raimâo was married now. His wife was Isabel, the daughter of Roberto's former master, the pretty child who had taken Roberto as her sweetheart and given him the thought of seeking wealth for her sake in foreign lands.

Her father had fallen on evil days. He had lost boat after boat, and then an injury to his spine in helping to rescue a wrecked crew had made him a confirmed invalid. Anna had cared for him in his destitution, and when he died, Raimâo had given his name and a home to the orphan maiden. All three lived together in peace and comparative comfort, for Anna and her daughter-in-law were expert at making and mending nets, and Raimâo was indefatigable in gathering in the harvest of the sea.

When Roberto arrived in Lessa da Palmeira on a lovely morning at the beginning of June, he was received with as much acclamation as Solomon is said to have extended to the Queen of Sheba. The day after his arrival, all the fishermen took a holiday by leave of the masters, and a great feast was arranged on the strand. Baskets of lobsters, crabs, roast chickens from the cottage poultry yards, early fruit, and in fact all the simple dainties available to such humble folk were contributed by the thirty fishermen and their families who came to do honour to the returned wanderer.

Roberto filled his goblet with wine, and rose to drink to the health of his friends.

" I cannot tell you all how glad I am to see you again," he said. " Fortune has not treated me ill all these years, but my greatest good luck has been to find myself here once more among you all, my friends, of whom I have always thought. I am so happy to see my relatives again,—my mother, my brother, and you who are all like brothers to me."

" Here is another relative whom you must not forget to speak of too," said Raimâo, resting his hand on Isabel's shoulder.

" Oh, forgive me, Raimâo. My brother's wife is my sister, and next to my mother, I love you two best in the world. Your wife has a sweet name, the name of a saint."

" See what you did by going to Brazil! " exclaimed Anna, laughing and kissing Roberto. " You lost your little sweetheart."

" How was that? " asked the fishermen.

Anna related the story of the jesting offer made by Isabel's father and the little girl's choice of Roberto as her future husband.

All laughed heartily at the little tale. Raimâo laughed as heartily as the others.

" Since then the wind has changed," said he, " and our good parish priest, giving us his blessing in the chapel of Our Lord of Mattosinhos, made me captain of this fair little bark, and we have sailed until this moment on a calm sea with favourable breezes to waft us through life."

Roberto looked suddenly at Isabel, and she seemed to avoid his gaze.

" To the health of the company! " he exclaimed, raising his glass.

" To the health of Roberto! " cried all, standing up and drinking.

" All this seems like a dream to me," cried the good Anna, wiping her eyes. " My darling boy back again in Lessa da Palmeira, rich and happy. Thanks be to the Christ of Mattosinhos! "

Roberto sat silent for a while as if dreaming. Then he rose with a sigh and embraced his mother tenderly.

" Are you happy, my boy? " asked Anna anxiously.

" Why should I not be happy when I am with my own dear mother? "

" And yet you left our mother for so long to hunt for riches," observed Raimâo, half reproachfully.

" You have not forgiven me that. Well, perhaps you are right. It is folly to wish to possess much in this life, for we must soon leave all behind us."

When Roberto knelt before his mother that evening to ask for her blessing, she said to him with strange meaning:

" May God protect you and keep you from temptation! "

IV

In spite of his good fortune in Brazil and of the welcome which he received everywhere in the little town Roberto went about sad and as if lost in thought. He often went into the chapel and gazed as if in reproach at the mysterious arm of the figure on the cross which had appeared to point out the way of destiny to him. Then he wandered along the shore and looked dreamily across the sea.

Anna watched her son closely, and almost unconsciously she watched her daughter-in-law at the same time. She noted that Roberto seldom spoke to Isabel, but when he did it was with an indescribable air of bitterness, and the young wife looked at him furtively with a preoccupied expression when she thought herself unobserved.

Some days after Roberto's return, the two women were sitting by the window of the cottage, looking out over the sea. The elder brother was out in his boat; the younger was wandering by the shore. Anna led the conversation to the subject of her two sons, remarking the difference in their dispositions and praising the qualities of each. Isabel knitted a sock for her husband and replied to her mother-in-law's observations.

Suddenly Anna said:

" Is it because Roberto is comparatively a stranger to you that you seem so much more interested in him than in Raimâo? "

The young woman hesitated, blushed, and said:

" Not that, mother,—but, you see—Roberto has qualities which Raimâo does not possess."

" That is not the reason either."

" Oh, indeed, mother. . . ."

" Listen to me, Isabel," said the elder woman in a grave tone; " it is just a week since Roberto came back unexpectedly, and in that week you have changed a great deal. You are twenty-one years of age and I am fifty-two. I have seen a great deal of human nature, though not of the world, and I know that you are in love

with Roberto. You never loved my poor Raimâo—you married
him to have a home and a shelter from the hardships of the world.
Can you deny it? ''

Isabel was silent. The night was an exquisite one. The murmur
of the stream blended with the placid melody of the waves and the
whisper of the breeze through the olive trees. The roses climbing
over the cottage and the lilies in the garden breathed their soft fragrance to the warm air, and the deep blue sky was brilliant with its
pattern of stars.

Anna, without removing her gaze from the fair face of her
daughter-in-law, continued:

'' Both are my sons and I love them both equally, but I love
still more the honour of my family, and that is now in your hands.
I have never had a daughter, but my son's wife is my daughter
now, and because I love you as a daughter I speak to you like
this. Roberto loves you. I believe he has always loved you in his
vague poetic way since the day when your childish choice fell on
him; but Raimâo loves you too. He is not poetic, he is not made
for great passions, but he is honest, kind, and good. If—Heaven
grant that it may not happen—but if anything should destroy his
faith in you, it might work a terrible change in him, for calm
natures are the worst when roused. Isabel, my child, I implore you to have a care—do not turn our little Paradise into
Hell.''

The younger woman wept softly and trembled. Then she raised
her head and murmured:

'' I do not know what to do, mother. He has asked me to meet
him this evening behind the cliff. I dare not refuse to go, but I
fear what he may have to say to me.''

'' Behind the cliff? ''

'' Yes, after supper. It is the first time he has ever asked me to
meet him. You know there is to be a dance on the sands to-night,
round the bonfires, and he insisted that I should meet him behind
the cliff while the others are dancing.''

'' Well, you will not go.''

'' But what am I to do? Must I deceive him, say nothing, and
let him wait there? ''

'' He will not wait in vain. Some one will meet him behind the
cliff—his mother! ''

'' But what can you? . . .''

'' I can put everything right. If I wait longer it may be too
late.''

'' Here he comes, mother, with Raimâo. At least do not be
cross with him now.''

'' Do not fear, my daughter. I have no idea of letting your
husband suspect what I know.''

V

The fishermen and their wives and daughters met after supper
to dance the night away, that exquisite June night, on the smooth
sands of Lessa da Palmeira. Raimâo, Anna, Isabel, and Roberto
joined the others round the bonfires of dry pine wood flaring in a
circle on the beach.

Every one was gay and happy, at least in seeming. The young
men and maidens laughed, jested, and danced in anticipation of the
beginning of the festival, which was held every June in honour of
the Christ of Mattosinhos. The elders talked apart and drank one
another's health in goblets of the red wine of the province, several
skins of which had been contributed by the fishermen. Roberto,
as a returned traveller, was the hero of the hour: he passed from
one group to another, chatting, relating his adventures beyond the
sea, and talking of what he meant to do for the glory of the little
town and the honour of the Christ of Mattosinhos with the riches
he had amassed in the years behind him—riches now lying safely
in the bank in Oporto. He would give a new red lamp of solid
gold to burn night and day at the foot of the crucifix; he would
purchase his mother's cottage and build a fine house in its place, a
house which would be the admiration of all the ladies and gentlemen who came from the city to breathe the sweet air of Lessa de
Palmeira.

Presently the flutes and violins struck up the *cadêa,* the dance
which always begins these rustic festivals, and the pairs formed up
round the bonfires. Fresh fuel was thrown on, and the elders
gathered round in groups on the sand to watch the dancers.

Roberto danced with Isabel, with some of the young wives of
the fishermen, and with a couple of the girls. Then, as the night
wore on, he slipped away behind the cliff.

Anna followed unperceived by the others, her heart torn by grief
at the knowledge of the task before her. Roberto, seeing the form
of a woman approaching in the shadow of the cliff, had no suspicion
that it could be any other than Isabel, and he exclaimed in a low
but penetrating voice:

" My love, how glad I am you have come. I cannot keep
silence any longer. I must reveal my soul to you to-night! "

Then, looking more closely at the woman who approached without uttering a word, he cried:

" Mother! What are you doing here, so far from the rest? "

" I might ask you the same question, Roberto, if I did not know
the reason for your being here."

" What? You know. . . ."

" I know everything."

There was a brief silence, broken by a sudden sound of sullen moaning from the sea, as if in harmony with the sadness which weighed down the minds of mother and son. The night grew darker, and heavy clouds began to surge up from the horizon.

" Roberto," said Anna at last, " you expected Isabel to meet you here, but it is your mother who keeps the tryst. Do not attempt to deny that you have asked Isabel to meet you to hear a declaration of love from you—Isabel, your brother's wife! "

" She should have been mine. She was my little sweetheart; he stole her from me while I was away working to win her."

Anna looked fixedly at her son as he spoke these passionate words, and then she answered slowly:

" My son, you must not stay here. Think of the honour of our family. Isabel does not love you; if she did, she would not have married your brother. It was Isabel who told me of your mad request to her to meet you here, and that is why I have come. If she loved you, would she have told me? "

" Oh, mother, do not say that. I know she loves me."

" Silence, Roberto. I have sworn to myself and promised to my daughter that peace and honour shall abide in our home. You will leave Lessa de Palmeira to-day after daybreak, and you will not return to it until you return in all sincerity as my dear son, and bring me your wife—another daughter to me."

" Impossible! "

" It is your mother who commands you, your mother who is here to defend the honour of her daughter. I will tell all our friends, and Raimâo too, that you are too restless to settle down here. They may smile at you; better that than condemn you as the destroyer of our home. You will go? "

" I will go, mother."

They returned in silence to the groups dancing round the bon-fires. Just before leaving the shadow of the cliff, Anna put her arms round Roberto's neck and kissed him tenderly.

The day was about to break, and the fishermen were unfastening their boats.

" What is this? " asked Roberto. " Going off to fish already? "

" Yes," answered his brother; " the tide is favourable and the catch should be fair. It will do us all good to rest and fish after our night's dancing."

" Raimâo, will you do me a favour? This night reminds me of my boyhood's days, when I fished for Isabel's father. Lend me your boat and do you go out in some other craft. I want to see what I can catch all alone."

" But can you manage the boat alone? "

" Oh, yes. I have no fear of that. But I have been so long a stranger to our fishing here that I would like to see if I can do as well as you who have spent all your life at it."

The men all clapped their hands, shouting:

" Long life to Roberto, the fisherman of Lessa da Palmeira! "

" To the sea, my first and last sweetheart! " cried Roberto.

He kissed his mother and knelt to ask her blessing. Then approaching Isabel, he bent to kiss her hand, and gave her a long look, before which she dropped her eyes.

All the fishermen set off in the boats, Roberto alone, as he had wished, in his brother's craft. The girls remained on the beach, dancing with one another and singing in unison with the receding songs of the fishermen.

Isabel withdrew from the others and sat on a rock, looking after the boats. Anna sat beside her and slipped an arm round her waist. Both women wept in silence.

The dance continued and the night gave place to dawn. The mother and Isabel rose to return to their cottage, and advanced to take leave of the others. Far away a voice was heard singing over the distant sea; a melancholy song of grief and farewell. Anna grew pale as she whispered:

" It is Roberto! "

Another voice answered it in a gay strain, chanting the Song of the Fishermen, and Anna, drawing Isabel closer to her, said smiling:

" And that is Raimâo, letting us know that all is well."

The light grew stronger and the last groups of the merry-makers broke up—women and the older men who had ceased their active lives as toilers of the sea, and now lived by mending nets and salting fish for sale in the city. Anna and Isabel paused at their cottage door to bid farewell to those who were going farther on, and Isabel cast a last lingering glance at the sea. Then she uttered a quick cry:

" Roberto's boat! Look, look, he is back already! "

The boat came nearer, but it was soon apparent that it was empty and was drifting at the mercy of the waves. It tossed about, now approaching the shore, now being driven out to sea.

As the distracted women ran towards the shore, a fishing smack with spread sail came swiftly to land. The men who stepped from her carried a burden, covered with oilskin, the nature of which was but too evident. Anna and Isabel threw themselves on the corpse which the fishermen laid gently at their feet, and the distressed mother raised her arms to Heaven:

" Our Lord of Mattosinhos, pity and pardon me," she moaned. " Roberto, my darling son, has lost his life, and through me, through me. Here in this spot, where he was to build a mansion, we have to build his tomb! "

Far in the distance the voice of Raimâo was heard, singing a merry strain.

THEOPHILO BRAGA

1843–1910

THE GREAT CLOCK OF STRASSBURG

Surely that strange, rich legendary lore of days gone by is for us the chief quality of the Middle Ages. Through this it is that we see history as through a stained-glass window; it gives us the life of men with all its colour and reality. Probably the greatest figure of the time was that of His Satanic Majesty, who certainly most attracted the mind and hand of the artist. This sinister figure, coming from Persian mythology, marked the highest development of the religion of that era. Its effect in art was a continual striving after the grotesque, the record in sculpture of much ancient heathen superstition, and that peculiarly elusive symbolism of the highest period of Gothic architecture. The same idealisation of the principle of evil resulted in much that was morbid in the stories of the saints.

We all know that in early Christian times secular human knowledge was feared, and often even forbidden. It was regarded as useless and very dangerous, as ministering to that pride to which we are so prone, and as a blemish upon the childlike simplicity which brings man near to God. It then seemed impious even to study the laws of Nature, so that Roger Bacon and Sylvester II. were accused of sorcery; and human enlightenment is marked throughout its progress with a long train of martyrdoms. All who know their Bible well will recall that this view is supported by very high authority: " I will destroy the wisdom of the wise, and will bring to nothing the understanding of the prudent."

Many legends have come down to us, showing with what rigour and cruelty the Church enforced her condemnation of profane learning, and through what agonies of suffering the human spirit attained its emancipation. The story of Faust is only one among thousands.

It was a glorious spring day in the middle of the fourteenth century; the sun blazed in a cloudless sky, streaming dazzling white upon the Cathedral of Strassburg and kindling it to a radiant brilliance, until the great church flamed like a white torch in the midst of a sordid world. The stained-glass windows gave back the light in beams of wonderful colours, as clear and vivid as those of the rainbow, and as mystically significant. Each stone, each separate bit of carving, each morsel of delicate lace-like tracery, in this masterpiece of inspired artistry, stood out in perfect beauty, and the lofty tower seemed to pierce the sky till its spires were lost in the everlasting blue.

In the great Square before the cathedral little groups of people were standing, talking idly, and these were joined by others, until at last a huge crowd had collected. A certain restlessness and expectancy was evident in all, as if they were waiting for some auspicious event which they knew was about to occur. They kept on looking upward, and furtive eager murmurings ran from group to group. It was clear that it was from the sky that they awaited some sign or apparition. Yet there was no eclipse, nor the dread visitation of a comet, things which in those days were full of awe and menace, and might have drawn all these folk together for the support which is given by mere numbers. What then could have caused the crowd to collect thus at mid-day?

In those ages of faith and worship there was nothing which more strongly appealed to the hearts and minds of the people than the great religious processions. For days before and afterward, nothing else would be thought or spoken of; and the fervour with which the whole population entered into these simple ceremonies made them the most poignantly touching expression of love and worship. But it was clear that these people were not collected for a procession.

Suddenly a horseman dashed up, and reined in his foaming steed at the very edge of the crowd. He wore the dark cloak and plumed hat of the nobility, and from the mingled curiosity and interest with which he watched the crowd, it was obvious that he was a stranger.

" What is all this fuss about? " he asked of a boy who stood near him, watching the scene with a sort of fearful apprehension. " This is no great festival nor saint's day. Your cathedral doors are not even open. Is there some great occasion in the town to-day? "

" What? " cried the boy. " Have you not heard the wonder of our great miracle? You must indeed have come from far! There is no more famous miracle anywhere in Germany than the great Clock of Strassburg. Do you see that fine statue of Our Lady up there on the tower? Well, in a few moments, when the clock sounds the first stroke of noon, you will see the Three Kings come out of the tower and kneel before that statue, offering their gifts; and on the last stroke, which sounds exactly as the sun reaches the zenith, the cock on the top of the spire will flap its wings and crow, and all the three figures will disappear."

Before the knight could reply, a sudden deep murmur, rising from the assembled crowd, warned them that something was about to occur, and the chimes rang out announcing the advent of noon. All waited in breathless silence, and every face was turned upward to the statue on the tower. Then came a sound like the rushing of mighty wings through the air, and a gentler whisper as of far-off voices. The knight sat fixed as a figure in stone, watching in entranced amazement this miraculous prodigy of the Three Kings, and holding all the time a tight rein upon his impatient charger.

The fame of this wonderful clock had already spread over many lands. Princes, bishops, and great noblemen would have given any price to obtain one like it for their palace, church, or castle; but the name and dwelling of the maker remained a secret, and all attempts to discover him had so far failed altogether. The clock was known everywhere as the Clock of Strassburg, and no word of its origin had ever been whispered at home or abroad.

For some moments the stranger was silent with astonishment. Then, turning to the boy who stood by his stirrup, " Do you know, my lad," he said, " who it was that made that extraordinary clock? Surely every city would wish to have the like! I have never heard the maker's name, but I have come all the way from France to see him."

" Sir," the boy replied; " I am very sorry, sir, but I may not tell his name. It is too dreadful—we are not allowed to say who made that clock. Oh yes, sir, I know who it was, but they threaten us with death if we tell. Sir—sir—it was my father." The tears were in the boy's eyes, and at the moment of his confession he broke into sobbing.

The cavalier leaped from his charger, and held out his hands to the boy. " But, my dear fellow, why did you not tell me? Where is your father? Do you weep because he is dead? I do not understand at all. His Majesty the King of France has sent me to find your father."

" Yes, sir, he is alive, if you can call it life. We often think it would have been happier for him if he had died before he had shown what wonderful things he could do. It was just his wonderful skill which brought him his misfortune."

By this time the crowd had separated, and the boy took the stranger knight to the little shop where his father lived. It was a clock-maker's workshop. An old man was seated on his bench with his face buried in his hands, over which fell his long wavy white hair. His attitude was that of profoundest thought or of extreme dejection.

The stranger threw his bridle over the hook beside the door, and then stood hesitating on the threshold, unwilling to break in upon the old man's melancholy. The boy went up to his father, put his hand upon his shoulder, and spoke some words in a low voice, glancing uneasily toward the figure in the doorway. The aged craftsman drew himself up, turned toward the door, and beckoned to the stranger with his hand.

"Your lordship has done me the honour to come and see me from the King of France?" he asked, rising from his seat, but hesitating to advance.

"Yes, sir," said the other, "I have come at His Majesty's command."

"What can His Majesty, who is lord of everything, want of me, who can do nothing?"

"His Majesty has heard of your wonderful skill, and wishes you to come to Paris and set up a clock on the Law Courts, so that the equal division of the hours may afford to his people an example of order and of justice."

"I am greatly honoured," replied the old man, "and would do anything to serve His Majesty, if daylight had not been taken from me for ever. Look at my eyelids, sir. It is sixteen years since our cruel people put my eyes out, and from that day my life has only lingered on. I cannot die, yet my days and nights are only suffering. The ideas that come to me are a torture, for of course I cannot work without my sight. The only comfort of my misery is that I can tell this dear boy the secrets of clock machinery, so that he may some day make some use of them. Thus I leave him all I have to bequeath. Every stroke of my great clock across there is to me a stroke of torment; it is like the voice of a devil's mockery. I cannot sleep of nights, but count the hours and say that one more hour has gone from the living death which is all my portion."

The old workman spoke in tones of mingled grief and pride, and the contrast between his genius and the unhappy frame which held it was pitiful to witness. His head was bent over the sunny locks of his son, who stood in silence beside the old man, gazing upon the floor.

The courtier was indignant, and exclaimed: "How could any one be so fiendishly cruel as to plunge your great and wonderful spirit into darkness? How did it happen? I suppose it was some one who was envious of the surpassing excellence of your work. But I am afraid I give you pain. You shall tell your story to His Majesty himself; I pledge my word that he will give you what help it lies in the power of man to give."

And then, slowly and quietly, the old man told his sad story, while his deft fingers played with the boy's golden hair.

"His Reverence the Bishop of Lichtenberg commissioned a large clock for the Strassburg tower. He demanded an absolute guaran-

tee of its accurate timekeeping, lest any irregularity should disturb
the services of the church. It took me two years of incessant work,
for I felt that all my reputation was bound up in that clock. I
tell you, my lord, that the art of clock-making could not go farther;
it even shows all the great feasts of the Church. Beside its dial
are panels in which the qualities of the seven planets are inscribed
in verse; and it includes a special movement giving the motions
of the sun and the phases of the moon. Above all is a statue of the
Blessed Virgin, and at the first stroke of every noon the figures
of the Three Kings come forth to adore her. Every one was
astonished at the perfection of my work, and every day the
Cathedral Square was crowded with people to see the prodigy of
this show. Soon we heard that other cities wanted as grand a
clock, and princes inquired for them for their palaces. You
must understand, my lord, that anything of that kind would have
detracted from the unique glory of Strassburg, and must at every
cost be prevented.

    " One night, tired with many hours of work, I was asleep in the
room above here when there came a loud knocking at the door.
I came down and opened it, and they told me that the clock had
stopped. I dressed and went out to the tower, and having climbed
the stairs found the clock going as well as ever. I turned to them
and said so, but even as I spoke, they had seized me and were
trying to throw me from the clock-tower into the market-place.
I struggled for my life, and they could not throw me down; but
presently I fell in a swoon. They then, it appears, decided to spare
my life, but they blinded me and left me wounded and helpless.
Then, as I screamed at their cruelty, they said that it had been
intended that I should be burned alive in the Square, under the
clock which they said I had made by black magic. They said
that my guilt was proved by words engraved on the wheels of
my clock-work, which I had set there, forsooth, as an invocation
to the devil. They brought me back here to my poor boy, and
so they left me."

    The poor old man was silent for a while, his mind revolving
that dreadful night. The courtly messenger then asked him
whether his son might not go to build the clock for the Law Courts
of Paris, but the clock-maker was difficult to persuade. His son,
he admitted, was perfectly qualified for the work, but he feared for
him a fate such as he himself had suffered. But the knight promised to protect the lad with his own life and to restore him safely
to his father's arms as soon as the great work should be completed. In due time, therefore, the clock was installed in the tower
of the Law Courts, and gave the desired example of order and of
justice. But this same clock, two centuries later, gave the signal
for the Massacre of St. Bartholomew.

The young workman returned to Strassburg to find his old father still in life. But now the unhappy man's poverty and grief were deeper and his spirit was darkened by the gloom of revenge. It was not long before he found his opportunity. Having groped his way up those stairs to where the great wheels were marking the hours, he wrecked the delicate mechanism, the offspring of his brain. And all the skill of Germany could not repair the great Clock of Strassburg.

JOSÉ MARIA EÇA DE QUEIROZ

1843–1900

THE THREE BROTHERS AND THE TREASURE

I

In the whole kingdom of Portugal the three Medranhos brothers, Rui, Guannes, and Rostabal, were the poorest and worst clad among the nobles.

In their dwelling of Medranhos, where the wind sweeping down from the mountain-side carried off roofs and dashed out windows, which they had no money to have repaired, they spent the winter afternoons, shivering under their rough garments made from goats' hair, walking about their bare kitchen and looking moodily at the great fireplace where for a long time past no spark of fire had burned, no meal had been cooked. When night came they devoured a lump of black bread, flavoured with garlic, and then, without a light, they crept across the courtyard, through the snow, to the stable, where they slept in the straw, taking advantage of the warmth they obtained from the company of their three miserable mares, which, as hungry as they were, roamed during the day trying to pick up a living on the bleak mountain-side. And their poverty made these gentlemen fiercer than wolves.

When spring came, one quiet Sunday morning the three brothers were wandering through the woods of Roquelanes trying to catch some wild creatures which they could use for food, or to find some of last autumn's fruit which they could add to their meagre meal of bread, while the three poor mares devoured the fresh April grass. Suddenly the three brothers came on a sort of cave in the rock, almost concealed by a thicket of brambles, and in the cave lay an old iron chest. It had three locks, and in each of them was a key. On the lid was an inscription in Arabic letters, hardly visible through the rust which covered the old box. And when the three locks were undone, it was full of gold pieces up to the brim!

The three brothers grew paler than wax at the sight of this unexpected treasure. Then plunging their hands feverishly into the

345

gold, they began to laugh—such peals of laughter that the leaves on the elms above them danced as if in harmony with their glee. And rising, they faced one another, breathing hard, and asking more by glances than by words what they were to do. Guannes and Rostabal began to dispute, but Rui, who was the most sensible of the three, as well as the tallest and strongest, raised his arms and gave his opinion that the gold, whether it came from God or from the devil, was their joint property, as it had been their joint find, and should be divided equally among them, after being weighed in a pair of scales.

This was agreed to. But now a difficulty arose. How were they to carry to Medranhos, up the slope of the mountain, a box so heavy as this was? After some consideration it was decided that Guannes should put some of the gold pieces in his pocket, and, as he was the lightest, should go to the neighbouring town of Retortilho and buy three large leather knapsacks, three loaves of barley bread, three lots of cooked meat, and three bottles of wine, so that they might refresh their weakened bodies, and then unpack and carry off the gold at their leisure. He was also to bring some corn for the mares, for in their joy at their good fortune they did not forget their poor beasts. They themselves had not had anything to eat since the day before, and they were weak and famished. The two remaining brothers would sit with their treasure and await the return of Guannes, and all could return home safely together when night fell, without any one being the wiser.

"A good idea," said Rostabal, who was tall and lean by nature, leaner still through hunger. "Now, Guannes, take some of the doubloons and be off."

But Guannes stood looking down at the shining contents of the box, nervously clasping and unclasping his fingers, and muttering discontentedly to himself. At last he said roughly:

"The box has three divisions, and each locks with a separate key. I will lock my division and take the key with me."

"Well, in that case, I will do the same," growled Rostabal.

Rui smiled.

"All right. No reason whatever to the contrary."

And each brother solemnly locked one of the divisions with its proper key, which he put in his pocket. Then Guannes, satisfied with this, leaped on his mare and rode off through the trees, singing as he went the refrain of an old ballad.

II

In the open space of the wood, opposite the shrubbery growth that had concealed the treasure and the brothers had cut away with their knives, a rivulet murmured its bright way through the rocks and widened into a still pool, from which it issued to fall in a cascade down the steep slope of the wooded hill. Beside this there was a rough granite column, weather-beaten and covered with moss. Rui and Rostabal seated themselves at the foot of this column, their swords between their knees, keeping watch over their treasure, while their two mares browsed on the sweet spring herbage, glittering with daisies and buttercups. The birds flitted about in the branches of the elms, and a breath of violets was drawn out from the floral carpet at their feet by the warm beams of the ascending sun.

Rui had taken off his hat and was endeavouring to arrange the old battered plumes of it with the aid of his knife, and as he did so he began to consider something which had just occurred to him. Guannes had not wished to accompany the other two that morning to the wood of Roquelanes. What a thing Fate was! If Guannes had stopped at home in Medranhos the box would have been discovered only by the other two, and they alone would have had the right to divide the gold. What a misfortune—and this was the greater because Guannes would be sure to get rid of his portion very soon. He was a born gambler, and his part of the fortune would very soon find its way into other hands in the clubs and wine-shops.

" Oh, Rostabal, just think. If Guannes had passed this place alone and had found this gold, I am sure he would not have shared it with us."

The other brother started, and plucked at his long black mous-tache.

" The devil he would! You are right there. Guannes is as selfish as can be. Do you remember last year, when he won a hundred ducats at dice from the sword-cutler in Fresno, he would not lend me even three ducats to buy a new knife? "

" You see now," growled Rui triumphantly.

Both brothers rose at once, as if struck with the same idea. The tall grasses rustled and bent beneath their hurried steps as they paced up and down.

Rui began to speak first.

" You know that Guannes is a very sick man," he said. " That cough of his is getting worse and worse, and he brings up a lot of blood every night when the cough shakes him. He will not last till next winter, Rostabal, but before then he will have found means to spend the good ducats which ought to be ours. He will spend them badly too, in dissipations which will only hasten his death instead of doing him any good. Now, if we had that money, we could restore the fortunes of our house. You could have proper clothes and horses and equipments, and even a train of retainers, such as is only fitting for the head of an ancient family. You are the head of our house, the great house of Medranhos."

" He ought to be dead. He ought to die to-day," exclaimed
Rostabal, throwing off all reserve. " What do you think? "

Rui grasped the arm of his brother and drew him along through
the elms in the direction in which Guannes had set off singing.

" Over there, at the bottom of the clearing, there is a good place,
right behind those shrubs. You must do it, Rostabal; you are the
strongest and most expert. A stroke between the ribs will settle
all at once. And it will only be an act of justice, for God knows
how often Guannes has sneered at you in the taverns and gaming-
houses, at you, the head of our great house, just because you
have no book-learning. He has called you a swine, a blockhead,
a . . ."

" To the devil with him," snarled Rostabal, his dark face
growing crimson with rage.

" Come."

They crept forward, hiding behind the shrubs, gay with spring
blossoms, while the birds sang and the bright sun warmed the
sweet-scented air. Rostabal took his sword from the scabbard
and held it behind his back. Rui, pulling his moustache, watched
the sun, which had now begun to descend over the slope of the
hills, and endeavoured to calculate the time. A flock of crows
passed over the tree-tops, cawing loudly in their flight. And Rostabal, watching them as they disappeared, began to grumble again
at the length of time that good-for-nothing Guannes was wasting
in the town, while they were there starving and longing for a
drink of wine.

At last! They could hear the strains of an old ballad sung
gaily in the distance; the same ballad which Guannes had chanted
as he went down the slope to the town.

Rui uttered an impatient exclamation. Now they could hear
the mare's hoofs resound on the silent mountain road, and presently
a red plume appeared waving from the rider's hat just round the
edge of the wood.

Rostabal slipped round silently under cover of the blossoming
shrubs, and as Guannes came level with him he uttered a loud cry
which caused the rider to start and turn in his saddle. In an instant
the sharp point of the finely-tempered weapon had entered his
throat, and with a hoarse moan he fell sidewards across his mare,
swayed helplessly, and tried to regain his balance. Rui sprang
forward and seized the bridle, whilst Rostabal, dragging the unfortunate man from the saddle, plunged his sword again and
again into his throat and chest.

The evil deed was done.

" The key! " cried Rui.

And snatching the key from the pocket of the dead man he led
the way towards the spot where the box was hidden, leading the

frightened mare. Rostabal cleansed his sword in the brook, and washed the blood from his clothes and face, for in dragging Guannes off his saddle the blood of the wounded man had poured all over him. Then, shaking the water from himself like a dog, he followed Rui to the granite pillar.

The mare began to graze, still laden with the bags containing the provisions and other stores which Guannes had purchased in Retortilho. Rostabal stopped at the spot where the brook broadened out into a still pool, and bent over it to see if his reflection showed any traces of what he had just done. Rui took out his knife, saying:

" I am going to open the parcels now, so that we can have something to eat before we do anything further."

Passing close behind the stooping figure of Rostabal he paused, and calmly, as if piercing a wine-skin, he drove the sharp blade between his shoulders, right through the heart.

Rostabal fell into the pool without uttering a sound. He lay face downwards, his hair floating on the still surface of the water. Rui caught hold of his leather belt, to take from it the key which had been placed in the pocket of the belt for safety, and the blood gushed from the wound in the dead man's back in a torrent over his hands and clothes.

III

The three keys of the box were his now, and his alone! And Rui, stretching out his arms, breathed his relief and joy. Then he packed the gold into the three wallets and slung one on the back of each mare, and having refreshed himself with the food and wine, and given his beasts a meal of corn, he set off, as night fell, for Medranhos, where he buried the gold in the cellar.

His joy was great. When only whitening bones, picked by the crows in the wood through which no one ever passed, should be left, he would remain the magnificent lord and master of Medranhos, and when the old house should be rebuilt and the ancient chapel restored he would have a private chaplain and would have masses said for the souls of his dead brothers, who had died suddenly in their sins.

He thought it all out as he sat drinking in the deserted hall, after he had carefully stabled the three mares. How would he account for the death of his two brothers? Well, of course they had died bravely, as sons of the house of Medranhos should, fighting for their country against the Turks. He alone was left to support the honour of the ancient house.

He opened the wallets, and let the gold coins slip through his fingers and rattle on the stones of the cellar. How lovely the gold was; how clear its tinkle! And it was all his own. But now he felt very hungry, and he searched in the bottom of the wallets to see if there was anything left to eat. In one he found a fat roast turkey, which no doubt Guannes had bought for his own private eating, and some more bottles of wine. How delightful to be able to eat and drink as much as he wished, and not have to share with any one!

He dug further into the wallet—it was the one which had been on Guannes' mare. More surprises; more delights. Guannes had certainly known how to cater. There was another parcel, containing fruit, sweet cakes, and chocolate. And a jar of olives. Lastly a flagon of clear bright wine.

Rui enjoyed his supper. He ate and drank to his entire satisfaction. The crows had long since gone to their roosts in the trees, and the mares slept in the stable, happy and satisfied with their day. The brook sang on its way to where the two corpses lay, silent and helpless, under the stars.

Rui lifted one of the bottles of wine and looked at it through the light of the wax candle which Guannes had not forgotten to add to his stores. The wine was amber and clear. Certainly it was good and could not have been bought cheap. He took off the seal, poured the wine into a beaker and drank slowly. How soon his blood was warmed through by this rare wine! He emptied the bottle and opened another. But suddenly a thought came to him. Next day he would not be able to leave the house, and he would need all the food and drink he could command. If he went out, who would guard the treasure?

He stretched himself on the floor and began to plan how he would refurnish the old house. Everything would be of the very best, and he might even think of marrying into one of the old families, and having heirs. Why not, since his two brothers had died nobly in defence of their country?

Suddenly a thought came to him. Why not take the gold back and bury it under the rock where it had lain for so long? No one alive had ever known it was there; no one could know now, since the only two who had been present at its discovery were dead. He rose and began to pack the gold into the wallets again, so that he could load the mares and take the treasure back to where no one would be able to find it. He could lock it all again in the box there and keep the three keys himself.

He would not wait until morning. It was too dangerous. Supposing some one found the bodies of his brothers. He would go at once and bury the corpses and then put the gold in the box.

But, first of all, he would have a draught of that last bottle of wine, which seemed so clear and bright, and which would give him strength for what he decided to do after his toilsome day. It was a smaller bottle than the others, so the wine must be stronger.

After all, he must give Guannes his due; he knew how to cater.
No doubt he had intended to keep this rare bottle of wine for himself—the greedy, selfish rascal.

Rui went out to see that all was quiet, and then came back, sat
down, and poured out a goblet of the amber wine. It had a
perfume which he did not know, but no doubt that was due to the
grapes. It was so long since he had tasted really good wine. And
he took a long draught.

Merciful Heavens, what was that?

A flame of fire seemed to consume him, tearing his very vitals.
He rose, staggered, could not collect his senses, and then rushed
out to drink from the brook, to try to cool his burning throat.
No use! The more he drank the more terrible the torture grew,
and as he ran on and on he was brought up in his rush by something soft. It was the body of his brother Rostabal, floating at
the edge of the pool and already torn by the beaks of the crows.

He dashed the body away and ran on, still gasping and clutching at his throat. Lower down the hill the sparkling cascade
murmured, and all was still and peaceful under the rising moon.

Rui fell on his hands and knees and crept onwards, moaning and
praying. Mother of Heaven, what had happened to him? He
rolled along in his agony, clutching at the grass until he was
stopped by something which lay on the side of the path. It was
the body of Guannes.

In a flash, Rui now understood. He rose to his feet by a
supreme effort. All was clear to him. The small bottle of bright
wine, the dainty food, the subtlety of the whole plan; and the
anxiety of Guannes to have his own key first of all! And lying
down in his torture he dug his nails into the stiffening face of his
brother and moaned with his last gasp:

" Traitor! Thief! Poisoner! "

. . . .

It was true. When the bodies were found and inquiries were
made, it was known that Guannes had gone first of all to a chemist
and bought a flask of poison, with which he said he wanted to
clear the old house of rats. He had next bought a bottle of rare
wine, had taken some of the wine out, and no doubt had mixed the
poison with the remainder. Then he had hidden the bottle amid
the daintiest of the food, in the certainty that his brothers would
want it first. Thus he alone would survive to get the three keys
and possess the treasure.

JOSÉ VALENTINE FIALHO D'ALMEIDA
1857–1911

HER SON

IT was early in the morning when she arrived at the station of Pampilhosa, the junction where the trains from Lisbon stopped on their way through the province of Beira. She was a little woman, aged more by hard work and privation than by years, sallow, small featured, and quick in her movements as a little grey mouse. She was dressed in poor but decent black, and her brown feet and legs were bare, after the custom of the peasant women of Beira. No one took much notice of her, and she gave but little heed to the persons at the station.

She carried a closed basket, and she had walked all the way from Vacariça, some five miles from the station, through the woods and fields, where the winter gorse bloomed and hurt her feet with its sharp prickly shoots, and the barberry brightened up the under-growth with its brilliant scarlet berries. As she came near the station a porter called out to her to keep away from the railway line, as it was dangerous: the train might come at any time.

Timidly, the little woman explained to him that she had come from the country; she did not mean any harm by walking near the rails, she wanted to get to the station, because her son, her only son, was coming by the train from Lisbon. It was thirty years since she had lost her husband, and her boy was then three years of age; he was all she had in the world, and he had been in Brazil for ten years. Now he was coming back to her by the train from Lisbon.

The porter took little heed of what she said. He indicated the entrance to the station and went about his business. In the station she looked about timidly everywhere, into the waiting-rooms, the refreshment room, the office, asking everywhere if any one had seen a tall young man, rather dark, with a scar on his right cheek, and short curly hair, because, if so, it was her son, who was to arrive at any moment by the train from Lisbon.

Some people did not answer her. Others smiled indulgently at the poor little peasant woman, and said the train from Lisbon had not come in yet. The one who showed her most civility was a soldier who was going to join his regiment in Luzo and had arrived at the junction by the train from Coimbra. His train would not arrive until night, and he had to spend the whole day at the station. So he was glad to make room for the little woman on the bench beside him and listen to her chatter to pass the weary hours.

The train from Lisbon rattled in, and the little woman rose trembling, her eyes eagerly fixed on the passengers descending from the carriages. There were not many of them, and none of them in the least resembled the expected traveller from Brazil.

" Never mind, mother," said the soldier kindly. " Better go home and come again when the next train from Lisbon is due."

" And when will that be? "

" Half-past five in the afternoon."

" Oh, I cannot go home. I will wait here. Supposing the train came in before I could get back, and I missed him! How disappointed he would be. For, you do not know—he is my only son, and he has been in Brazil for ten years."

So she sat down again, and the soldier heard all her poor little history: how her husband had died, leaving her with this boy, whom she had brought up so carefully; how he too had been a soldier, and how she had worked to live and send him a little money while he servèd; how they had both worked afterwards, but the country was so poor and money was so hard to get; how at twenty-three years of age he had emigrated to Brazil, but he had not had good luck there either; he was not strong, and he had tried all sorts of things without much success. Lately his letters had all been full of longing to get home and work for his mother in his own country; he had been very ill with that dreadful fever, and he had managed to save enough money for the voyage home and for his mother to live on until he should be well again. Oh, but he would soon be well now; she would take such care of him, and the good air of his native village would set him up after the bad climate in which he had fallen so ill.

The soldier offered her some food from his knapsack, but the little woman refused with profuse thanks. She was not hungry; she was accustomed to do with so little, and she had plenty of food in her basket—a chicken, some cheese, and a loaf, and a small skin of wine. It was for her son, and when he came, if the soldier would accept, they would all eat together. It would be so pleasant for all of them, and she was sure he would like her son, who had been a soldier too. But did he think her son would come by the afternoon train?

The soldier tried to assure her that no doubt he would, and gave her his arm to walk along the platform a little. Some of the passengers in the waiting-rooms slept on the benches; others gossiped to while away the hours of waiting, for all were waiting for one train or another. The children ran about gaily, looking at every-

thing: at the clocks, the semaphores, the telegraphic apparatus, the
first-class refreshment room gay with winter flowers, the cottages
of the railway officials with their fanciful little gardens.   A few
young girls joined their voices in one of the old folk-songs of
penetrating sadness, blended with simple sweetness, which still
linger in that sacred land of Beira, nucleus of the strength of the
Portuguese nation, and still the centre of all that is purest in the
humble charities of family life.

Two or three small trains came in, each as it whistled on its
approach causing the little woman to start and tremble.   As the
last of these departed she ventured to approach the station-master.

" You will pardon me, sir.   But when will he come? "

" When will who come? "

" My son.   But you do not know. . . ."

" No, indeed, I do not know.   Where is he coming from? "

" From Brazil, sir."

" Train from Lisbon, half-past five this afternoon."

" And . . . if he does not come to-day, when will he come to-
morrow? "

" But woman, dear, the trains from Lisbon will be the same to-
morrow as to-day."   The station-master smiled.

" Please pardon me, sir.   I am from the country, and I am
expecting my son.   A tall young man, rather dark, with a scar
on his right cheek. . . ."

The station-master hurried off to see to the arrival of another
local train.   The little woman seemed to grow smaller still, as she
sank down on a bench and rested her basket on the platform.   The
soldier was some way off, chatting to a stray acquaintance.

The December day wore on, grey and misty, one of those days
which seem to be all one long vista of sky and earth, with no inter-
vening horizon to break the colourless monotony.   Even the
sparrows were depressed, and shivered in close groups on the station
roof, and the dull clouds hung in the windless air.

At one o'clock the soldier unbuckled his knapsack, calling out
gaily:

" Dinner-time, all the company! "

At the word " dinner " all roused themselves.   The better-class
passengers went to the refreshment rooms; the poorer ones took
out parcels of various sizes and shapes.   Some of the women went
off some way from the station to pick up sticks and make a fire
with which to heat their tins of coffee or soup.   And the occupation
resulted in a general loosening of tongues.

" Come, mother," said the soldier.   " I have enough for two."

But the little woman refused.   When her son came, then she
would be able to eat; they would all eat together.   Just now she
was not hungry.   But she had a chicken, cheese, bread, and wine:

they would have a feast together. She had a pig at home, but she did not want to have it killed until her son came; he would enjoy the hams and the sausages. And she had chickens and ducks too, all waiting for him. She herself required so little. An old woman is not like a young man, and he had been ill too—he must have good food to bring him round. No, she could not eat, not until she had seen him, her son, her only son, whom she had not seen for ten years.

The soldier ate his dinner with a good appetite. He had barley bread, goat's milk cheese, and dried codfish stewed with tomatoes, vinegar and a trifle of garlic, in an earthenware jar. When he had eaten he threw the crumbs to the shivering sparrows and went off to the refreshment room. The little woman sat patiently waiting, her gaze fixed on the dull grey sky.

" Here, mother," said the soldier. " A finger of wine. You must take it, just to drink your son's health."

She smiled humbly, hesitated, and then accepted gently.

" My son's health, soldier, and yours too."

" Ten years is a long time, mother. Your son will have altered a good deal! "

She looked up startled.

Altered? Her son altered? She had never thought of such a thing.

To her in her thoughts, in her prayers, he had always been the same. A tall lad of twenty-three, dark of complexion but with blue eyes, never strong—he had had too little to eat in his childhood to grow strong—but her own boy, her only one. In what way could he alter?

She began to tell the soldier what she knew of his life in Brazil: how, when he went out first, he had good luck. He found work in a tannery. Then the hope of earning more money led him to go to the interior, and his letters grew rarer; perhaps two or three in a year. There were so many reasons for this: the distance was so great, he had to work such long hours for so little money; the climate was bad and he was often ill. No comforting words ever came; only hopes that things might improve, and they never did. He begged his mother to pray that he might live to see her again, that he might get better work, that he might grow strong and bring her back enough to keep her from misery in her latter days.

" Do have a mouthful, mother. This cod with tomatoes is so good."

She shook her head and went on talking, as if to keep her son before her eyes. A good lad, no one could say that she had not brought him up well, but they were so poor, and he had never been strong. Now, perhaps, his native air would do him good.

" And he will bring you back a few dollars, no doubt."

" Whatever he may bring, it will be riches to one who has nothing but the blessed day and night, which God gives us and no one can take away. Let him only come himself; that will be enough. Because, you see, he is my only son, and I lost his father when he was three years old."

An electric bell rang and she started up.

" Is it the train from Lisbon? "

All the children laughed, and the soldier smiled too.

" It is only two o'clock, mother. The train comes at half-past five."

The slow afternoon passed by, and the early December darkness closed in. The soldier's cigarette went out and he slept on the bench. Still the little woman stared wistfully into the growing night, her eyes wide open, though she had been awake since dawn.

The station lamps were lighted, and the afternoon trains began to arrive at the junction, each heralded by the rattle of the points and the shrill whistle of the approaching engine.

First a local train came sweeping through the pine woods of Valdoeiro, then the train from Figueira whistled in the far-off darkness, and the next to arrive was the Oporto express with its great white and crimson eyes gleaming as it rushed in.

Ten minutes to wait for coal and water. The hungry passengers rushed to the refreshment rooms, and the porters were busy answering questions, carrying wraps, opening and shutting doors. The little woman stopped one of them timidly.

" And the train from Lisbon, sir? "

" Half-past five. Next train in. Stand back, please."

The long Oporto express thundered off, and the little woman, half sobbing with excitement, strained her eyes in the direction of Lisbon. The train was coming. It seemed too good to be true.

The soldier spoke some cheering words, but she did not hear him. All her faculties were centred in the watch for the coming son. Her hands clasped and unclasped unconsciously. At last the whistle sounded, faint at first, and growing clearer and higher across the pine woods.

The train thundered alongside the platform. There was an indescribable noise: porters shouting; passengers talking excitedly; men selling water, selling cakes, newspapers, chocolate, oranges. The little woman dashed among them, scanning the faces of the third-class passengers as they got out—pushed aside and almost trampled on as she ran, unaware of anything but that here in this very train was her son, her only son, whom she had not seen for ten years. He must be cold, perhaps hungry; she must find him and take him home at once. It would be a long walk, but at least they would be together. And when they got home, she would

light the fire which she had left ready laid, would make hot coffee,
and how happy they would be at their evening meal.

A stout middle-aged man nearly fell over the little woman as she
ran on, and with an exclamation he seized her arm to steady her,
muttering an apology. Suddenly he exclaimed:

" Why, Rosa! It is Rosa of Vacariça."

She looked up at him uncomprehendingly.

" Don't you remember me, Rosa? Clemente, your former
neighbour. I have just come from Brazil to see the old home
again. Ah, woman, if you knew how glad I am to see the old place
again! "

He laughed, adding:

" There is no one here to meet me, for I did not say I was
coming. I wanted to give every one a surprise. How glad they
will all be, for I have done well out there."

" But my son? Is he still in the train? You must have come
together."

Clemente uttered a stifled exclamation.

" Come and have something to eat with me."

" Thanks, I will. But I must wait for my son. You know
where he is. Perhaps he did not think I would come to meet him.
Go and tell him, Clemente. I will wait here, and then we can all
have dinner. I have brought it with me. Make haste, Clemente,
please. Tell him his mother is waiting here."

Clemente hesitated, and pulled his hat further over his eyes as if
to hide the sudden pallor of his face. And as the little woman
raised her eyes to his again, he put his arms round her thin
shoulders and stooped to look into her anxious face.

" Rosa, my dear woman, old neighbour. I had forgotten that
you could not know. It breaks my heart to tell you, but you must
learn it somehow. Your son . . . your son died on the voyage
over."

Not a sob, not a cry did she utter. She pulled her thin black
shawl closer round her shoulders, and her basket still in her hand,
her head down, walked quickly out of the station.

Clemente was about to follow her, but he hesitated. He would
see to his luggage, get a cab, and take her home. He would be
sure to overtake her on the road.

On, on the little woman went, seeing nothing, hearing nothing.
The lights and noise of the station were left behind as she hurried
on, her bare feet making no sound on the mist-clogged road. She
passed on to the common where the gorse pricked her ankles, but
she felt nothing. She went on without taking note of where she was
going.

The train from Lisbon had left the station, whistling as it went,

and now it came rushing with gathering speed along the edge of the
pine woods. Its great eyes gleamed redly into the night; and the
plume of smoke bent backwards over its length gave it the likeness
of some gigantic infernal horse, let loose to bring death and destruction on the world. On it came round the curve of the rails, and its
red eyes seemed to fascinate the little woman, to call her to themselves with irresistible force. She thought of nothing, she went on,
on where those eyes called her.

When daylight came, they found all that was left of the little
woman. Her basket lay at some distance from the rails, still full
of the dinner she had brought for her son.

AFFONSO BOTELHO

19TH CENTURY

THE CUP OF TEA

I

IT is not very many years ago that the journey from Oporto to Regoa had to be made partly by stage-coach and partly by rail, as the country permitted.

The stage-coach, drawn by six powerful horses, stood at the point of departure from the offices of the Coaching Company in Oporto, awaiting the final arrivals. A wild tumult was going on round the coach, some passengers declaring they could not get the places they had booked, others claiming luggage which they could not see in the imperial. The not exactly edifying observations of the porters punctuated the general turmoil.

A young man sat in one of the places near the door. He had taken his seat early, and his luggage was all in order. The other places were all filled, with the exception of the one opposite to him, which appeared to be reserved for some passenger who had not been able to arrive in time. The driver gathered up his reins, and the guard began to sound the signal for departure on his horn.

Suddenly a strange apparition came round the corner—a fat man, waddling like a duck, puffing in his haste, and waving an enormous umbrella in the direction of the coach. After him two porters toiled along under a load of luggage.

The guard swore heartily, causing an abrupt diversion in the melody he was just extracting from his horn. The luggage was hauled up to the imperial, and the fat passenger climbed into the vacant place. He found room with difficulty for his umbrella and for an ample rain-cloak.

The guard resumed his broken melody and the horses set off, rattling along the stony streets of Oporto in the direction of the road leading to the railway station of the Minho-Douro line. The fat passenger seemed to be annoyed about something, for he muttered impatiently to himself and fidgeted in his seat. At last he caught the eye of the young man opposite, João de Sousa.

" It is too bad, sir," he exclaimed. " Just think, I could not get my cup of tea ! "

359

João de Sousa did not answer, but looked interrogatively at the
fat man, who, thus encouraged, went on:

" You see it has always been my custom to take a cup of tea
after my luncheon. Just a cup of strong black tea. I was in such
a hurry to catch the coach that I did not wait for tea just now. I
cannot tell you how I miss it. You see, sir, when a man comes
to my age habits are everything, and it is really dreadful to have to
break through your habits. Now I know I shall be miserable
throughout this whole journey because I could not have my cup of
tea. You are young, sir, but take the advice of a man who is of
regular steady habits. When once you form a steady habit, do not
let anything put you off it."

João de Sousa felt amused at the communicative nature of his
opposite neighbour. Wishing to humour him into further talk he
said:

" But when we get to the railway station you will be able to get
tea in the refreshment room."

" To be sure. I had not thought of that. It will be a little bit
late after my luncheon, but still it will be something."

When they got to the station the train was already at the platform. All rushed into the refreshment room to prepare for the train
journey, some by drinking a glass of wine and eating some bread
and fruit, others by purchasing food at the counter to eat in the
train.

The fat man sat down at one of the tables and looked round for
a waiter. There were few waiters and many customers. At last
he attracted the attention of a waiter and ordered a cup of tea. He
was about to go into particulars about the tea, but the busy waiter
had to attend to other orders. At last João de Sousa, when going
off to take his place in the train, saw the fat man preparing to enjoy
his favourite beverage.

Presently he came rushing out and climbed into the train just as
the whistle sounded. He took the seat opposite to João de Sousa,
and wiped his face with a brilliant silk handkerchief.

" Well? " João de Sousa smiled his inquiry.

" My dear boy, it was green tea the waiter brought me. I can
never drink green tea! "

II

The train passed through the magnificent landscape of the North.
The mountains, clad with pine and larch woods and crested with
snow, looked down on the undulating fields, broken here and there
by tile-roofed farms, and brightened by the silvery gleam of the
mountain brooks.

Night was coming on. The setting sun had gone below the line

of hills which formed the continuation of the mountain chain, and
the evening mists crept up in the valley.

The fat passenger saw no beauty in the scene. He yawned and
fidgeted, and uttered impatient exclamations under his breath.

João de Sousa turned from the window where he had been feasting his eyes on the passing panorama. He overheard a moan,
ending in the single word " tea."

" Still thinking of tea? " he asked with a smile.

" My dear sir, when one has formed a habit, it is impossible to
lay it aside. Let me advise you never to allow anything to break
through your habits. And that blockhead of a waiter brought me
green tea. I can only drink black tea."

" Well, you can soon have your cup of tea, all the same."

" Where? "

" We leave the train at Cahide and take another stage-coach."

" Ah, so we do! I had not thought of it. Many thanks for
reminding me. I can get tea at the inn where the coach starts."

And the fat passenger began to hum contentedly to himself, until
he fell into a heavy doze, lulled by the motion of the train. He did
not open his eyes again until roused by a gentle shake given by
João de Sousa.

" What is it? Where are we? "

" We are at Cahide, and we must get out here and take the
coach."

" You are very kind, sir."

And he began to gather up his luggage.

Two stage-coaches were drawn up outside the inn, one on the way
to Villa Real and the other to Regoa. Passing the restaurant on
his way to the coaches, João de Sousa came on the fat passenger
engaged in a violent argument with the waiter. He stopped to ask
if he was going to Regoa or to Villa Real.

" I am going to Regoa, sir. Just fancy, what an awful thing!
I cannot get my cup of tea! "

" That is a very serious matter indeed," returned the young man
gravely.

" Serious! I believe you. What sort of a restaurant is this?
What sort of people keep the inn, I ask you? There is not a grain
of black tea in the place."

" All passengers for Regoa take their places, please," called out
the guard, who was a picturesque figure in the old coaching costume
of the province: short astrakhan jacket, high boots reaching to the
knee, velveteen breeches, and fur cap.

The fat passenger again seated himself opposite to João de Sousa.

" So that you have been disappointed again, sir? "

" Do not speak of it. It is too awful. What a journey to make
without my cup of tea! "

" But you will soon have another chance of getting tea."

" Oh, where? "

The poor man brightened up a little.

" In Amarante, where we change the team."

" Oh, I am glad. You are very good, sir."

The coach rattled on through the country roads. The passengers slept in various attitudes, in spite of the jolting of the vehicle and the loud cracking of the whip with which the driver encouraged his steeds. João de Sousa alone remained awake, watching the landscape flit by under the gleam of the moon, the trees, the hedges, the lines of light from the houses of a village perched on the hill-side. The dogs at a farm barked at the coach as it thundered by.

Presently they came to the ancient bridge of Amarante, the origin of which is lost in the mists of antiquity, and the coach passed into the narrow stony street, and pulled up outside the celebrated old coaching inn of the Capadeira.

The dining-room of the inn was full of tobacco smoke and the odour of chocolate and warm oil. The waiter advanced, bowing and smiling, to show the travellers to their seats, and presently a really excellent supper was served.

João de Sousa did ample justice to the stewed capon and good wine of Valdepenas, and looking round he caught a glimpse of the fat passenger sitting at a corner of the table, waiting anxiously to get speech with the busy waiter.

" Waiter, I want a cup of tea, strong black tea, mind. No other will do."

" Sir, in an instant. I must just serve the supper, and then I will order the tea for you. What will you have for supper, sir, stewed capon or roast mutton? "

" I cannot eat anything until I have had my tea. Don't forget now, strong black tea."

The waiter continued serving the great tureens full of capons stewed with all manner of succulent additions, and soon tongues began to be loosened, and a buzz of general conversation could be heard. Great hilarity prevailed in the neighbourhood of a jolly priest from Douro, who told rollicking stories to the delight of the company. The waiter stopped to listen too in the intervals of his service, and the bottles of good wine were passed merrily round the board.

The fat passenger, wrapped in his cloak, waited patiently in his corner.

Presently the landlord of the inn made his appearance in the doorway.

" Ladies and gentlemen, the coach will start in five minutes. The team is in, and the luggage is being put in the imperial."

There was great excitement and confusion. The jolly priest

called the waiter and ordered some provisions to be put in a basket for use on the journey. Every one rushed to secure places in the coach. As João de Sousa rose with the others, he heard the distressed voice of the fat passenger:

" And my tea? Waiter, what about that tea? "

" In one minute, sir. I will bring it as soon as I can."

All had taken their places except the fat passenger, who stood at the inn door stamping with impatience. The coachman cracked his whip, and the guard blew a resounding blast on his horn. As the coach had to climb the mountain for some distance a strong team of twelve oxen had been yoked, gay with their scarlet head-fringes and jingling brass bells. When the stiffest part of the ascent was over, they would be replaced by horses at the next stage.

The guard called to the fat passenger:

" Take your place, sir, please. I can wait no longer."

He was just beginning to sound the signal for the start, when the waiter came running, a steaming cup of tea on a tray carried in both hands.

The fat passenger had one foot on the step of the coach. He uttered a cry of joy as he seized the cup and raised it to his lips. But the next instant he cried out in distress, and put the cup back on the tray.

" Impossible to drink this tea, waiter. It is simply boiling hot. What do you bring it like that for, with the coach just starting? "

And he climbed into his place opposite João de Sousa, tears of pain and annoyance starting from his eyes.

The young man looked at him sympathetically.

" And to think," moaned the fat passenger, wiping his scalded mouth, " that I have not been able to get my tea! "

III

The stage-coach climbed the hill slowly for five hours, dragged by the slow but powerful oxen. A fine rain fell, and the landscape was cold and rather depressing. Enormous old chestnut trees bordered the mountain road, the rain pattering on their leaves, and the wind whistling through their branches. Here and there streamlets ran from the mountain snows to feed larger brooks in the plain leading to the mighty Douro.

The driver walked beside the leader of the team, encouraging the oxen, and directing them with stick and voice. His monotonous " Ola! " and " Arre! " were the only sounds which broke the stillness except the movement of wind and water. All the passengers slept, lulled by the slow motion of the coach, except João de Sousa, who watched the passing scene. Near the road they passed a granite house, with two immense cactuses, twisted like serpents, climbing at each side of the porch up to the roof, on which the moon, emerging from the racing clouds, cast strange fantastic reflections.

It was the chill moment of the turn of the night, forerunner of the dawn.

A little higher up they passed a thatched cottage perched on a spur of the mountain and overhung by a massive block of stone, which looked as if it might fall at any moment. The guard told João de Sousa that a witch lived there.

The road grew narrower and the trees more stunted as they neared the summit. The grey light in the sky gave place by degrees to a clearer tint, and at last the sun broke through the clouds, bathing the mountain in many-coloured beams, purple, pink, yellow, all the hues of an Alpine sunrise.

The coach rounded the corner of the mountain shoulder and drew up at an inn. The village lay beyond, the village of Quintella, scattered along the crest of the rocky slope. The oxen were removed from the yoke, the yoke itself taken off the coach, and those of the passengers who were awake descended to stretch their legs and to breathe the pure morning air, so exhilarating after the close atmosphere of the coach during the night.

João de Sousa walked along admiring the wild grandeur of the mountain scenery. Far as the eye could reach, peak after peak extended, changing their outlines with every step taken, and losing themselves in the blue mists of the distance. Lower down at the foot of the slope before them shimmered a wide expanse of water, and the rustling trees framed the whole lovely picture. Villages and single cottages seemed like toy houses dropped by children at their play. And the great crest of the Cordilheira do Marão looked down on the scene, as if guarding it against the invasion of the north wind.

As the young man paused to draw a breath of sheer delight, he heard a slow step approaching, and a long-drawn-out yawn ending in a moan of utter boredom sounded close to his ear.

It was the fat passenger, still half asleep, sighing and rubbing his eyes. João de Sousa smiled at the sight, so different from the glory of the new morning.

" Well, sir, how are you? What about your tea now? "

" Oh, my dear young friend, I have really lost all hope. I have been round to that miserable little den that calls itself an inn, but there is no tea of any sort to be had there. They say no one ever asks for such a thing."

The horses had been put into the coach, and the guard gave the signal for the start. The descent of the steep mountain-side was begun at a breakneck pace, for the horses were fresh and had been given a good meal of oats. The dark forest of pine trees opened on

each side, letting the long white road appear, and soon other kinds
of vegetation came into sight as the coach went downwards: olives,
cork oaks, and orange trees. The vines were higher and thicker as
the valley came in sight now, and presently the travellers were passing through the luxuriant vineyard country of the Douro.

The road curved along to the mountain foot, through hamlets
and villages, continuing its course along one of the banks of the
broad river which gives its name to the province. The slow majestic Douro kept them company with its silvery flood for many a mile,
until the houses grew thicker and the vineyards gave place to gardens and orchards. At last with a rattle and a loud blast of the
horn the coach entered the white streets of Regoa. It was just half-
past eight in the morning, the right hour for breakfast.

As the coach drew up at the hotel—no country inn now, but an
imposing three-storeyed building with green shutters and a vine-
shaded verandah—the fat passenger turned to João de Sousa with
a beaming smile.

"I am infinitely obliged to you, sir, for all your courtesy. I
should have had a dreadful journey indeed if it had not been for
your agreeable company. I cannot tell you how much I have
suffered by the series of misfortunes which have deprived me of my
cup of tea, which I have missed so terribly. It does not do to give
up any of one's regular habits at my age. Take my advice, sir,
and do not allow anything to interfere with a habit you have
formed, when it is a good one. I do so love a cup of tea after my
luncheon. Now I am going to get it at last. It is late, it is true,
but better late than never. Permit me to introduce myself, sir.
My name is Barnabé dos Anjos; I am a native of the town of Freixo-
de-Espada-à-Cinta, and I am travelling to Douro on business. I
hope to meet you again, sir, and in any case I am always at your
service. I wish you good luck and all prosperity, and a safe journey all along; and now I am off, my dear young friend, to drink
your health in a cup of tea!"

JOAQUIM MARIA MACHADO DE ASSIZ

1839–1908

THE SICK NURSE

So you really think that what happened in my life in 1860 might form part of a book. Well, you are welcome to make what use you like of it, provided only you do not publish a word of it whilst I am still alive. That is not much to ask, for I think I may have only a week to live—perhaps even less. I am very near the end, at any rate.

Of course I could tell you the story of my whole life, which has many interesting things in it; but for that I would need time, energy, and paper, and of those three things I have only paper: my energy is gone, and my time is like a night-light at dawn. The sun of another day it at hand, but as yet it is hidden by mists, soon to be dispelled. Farewell, my dear friend; pardon my faults and think of me kindly when I see you no longer. You have asked me for a human document, and here it is. Do not ask me for the Empire of the Grand Mogul or for the portrait of the Maccabees, for I cannot give them to you. But if you care to have dead men's shoes you can soon have mine, and no one else will get them if you want them.

You know already that what I am going to tell you happened in 1860. The year before that I was forty-two years of age in the month of August, and I became a theologian. That is to say, I copied out theological works for a certain Father de Nitheroy, who had been a colleague of mine at college, in return for which service he gave me shelter and food.

One day my patron, the priest, received a letter from the parish priest of a small provincial town, asking if he could recommend some discreet, experienced, and patient person who would go as sick nurse to Colonel Felisberto, of his parish, in return for a good salary. The priest asked me if I would like to go, and I gladly agreed, being already heartily tired of copying Latin texts and Church dogmas. I went to the capital to see my brother, and then I went on to the provincial town.

There I learned something more about the Colonel. He was, it

seemed, an awful man, ill-tempered, selfish, and overbearing, so
that no one liked him, not even his own circle of acquaintances.
He used up more nurses than medicines. He had given a sound
thrashing to two of them. In reply to all this I said that I was not
afraid of any one in good health, let alone of an invalid, and after
a conversation with the parish priest, who confirmed all I had been
told of the Colonel, and recommended me to be patient and
charitable in my new undertaking, I set out for the Colonel's house.

He was sitting on the verandah in an arm-chair, and his reception
of me was not disagreeable. At first he did not say anything, but
looked me over narrowly. Then a sort of malicious grin distorted
his hard features, and he began to talk. He talked about his
previous nurses, none of whom, he said, were good for anything.
All they could do was sleep and idle away their time, and he was
glad to get rid of them all.

" Are you a lazy dog too? " he asked.

" No, sir," I replied to this delicate question.

He asked me my name, and I told him it was Procopio José
Gomes Valongo. He made a gesture of horror, saying that it was
not a name for a Christian man, but that he would call me
Procopio, to which I answered that he could call me what he
wished. I do not know why I chronicle this trifle, but I think the
Colonel had a better opinion of me after I had given him this reply.
At any rate, I found afterwards that he told the parish priest that he
liked me better at first sight than any of the nurses he had had so
far. And for at least a week we got on together like turtle-
doves.

After that my life began to resemble that of my predecessors: a
dog's life, neither more nor less. No peace for a moment, no sleep
at night, and insults hurled at me all the time. I usually smiled
at these, and I found that this seemed to flatter my tyrant. He
considered it a tribute to his ingenuity in inventing forms of abuse.
I did not really resent his behaviour, for I knew that it was caused
by his illness and his peculiar temperament. The illness was a
complicated one, almost a rosary of evils—aneurism, rheumatism,
and half-a-dozen other attendant diseases. He was nearly sixty
years of age, and he had been spoiled all his life, as child, boy,
and man. If he had been merely wilful, it would have been bad
enough, but he was that and more. He had naturally an evil
disposition, delighting in inflicting and witnessing suffering and
humiliation on all who came within his reach. At the end of three
months, in spite of my philosophy, I began to find the strain too
great, so I just awaited the opportunity of making my escape.

The opportunity was not long in coming. One morning I had
made his poultice a little warmer than he liked, and he jumped out
of bed, seized his stick, and struck me several blows. I gave him

notice at once, and went to my room to pack my clothes. To my
surprise he followed me, knocking at the door and asking humbly
if he might come in.

He begged me to stay, urging that he was old and lonely, and
that it was not worth my while to leave him just because of a
temper which was not really his own, but had been inherited from
others, and which he had never been trained to curb. I saw the
logic of this, and I agreed to stay.

" It will not last long, Procopio," he said to me. " I am too ill
to live much longer. I am here, but I shall soon be in my coffin,
and you will have the pleasure of being at my funeral and knowing
that I am powerless to annoy you any more. Perhaps you will
say a prayer for my repose in the next world, for I shall need it.
I have never had any rest here. If you do not come and pray
for me, I swear that I will come back from the grave and haunt
you. Do you believe that souls can come back from the other
world, Procopio? "

" No, I do not."

" Then you are a fool! Why should you not believe it? Anyhow, it does not matter what idiots like you believe or do not
believe. That does not alter facts. I will come back from the
other world, if only to show you what an ass you are! "

That was how we made our peace, so you can imagine what our
war had been like. He did not strike me again, but he overwhelmed me with abuse and bad names His temper seemed to
grow worse from day to day. I made up my mind to take no
notice, and I even amused myself by making a list of the names I
was called. Never had any attendant on a cranky invalid such
an assortment of titles. I was an ass, a camel, a son of an ass, an
idiot, a monkey; in fact, in my own person, according to my gentle
employer, I could have filled a whole menagerie.

The Colonel had no relatives; he was really quite alone in the
world. He had a few acquaintances who came now and then to
pay him a visit of a few minutes' duration, to inquire how he was,
and then to depart after hearing a catalogue of his troubles. I
sometimes thought they came for the fun of the thing, to be able
to laugh at him afterwards at their Club. Certainly they did not
come for pleasure in his company.

I felt terribly lonely, and more than once I made up my mind to
leave. But each time I went to see the parish priest, and he always
advised me to remain.

One of my troubles was that there did not really seem to be any
prospect of release in the way of which my patient sometimes
spoke. The chain of his diseases seemed to bind him closer to life
instead of freeing him from what was a burden to himself and a
misery to others. I was myself forty-two years of age, and did not

want to waste all my life in bearing the ferocity of a tyrannical invalid in the seclusion of a little country town.

To give you an idea of my loneliness, I could not even see a newspaper, for the Colonel would not suffer any in his house. He took no interest in anything except his own afflictions, and it was only when the parish priest showed me his own newspaper that I had any idea of what was going on in the outer world. I had not even an opportunity of spending my salary, which the Colonel paid me regularly. Meanness was not one of his many faults.

In spite of the parish priest, I had made up my mind to go, when suddenly the Colonel grew worse. He decided to make his will, and that was a terrible business, for he insulted the lawyer almost as much as he was in the habit of insulting me. From that time onwards he never had any intervals of rest at all, nor did he give me a moment's peace. I was unable to control my nerves; I conceived an abhorrence of him which was an absolute torture to me, and I considered that, as a Christian man, it was my plain duty to leave him. I told the parish priest that I would go in a month's time; and, after vainly endeavouring to make me change my mind, he agreed to look out for a successor to me.

What I am going to tell you now happened on the twenty-fourth of August, at night. The Colonel was in his usual fit of rage. He called me every name he could put his tongue to, threatened to break my neck, and flung a plate of soup at me, because he said it was cold. I had brought it to him warm, and he had let it grow cold purposely. The plate missed me and struck the wall, breaking in pieces, and scattering the soup over the carpet.

About eleven o'clock he raved himself to sleep. I had borrowed a novel from the parish priest, an old romance by d'Arlincourt, and I sat reading it in the Colonel's room, near his bed, for I should have to wake him during the night to give him his medicine. But before I had read two pages, the letters swam before my eyes, and I must have fallen asleep.

I was awakened by the shouts of the Colonel, and I sprang up in terror. He continued to call out, apparently in delirium; and as I approached him, dazed with sleep, he stretched out his hand, seized his stout stick, and struck me with all his might across the face.

I was blinded and maddened by the force of the blow. I was in such a mad fury that I sprang on my patient; we struggled together, and I seized him by the throat and put my knee on his chest. He ceased to struggle, moaned feebly, and lay still. When I drew back and looked at him, I saw that he was dead.

I uttered a cry of horror, but no one heard me. I returned to the bedside and did all in my power to restore animation, but in vain. His aneurism had burst, and the Colonel was dead. I went into the next room and stayed there for two hours, not daring to move, waiting, waiting. I cannot even tell you what I felt during all this time, for I seemed to be stupefied, dazed, and only half conscious. I seemed to see figures bending towards me from the walls, and hoarse voices cried out to me. The cries of my victim, both before and during the struggle, resounded in my ears unceasingly, and the very air appeared heavy and full of throbbing forms. I am sure I did not imagine all this; the whole place was full of menacing shapes, and of voices which called out to me, " Murderer, murderer! "

In the next room all was still. The slow ticking of the clock seemed to accentuate the stillness, so distinct did it sound. I listened in vain, not daring to go in. There was no movement, no sigh. How gladly I would have welcomed a word of insult, a cry of abuse, such as I had for so long been used to hear. But nothing came to reassure me, to ease my conscience, and still my terror and remorse. I walked up and down the room, stopping to listen every now and then, and wishing I had never been born. Why had I ever taken such a place? What was left to me to do now? And still the moving shapes, the accusing voices!

I blamed myself, the parish priest, the doctor, even Father de Nitheroy, who had first told me of this awful task. They were all my partners in guilt, I thought. All had led up to the awful death of the Colonel.

I ventured to open one of the windows to listen to sounds from without, but all was deathly still; not even a breath of wind stirred. The night was calm; the stars shone in their aloofness from all earthly trouble, indifferent to everything here below. I lay down on the couch and began to go over all that had happened in my life, so as to get some momentary escape from the present misery. It was only then that the thought came into my mind that I should be punished for what I had done. Fear came to add to remorse; and I felt what it was to have a crime on my conscience, and to know that I must certainly pay the penalty of having committed it. I seemed to see the shadowy forms still wandering round me, and then mounting and disappearing into the air, only to return and look at me malevolently, with murmurs of reproach.

I bathed and dressed my wounded face, and then I thought I would venture to go into the Colonel's room once more. I hesitated at the door, shrank back several times, and clung to the handle of the door, trying to steady my trembling limbs, to quiet my throbbing heart. I thought of flight, but I had sense enough to know that such a course would convict me irrefutably. Better stay and see what could be done.

I forced myself to look at the Colonel. He lay back with eyes glazed and mouth wide open, as if to speak the accusing words which have echoed down the centuries: " Cain, what hast thou done to thy brother? "

I could see the marks of my fingers on his throat. Almost without knowing what I did, I buttoned up his night-shirt and drew the sheet up to his chin. Then summoning all my resolution, I called a servant, told him that my patient had died suddenly in the night, and told him to fetch the doctor and the parish priest.

I thought first of all of going away before they could arrive, under the pretext that my brother was very ill, and that I was obliged to go to him at once. Indeed, they knew that he was ill, for I had received a letter to that effect a couple of days before, and had told the parish priest that it gave me an additional reason for wishing to leave the Colonel's service. But no, I could not risk awakening suspicion, so I stayed.

To my great surprise the doctor did not examine the corpse, beyond ascertaining that life was gone. He took my word for the fact that the Colonel had awakened from sleep, shouting as if in pain, and had died as soon as I reached the bedside. He had long been dangerously ill, and an aneurism may be fatal at any time. So he certified the death, and all preparations were made for the funeral.

I prepared the corpse for the coffin myself, with the aid of an old negress who was almost blind and performed her task almost instinctively from long habit. I did not dare to leave the death chamber, dreading that some discovery would be made. I watched the faces of those who came and went, in furtive anxiety, seeking to read what they thought. Everything made me impatient; the coming and going of the servants, of the doctor, the prayers of the parish priest, all the sad ceremonies which herald the final disappearance.

At last the hour arrived; the coffin was brought in, and I lifted the corpse into it myself and closed the lid with hands which trembled, so that one of the persons present whispered to another:

" See that poor man who was the Colonel's nurse. He has a good heart, for he seems so grieved, although every one knows that he has suffered a great deal at the old man's hands "

How I longed for the whole thing to be over, before I lost self-control and risked being found out. Heaven knew I had not intended to kill my employer, but who would believe it? The men came to bear the coffin to the hearse, and we passed into the street. The bright daylight after the gloom of the house of death struck me like a blow. I felt as if all must be made clear, as if even the secrets of the closed coffin would be revealed by that brilliant daylight.

I paced along beside the hearse. I have already said that the Colonel had no relatives; so there were no mourners but myself, the parish priest, the doctor, and the couple of servants who had lived in another part of the house. A few of the dead man's acquaintances accompanied the funeral, more out of idleness than out of respect for the Colonel, who had never won any man's friendship.

At last all was over. I left the grave-side with an immense feeling of relief. I was at peace with men, though not with God or my conscience, and for several nights I could not sleep. I left the little town as soon as possible, and came to Rio de Janeiro, where I lived almost in seclusion, eating little, scarcely speaking, never smiling, and a prey to the strangest visions and delusions.

" It is wrong of you to take things like that," said my acquaintances to me. " You did your duty to the dead man, and you should not grieve for him so much."

I kept up the idea of inordinate grief for my late employer. I praised him continually, saying that he was a good soul, a little rough and hasty, like so many old soldiers, but truly kind at heart and tried by much suffering. And by constantly repeating this, I succeeded in partly believing it myself, at any rate at times.

I have never been really a religious man, but oddly enough I felt some little consolation from being able to have a mass said for the repose of the Colonel's soul in the Church of the Holy Sacrament. I said nothing to any one but the priest about this; I had the mass said early in the morning, and I alone formed the congregation. I remained on my knees the whole time, praying fervently, and frequently making the sign of the Cross. I prayed for the repose of the dead man's soul and for my own living one. I doubled the priest's fee and put alms in all the church collection boxes. I did not do this to impress any one, for no one was there to see it. I did it to try to ease my own tortured mind.

After this, I always appeared to cease to regret the Colonel, and I never spoke of his death with sadness or said " Lord have mercy on him," as we do here in speaking of the dead. I spoke of him often, but always to tell some amusing anecdote of his ways, or to recount some imaginary good deed he had done. In this way I tried to cheat myself into the belief that he was at rest, and that no real harm had been wrought by me.

A week after my arrival in Rio de Janeiro I received the letter from the parish priest which I have already shown you, telling me that the Colonel's will had been opened and that he had made me his sole heir. Imagine my surprise. I could not think I had understood aright, so I took the letter to my brother and to my friends; all read it in the same way. There was no doubt about it; the Colonel had left me everything he possessed.

At first I imagined that this was a trick, and that the unfortunate incidents of the Colonel's death had been discovered; but I soon reflected that there would be simpler means of trapping me than this. And the parish priest was honesty and probity personified, so that he would never lend himself to a subterfuge of this kind. I read and re-read the letter many times; its contents were plain enough.

" How much did he leave? " my brother asked me.

" I do not know, but he was believed to be rich."

" Well, he must have liked you "

" I suppose he did. . . . I did not know."

And so in this unexpected way the Colonel's possessions came into my hands. I wondered whether I ought not to refuse the legacy. It seemed hateful to me to receive it in such a way; I felt even meaner than if I had stolen the old man's money in his lifetime, for then he would have known of it. I considered the whole thing for three days, and finally decided that if I refused the legacy, my doing so might arouse some kind of suspicion. I resolved to effect a compromise with my conscience; I would accept the legacy, but I would secretly give it all away in charity, and with the intention of appeasing the Colonel's spirit, if he should know what had occurred. It would all be offered for the repose of his soul. I must tell you that I did not decide in this way through any real scruple, but because I thought my crime might be wiped out by an act of self-sacrifice. In this way accounts would be squared.

I prepared to start for the little provincial town to claim my inheritance. Everything seemed to come back to me as I approached the place; the whole tragedy rushed back into my mind, and every bush I passed appeared to conceal the shadow of the Colonel. In imagination I went over all the horror, the despair, of that awful night on which I had committed the crime.

Was it really a crime or a justifiable homicide? As a matter of fact, the Colonel had attacked me, and as he was in delirium, I had but tried to defend myself from his fury. It was an unfortunate struggle, for it ended in a swift tragedy. I resolved to keep this idea before me; and I summed up all the sufferings I had undergone in that man's service; all the insults, all the miseries of my lonely life. I had wished to leave him, and he had prevented it. Was it not the hand of Fate which had struck him down, using me as the instrument only?

As the station of the little town came near, I felt that I would not leave it. I would take the next train back to the capital. However, I crushed down this idea too, and went to the house of the parish priest, where I was made very welcome. He told me the dispositions of the will, the charges which it enjoined on me, and he went on to praise the Christian patience and the self-sacrifice with which I had performed a task which had earned so much

gratitude from a man of the Colonel's hard and exacting temperament. I must often have found the position unbearable, but at
any rate I had the comfort of knowing I had done my duty.

" Yes . . . no doubt," I said, looking away out of the window.

Every one else spoke to me in the same way. All were glad that
my great patience and devotion had been rewarded. I had to hear
this constantly, for the requirements of the administration of the
property obliged me to remain for some time in the town. I appointed a lawyer to act for me, and everything seemed to go on
smoothly. The lawyer had known the Colonel well, and he spoke
of him to me very often, but without the moderation of the parish
priest.

I defended my old master. It was the least I could do.

" He was not really bad natured. It is true he was a trifle
severe."

" Severe, indeed! It was high time he died. He was just a
devil, neither more nor less."

He went on to tell me many things which had happened before I
had come to the place, incivilities of the Colonel's, brutalities
towards his servants and his nurses. I listened to all and felt a
strange pleasure in excusing all, finding reasons for all, perhaps
local jealousies because he did not belong to the place, and the
people had not known how to appreciate him. He was a little
violent in his ways, but that was only his manner, and so on.

Every one was of the same opinion. The dead Colonel was a
poisonous serpent, and his behaviour had always been atrocious.
He had not a single friend; what would have become of him if it
had not been for my care? If he did leave me his property, he
had good reason to do so. Who else would have remained with
him so long and closed his eyes with such pious devotion at the last?

All this praise had its effect on me. I began to feel that they
were right. The Colonel was well out of the world, and his money
was in good hands now.

The task of making out the list of property occupied and interested me, and I remained on in the town, even spending some time
every day in the house from which I had been so glad to make my
escape not long before. It had been left to me with the other
property, and I intended to sell it and return to live in the capital,
when I had realised all my possessions and converted all into money
and investments.

After some months had passed, I had become so much accustomed
to the house where I had lived more and more regularly, that I
no longer thought of disposing of it. I did not even think seriously
now of giving away all my legacy in charity. I began to think
that this would be a piece of needless affectation. I would rebuild
some of the cottages in the village, give a sum to the local schools,

and have a grand High Mass said by the parish priest publicly for the repose of the soul of my lamented benefactor, as I had come to speak of him and indeed to regard him. And I sent to Rio for a celebrated sculptor, a Neapolitan, who was working at the cathedral there, and got him to erect a fine marble tomb in the graveyard over that grave where I had stood some months before in fear and trembling. No fear of the Colonel's bones being disturbed now!

Years went by in this way, and the memory of my first agony of grief and remorse had long since grown dim. I had come to think kindly of the dead man, who had rewarded my faithful services so justly. I no longer thought of him with terror or remorse; scarcely even with regret. I often spoke of him to those who had not known him, always in terms of praise. When chance brought me in the path of a doctor, I recounted to him my patient's illness and the details of his sufferings. All agreed that he could not have lasted longer; it was only by a miracle and on account of the patient care I gave him that he had lasted even so long.

Did I exaggerate his symptoms when I described them? I do not really know. It is certain that the more I thought of them and the oftener I spoke of them to those who were in a position to judge, the more certain it became that the man could not have lived another day, even if I had not had that terrible experience.

Farewell, my dear friend. If you find that this confession of mine is of any interest to you, I beg you to reward me by giving me also a marble tomb, on which you will have engraved that promise from the Divine Sermon on the Mount:

" Blessed are they that mourn, for they shall be comforted."